About the Author

Catriona King trained as a doctor and a police Forensic Medical examiner in London, where she worked for many years. She worked closely with the Metropolitan Police on several occasions. In recent years, she has returned to live in Belfast.

She has written since childhood; fiction, fact and reporting.

'*The Slowest Cut*' is the sixth novel in the modern Craig Crime Series. It follows Superintendent Marc Craig and his team through the streets of Northern Ireland on the trail of the worst corruption they have ever experienced.

Books number seven and eight in the Craig series are in edits.

Acknowledgements

My thanks to Northern Ireland for providing the inspiration for my books.

I would like to thank Crooked Cat Publishing for being so unfailingly supportive and cheerful.

And I would like to thank all of the police officers that I have ever worked with, anywhere, for their unfailing professionalism, wit and compassion.

Catriona King
Belfast, June 2014

Also by Catriona King

The Craig Modern Thriller Series

A Limited Justice
The Grass Tattoo
The Visitor
The Waiting Room
The Broken Shore
The Slowest Cut
The Coercion Key
The Careless Word

Discover more at: **www.catrionakingbooks.com**

The Slowest Cut

Chapter One

Midnight. Sunday. 2nd February 2014. Belfast

The body swung and twisted in the wind, until the chain's tension stilled it momentarily, suspending the woman's arms above her head like a ballerina poised mid-pirouette. The moment passed and the iron rope uncoiled, turning slowly at first in a graceful arc, then faster as the tension rebuilt, repeating the macabre dance.

The girl smiled at her work, admiring the flashes of red as the bloodied corpse turned. She took a photograph with her mobile phone and saved the image like a holiday snap. Then she walked away satisfied, certain that what she had done was right. The jet-black silence hinted at its agreement and the waiting man nodded and took her hand, letting the steel gate slide closed behind them. They were almost free.

***

Monday. 12.30 p.m. Docklands Coordinated Crime Unit. The Murder Squad.

D.C.I. Liam Cullen scrunched-up his plastic cup and threw it backwards over his head, missing the bin by a mile. Davy Walsh glanced up from his horseshoe of computers and laughed. It was the fifth time in a row that Liam had missed; something was seriously spoiling his game. Davy glanced at Jake

McLean, the Squad's sergeant, to see if he'd noticed, but he was tapping furiously on his computer keys and frowning. Only Nicky, Craig's P.A. met his eyes, her rueful shrug saying what Davy already knew; that the whole place was out of kilter because of the boss.

Marc Craig was one of the easiest bosses that he'd ever had. Mostly polite, except when the pressure was on, then the 'pleases' and 'thank-yous' got dropped in favour of 'do it now and ask questions later'. Sure, he lost his rag the odd time, usually on the phone with some barrister and then you could hear him yelling halfway to the lift. And he threw the occasional punch on a job, but always at a perp. So mostly they couldn't complain. Until now. Craig had been like a bear with a migraine since Christmas, and even the usually amiable Nicky had finally had enough.

Davy watched in awe as she stood up, smoothed down her 'this season's' tie-dye skirt, poured out a mug of black coffee and raised her small fist to knock on Craig's office door. Liam turned just as her hand was poised to fall and the speed he moved at made Davy think of an Olympic sprinter, except more overweight. Liam crossed the floor in two giant lopes, a drawn-out 'NO...' echoing through the room. Just as he reached Nicky the office door opened and a stunned looking Craig surveyed the scene.

Liam skidded to a halt and Nicky's fist knocked on his chest instead of Craig's door, surprising them both and spilling the coffee everywhere. Liam felt Nicky's words before he heard them.

"You clumsy big..."

Craig smiled at the scene, bemused and Nicky blushed and dropped her hand down by her waist.

"Was that coffee for me, Nicky? Because generally it tastes better from a cup than the carpet."

To Liam's horror Nicky drew herself to her full five-foot odds and thumped the mug down on her desk then she placed her

4

hands on her hips and let rip.

"Yes, it was for you...sir, but you don't deserve it. This place has been like a funeral parlour for months, with everyone tiptoeing around in case they annoy you."

She waved her hand around the room as if indicating support, but she was sorely disappointed. Jake was still tapping away furiously hard on his keyboard, Davy had discovered something fascinating beneath his desk and Liam was hotfooting it back to his desk-basketball.

"Come you back here, Liam Cullen and back me up. Or..." Nicky searched for a suitable punishment. "Or you'll be doing your own expenses in future, and...and you'll never get another biscuit from me again!"

Liam froze mid-retreat and considered his options. The thought of years of filling in expenses claims overcame his urge to run and he turned reluctantly back to the fray, shrugging an apology at Craig. Nicky drew breath for her next tirade and Craig raised his hand, beckoning them all to pull up a chair and sit down.

"Right. First of all, I'm sorry. I've been a grumpy bastard for weeks. Some of you already know what it's about and I'd rather not discuss it, but there's still no excuse for me bringing my problems into work. Apologies."

Liam nodded. He knew what Craig's mood had been about; the end of his relationship with Julia McNulty. They'd been together for over a year and most people had been expecting wedding bells, but a combination of career, geography and joint intransigence had sunk them deeper than a torpedoed sub. He wasn't sad she'd gone. McNulty had been a looker all right but she'd a tongue on her like a knife. The boss deserved better.

Craig was still talking. "Secondly, it hasn't been helped by us not having much to do except court appearances since Christmas. But that's about to change."

Jake stopped gazing longingly towards his computer and Liam sat forward eagerly, a grin brightening his pale face.

Craig scanned the open-plan office. "Anyone know where Annette is?"

Annette McElroy was the Squad's Detective Inspector and she was normally at her desk. Nicky nodded.

"She's taken Jordan to some special event at Queens. He wants to get in next year, to do drama. She'll be back at three."

Craig smiled. "OK, Liam can catch her up later. Let me tell you what we've got. At six o'clock this morning a primary-school caretaker on the Lisburn Road went to check the playground before kids started arriving for class. What he found there closed the school and the C.S.I.s have been there since. John's just called me."

Dr John Winter had been Craig's friend since grammar school. Now he was the Head Forensic Pathologist for Northern Ireland and, as Liam would have put it, 'a brain on legs'.

Liam leaned forward, interrupting. "Let me guess. He found a body."

Craig nodded. "Not just any body. The school's headmistress; a Mrs Eileen Carragher."

Davy cut in confidently. "How did s...she die?"

Davy was the team's analyst and brilliant at his job, but when he'd started with them two years earlier he'd been so shy he would barely speak to Craig. Now his stutter on 's' and 'w', once so prevalent, was only there occasionally, and he often queried things, showing how comfortable he now felt with them all.

Craig shot a wary glance at Nicky before he answered the question, knowing she didn't like the gory bits of their work. She waved him on graciously, so glad that he'd emerged from the doldrums that she'd forgive him just this once.

"Badly, Davy. John's sending over some preliminary photos and they won't be pretty; his description was bad enough. She was found hanging from the chain of one of the swings in the playground."

Liam interjected knowingly. "Strangulation. Wrapped

around her neck."

Craig shook his head. "'Fraid not. She was hung up by her wrists."

Liam sniffed huffily. "What killed her then?"

Craig winced. "A razor-sharp knife."

"Her throat, sir?" Jake tapped his neck without thinking as he asked the question. It was too graphic for Nicky and she glanced away.

"Eventually, Jake, but not before she'd been slashed everywhere else first. They cut her so many times that John lost count. The blood loss would have killed her eventually, if the cut to her throat hadn't done the job first."

Liam whistled. "God, she'd pissed someone off and no mistake."

Craig nodded. "Definitely. It reminded me of the Britt Ackerman case, except John didn't feel that these cuts were staged. The depth made them feel frenzied."

He stood and turned towards his office. "Liam, Jake, come with me. We're heading to the morgue to meet John. Nicky, could you ask Annette to meet us at the school at three-thirty. The address is on my desk."

Craig smiled and grabbed his jacket, swinging it on over his head, then he headed for the double-doors to the lifts. He felt more like himself than he had for months and it had taken a murder to do it. He didn't want to think about what that said about him.

Chapter Two

Craig pushed his way through the PVC doors into the lab and entered John Winter's rosy-hued outer office. He and Liam were long past being shocked by John's Montmartre-brothel décor, but Jake had only joined the team in November so this was his first time. The look on his face was priceless. They watched as his jaw dropped like a character in a children's cartoon and he turned full circle, taking in the drapes and artwork in John's boudoir. It wasn't his boudoir of course, but it was his empire and a real step back in time. It wouldn't have surprised Craig if a can-can girl had wandered past them.

Jake's daze was shattered by the loud blast of the brass band that heralded the finale of Tchaikovsky's 1812 overture, and John's sudden appearance through a door in one corner of the room. He looked rough, and Craig said so. John took off his wire glasses and rubbed his eyes; they were bright red against his pale skin. With the background setting he would have fitted in a horror film.

Craig smiled ruefully. "Bad hangover?"

John nodded slightly then winced. A harder nod would have set his head throbbing. They'd all been there.

"Natalie decided to make cocktails last night. She was practicing for some friend's hen-do. I doubt that the poor girl will ever reach her wedding."

Natalie Ingrams was John's girlfriend/partner/significant other, whatever the correct term was when you were middle-aged and way past the first-date stage. She was a no-nonsense surgeon with a wicked sense of humour, and she'd dragged the quiet, professorial John into the twenty-first century with a bang, despite many protests. Craig had known John since he was twelve and even then he'd had a Victorian air.

Craig smiled benignly at his friend. "I would have thought Tchaikovsky was a bit much then."

"Opposition therapy. The louder the music the less I can hear the banging inside my head."

John smiled vaguely at Liam in greeting and then glanced at Jake. He was wandering around the lab, touching the pictures and antique items of medical equipment that John had arranged artfully around the room.

Lima nodded sagely. "Don't mind him, Doc. He doesn't get out much."

The irony of an almost-fifty father of toddlers saying that about a twenty-eight-year-old clubber made them all laugh; John very gently, and holding his head as he did. He beckoned them into his small office and found everyone seats, then he pointed Craig at the percolator and sat down.

Two minutes of banter and coffee later Craig cut to the chase. "What have you got for us, John? Take your time; we're not in a hurry. We're not meeting Annette at the scene for two hours."

Winter reached into his desk drawer and pulled out a buff-coloured file. It remained closed while he brought them up to speed.

"Right. The victim was a fifty-five-year-old school teacher called Eileen Carragher. Married, two grown-up kids. One of them, Ryan, runs a restaurant in the centre of town."

Liam leaned forward, interrupting. "Which one?"

Liam's natural voice was so deep that it would have been almost inaudible at times, if it hadn't been for the volume that usually accompanied it. If a dog's hearing allowed them to hear high-pitched sounds, then hearing Liam when he whispered would have required the exact opposite. Except that he never whispered. Ever. When he was interviewing a suspect, he deafened them into submission. Even his softer tone, the one he was employing now, would make a brave man sit up and take note.

John's response was to stick his fingers in his hung-over ears and slink further under his desk, until the look of pain on his face passed. Then he muttered. "The Lebanese one on the Ormeau Road. Tagine."

Amusing though the scene was, unless John took his fingers out of his ears they would get nothing done, so Craig took back the questioning.

"What does her husband do?"

"Surveyor at Taylors in town."

"And she was the headmistress of the school where she was found?"

John half-smiled in assent.

"You said she was suspended by the chain of a swing, but that wasn't what killed her?""

"No. She died from her carotids being severed, but not until she'd almost bled out from the cuts all over her body." He opened the file and spread the pictures inside it across the desk. "I'll take you to see the body in a moment, but here are just some of the injuries."

Craig lifted the sheaf of photographs and handed them around the group in silence. The only sounds in the room were John's coffee-machine perking and Jake's loud gasp. The blood drained from his face and for one minute Craig thought he might be sick. Jake had asked to be seconded to Murder and he was bloody good at the job, but he hated the gory scenes. It was something he had in common with Annette, despite her nursing background. In fact everyone hated them except Liam and him. They had too many years on the clock.

Craig stared at the photograph in his hand. It showed the teacher's back, what was left of it. It was a bloody mess and he struggled to find the normal anatomical landmarks. The whole space from the nape of her neck to the top of her hips had been stripped of skin, and not in one neat cut. Small remnants of flayed flesh sat like islands in a sea of red and purple where her muscles had been ripped and torn, like badly tenderised steak. The only hints to exactly what had caused the damage were occasional deep slices from what looked like a large, sharp blade. He passed the photograph to Liam and took another one from Jake.

Craig could see now what had made Jake gasp. It was what was left of Eileen Carragher's face. Beneath the short-layered brown hairstyle so loved by female teachers from his youth, sat a pair of pale blue eyes, lidless and glazed, staring out at them from a ruddy mass. Craig set the photograph face-down on the desk and stood up, ostensibly to top up his espresso, but John knew that he was shutting out the image and formulating questions to ask.

"Her face looks like it was dissected professionally, John. Was it?"

Winter shook his head. "No. I can see how you might think that. Superficially it looks like anatomy dissections of the face, but it isn't." He reached enthusiastically for the photo. "I could show you in detail."

"No thanks. Just the un-illustrated highlights at the moment."

"OK. The body was almost stripped of skin from head to foot, but it wasn't done in any orderly way e.g. the skin wasn't flayed off in sheets. It was sliced off randomly, hence the small pieces of skin you can see here and there. The cuts were frenzied."

"Over how long a period, Doc?"

"I can't be sure yet, Liam. But we're talking days, perhaps even a week."

"Shit! She must have annoyed the P.T.A. big time."

John laughed, despite himself. "She annoyed someone, that's for sure. The pattern of clotting and muscle necrosis shows that when skin was removed she was left long enough to clot, then she was cut again." He indicated the photograph that Craig had left on the desk. "Her eyelids were cut off early."

"So she had to watch, Doctor Winter?"

John stared at Jake in surprise. "You're right Jake. I hadn't thought of that. I was thinking more of the pain it would have caused her, and the fact she wouldn't have been able to rest because she couldn't have shut out the light. But you're right; she would have been able to see what they were doing to her, at least until her corneas became damaged through lack of tears."

Craig looked thoughtful. "What if they were lubricating her eyes, John? Could she have seen everything then?"

John tutted, frustrated that he hadn't thought of it. "Yes. If they'd bought artificial tears and put them in regularly then she'd have been witness to her own death. I'll test the corneas for chemicals."

Craig smiled at his friend, seeing that he was getting annoyed with himself. John would normally have anticipated all their questions and he'd have got there today, eventually, once his blood alcohol dropped. Craig could see him composing a lecture to Natalie inside his head, entitled 'don't lead me astray on a work night.' She would ignore him as usual and Craig was glad. John was too work-focused, even more than he was at times. Natalie brought him back to the real world.

"OK. So perhaps Eileen Carragher watched herself die, and perhaps she didn't. Any idea what sort of knife did this?"

John smiled, on steadier ground. "Razor sharp with a broad blade. Some of the sideways cuts sliced deep into the muscle. Hang on and I'll call Des. He'll have a book about it for sure."

Five minutes later the bearded figure of Dr Des Marsham, Head of Forensic Science, strolled through the door. He was carrying two thick, leather-bound volumes. Craig stood up to greet him.

"Long time no see, Des. How are Annie and the baby?"

"Not so much a baby now, more a holy terror. I swear to God that child rules us both with a rod of iron."

Liam felt his pain. Des' son Rafferty was only four months older than his own, Rory, and he hadn't had any sleep for months. "Did you ever wish that someone should invent boarding kennels for babies?"

"Brilliant idea, but don't say that in Annie's hearing. She thinks the sun shines out of his nappies."

Liam nodded and rubbed his eyes, looking for sympathy. "Danni's the same. The last time I had a decent night's sleep was during that case in Portstewart last November."

Jake put an imaginary handkerchief to his eye and sniffed and Liam batted his hand away. Craig waved Des to his seat and took up position against the wall behind John.

Des tapped the two books on his lap, then shot Craig a warning look. "Now, because you're a mate I'm going to lend you these books, for Davy to check out the knife. But I want them back in mint condition. They're original editions from the 1950s." He stroked the leather lovingly and smiled at John. "Nothing they've produced since touches them, for the range and accuracy of the descriptions."

Liam interjected. "Aye, and that would all be dead interesting, Doc, if this was an episode of the Antiques Roadshow. What about the case?"

Des punched Liam in the arm hard enough to make him jump. "You're in our town now, Cullen. Show some respect." He held out the books, pushing past Liam's outstretched hand to give them to Craig.

Craig nodded his thanks. "Davy will take good care of them. Any first opinions on the knife?"

"Razor thin, broad blade and serrated edge. I've slipped a list of possibilities inside the front cover. If we get anything more on it, I'll call you."

John rose to take them to the mortuary, and Jake ventured a question.

"Have you ever seen this method of killing before, Dr Winter?"

"Not here. But…"

Craig cut in. "Where, John?"

"I'm not certain, but I know that I've seen it somewhere. Outside Northern Ireland." John thought hard for a moment then shook his head. "The problem is I've been a lot of places over the years, Marc. The U.S., Eastern Europe, China, Australia. It could have been in any one of them. I'll have a think."

John was internationally respected in forensic pathology and he'd been asked to consult on hundreds of atrocities over the years, from war crimes to serial killers.

"It'll come back to me."

They descended the stairs to the ice-cold mortuary and John crossed to a steel table in the centre that held the familiar shape of a body. He pulled back the sheet and the sight that greeted them was even worse than Craig had feared. Even Liam was silenced by what he saw.

The woman's body was short and thick set. It was a woman, but if they hadn't already known that the body was female only the hair style would have given them a clue. There wasn't even enough left of Eileen Carragher to say which was the front of her body and which the back. All that remained was three-square-feet of raw meat with limbs attached. Jake didn't just look sick this time, he actually was. He bolted from the room and they heard him retching in the corridor outside. John left for a moment to steer him towards the bathroom, then returned and started reporting like the professional he was.

"Female, approximately forty to sixty." It fitted with Eileen Carragher's known age of fifty-five. "Naked when found, suspended vertically by the wrists from the chain of a child's swing in the playground of Fitzwilliam Primary School on the Lisburn Road."

Craig raised a hand, interrupting. "How was she I.D.ed if she was naked? It's impossible to say who she is from her face."

John shook his head and Craig knew he was frustrated with

himself again for forgetting.

"Sorry, I should have said. Her wedding ring, driving licence and purse were laid out at her feet. There was a note inside the purse. You'll see it when forensics have finished. Des has photocopies of everything for you upstairs."

"What did the note say?"

"It was succinct. 'The bitch got what she deserved.'"

"Written?"

"Typed; sorry. We're checking it for prints. Obviously we'll check the victim's DNA to confirm the I.D."

He turned back to the body and carried on. "OK. Cause of death was exsanguination from a single cut to the throat that severed both carotid arteries. Lividity says she was vertical when she was killed and had remained that way for at least six hours. Until she was taken down this morning."

"She was suspended before death?"

"Before, but the marks on her wrists say not long before. There's no bleeding at the wrists; the skin wasn't broken, which it would have been if she'd been suspended by an iron chain for more than a few hours. Her throat was definitely cut while she was hanging. Blood spray on the playground matches that expected from carotid bleeding, but not from any of the older wounds. I'd say her other wounds had clotted before she was brought there. So on balance, she was tortured elsewhere and brought to the playground to die."

Craig nodded. "We'll narrow down the timings later, but it's likely she was brought there after dark last night, to prevent the killers being seen, and we know she was found this morning at six o'clock. That leaves us with a tight window to bring her there, string her up and kill her."

He turned to Liam. "Liam, can you get Davy to check sunset and sunrise times, and start the Uniforms on door-to-door, especially any buildings overlooking the playground. CCTV and traffic cams as well please." He nodded John on.

"OK. The cuts on her body are a mixture of superficial and

deep."

"Hesitation?"

"No, there are no sign of rehearsal cuts anywhere, and you normally get those with hesitation. I'd say that any superficial cuts were deliberate, to cause pain, as were the deeper ones. I'll do my best to give you timings, but I'd say she was kept somewhere for a few days while they played with her. If they didn't want her to die quickly, then they could have kept the cuts superficial initially then deepened them as time went on."

Just then Jake re-entered, the pallor of his skin blending with his fair hair to make him look like a ghost. Liam nodded 'all right?' and Jake nodded back, averting his eyes from the mass on the table.

"She must have lost a lot of blood in those days, John. Why didn't it kill her?"

"Because she was a strongly built woman and because they definitely knew what they were doing. They knew just how far to go to avoid killing her." He thought for a moment. "They could have butchery training."

"Any possibility that they're medically trained?"

John shook his head. "No. The cuts are too random and imprecise."

"Maybe they'd done it before, sir."

Craig turned towards Jake and smiled. "You're right, Jake, maybe they had. OK, add-in similar cases to Davy's search list. But not just UK or local, widen the search to worldwide." He turned back to John. "When you remember where you've seen this before let us know. It'll help narrow Davy's search."

John continued. "OK. The killers could be experienced in torture, or not, but they definitely knew how to keep her alive while she bled, so they may have used a clotting agent. I'll check."

"If you could check for eye drops on her corneas first then we can start looking for recent purchases of those."

John shook his head. "They can be bought over the counter,

so unless they used a credit card…" Craig nodded. "I know it's a long shot but anything's worth a try." Craig stared at the corpse thoughtfully for a moment. "How much does she weigh?"

"She wasn't a thin woman. I'd say around seventy kilograms."

"What's that in real money, Doc?"

"About eleven stone."

Craig nodded. "OK, then how did one person lift her? I can just about see a strong man carrying her to the playground from a vehicle, but holding her vertical long enough to wrap her wrists in chains? I doubt it."

John rubbed his eyes then stared into space. "I'm trying to think if any of us could hold seventy kilos vertical for long enough to wrap a chain around it."

"I could."

Craig glanced at Liam. At six-feet-six he was probably the only one of them that could have managed it, but how many six-feet-six men were there around?

"We'll all six–feet or thereabouts and we couldn't, Liam. Were her feet resting on the seat of the swing, John?"

"No. The seat was twisted up near her face."

"So they didn't even stand her on the seat and then tie her hands with the chain. That means she was lifted as a dead weight." Craig nodded to himself, then realised from their blank faces that he needed to say his thoughts out loud. "We're looking for two people."

"You mean two men, boss."

"Not necessarily, Liam, no. I agree two men are more likely than two women, but a man and a woman, provided they were both fit might have managed it. Either way, at least one man was involved."

John cut in. "None of this answers the main question, Marc. Why? By all accounts Eileen Carragher was just a wife, mother and teacher, hardly the profile of a person someone would want to do this to, is it?"

17

"Except she obviously wasn't just those things." Craig nodded towards the door. "Let's grab a seat outside."

He led the way while John covered up his charge, then they took a seat in the mortuary office, perching on steel stools designed to discourage their occupants from staying too long.

"OK. I'll get Davy to look for the knives, similar M.O., the note and sun times. Jake, can you liaise with sergeants Harris at High Street and Maguire at Stranmillis and make sure that we have plenty of Uniforms on the streets near the school over the next few days. In particular I want a door-to-door on any houses with a bird's eye view, including blocks of flats that might have the school in their line of sight. Liam, you take the grieving widower and the kids. Annette can take the rest of the teachers; we can use her diplomacy on this one."

Liam sat forward indignantly, almost sliding off his stool. "Here, are you saying I can't be subtle when it's called for, boss?"

"That's exactly what I'm saying, and don't pretend that you're offended. You should be grateful. I don't think a school full of traumatised teachers is quite your thing. Find out when and where Eileen Carragher was last seen, and if she's been missing for days then find out why no-one reported her gone. I'm going to dig into Mrs Carragher's life in other ways." He turned to John. "You were right when you said Eileen Carragher didn't have the profile of a person someone would want to do this to. But that means she was more than the obvious information tells us about her."

"A secret life?"

"Everyone has things they'd rather weren't made public. Including all of us."

Liam harrumphed. "Not me, I'm an open book."

Craig shot him a sceptical look. "Two words, Liam. Ray Mercer."

Ray Mercer was an unscrupulous reporter at the Belfast Chronicle who made their lives hell on nearly every case. Liam had been about to punch him in an interview room some months earlier when Craig had intervened. Only he and Craig knew about the incident.

John arched his eyebrow curiously and Liam blushed. "Aye, well. I meant…"

"None of us are angels, Liam, including me. We all have things that we'd rather didn't leak out. I'm betting that Eileen Carragher had as well."

John looked sceptical. "Something bad enough to warrant this, Marc?"

"Obviously the answer to that is yes."

Chapter Three

The meat slid off the bone like oil from a blade and Mai heaped the plate high with dark-red slices. She handed it to her lover proudly, nodding him towards the ramekin of sauce.

"This looks great, pet. Even better than the beef last week."

She smiled at him, wrinkling her nose prettily. "The secret's in the marinade. At least two days."

They both laughed as she poured a glass of ruby merlot and carried her own plate to the table. The young man took her hand gently. She felt relaxed, but he knew it wouldn't be that easy after all the years of pain. He could smell freedom after so many trapped years. He corrected himself. Almost smell it. There were still two more left to die.

***

3 p.m.

John turned his head slowly, testing his hangover; it was definitely getting better. It was down to a small twinge at the end of the turn now, from a head that had needed holding when he'd brushed his teeth that morning. He'd deliberately used his old toothbrush, worn but silent. The thought of an electric head buffeting his gums and assaulting his ears with its whining had been too much. Now it was three p.m. and he could almost consider starting Eileen Carragher's post-mortem, with all the bone cracking and saw whirring that implied.

He poured himself another cup of coffee and sat down again,

thinking of Natalie as he sipped. He smiled as he remembered her leaping energetically out of bed that morning, completely untouched by the excess alcohol of the night before. He would never be much of a drinker and she normally respected that, but now and again she deliberately engineered a heavy session, just to show him that she was made of sterner stuff. She didn't need to prove it; he'd never had any doubt. She'd made it to Consultant Surgeon at thirty-five in a world dominated by men; Boadicea would have been proud.

And yet…When they were alone and all the bantering had stopped, he saw Natalie for the woman she was. Playful and loving, tender-hearted and absolutely desperate to do some good in the world. At first he'd wondered why she'd hit it off so well with Craig's sister Lucia, much more than she ever had with Julia McNulty, his ex. But now he knew. She was just like the gentle Lucia; always trying to help people, marching for every good cause, collecting waifs and strays wherever she went.

Natalie might not have Lucia's gentle ways and girly looks but she was exactly the same, just with a layer of spit and vinegar on top. Julia had been a different type entirely; defensive and moody and self-absorbed. He wasn't sad that she and Craig had split up. He knew Craig missed her but he needed someone who wasn't constantly fighting the world.

John turned his head again and smiled; the twinge had all but gone. Last night's drinking session had been Natalie's rehearsal for a friend's hen-night. That meant another spring and summer of weddings. His mind went straight to 'boring', but his heart surprised him by whispering 'what if?' John jerked upright, startled by the thought. What if what? He answered himself out loud. "What if it was Natalie and me getting married?"

John started to turn away from the words as soon as they hit the air, then he stopped, letting himself imagine what they meant. For the first time ever it didn't frighten him. After years of cold sweats in churches, listening to Mendelssohn's Bridal

March and thanking God it was some other poor sod trussed-up in tails and signing his life away, John wondered. He wondered for a whole five minutes, half-smiling as he did and then he walked back into the mortuary to discover what he could about Eileen Carragher's death.

***

Craig paced the small playground in silence, taking in the chalked lines for hopscotch and football, and the climbing frame and elderly row of swings. The concrete school building was quiet; no children's chatter or timing bells to disturb his thoughts. An anxious looking man stood in one corner with Annette, answering her questions distractedly, while all the time watching Craig as if he was going to find fault.

Annette smiled to herself. The presence of the police affected people in different ways; bravado or fear were the common two, with a long list of subsets for each. Physically that usually meant fight or flight. Mentally it ranged from mute panic, through vagueness, to an all-out faint.

She watched the thin man beside her to see which one he would fit. If he fainted she could catch him, he was only her height and weight; ten stone. She admitted it ruefully, knowing at her height she needed to lose fourteen pounds. She felt she should set an example for fitness now that she held an inspecting rank, but people's tendency to bring cakes into the office had so far thwarted her good intent.

Annette sucked in her stomach and stared at George Harlston again. Mr Harlston or Sir, to the children that roamed the halls. She smiled, remembering the tiny chairs and desks in the classroom when she'd gone to knock his door. It was the coat pegs that had touched her most. Three feet from the ground with names scribbled underneath, declaring that they belonged to Kevin or Jay. She'd seen them before of course, with her own kids, Amy and Jordan, but her nostalgia went further back today. To her own childhood, when she was small enough to have fitted in one of the forgotten coats.

She shook herself and opened her notebook to a fresh page, getting ready to scribe.

"Now, Mr Harlston. What can you tell me about Mrs Carragher?"

George Harlston stared at Annette with a haunted look, as if he could see the dead headmistress beside her, hovering like Banquo's ghost. He was a man somewhere in his forties, not unattractive in a miniature way, but the pallor of his skin matched his translucent eyes, and made him look as if he would faint. Only the vibrant orange of his tie added any colour to him at all.

He spoke hesitantly, as if he was sure there was a right answer; an answer that he should somehow know. Years of tests and inspections had taught him that there was always one answer more correct.

"I…I would say she was nice."

'I would say she was nice'. How much more damned by faint praise was it possible to get? Annette prompted him gently, afraid that a harsh approach to questioning might make him run away.

"And? Could you tell me when you saw her last? What she was like to work with? Any more details?"

"I saw her last Friday, at approximately four-thirty. She was just walking to her car and she turned and waved."

"Good. What did she drive?"

"A small saloon. I'm afraid I'm not good with makes. I can tell you that it was blue. Dark blue."

"Excellent, thank you. Did you speak to her again after that? Over the weekend perhaps?"

Annette's husband Pete was a teacher and she knew that they were like most professionals, always remembering something that they had to check or ask outside working hours. Harlston frowned as if trying to remember, but his eyes said that he already had. Annette waited through his mime then nodded him on.

"I called her at home. On Saturday at six p.m. To ask about a child who I'd referred for counselling."

"And?"

"She wasn't there. Her husband said she'd gone into town to meet an old friend and he was expecting her back at seven. But I called back at nine and she wasn't there then either."

Annette made a mental note to check with the husband, and continued her questions, occasionally glancing over at Craig. She'd watched him pacing out the playground from the side of her eye, now she saw him beckon Liam and Jake over for a chat. She felt left out. She asked her next questions impatiently.

"Did he say who she was meeting? Did you speak to her at all after that?"

"No, no. Neither of those. I didn't ask who she was meeting and he didn't say. She didn't return my call, so I thought I would just talk to her about it at school this morning…"

Harlston's voice tailed off and Annette knew there was only one question left to ask, and that it would knock him for six.

"Why didn't you like Mrs Carragher, Mr Harlston?"

George Harlston's eyes widened and he blushed from brow to chin, objecting strenuously. "I didn't say that I didn't like her…"

Annette interrupted quickly. "Call it a hunch then. But you didn't. Like her, I mean. Did you?"

She watched as Harlston's thin face turned a deeper red and panic filled his eyes. She could see him doing the calculations. Tell the truth and slot himself into a suspect box. Or lie, certain that the police had mind-reading talents that would make him confess, or bright lights in an interview room that would have the same effect. He decided to tell the truth. He shook his head firmly.

"No. I didn't like her. Very few of the teachers did. Or the parents. She was hard. She bullied her staff and was rude to parents. In fact the only people she was nice to were the kids, and a lot of them didn't like her either."

"Any idea why?"

He stared into the distance vaguely. "I'm not sure. There was something about her. If I was ten I would call it creepy, that's what the kids said and I could see what they meant. Let's just say that she wasn't a comfortable person to be around."

"Who did like her?"

"What?"

"You said very few of the teachers did, that implies that at least one must have."

Harlston looked shocked at Annette picking him up on two words.

"Oh. Yes, I suppose it did. There was really only one. Alan Rooney. He teaches the transfer year; ten and eleven year olds. He seemed to get on very well with Mrs Carragher; they often had lunch together or went off into a huddle in her office. No-one likes him much either. And of course, the school governors liked her. She was good at hitting targets and keeping within budget. They like all that stuff. Plus, she could smooze with the best of them."

He stopped suddenly and Annette wasn't sure if it was because he had nothing more to say, or because he just wasn't saying anything more. They'd find out later when they interviewed the rest of the staff. She closed her notebook and slipped it inside her bag, impatient to join the huddle fifty metres away.

"Thank you, Mr Harlston. That's all for now."

The relief that covered Harlston's face almost made her laugh. The last time she'd seen someone look so grateful was when they'd been acquitted of murder. Harlston turned on his heel and was halfway towards the school when he remembered his manners and shouted "thank you". Then he put his head down and kept on walking, moving faster than any teacher Annette had ever seen. She hurried across to the small group

25

just in time to catch the end of one of Liam's jokes.

Craig greeted her, laughing. "Did you get anything from the teacher, Annette?"

She smiled. "Yes, sir. He didn't like Carragher much. Apparently no-one did, except for the school governors and a Mr Rooney who teaches the oldest class. Seems they were quite close. Harlston last saw Eileen Carragher on Friday at four-thirty. She was getting into her car, some sort of blue saloon. He phoned to speak to her about a child on Saturday night but her husband said she was in town meeting an old friend and he was expecting her back at seven. He called back at nine o'clock, but she still wasn't home." She turned to Liam. "Has anyone spoken to the husband yet?

Liam looked sheepish. "Not yet. I called but he was at work."

"Work? When his wife's body's just been found!"

Craig interjected. "He won't know yet, Annette. Remember we don't have a definitive I.D."

Liam shook his head. "Aye, well, even allowing for that, boss, I thought it was a bit odd as well. Uniform called him and hinted something was up this morning, but he still went into work. Still, there's nought as queer as folk. He said he'd be home at five so I'll head round there then."

"Harlston said he was going to speak to Mrs Carragher this morning when school started, but..."

"OK, thanks, Annette. Liam, check if she was reported missing before you go to speak to the husband. If he didn't report her on Saturday night then I want to know why. Annette, you and Jake interview all the teachers. Question Rooney especially and see what their 'special relationship' was all about."

"Are we interviewing any of the kids or parents, sir? It's just that Harlston said Carragher was rude to the parents but nice to the kids, and the kids though she was creepy."

Liam boomed so loudly that Annette jumped back. "If any teacher's rude to me when our Erin and Rory start school, they'll be sorry."

Jake shot Liam a sceptical look and turned to Craig. "Some parents can be a real pain, sir. My mum's a teacher and she said some of them want to do her job, and they all think they can do it better."

"Does your mother teach primary or secondary?"

"Secondary, sir. But kids are kids."

"True. Ask her what normally warrants the description 'creepy' applied to a teacher."

Liam interrupted. "Strange clothes or haircut, bad breath. The usual nerd behaviour. We had a teacher once…"

Craig shook his head. "No. It doesn't feel like that here. Ask for me Jake, please, and Annette, go back to Harlston and see if there are a couple of children who are willing to talk to us about why they didn't like her. I'll get Davy to dig into Carragher's background and see which schools she worked at before here, and why she left them."

"So we're making the victim the suspect?" Annette asked the question quietly but the point was well made.

Craig nodded. "Yes, unfortunately we are, until we can rule out that her lifestyle had anything to do with why she was killed. If this had been death associated with a mugging, rape or a myriad of other things, then no. The victim would be the victim, pure and simple. Chosen at random, or wrong time wrong place. But this was much too deliberate and too well-planned, Annette. There was nothing random about why Eileen Carragher was chosen, the note tells us that, or why her body was displayed here in the way it was. She was the reason for the crime and we need to find out why."

"In case it happens again, boss?"

"Perhaps. Or perhaps it won't, but either way there's a story behind this murder and every part of me is screaming that someone thought Eileen Carragher did something to bring this on herself. And my hunch is this case is going to get much darker than we think."

Chapter Four

John cast a final glance at the cadaver, then pulled off his gloves and ripped the plastic apron from around his waist. Eileen Carragher's body had given up every secret that it held; her mind was Marc's business. Davy and Des would tell them what sort of knife had done the damage, and the swabs, bloods and stomach contents would say if she's been sedated, or given pain relief while she'd been hacked to death. His money was on no. Something about the brutality of Carragher's end said that her killer would have wanted her to feel every slice. They'd wanted her to suffer and she had.

John walked towards his office to leave the post-mortem recording for typing-up, then slung his suit jacket over his shoulder and headed for the car and home. Natalie was working tonight so he'd get a good night's sleep to clear his head and he would look at the case again tomorrow, refreshed. All the signs said the body belonged to Eileen Carragher, but until they had a formal identification he couldn't sign her off. There was no way her husband could I.D the raw meat on the table as his wife, so it would be down to DNA.

John stopped in his tracks, shocked again at his forgetfulness that day. He'd forgotten to ask Liam to get her toothbrush or hairbrush for a DNA match! Then he smiled. Liam would do it instinctively. Sadly he was too well versed in identifying bomb-blasted remains not to know the drill.

John started the engine of his Chrysler Crossfire and drove slowly towards the Lisburn Road and past Fitzwilliam Primary School on his way home. He was thinking of food and bed, but at the back of his head another, more personal, topic was lurking. He'd think about it tomorrow. Once he was sure his hangover hadn't been making him sentimental and leading him astray.

***

Liam looked at the steep flight of stairs in front of him and sighed. He was getting to the age where bungalows had started to look appealing, the last thing he needed was to have to climb twenty steps up to someone's front door. What eejit had designed town houses anyway? With the garage and kitchen at ground level and the front door a storey above. It wasn't natural. His daughter Erin had a picture book about an upside-down house and that's where they belonged.

Liam clambered laboriously up the high steps, his one concession to keeping fit not to hold onto the rail. If he could still ascend without doing that, then the Zimmer frame was a few years away yet. He'd just raised his hand to knock when the door opened inwards and a sixty-something man with a bad comb-over stood in front of him. Liam dwarfed him, but then at his height he dwarfed nearly everyone.

"Mr Carragher?"

"Yes. You must be D.C.I. Cullen. Please come in."

Liam composed his face in an appropriately solemn expression and entered a long, carpeted hall. Ian Carragher nodded him into the small front room and turned to go. "I won't be a moment. I'll just make the tea." He scurried off down the stairs into the kitchen, upsetting Liam's sense of spatial rightness once again and leaving him to wander around the modern living room, examining papers and ornaments with a well-trained eye. When he heard Carragher's footsteps on the stairs again Liam sat down in an armchair, with an innocent look on his face.

"I hope you like cake, Mr Cullen. Eileen made some last

week."

It was said matter-of-factly, without any sign of grief, confirming Craig's earlier opinion. Carragher didn't know his wife was dead. He hadn't been asked to I.D. the corpse they'd seen earlier that day, so as far as he was concerned she was probably just missing. Liam made a note to ask him for her toothbrush and gratefully accepted the proffered tea.

After a few seconds of sipping and two pieces of cake, Liam reminded himself why he was there and set down his cup. He removed his tiny notebook from his pocket and readied himself to ask questions in a way that implied he didn't already know the answers.

"Did you see your wife over the weekend, Mr Carragher?"

"Yes, on Friday night and Saturday morning. She went into town in the afternoon to meet a friend. When she didn't come back I reported her missing."

Liam nodded. He'd already checked whether Carragher had reported her missing, so that his other questions wouldn't sound out of place. He had; on Sunday. Liam asked another question whose answer he already knew.

"When was that?"

"Yesterday, at about two p.m."

"Who did you speak to?"

"A Sergeant Harris at High Street station. I thought as Eileen had disappeared in town that I should report it there. Was that OK?"

"Yes, quite OK."

It was more than OK, it was positively handy. Jack Harris was a mate of his from training college and Craig often used his interview rooms on a case. He'd get far more than facts from Jack; he'd get his impression of Ian Carragher's guilt or innocence, and what state he'd been in when he'd reported his wife gone.

He turned back to Carragher, scrutinising his round face. He didn't look like a man who'd offed his wife, but you never knew.

Murderers rarely looked like murderers. That comb-over could be concealing evil thoughts.

"Who was your wife meeting in town on Saturday?"

"An old friend."

"Male or female?"

Liam asked it deliberately provocatively, to see if jealousy might play an element in the case. He wouldn't like it if Danni was meeting an old male friend, and he thought that it would niggle at most men. Not Ian Carragher.

"Male. I think his name was Gerry Warner. Something that started with a 'W' anyway."

"And that didn't bother you?"

Carragher looked blank. "What?"

"That she was meeting another man?"

Carragher looked at Liam as if he was a Neanderthal and Liam suddenly blushed. Danni was always telling him he was old-fashioned and even Craig had hinted at it once or twice, although his Italian half seemed to understand jealousy. But in front of this older man with bad hair Liam felt almost embarrassed. Carragher's tone became frosty.

"I trust my wife implicitly. She can be friends with whomever she wishes."

Liam bristled. "Aye, that's all very well. But you didn't report her missing until two o'clock yesterday. Does that trust extend to her being out all Saturday night?"

Carragher sat back in his chair and the movement told Liam that something he'd said had hit a nerve. When Carragher spoke again his modulated tenor had risen several tones.

"Yes. Of course it does. She probably wanted to continue their chat and then realised the time and decided to stay in town. Perhaps they had breakfast together."

"I don't believe that, Mr Carragher, and neither do you, or you wouldn't have reported her missing at all." Liam paused and shifted tack. "What do you do, Mr Carragher?"

"I'm a surveyor. I work for Taylors in town."

"So you wouldn't have met any of your wife's old college friends?"

"Yes, I've met them. We've gone to reunions over the years."

"And this Gerry? Had you met him?"

Carragher paused, as if he was considering what to say. The answer was yes or no. Simple. Except that the look on Carragher's face said he was working out the ramifications of each. Interesting. After a moment he plumped for yes.

"Yes, I met him several times at college dos. He was on the organising committee."

Good. That would make him easier to find. Now came the bit that Liam hated. He altered his posture and softened his deep voice to mimic sympathy, except that he didn't feel any for the man in front of him and he couldn't quite work out why. His wife was dead and he'd done everything right. Ian Carragher was an easy-going husband who didn't mind his wife meeting male friends for a catch-up. He went to boring college reunions and supported her career, and he'd reported her missing within a reasonable time. So why didn't he believe that he was completely guiltless in her death? Liam shrugged. Maybe it was just his suspicious mind.

"Mr Carragher, I have some potentially bad news."

Carragher's eyes widened and he lurched forward in his seat. "What? Have you found Eileen? Is she hurt?"

The questions and reactions of an innocent man. They felt real. Ian Carragher hadn't killed his wife after all, but did he know who had?

Liam restarted more slowly; certain now that he was dealing with a widower not a murderer.

"We've found a body."

"Is it Eileen? Is it?"

Carragher's voice was reaching screeching pitch and Liam tried to calm him down. "We don't have an identification yet, Mr Carragher. It wasn't possible. So we're going to have to use DNA. Could I have something of your wife's to compare? Her toothbrush or perhaps a comb?"

But there was no calming the man opposite. "What do you mean it wasn't possible? Either it looks like my wife or it doesn't."

Carragher stood up so quickly that Liam recoiled, immediately preparing for an attack. But he merely rushed past Liam to the mantelpiece and lifted a picture of a couple, thrusting it in his face. It was Carragher and his wife. It was the first time Liam had seen Eileen Carragher's face, other than as a mutilated corpse. She looked pleasant. A plump-faced woman wearing a floral dress and a smile. Nothing like the cadaver he'd seen earlier that day.

Liam shook his head, not wanting to tell the man the full horror of their discovery.

"I'm sorry, Mr Carragher. It isn't possible to say that the body we've found resembles this lady."

Carragher screamed in Liam's face. "So what makes you think this body has anything to do with Eileen at all? It could be anyone, but you come in here randomly, scaring the life out of me and asking for samples of DNA. You ought to be ashamed…"

Liam let him rant for a moment then stood and placed his hands gently on Carragher's shoulders, pressing him to sit down.

"It isn't a random visit, Mr Carragher, and I'll tell you why. The reason we feel this might have something to do with your wife is because of where and how the body was found."

Carragher went to ask where, but Liam stilled him with a look.

"I can't tell you any more, sir. I'm sorry. Please just give me the samples I've asked for and then let me get someone to come and stay with you until we find some answers. Is there anyone you can call?"

Carragher stared at the ground for so long that Liam thought he'd been struck dumb. Finally he whispered "My son, Ryan.

He lives off the Ormeau Road."

"Good, give me his number. I'll call him and explain, while you get those items for me."

Carragher motioned Liam towards an address book then stood slowly, heading for the bedroom with his energy seeping visibly away. Liam compared him to the cheerful man who'd answered the door and made the tea thirty minutes before, and shook his head for the thousandth time at the power of grief.

***

Craig hung up the phone and pulled open his office door, walking out onto the squad-room floor. He really wanted to gaze out his window at the river, but he avoided it these days. Since he'd split with Julia it made him maudlin, the Lagan's water too dark a place to go. He strode across to Davy's desk.

"Do you have a minute, Davy?"

Davy spun round from his computer so quickly that his long hair caught in his mouth. As he pulled it out Craig noticed that his nails were unpainted these days. He stared at him more closely; something else was different as well. It took him a while to work out what it was and then finally he did; he was wearing a shirt and tie! Davy's usual office attire was a T-shirt and jeans and always dark, but today he was wearing a white shirt, a red tie and if Craig wasn't mistaken his trousers were part of a suit. His heart sank. It could only mean one thing; Davy had an interview. He kept his tone light and asked.

"Are you leaving us, Davy?"

Davy shot him a puzzled look and Craig went on.

"The way you're dressed. It's not your usual gear. That usually means interviews."

Davy stared blankly at him then glanced down at his shirt and laughed. "This? No, it's not for an interview. Maggie's been nagging me to s...smarten up, so I finally have."

Davy had been dating Maggie Clarke; a reporter with the

Belfast Chronicle, for over a year and her influence on him so far had all been good. Nicky overheard their conversation and wandered across the floor.

"I think it suits him. Don't you?"

Craig grinned. "Yes, I do. Even more now that he's not thinking of leaving us."

Davy was only twenty-six but he was the best analyst that Craig had ever worked with. And, while he knew they couldn't hold onto him forever, he was going to give it a damn good try.

Davy smiled mysteriously. "Ah, now. I didn't s...say that, chief."

Nicky saw Craig's face fall and she clipped Davy playfully around the ear. "For God's sake don't wind him up. He's been hard enough to live with lately."

As soon as the words were out Nicky realised what she'd said and scrambled frantically for a retreat. Craig smiled at her confusion and raised a hand, calming her down.

"Don't panic, Nick. You're right. Like I said this morning, I know I've been a pain in the ass since before Christmas. I'm surprised no-one called me on it weeks ago."

Davy interjected. "W...we were going to draw straws this week for it. Nicky had them all ready to go, but then you got better by yourself."

Nicky flushed. "Davy Walsh! I'm never telling you a secret again. You just wait. I'm going to tell Maggie everything you've ever said about her."

Craig smiled then pulled over a chair and sat down at Davy's desk. "Like I said, I'm surprised you didn't draw lots after New Year. Now go away, Nicky. Davy and I have work to do."

Craig turned towards Davy, knowing that Nicky was returning to her desk drawing a finger across her throat for Davy to see.

"You've got the books from Des, and I know you've been looking at the mode of death." He gave him a hopeful smile. "Anything so far?"

"Not on the knife yet, chief, I'm waiting for Dr W… Winter's post-mortem report. But the M.O. was easy to check. There's nothing similar anywhere in the Americas or Western Europe, I'm still waiting for the reports from further afield. I'm s…sure I read about a similar death in a journal years ago, but I can't remember where."

"How about the sun times?"

"Yes, I've got those. Sunset yesterday was at five p.m. and s… sunrise this morning was at eight o'clock."

"That means theoretically the body could have been left there between five o' clock last night and eight o'clock this morning. To be safe they probably would have waited until the locals were asleep, say eleven p.m., and the caretaker found her at six this morning. That gives a window of seven hours for them to bring Eileen Carragher to the school, kill and display her. "

"The temperature dropped to zero over-night, so that would explain why she was so stiff when Dr Winter got her down."

Craig made a face. "Damn. That'll make death harder to time."

Davy shook his head. "Dr W…Winter will be able to compensate. He's used to it. The blood splatter at the s…scene was definitely arterial. If she spurted arterial blood then she was still alive when they cut her throat. Time of death had to be sometime between eleven and six a.m."

Lividity showed that Eileen Carragher had been hanging for at least six hours after death, so that meant she had to have been killed no later than midnight. Craig raked his hair thoughtfully and Davy did the same. Nicky smiled at his mimicry then checked herself; she hadn't forgiven Davy by a long chalk.

"This is a strange case. The note implied that Eileen Carragher was killed for something that she'd done to someone."

"Revenge."

Craig shook his head slowly. "Yes and no. It feels more like punishment. The way she was displayed was almost like a public hanging, as if they wanted to shame her as well as kill her. Anything on the note?"

"Nothing. Typed, standard font and paper that can be found in any office. I'm running the w...words to s...see if I get any hits on the phrasing, but I'm not holding my breath."

Craig wasn't holding his either. The note would give them nothing, he already knew that. He glanced at the clock. It was nearly six o'clock. He stood up briskly. "Go home, Davy. We need to come fresh to this tomorrow." He glanced over his shoulder at Nicky. "And I'd advise you to run because that's a paper knife in Nicky's hand."

Chapter Five

8 p.m.

Nicky stared at the pile of receipts in front of her, trying to make sense of the mess. Gary was a good husband and an excellent mechanic, but as far as managing their haulage business went, he was a non-starter. She sipped at her cold tea and screwed up her face, wandering into the kitchen to make a fresh pot. She gazed out at the garden as it brewed, and smiled as her son Jonny waved and then kicked the football back to his dad.

Gary looked as if he hadn't a care in the world. She was no accountant but one look at his paperwork had told her that they were in deep trouble with the taxman. There was unpaid VAT going back for three years, and set against the meagre profits the business made it would almost wipe them out.

Nicky carried her cup back into the living room, sighing as she set it down, then she started dividing the receipts into two piles that she knew would divide into more. She prayed that her first impressions were wrong because if they weren't then none of them would be smiling for long.

***

The C.C.U. Tuesday. 9 a.m.

"Right. Here's what we've got so far. A woman, tortured by being slashed multiple times with a sharp blade then strung up by her wrists and finally killed with a single cut to her throat."

Liam leaned forward, interrupting. "Do we know how long she was killed before she was found, boss?"

Craig shook his head. "Not exactly. John's working on it but it was cold last night, so body temperature won't be as much help as it should." He gave a fleeting smile. "But he'll get there. We know from Davy's sunset and rise times that she was most likely brought there between eleven p.m. and six a.m. Death was definitely during that time, and Lividity says it was at midnight or earlier. Right now I'm less interested in the time of death than the method."

Jake indicated to speak and Craig waved him on. "I hope you don't mind me saying, sir. But this feels like full on torture. Punishment for something and humiliation."

Davy nodded at Craig. "That's w...what you said yesterday. That this was like a public flogging."

Craig rubbed his chin thoughtfully. "Punishment yes, shame after death, OK, but you really think humiliation of the victim was part of it?"

"Don't you?"

"Maybe, but if humiliation was the main aim then the torture would have been done in front of an audience while she was alive, not in private before she was brought there."

Liam joined in. "How do we know it wasn't, boss? It might have been done somewhere else where people could have watched."

It was a good point.

"Good thinking. OK, let's run with that for a moment. If she was tortured to humiliate her, then what sort of audience would it have had?"

"People who hated her?"

"Maybe. Anyone else?"

Annette leaned in to speak, averting her eyes from the photographs strewn across Davy's desk. She'd signed up to maintain law and order, not be a C.S.I.

"People who the killers were sure weren't going to rescue her, or go to the police."

Craig stared at her, admiring the way her mind worked. She'd gone from the torture's audience being passive, to them having an active, supportive role.

"Go on."

Annette put down the handbag she was clutching on her knee and warmed to her theme. "Well, just think. The audience could have hated Eileen Carragher as well, which could go to the motive for her murder. Or they could simply be sadists who'd paid to watch tortured in front of them."

Liam interrupted, earning Annette's scowl. "You mean like some sort of snuff movie?"

"Perhaps, or perhaps not. I just think that until we find the reason that someone hated her enough to do this, we should keep an open mind."

"So you think this could have been filmed, Annette? And distributed to a chosen few?"

"Or put out on the internet live for money, sir. Who knows?"

Craig turned to Davy. "Can you add that to your list, Davy? See if there's a cyber-trail for this."

Davy nodded and Craig smiled at the group. He loved this part of the job. Not the murders, and most definitely not the victims, but getting his team to think outside the box.

"So you're saying that the motive mightn't just have been something that Eileen Carragher did, Annette? There could be a commercial slant?"

"It's possible."

"And they decided to leave her in the playground because they'd found her I.D. and thought it would add to the after effect?"

"Mmm… I'd need to think that through, sir. The location seems a bit too strange unless she was chosen specifically. But even if she was chosen because of something she'd done, that doesn't remove the possibility of a group audience."

Liam raised his eyebrow sceptically. "If she was lifted to provide sport for a bunch of weirdoes who get off on watching people die, then we're looking at some sort of cult, boss. How likely is that?"

Craig shook his head. "Before the trafficking ring we busted last June I'd have said that kind of group mentality was more likely in a country the size of the U.S., but now…"

"And if they've done it once with Eileen Carragher, sir, then they could do it again."

"They could, Jake, but let's not get ahead of ourselves. We agree Eileen Carragher was tortured in a way that feels like punishment, and whether she was chosen particularly or at random will come out in the investigation. We know it would have taken two people to suspend her in the playground, so even if we're not looking for a group, we're looking for more than one person. We know they knew her identity, either before they took her or after."

Liam interrupted. "The note implied they knew her."

"The note was so generic they could have written it about any woman, Liam. They could be trying to imply they knew her, which isn't the same thing. OK. We also have a tight window for her time of death and we can't rule out that her torture was filmed for private or commercial use." He sipped his coffee and turned to Liam. "What did you make of the husband?"

Liam sniffed and pulled out his small notebook, shooting Annette a sideways glance. He didn't mind people speculating up to wazoo, but when it came to getting the work done it was walking the streets that gave answers. Annette caught the look and so did Craig, strangely reassured that their sibling rivalry was still alive and well. They might have gone up in rank from their Sergeant/Inspector pairing to Inspector and D.C.I. but everything else was business as usual. Liam started reporting.

"Aye well, Ian Carragher. He was a pleasant enough being.

Older than the wife by about ten years and no oil painting." He pointed to his own full head of hair. "Had one of those comb-overs, a full-on Bobby Charlton. He was pleasant enough and seemed supportive of the wife's career, went to her college reunions and all that stuff." He sniffed meaningfully. "Mind you, he was way too broad-minded in my opinion."

Jake interjected eagerly, in awe of Liam's street sense. Liam could sniff out a perpetrator quicker than any dog and it was a skill he was keen to learn. "Why, Liam? Did they have sex parties and stuff?"

Liam's eyebrows shot up to his hairline and Craig was certain he could see the beginnings of a blush. "Here, none of that, now, son. There are ladies present. I just meant he let his wife meet up with her men friends without him. Sex parties indeed."

Craig laughed and Annette gave 'Chivalrous' Cullen a sceptical look. Liam was only chivalrous when it suited him in her book, but he was an old-fashioned cave-man all the time. Liam was still talking.

"She'd gone to Belfast to meet this old friend called Gerry Warner, or something close. Carragher said he'd met him at a teacher training reunion so he was something to do with her college. Anyway, Carragher was expecting her back at seven and she didn't come."

"That fits with what George Harlston told me, sir. He said the husband told him that she'd be back at seven, but she wasn't, so he waited until Monday, to see her at school."

"Did the husband report her missing on Saturday night, Liam?"

"No, that's the weird thing. He said that time must have run away with her and she was probably just talking half the night, catching up like, and she must have booked herself into a hotel in town."

Craig threw him a sceptical look. "Instead of driving the three miles home?"

"Maybe she'd been drinking."

"OK then, instead of calling a taxi home? Hardly."

"Aye, well. The husband seemed to believe it was possible, although he didn't say that she'd done it before. That's what I mean about being broad-minded. If Danni ever…"

Craig interrupted before Liam started thumping his chest. "What time did he eventually report her missing?"

Liam squinted at Craig, peeved that he'd been interrupted mid-rant. "Two o'clock, Sunday afternoon." His face brightened. "But here, we had a stroke of luck there. He reported it to Jack Harris at High Street."

Craig and Annette smiled simultaneously. Jack Harris was well liked. He'd been the desk sergeant at High Street station all through The Troubles and there was nothing that he hadn't seen. He was like everyone's dad and he remembered enough about Liam when he was young to keep them all amused.

"Excellent. Go and see him and find out how Carragher seemed when he came in. Take Jake. It's about time he heard all about your misspent youth."

Liam laughed and the loudness of it roused Nicky from her day-dream. She'd been staring into space all morning. She normally joined their briefings but this time she'd stayed put at her computer and Craig knew she was thinking about something else. She gazed over at the group blankly, as if she didn't really see them, and then turned back to her screen.

"Anyway, Carragher was fair cut-up when I said we'd found a body and it might be her. Nearly went berserk when I asked for her toothbrush for DNA."

"Well you would, wouldn't you? That could only mean she didn't have a recognisable face."

"And the rest. I didn't give him any detail. Just said we'd be in touch. But he seemed genuinely concerned, right enough."

Craig stared at him. "What does your gut say, Liam? Guilty of her murder or not?"

Jake gawped. The boss trusted Liam's gut enough to base decisions on it!

Liam shook his head. "Not guilty of her murder, but God knows what else the pair of them got up to."

"That's my feeling too. We'll play this as a punishment killing by two or more perpetrators, and investigate the random and audience aspects that Annette suggested. But my instinct says Eileen Carragher did something to cause this."

"I don't think the husband was thinking any of that when I saw him, boss. He looked pretty blank. Mind you, I didn't ask him if anyone had a motive to harm his wife. Didn't like to until we'd confirmed the I.D."

"That's fine, Liam. When we get Mrs Carragher I.D.ed we'll interview him again. Meanwhile…"

Craig paused and they waited to hear what came next. Liam broke the silence, knowing exactly what he was thinking.

"Meanwhile, if Carragher's not a suspect and someone else killed his wife, is that it over? Or is he going to be next?"

Chapter Six

John shook his head at the numbers in front of him, trying to calculate Eileen Carragher's time of death. He knew it was at least six hours before she was found at six a.m. because of the Lividity, just not exactly when. The temperature had dropped to zero at midnight. That mean the body might have been in freezing temperatures for six hours before it had been found, complicating things. He shook his head. What did it matter anyway? They had a time range for her death. That would just have to do.

John sat back suddenly, astounded with himself for even thinking it. Accuracy was his middle name. Well not really, his middle name was much more embarrassing, but no-one, not even Craig knew what. But he'd never, in all his years in pathology, dismissed a time of death so casually. He must be sick. As soon as John thought it he knew that he wasn't. He wasn't sick, he was stressed. But by what?

He ran through the day-to-day stressors that affected every life. Work; no. Money; no. Family illness; no. His parents had died more than ten years before and he was an only child. Their death had left him with no-one but his elderly aunt Mamie in Dublin, who was so healthy that she played golf every day, and the Craigs, who had basically adopted him.

His health; no, he was fit as a fiddle despite Natalie telling him that he needed to jog more. As soon as John thought Natalie's name his pulse raced and he had his answer. Natalie! Natalie was stressing him. She wasn't even with him and he felt stressed.

Why? He loved her; he'd known that for months. She didn't nag him, well not really, not unless you counted dragging him out of his hermit-like existence to parties where he might enjoy himself, or making him look up from his microscope at real life. He quite enjoyed all that, it made him feel normal, and loved. He could talk to Natalie about anything and everything, and she bore a disconcerting resemblance to his late mum Veronica who he'd loved; in looks as well as eccentricity. That was supposed to be good, wasn't it? Dating someone who reminded you of a family member.

Natalie never dragged him clothes shopping on Saturdays, or pressured him for commitment like most women did, so what did he have to be stressed about? Nothing; that was what. So why was he?

The answer came to John with a jolt so sudden that he slid off his stool at the workbench onto the polymer floor, pulling a microscope down with him. He hit the floor with a thump then the microscope landed on his chest, giving him another one. As John lay there rubbing his head and his ribs in sequence he knew that there was no treatment for the stress he felt; it would gnaw away at him until he dealt with it.

He was feeling guilty about not making a formal commitment to Natalie. She might not be pressuring him to make an honest woman of her, but he was. He was feeling so guilty that John knew there were only two things he could do. Propose, or break up with her. He didn't want to do either, so he would do what he always did at times like this, he would go for a drink with Craig.

***

Craig stared at the hand set, puzzled. It wasn't like John to want to go drinking straight after work, well at least not at six o'clock. But who was he to complain?

"OK. Six o'clock at Bar Red. Let me know when you have

time of death or anything else, John."

Craig clicked the phone off, knowing that something was up with his friend. He shrugged. That was this evening's problem, right now he had a murder to solve and an unhappy P.A. to deal with. He opened the door of his office and beckoned Nicky in. She dragged her feet, no mean achievement in five-inch heels, and sat down reluctantly at his desk. The look on Nicky's face said she thought she was in trouble. Craig never summoned her; she usually anticipated his needs before even he knew them.

Craig read her expression and jumped in before Nicky had time to speak. "You're not in trouble, Nicky. I just noticed you looking out of sorts and wondered if it was something that I'd said or done?"

She shook her head vaguely. "Nothing to do with work, sir. Just life."

"Do you want to tell me about it?"

"No, not really. There's nothing you can do." Nicky stood up and pushed her chair against his desk. "Was there anything else?"

Craig scanned her face. It was blank; no hint of what was troubling her written there. There was no point trying to force it out of her. He would have to find out some other way.

"No. That's fine, Nicky. Thanks for coming in."

Nicky dragged her feet back to her desk and Craig watched her hunch forward over her work, her shoulders slanted in defeat. He knew that whatever was bothering her was none of his business, except that he was fond of her and she needed help. So she would get it, even if she didn't ask for it. That made two of his friends who were having difficulties with their day.

***

"Gerry Warner."

Liam boomed the name across the open-plan office as if he

was announcing the winner of a Grand Prix. Davy took the bait.

"W…Who's he, when he's at home?"

"The bloke Eileen Carragher was having dinner with on Saturday night."

"Right. I s…suppose you want me to run his name now?"

"Aye. You do that while I get us coffee. He trained at Brookville College between '76 and 78'. He's a teacher, don't know what of, and he's on the college fund-raising committee."

"Fine. That's all I need."

By the time Liam returned with two white coffees Davy had pressed print. He handed him a warm sheet of paper and Liam perched on his desk, reading it as they drank. Gerry Warner, Head of science at Maurena Grammar School in Lisburn, eleven miles away. He was sixty-four years of age, divorced with two kids, both grown up and away. Liam stopped reading halfway down the page and tapped urgently on Davy's screen. Davy pushed his hand away protectively.

"Get your grubby mitts off my touch-screen. It took me a year to get the boss to fund that."

"I need you to check something else for me."

"W…What?"

"A hunch. Find out where Gerry Warner and Ian Carragher did their degrees."

"Please."

Liam squinted at him then squeezed the word out. "Pleeease."

Davy's fingers flew across the screen then he sat back and gawped. "How the hell did you know that?"

"Now, now. Watch your language. I'm a sensitive soul."

Jake had joined them out of curiosity. Liam knew Annette was sitting stubbornly at her desk, dying to know what he'd discovered, but she wouldn't give him the pleasure of showing it.

"Liam's just found out that this guy Gerry W…Warner and

Ian Carragher, the victim's husband, went to Queens at the same time to do their Physics degrees. Warner went on to do a doctorate and teaching certificate, and Carragher became a s... surveyor."

Jake beamed at Liam as proudly as if he was his Dad. "Well done, sir."

"Well done for what, Liam?"

They turned at the sound of Craig's voice and Jake beckoned him across the floor.

"Liam had a hunch, sir."

"Another one! You're batting one hundred today, Liam. What's this one about?"

"Carragher lied. He knows Gerry Warner a damn sight better than he let on."

"Update me."

Liam ran through what they'd found, ending with. "He lied for a reason, boss."

Craig nodded. "You're right. There's dirt here somewhere and both the Carraghers and Gerry Warner are involved. Get Warner in for interview, Liam."

"What about Ian Carragher? He lied to me."

Crag shook his head. "No, not yet. Not until we have his wife's I.D. Even then we need to remember that he's a victim's relative. He could run screaming to the press about police brutality and we need that like a hole in the head."

"Sir?"

Craig turned towards Jake, half-expecting him to raise his hand. "Yes?"

"If Carragher is a possible next victim then don't we have to protect him, just in case?"

"It's a valid point, but it's just speculation at the moment that there will be any more deaths. All we can do is tell him to take care. Do that please, Jake, but subtly. Remember we haven't even confirmed that our body is his wife yet." He turned back to Liam. "Liam, you and Annette lift Warner. Jake will go back to see Carragher and put him on alert. But Jake..."

"Yes, sir?"

"Don't give him any reason to think he's a suspect. If there's any evidence in that house I want it still there, if or when we get a search warrant. Emphasise the concern for his welfare aspect for now. Understood?"

***

Mai stroked the young man's naked back and he turned towards her and smiled. He wrapped his muscular arms around her waist and pulled her close, feeling his excitement grow. She laughed and pushed him away, nodding at the clock.

"It's nearly noon. We have to get up."

He smiled down at her and ran a hand through her poker-straight black hair. He lifted the silky strands, burying his face in them and marvelling at their sheen; his own hair was coarse and dull in comparison. He smiled again and moved in for a kiss. Mai returned it gently then slipped quickly out of bed. They had work to do, and it had to be completed soon.

"Can't it wait, Mai? Until the trail on the woman goes cold at least."

Mai shook her head vehemently. "They aren't stupid. They'll realise soon and then they'll come looking for us. Punish the innocent for punishing the guilty; that's what passes for justice in this country."

"We have time. They aren't that good."

She shook her head again, her black bell of hair swinging around her neck. "We have two days at most. Then we have to leave." Her voice changed to a command. "Now get up, and don't make me tell you again."

***

Liam stared at the school's modern façade and whistled. It

was high tech all right; good to see his taxes were paying for something worthwhile. Annette gestured towards the sports hall, halfway across the recreation ground.

"Pete has to teach P.E. in a wooden hut." Annette's husband taught sports in a school near Newtownards. "He would give his right arm for facilities like this."

"He wouldn't be much use on the vaulting horse then."

Liam laughed at his own joke and thanked God Craig wasn't there to tell him off for being politically incorrect. Annette did it instead.

"Liam, that's shocking, even for you."

"OK, OK, don't start giving me grief. I've enough to contend with, with Danni at home."

Annette didn't answer, just walked towards the school's entrance and headed for the Headmaster's suite. They needed to find out which class Gerry Warner was teaching, so they could wait for him at the end. She verbalised her thoughts and Liam shook his head.

"When we find out which class he's in, we go in and get him. None of that 'waiting for class to end' rubbish. He's being brought in for interview, not afternoon tea."

"That's not necessary and it'll disrupt the kids."

Liam raised an eyebrow at Annette disagreeing, "It might not be necessary, Inspector, but it's what we're going to do. I want Warner good and scared by the time he reaches High Street. Remember that a woman's dead and he was with her the night before."

Annette flushed red at his pulling rank and stormed ahead. By the time they'd reached the Headmaster's office, the 'Headmaster' had morphed into a Headmistress and Annette face had cooled to a dull pink.

The woman that came out to greet them was small and round, with a cheerful expression that said years of recalcitrant teenagers hadn't managed to wear her down. Liam led from the hip.

"Mrs…?"

"Willoughby. Ann Willoughby. And you are?"

Liam whipped out his badge, signalling Annette to do the same. "Detective Chief Inspector Liam Cullen and Inspector Annette McElroy. We're here to speak to a Mr Gerry Warner in connection with a case. We hope he can provide us with some information."

Willoughby's smile dropped. Liam had managed to wipe it off her face where eons of children had failed.

"Dr Warner is in class at the moment, I'm afraid. Can't you come back at the end of the day?"

'Dr' Warner. He'd forgotten about the doctorate. It made no difference. PhD's were no protection against prison. Liam shook his head.

"No, I'm afraid not, Mrs Willoughby. This is a murder enquiry." Her eyes widened in alarm but Liam ploughed on. "Can you tell us which classroom he's in, please? And you should find someone to cover the rest of his day. He'll be with us for some time."

Annette tutted inwardly. Liam's scare tactics might work but they weren't very nice.

Ann Willoughby rushed to her secretary's desk and studied a diary on the wall. "He's taking double chemistry in Block A. Across the quadrangle, room sixty-one. But…"

Liam was at the door before she finished the sentence. "Thank you, Mrs Willoughby. And please don't phone Mr Warner to try to warn him. That would be a serious offence."

Liam was down the corridor and across the quad before Annette had time to object. She ran behind him, struggling to keep up with his long strides and finally caught up with him outside the room.

"Liam, Liam, slow down a minute. Remember there are children in there and they'll be scared if you go crashing in. Let me bring him out."

She panted, trying to catch her breath. Liam thought for a

moment then nodded. Perps were fair game but kids were another thing. Annette wasn't right about treating Warner gently, but she was right about this.

He dropped his voice to as close to a whisper as he ever got. "OK. Knock and go in. Say you've come from the Headmistress and there's an urgent matter for him to deal with. Walk him to the end of the hall and I'll meet you there. But if he tries to leg it the cuffs go on."

Annette nodded then watched as Liam walked slowly back to the corner and stood in the shadows, out of sight. She took a deep breath and knocked on the half-glass door, entering on Gerry Warner's "come in".

The classroom was long and bright, with high wooden workbenches, strewn with glass flasks and microscopes. Boys and girls in their late teens were seated or walking around the room, working on some experiment and chatting each other up. Gerry Warner was seated behind the front desk, scribbling on a notebook from a pile beside him. It reminded Annette of her own school days and she wondered if anything ever really changed.

Warner placed the notebook back on the pile and stood up with a puzzled look. "Yes? Can I help you?"

"Hello, Dr Warner. I've come from the Headmistress to tell you that there's an urgent matter you need to come and attend to."

"Urgent? What is it?"

Annette lied and asked for forgiveness in her mind. "I'm sorry, sir, I don't know."

"I can't leave my class unattended."

"Mrs Willoughby's arranging cover for you."

Warner's expression changed from puzzle to suspicion and he glanced quickly towards the window. For one moment Annette thought that he was going to jump, except that they were six floors up and it was almost certain death. Warner must have realised it as well, because finally he shrugged in defeat.

He lifted a textbook and scrawled a list of page numbers on the board, then barked. "Read those before I come back. There'll be a quiz." It was followed by a quieter. "Someone will be along in a moment to supervise you." Then he walked coolly past Annette into the corridor.

For a moment Annette thought it had all gone to plan but once outside the classroom Gerry Warner shoved her to the floor and sprinted off in the direction of the stairs. Thirty seconds later she heard an almighty thud and she knew that he'd been stopped by Liam's foot or fist. It didn't matter which; Liam had been right. Warner wasn't behaving like an innocent man, so they wouldn't treat him like one.

Chapter Seven

John was meeting Craig at six o'clock, which left him with four hours to fill and he thought he might as well fill them with the case. It would give them a conversation opener before he bored the ass off Craig about Natalie. He flicked on his computer and scrolled through the latest lab results; nothing. Although that didn't mean that they weren't available. It sometimes took hours for things to be put on the intranet.

There was only one real way to find out if they were ready, so John voted with his feet and took the lift to the fifth floor. He was so deep in thought when the doors slid open that he stepped out without looking. John's lack of attention was rewarded by a feminine sounding yelp and the clatter of papers falling to the floor. A slim woman with long blonde hair was standing in front of him, holding her nose and gazing dolefully down at the shambles John had made of her files.

"Oh God, I'm sorry. Did I hurt you?"

The woman lifted her eyes from the mess at her feet and half-smiled, removing her hand gingerly from her face for him to look.

"Is it bleeding? Only I'd rather not have a nose-job this afternoon."

John stared at the woman's face, horrified by the appearance of a bruise. He touched her reddening nose warily with one finger, his practiced medical hand able to tell that it wasn't broken. He exhaled gratefully and smiled.

"No fracture, thank goodness. But you'll definitely have a black eye."

John hunkered down quickly to gather her notes and handed them to her in an unruly heap, babbling in a flustered tone. "I hope they weren't for something important? I'll help you rearrange them, if you've got the time?"

The woman smiled at his obvious embarrassment and extended her free hand. "Katy Stevens. I'm an endocrinologist at St Mary's Trust."

John stared at her for a moment then realised that he'd left her hand hanging rudely in mid-air. He grasped it so firmly it made her wince and he apologised again. John waved her to a bench beside the lift.

"Katy Stevens? You know my girlfriend, Natalie Ingrams, don't you?"

A smile spread across the woman's small face, throwing the darkening bruise into stark relief against her tan. John winced again. She looked like someone had punched her.

"Yes, we're great friends. We see each other practically every day at the M.P.E. on the Lisburn Road." Katy's smile became a grin and she nodded. "You must be John. She talks about you a lot."

The mix of pride and concern that John felt at being discussed showed on his face.

She laughed. "It's all good, I promise. Natalie thinks you're wonderful. Although for God's sake don't tell her I told you that. She'll kill me." She glanced around the lab, indicating the rows of steel machines. "Do you work here?"

"Downstairs. I deal with the dead, I'm afraid."

"Does that mean you're afraid of the dead? Or you're apologising for dealing with them?"

John laughed. "The latter. It doesn't make for great dinner party conversation."

"Unless you're with doctors, in which case we're all fascinated."

"Or the police. They're even more fascinated, trust me."

John glanced at Katy's face again, marvelling at how pretty

she was, even with an enormous bruise. Her next words surprised him; they were accompanied by a rueful frown.

"I dealt with the police last year. About the death of a young mother. After I got over the shock of being interrogated, I have to say they did a good job."

"Oh? Who 'interrogated' you?" He emphasised the word in an amused tone.

"A D.C.I. Craig. He was nice. Natalie knows him. I bumped into him again just before Christmas at an art gallery."

"That would be Marc. He was always the arty romantic sort."

"Actually, I believe he was on a case."

The Trainor murder. John smiled and stood up.

"How does your nose feel now?"

"How does it look?"

"Nice shape. Pity about the colour."

Katy reached into her handbag, withdrawing a small mirror and grimacing at her reflection. She touched her nose cautiously then gave John a reassuring look.

"It looks worse than it feels, honestly. Don't worry. But I'll make sure to tell Natalie that her boyfriend hit me. It should be good for a rant or two." She laughed at John's crestfallen face. "I'm joking. Walking into a door makes me sound much less stupid." She rose and turned towards the lift. "Well, perhaps I'll see you again sometime, under better circumstances. Goodbye."

John watched as Katy walked away then he had a thought. He went to the reception desk and gathered his expected results, then went back to his office to lay his plan.

***

Jake walked away from Ian Carragher's business place in Academy Street, scratching his head. Liam had said Carragher was upset at the thought of what might have happened to his wife, and he was still that, although he'd continued to work. But what Liam hadn't said was how cool a character he was.

When he'd tried to explain that he might be at risk Carragher had just shrugged and said. "It's the price you pay." The price you pay for what?

He'd heard similar things said by guys in the military and armed response, even from some criminals. He could understand it from all of them; they took chances every day. But Ian Carragher wasn't in a high risk occupation; surveying was hardly cutting edge stuff. The fact that Carragher had said it meant he thought he was taking risks he might have to pay for, and if they weren't at work then that meant they were somewhere else in his life. Perhaps in an area that had involved his wife?

Jake climbed back in the car and drove down the Dunbar Link, heading back towards the C.C.U. He was going to take a close look at Mr and Mrs Carragher, a very close look, and he had a hunch that something very nasty was going to turn up.

***

"Is Warner saying anything, Liam?"

"Not a dicky bird, boss. Clammed up as soon as we got him into the car."

Craig gazed through the two-way mirror at the man lounging on the interview room chair at High Street Station.

"What did he say before then?"

Liam sniffed. "A delicate combination of four letter words, and the grammar school teacher's equivalent of 'you'll never make anything stick.'"

"Like what?"

"Ah well, that's it exactly, isn't it? We hadn't accused him of anything, just said we needed him to come in and help us with our enquiries. I didn't even say it was anything to do with Eileen Carragher's death. But he's feeling as guilty as hell about something."

Craig peered through the glass then gave Liam a rueful look.

"How did he get that fat lip?"

Liam glanced at him sheepishly. "Well… Annette was asking him to come and help with an urgent matter, and he pushed her to the ground then legged it down the corridor, where…"

Craig interrupted. "Where, let me guess, you were waiting to stop him? Gently, of course."

"Got it in one." He threw Warner a menacing glance. "He shouldn't have hit a woman."

Craig nodded. "Is Annette OK?"

"Aye, pretty much."

Craig stared at the glass, anticipating the chat they were about to have with Warner. "You go in first, Liam. I want to see how he reacts to you. I'll be there in a moment."

Liam pulled open the viewing-room door and ten seconds later he appeared on the other side of the glass. Craig could hear his booming voice without the microphone, but he turned it on anyway, to catch Warner's much softer words. After Liam ran through the formalities of name, address and whatever, he sat back in silence, folding his hands demurely on the table top.

Craig stared at their suspect, wondering what made him tick. Gerry Warner looked for all the world like an ordinary bloke. A school teacher; average shirt, average tie, average height. Sixty but looking late forties. Steel-grey hair, still all his own and not bad looking in a gaunt, sharp-jawed way. No-one would have looked twice at him in the street. Nothing about Warner said 'killer of middle-aged headmistresses', but then Craig didn't believe for one moment that he was.

Gerry Warner hadn't killed Eileen Carragher, any more than her husband had. But he was up to his ears in something, and whatever it was had led to Eileen Carragher's death. Craig watched the two men sit in silence for a moment then he entered the interview room, taking a seat beside Liam and introducing himself for the tape. Warner's expression soured when he heard Craig's rank and his sarcastic tone matched.

"Oh my. Here come the judge."

Craig smiled slightly, recognising the reference to a 1960s song. It would have been released when Warner was young. Warner had managed to summarise his obvious contempt for authority in one brief phrase. Despite the fact he was a teacher, Gerry Warner obviously didn't see himself as 'the man'. Craig imagined him as an anarchic student, wild, free and protesting every cause, until life and a mortgage had forced him to get a job and join the herd. What a blow reality was to some people.

"Good afternoon, Dr Warner. Thank you for helping us with our enquiries."

Warner snorted. "I didn't have much sodding choice, did I?" He gestured towards Liam. "King Kong here invited me with his fists."

Craig's tone was cool but firm. "Now, that's not strictly true, Dr Warner, is it? Inspector McElroy asked you politely and you chose to assault her. The moment you did that you committed a crime. D.C.I. Cullen was merely impeding a criminal's flight."

"Call it what you want, Craig. I'm getting my union lawyers on the job and I'll make sure this is in the press."

"Whatever you wish. Now, we originally asked you here to help us with an urgent matter. Aren't you at all curious what that might be?"

"Shortage of brain cells in the police force I suppose. Sorry, I can't help you with that. I need all of mine."

Craig saw Liam's fists whiten and shot him a look that said 'stand down'. He continued speaking in mellifluous tones.

"Very amusing, Dr Warner, but it's something much more serious than that. I understand that you know a Mrs Eileen Carragher?"

Warner scanned Craig's face suspiciously, certain that everything he said was a trap. When he'd run out of ways that Craig's question might have been one, he answered.

"Yes. I know her. We went to college together to do our P.G.C.E."

"P.G.C.E.?"

"Post graduate certificate of education. To teach."

"Ah." Craig deliberately paused for too long, just to make Warner sweat. He was rewarded by droplets forming on his top lip. "But you've seen her since. At college reunions for instance?"

"Yes. I saw her on Saturday for drinks." Warner glared at Craig and then Liam, then gave an exasperated sigh. "Look, what is this about?"

Craig leaned forward and watched as Warner leaned back to match, maintaining the distance between them.

"We have reason to believe that Mrs Carragher may have been the victim of a brutal assault sometime between Saturday and Sunday. We're trying to establish her whereabouts on those days."

Warner's eyes widened in shock, and something more. Craig recognised it immediately and Liam threw him a glance that said he had too. It was fear. Gerry Warner was afraid of something. Something to do with Eileen Carragher's assault. His shock said he hadn't known that Eileen Carragher had been attacked, and more, that he hadn't done it. But his fear said that the reasons behind her attack might apply to him as well.

"HOW?"

The word was shouted so loudly that Liam jumped, anticipating a flying fist. It didn't come. Instead Gerry Warner's eyes were frantic. He was desperate for an answer.

"A woman's body was found, with severe injuries. The location and items found lead us to believe it may have been Mrs Carragher. We're still waiting for a formal identification, but…"

"You can't tell from her face? Why can't you tell from her face?"

Warner's voice rose in volume as he repeated the question in differing permutations, until finally Craig shook his head. She had no face. Warner slumped back in his chair like he'd been punched in the chest and put his head in his hands, saying "my

God" again and again.

Craig asked him several more questions without success, nodding Liam to try the same, but they'd got all they were going to get from Gerry Warner for today. Craig called Jack Harris to put him back in a cell and get the on-call doctor to check him out. The last thing they needed was Warner topping himself in the station. They wandered into the staff-room and Liam put the kettle on to boil.

"Well, that was useless, boss."

Craig shook his head. "Not completely. We know that he saw her on Saturday, but my money says she was alive when they parted, whatever time that was. He was too shocked by her death to have had anything to do with it." He paused, remembering Gerry Warner's reaction. "Did you see how frightened he was?"

"Aye. What was that all about?"

"Whatever the reason was for Eileen Carragher being killed, Warner's afraid that it applies to him as well. He thinks he's next and he's scared stiff."

Chapter Eight

The moment Craig and Liam walked onto the squad-room floor, Jake beckoned them over to his desk. He started speaking before they had time to say hello.

"I went to see Ian Carragher. Ask me what I found out?"

Liam humoured him. "What did you find out?"

"He's expecting the worst to happen to him. He's expecting the same fate as his wife."

Craig pulled up a chair. "What makes you think that, Jake?"

"Something he said. 'It's the price you pay.' So I thought; the price you pay for what?"

Liam looked puzzled, but Craig could see where Jake was heading. He waved him on.

"People who say that usually work in risky jobs, or take risks somewhere else in life. Yes?"

Craig nodded.

"Well Carragher's a house surveyor, so there's no risk there, is there? I suppose he could indulge in high-risk pastimes outside work, like gambling or bungee-jumping, but he doesn't seem the type. And he said it when I warned him he could be in danger linked to his wife's death, so..."

Liam finished the sentence. "So you reckon that whatever got the wife killed was high risk and he was part of it?"

Jake glared at him; put-out that Liam had stolen his punch line. His sunny demeanour returned quickly and he nodded. "Yes, that's exactly it. I think that whatever got his wife killed, he was part of it as well."

Craig smiled. Jake was as good as he'd thought he was when

they'd met on the Ackerman case. It had been his initiative then that had helped them make essential links.

"So what have you been doing with your theory?"

Jake pointed to a pile of print-outs and beckoned Davy over from his desk. "Davy kindly ran a whole host of background checks for me on Ian and Eileen Carragher, separately and together. Something very interesting has come up."

Davy ambled over holding his computer tablet and Craig hoped it would have Jake's print-outs collated in one neat table. He wasn't disappointed. Davy tapped the screen and a table popped up, showing everything relevant in the Carragher's lives.

They didn't gamble, they didn't even have credit cards. If anything they were careful with money, pouring everything into paying off the mortgage on the townhouse Liam had visited the day before. There were no criminal records; in fact there was nothing that seemed a motive to kill them. And Ian Carragher definitely didn't bungee-jump.

Liam snorted. "Mr and Mrs exciting, not."

Craig hid a smile at the modern expression. Davy and Jake were rubbing off on him.

"Don't be so quick, Liam." Craig pointed to a line on the table. "What's that, Davy?"

"Glad you noticed it. That's the Carragher's little hideaway. A house in Newcastle, near the Mourne Mountains. And not a s...small one either. Quite the mansion if the estate agents blurb from its s...sale in 1995 is to be believed. It cost one hundred and fifty thousand back then."

Liam whistled. "Mortgage?"

Davy shook his head. "Bought outright with cash."

Liam sat forward, suddenly interested. "Now you're talking, lad. A teacher and a surveyor affording that? Something stinks."

Craig interjected and pointed at another line.

Davy smiled again. "That's when they got married. 1995, two months before they bought the house."

"Any idea where they met?"

"Every idea, boss. From 1989 until 2004 they worked together at a private school in Bangor."

"I can see why she might have been teaching there, but what was a surveyor like Ian Carragher doing at a school?"

"He didn't w...work there. He was on the Board of Governors."

Liam sat back, disinterested in the Carraghers' romance. "That's fair enough, boss. Lots of people meet at work."

"True, but how many buy a mansion for cash two months after they get married?"

Craig turned to Jake and Davy in turn. "Excellent work, both of you. Now, I need to you do something else..."

***

Bar Red. 6 p.m.

The interior of Bar Red was full of wood and welcoming leather chairs that just begged to play host to conversations; deep or trivial depending upon the occupant's mood. They'd certainly witnessed several of John and Craig's meaning-of-life discussions through the years, and they were about to witness another one now. John was standing at the long curved bar when Craig arrived, his loosened tie and swiftly removed jacket saying that it was evening louder than any clock.

"Hi, John."

"The usual?"

"Thanks." Craig scanned the room. "Let's sit down. There are some chairs over there."

"Bad day?"

Craig laughed. "No. But my back's a wreck. Lucia had me under her car all day Saturday, fixing a leak in the petrol tank."

Lucia was Craig's younger sister by eleven years and she worked for a charity. Her fifteen-year-old car had deserved a decent burial years before, but she didn't earn enough money to replace it and she was too stubborn to let her family buy her another one, so big brother had got roped in.

John grabbed the drinks and carried them across to two seats by the window. Craig threw his jacket down and took a deep drink of cold beer, like a man dying of thirst.

"Do you fancy eating here or going on, Marc? There's a new restaurant I fancy trying."

Craig laughed. John was always finding unusual new places to eat. He bowed his head in mock submission. "Whatever you want. What is it this time? Bolivian or Eskimo?"

"Vegetarian. There's a great place called Archana on the Dublin Road. Did you know there're thousands of vegetarians living in Belfast now? A girl told me the other day in the bank."

"Good looking, was she?"

John liked pretty women. Didn't they all? But whereas most men had an agenda, John just talked to them. It was as if a conversation signalled that they found him attractive and he didn't need to pursue it any further. Natalie was quite safe.

Craig set down his beer and wrenched his tie lower; oblivious to the fact that he'd was revealing some dark chest hair. The women sitting to their right weren't quite so oblivious. Craig decided to start the real conversation, knowing it would take John an hour to get round to it.

"So what was so bad that you wanted to start drinking at six o'clock, without even taking time to change?"

John stared into his beer, unconsciously tapping a rhythm against the glass with his thumb. Craig watched him absentmindedly for a moment, then his eyes widened in astonishment.

"My God! You're getting married."

John looked at Craig, aghast, unsure how he'd guessed what he wanted to talk about. "What? No. No I'm not. I'm definitely not getting married. Where the hell did you get that idea?"

Craig grinned and pointed at his hand. "You've just been tapping the wedding march against the side of the glass. Da-

dat-da-da."

"I wasn't!" John stared at his errant thumb as if it belonged to someone else. "Was I?"

"Yep!"

"Bloody hell. My subconscious should know better than to tap that in front of someone who's Mum played classical music to him in the womb."

Craig's Italian mother Mirella had been a concert pianist and she'd force-fed her children classical music all their lives.

"My Mum has nothing to do with it. A man on a galloping horse could have worked that one out." Craig lifted his class in salute. "When's the big day?"

"What? Don't talk rubbish! There's no big day, and for God's sake don't say that in front of Natalie or I'll be fitted for tails before I can blink. I haven't asked her."

"Yet."

John furrowed his brow and Craig knew that was what he'd wanted to discuss.

"If you want my opinion on whether or not you should propose to Natalie, then the answer's yes."

John blustered. "Now hang on, I didn't say that."

"Look mate. If you're even thinking about doing it, that means you want to, and in my opinion it would be a bloody good thing."

John scowled. "I didn't ask your opinion."

Craig was unoffended, but now that the horse had got to water he wasn't going to let it die of thirst. He continued undeterred.

"What did you want to ask me then?"

"Well...I feel..."

John stopped mid-sentence and Craig filled in the gap. "Confused?" He glanced at the clock and laughed, amused at his friend's discomfort. "Hungry?"

"What? No. I'm not hungry... Well I am." John was always hungry. "But that's not it. I...I feel guilty."

67

Craig gawped at him. What did he have to feel guilty about?

"I feel I should make some sort of commitment to her. After all, we've been together for well over a year. It doesn't seem right to keep on living in sin."

"You're not. She has her own place."

John shot him an anguished glance. "You know what I mean."

Craig could see that he was genuinely upset so he eased up on the banter. "You mean that you love her too much not to make a commitment."

John nodded. "Does that sound all Jane Austen and shit?"

Craig laughed. "And shit? Any minute now you're going to break into a rap. No, it doesn't sound all Jane Austen and shit. Or maybe it does, but so what? Natalie's perfect for you. You love her and you want to be fair to her. There's nothing wrong with that."

John gulped down a mouthful of beer, then gazed warily at Craig over the top of the glass.

"So you think that I should?"

"Well, I'm hardly a success story romantically, but if you want my opinion I think you should do what will make you happy. You're obviously not happy just dating Natalie anymore, so you either need to formalise things or break up. Do you want to break up with her?"

John's face dropped. "God no. I'd..."

Craig didn't make him say it. "OK, then breaking-up's not an option. Marriage then? Or co-habiting."

"No."

The 'no' was so firm it took Craig a moment to realise that he didn't know which 'no' John had meant.

"No to co-habiting, or no to marriage?"

"No to co-habiting. I don't like it. It's a cop-out. And all the research from Scandinavian countries shows it leads to a higher divorce rate later on."

Craig nodded. He didn't much like the thought of it either.

It felt like dipping one foot into the lake, instead of having the balls to take the plunge. He and Julia had discussed it, but that was because of geography. He and Camille had actually done it, but they were young and poor. At forty-three there was just no reason that seemed to fit.

"OK then. You don't want to be without her, you love her and you don't want to co-habit. Marriage it is then. Go for it."

John blanched visibly. Craig left him to it and went to bar for another round of drinks. When he got back John's fingers were tapping again, more cheerfully this time. Craig watched the thoughts running across his friend's face and knew exactly what they were. He'd had them himself just before he'd proposed to Camille.

"Don't worry about where you ask her; just ask her when it feels right. And for God's sake don't actually buy an engagement ring. By all means look and have an idea, but she'll want to choose her own."

John's face fell suddenly. "What'll I do if she says no?"

Craig shook his head, laughing. "She won't. Julia told me Natalie knew you were the man for her after your second date. Don't ask me how they know these things but women seem to."

Craig fell quiet for a moment, remembering Julia. He missed her. They'd broken up just before Christmas. It was the worst time of year for a split, but was there ever a good one? They'd agreed not to see or call each other for at least six months, so they could adjust to being colleagues again instead of lovers, but it was hard. He seemed to have too many weekends to fill now.

John stared at Craig's handsome face then glanced at the girls to his right. They were smiling across at them flirtatiously so John asked the question.

"Those girls seem to like us. Do you want to send them over a drink?"

Craig laughed loudly. "Do I have 'sad lonely man' tattooed that obviously across my forehead? Thanks, but no thanks. I'm not looking for another relationship. Besides, it's you we're here to sort out."

"Well, if you're not interested in a relationship then you won't want to hear who I met today in the lab."

"Who?"

"You said you weren't interested."

Craig squinted at John like a member of MI5 and he caved in.

"Katy Stevens. You met her during the case at St Mary's last year. She said you interrogated her. I bet you gave her that exact look."

"I didn't interrogate her! I interviewed her like several others."

"Well, she remembers you well. She must have enjoyed it" He smirked. "You didn't tell me you bumped into her on the Trainor case as well."

Craig squinted at him. "Who are you? My mother? I chatted to her in an art gallery for all of two minutes. I'd completely forgotten about it until now."

It was John's turn to laugh. "Don't ever commit a crime, Marc, because you're a lousy liar."

Craig stared into his glass, rubbing the rim irritatingly until it whined. Finally he spoke without looking up. "How did she look?"

"Better before I accidentally walked into her and almost broke her nose."

Craig gawped at him. "You did what?"

John folded his arms defensively. "I didn't mean to. I was thinking about Natalie and I walked out of the lift straight into her…she was very good about it, but she's got a huge bruise."

Craig didn't know whether to thump John or laugh, so he did both.

"Ow! Anyway. I think she likes you, so why don't I get Natalie to organise a double date?"

"Not unless you want me to let slip that you're planning to propose…"

Chapter Nine

The C.C.U. Wednesday. 8 a.m.

John had meant to tell Craig about the lab results the night before, but he'd forgotten when their early evening banter had turned into another drunken night. He dialled the Murder Squad's office and was greeted by Nicky's voice. She sounded flat and sad, completely unlike her usual lively self.

"Hi, Nicky. Is Marc there?"

"I'll just put you through, Dr Winter."

Before John could enquire how she was, Craig's voice was on the phone. "Hi, what did you forget to tell me last night?"

"The lab results. And it's your fault. You moved us onto whiskey."

Craig laughed, pushing his hangover to its edge. "Fire away."

"We were right. Eileen Carragher's corneas were being lubricated using artificial tears. Check with the husband that she didn't use them for any other reason, but if not, they lubricated her eyes after they cut off her eyelids, so she could watch. I've sent the chemical composition over to Davy, but good luck with finding out where they were bought, they're pretty common. I also found a clotting agent on her. They must have used it to stem the blood so she didn't die too soon."

"Great. Any more good news?"

"Yes actually. I think Des and Davy may have found your knife, but I'll leave Davy to tell you about that. And the C.S.I's lifted a print from one of the items at Eileen Carragher's feet."

Craig interrupted eagerly. "A print? I don't suppose you've

found a match?"

"Sorry, no. But I can tell you it came from someone tiny. I'm talking Natalie tiny."

Natalie Ingrams was only five-feet-tall. Craig smiled. He'd wondered how long it would take John to drop her name into the conversation. John was still reporting.

"I've compared it to standard sizes and it matches a child of either sex up to the age of eleven, or an adult with very tiny hands – probably a small woman. With hands that small you're looking at a shoe size of around a ladies' three, and surprise, surprise, the C.S.I.'s found a lady's size two-and-a-half shoe print at the scene."

"Couldn't it have been from someone using the playground the day before?"

John shook his head, and then realised that Craig couldn't see him. "No. It's not a child's shoe, it had a stiletto heel. And it was in the arterial blood spray. It was definitely made after Eileen Carragher's throat was cut and no-one but the caretaker would have been in the playground before we were called. It's locked at night."

If the playground was locked how had their perps got in? Craig parked the query and carried on.

"So one of Eileen Carragher's murderers was a tiny woman or a young girl?"

"Seems so. A woman's more likely. It's a primary school so it's unlikely any ten-year-old would be wearing stiletto heels. A small woman would explain why it would have taken more than one person to do the job."

"I suppose."

John heard the thoughtful tone in Craig's voice. "What? You've got a theory, haven't you?"

"Maybe. But nothing that I'm ready to share."

John paused for so long that Craig thought he'd lost the call. "John? Are you still there?"

"I'm here. Look… it's not my business, but is Nicky all right?

She sounds miserable."

"I know, but she won't talk about it. Don't worry; I'm digging around to see what I can find out. Send over the print, will you; I want Davy to check it out. Now, go and do some work. I'm off to see what else he's found."

***

They'd rested for long enough, now it was time to move. Yesterday had been about watching and waiting for news about the bitch's death, and gathering together the things for tonight's kill. The local news had been quiet. Nothing except 'the body of a fifty-five-year-old woman was found in south Belfast'. No name, nothing about the school and nothing about the way she'd died.

Mai wasn't surprised. Typical bloody authorities, never there when you needed them. She'd found that out too often to her cost. She ruffled her dark hair and gazed in the mirror. She was pretty, she knew that. She'd caught men's admiring glances all her life and they were hard to miss. Slavering dogs the lot of them. The women weren't much better. Something about her doll-like prettiness had drawn their hatred, making them cling desperately onto their men whenever she entered a room.

They were stupid. All she'd ever wanted was their friendship, not their ugly men. But it didn't matter now. She was beyond all that. Once they'd completed their task they would go somewhere that no-one could touch them anymore.

***

8.30 a.m.

"Tell me about the knife, Davy."

Davy jumped. He'd been surfing men's fashion sites and hadn't heard Craig walking up behind him. Craig leaned over his shoulder and clicked on an image. It was a slim-cut black suit paired with a dark red shirt. It was like something he would have worn, tieless, into the office in London. Now he only got to wear it on a big night out. Belfast fashion had a way to go.

"That would suit you. If you're trying to impress Maggie, that is."

Davy swivelled his chair round to face his boss, flustered by being caught out. He hid his embarrassment, not as he'd done for years, by blushing and stammering, but behind a show of detailed forensic knowledge that said he was all grown up.

"The knife's very unusual, chief."

Craig smiled inwardly. Gone were the 'sirs' that once preceded every conversation between them, often elongated for so long by Davy's stutter that Craig had been tempted to tell him to call him Marc, just to ease his pain. He hadn't, for one reason. Not because he liked standing on ceremony or because he was impressed by his own rank, but because Nicky had scolded him for a year before Davy had joined for telling people to do just that. He remembered her words being forced out through pursed lips.

"This isn't London and it isn't The Met, sir. You can't come back here after fifteen years away, all cool and 'street' and expect everyone in Northern Ireland to suddenly understand. It's traditional here, remember that. You're the boss, not everyone's best friend."

Craig had railed against it, having angry words with her the first few times that she'd told him off. If he was the boss then it was his house, his rules. Finally he'd realised that she was right. They might be his rules, but the first time one of his sergeants had said "as soon as I'm ready, Marc," when he'd given an order during an armed assault, Craig knew that Nicky had been spot-on. Calling him 'sir' might be a pain in the office, but in a shoot-out it might be the only thing that saved lives.

Craig was shaken out of his reminiscing by Davy pulling a photograph up on the screen. At first glance it looked like raw sausage meat; Craig didn't want to think what part of the human body it was. Davy leaned in and pointed to a slash down its centre.

"Can you see how deep that cut is?"

"Yes."

"And that it penetrates s…sideways as well?"

"Sure. And?"

"That's because the blade was broad and they angled it as it went in. Des has made a cast of it."

Craig realised he was staring at a piece of Eileen Carragher so he quickly stared at Davy instead. "What does it show?"

"The blade was twenty-two centimetres long and eight point five deep." Davy tapped a second screen to his left and a page of images pulled up. They were meat cleavers. "The cut was uniform all the way through s…so the blade didn't narrow from hilt to tip."

Craig peered at the screen. "Like a meat cleaver."

"Yes. But there was s…something else unusual about it. The edge was s…serrated."

"How could Des tell?"

"Tiny tears in the muscle. It wasn't just serrated, boss. It was razor-edged. Like it had been s…sharpened especially. If Mrs Carragher w…was awake the pain would have been unbearable."

Craig glanced at him. "My guess is she was awake the whole time."

Davy shook his head. "No. You're w…wrong. She couldn't have been."

His voice was adamant and Craig stared at him curiously. Even if he was still young enough to overreact emotionally Davy was a scientist. If he said 'no' that firmly they'd better listen.

"Why not?"

Davy pointed to the knives. "Look at the razor-edges." He pointed back to the other image. "Now look at how deep the cut in her muscle was." He stared at Craig. "Do you really think anyone could cope with that level of pain unless they were anaesthetised? They would die from s...shock."

Craig's eyes widened. He was right! He'd missed it. John had missed it. They'd all missed it except Davy.

"Davy, you're brilliant!"

Davy blushed, then realised that he hadn't asked why. Liam asked for him. He'd entered the squad a moment before and heard the last part of their debate.

"Why's he brilliant, boss?"

Craig beckoned him across and brought him up to speed with the blade and Davy's theory that Eileen Carragher had to have been anaesthetised as they cut. Liam shook his head.

"It wouldn't have been a punishment then, lad. And these bastards wanted her to suffer."

"But s...she'd have blacked out from the pain."

"He's right, Liam she would. Unless..."

They gazed at Craig. He contemplated drawing out his explanation to make himself look good then decided against it.

"Davy's right. The only way that Eileen Carragher would have been awake for long enough to suffer was if, either she was anaesthetised locally in each area while they cut her..."

Liam shook his head. "Too kind."

"Too kind to make you w...watch while they hacked away bits of you one by one! I'd hate to be your enemy, Liam!"

Craig pushed on. "Or if they didn't anaesthetise her but let her black out, then revived her again."

"They w...would have had to resuscitate her, chief. The risks of cardiac arrest would have been very high."

"Good thinking. So either she passed out or she arrested, but either way they resuscitated her every time. That means they had equipment and the location to do it in."

"A hospital? Clinic?"

Craig shook his head. "They aren't medical. John said the cuts showed they had a limited knowledge of anatomy. Besides, everyone's seen people being resuscitated on TV. They could have bought everything they needed over the internet. All they needed was enough space and privacy so that no-one heard her scream."

He leaned in and typed a few words on Davy's keyboard. The lab report from John's eye-drops popped up.

"John says her eyes were lubricated regularly using these. Can you run them through the usual databases, Davy? John says they're common so he doesn't hold out much hope they'll give us a lead, but you never know."

Liam pulled up a chair and sat down, resting his long legs up on a nearby desk. "So let me get this right, boss. They kidnapped her sometime between Saturday and Sunday and cut off her eyelids so she was forced to watch everything they did to her. Then they chopped her up while she was awake and feeling everything, and resuscitated her each time she collapsed?"

"Until they were ready to let her die, then they cut her throat. Yes."

Liam puffed out his cheeks, deep in thought, and Craig smiled as Davy unconsciously mimicked the look and wrinkled his brow. Davy secretly fancied himself as a detective but every time Craig raised the idea of training for the police, the thorny question of physical danger popped up and Day decided that he preferred his desk. Instead he lived vicariously through their adventures.

Liam dropped his feet to the floor with a thud and exclaimed. "BDSM!"

Craig's automatic response was to crack a joke. "Not just at the moment, thanks." Then he wrinkled his brow in thought. Liam was right. Just then Annette and Jake arrived, looking puzzled. They'd heard Liam's shout all the way from the hall so Annette asked the obvious question.

"What's BSDM when it's at home?"

Liam gave her a pitying look and adopted a posture befitting a man of the world. "BDSM. Bondage, domination, sadism and masochism. Sex games."

Jake shook his head knowledgeably. "You've missed out two. Discipline and submission."

Liam sniffed, put out. "When did it change?"

Annette interjected like lightening. "Around the time you started pretending you'd tried it, I expect." Her tone was so dry that even Nicky laughed.

"Whatever it stands for Liam is right. BDSM fits."

Craig ran quickly through their earlier discussion, much to Annette's disgust, then he theorised further about their killers.

"Only someone who has knowledge of restraints and torture would have been able to do this. And they'd need a particular mind-set. It's all very well reading about BDSM, but actually hurting another human being for hours and being oblivious to their pain requires something else."

"Aye, sadism, boss. Real sadism, not your 'tie me up with a silk scarf and whack me on the backside on a Saturday night sort'."

Annette arched one eyebrow. "And you know this how, Liam?"

"Ah now. Beneath this sophisticated exterior…"

The sound of Nicky snorting loudly made them all laugh again.

"Seriously, Liam. Annette's right. How do you know so much about the BDSM scene?"

Liam smiled as if he was remembering something. "During the Troubles one of the big loyalist paramilitaries had a BDSM club in Smithfield market that he used as a front for his little war games. We staked it out for months, then Jack Harris and I went undercover inside."

"Jack Harris! Our Jack Harris, everybody's Dad?"

Jake's words echoed everyone's thoughts. Craig looked around the group. Every face was screwed up; trying to imagine Jack Harris dressed as a leather gimp. It was like hearing that Santa Claus wore stockings and suspenders under his suit.

"Here. How come you're shocked at the thought of Jack doing it, but not me?"

Craig gestured him to get on with it before the conversation deteriorated even further.

"Aye well, we went under cover for two weeks and I saw more in those two weeks than I ever want to see again. Suffice it to say there's plenty up at Stormont that have stripes on their backs. Anyway, most of the stuff was mild but there was a back room where the rough stuff went on, and more than once an ambulance had to be called when things went too far."

Craig interrupted. "OK then, let's say that Liam's right. Let's say that no-one goes from 'normal', whatever that is, to performing the level of torture that Eileen Carragher endured, without some practice. No matter how much they hated her it would have been hard to listen to screams, unless you'd been sadistic before."

He turned to Davy. "Davy, get onto D.C.I. Hughes in Vice and see what he can tell you about the BDSM scene in Northern Ireland. There must be clubs for it, some well-known, some less so. Vice will know where they are. When you're talking to him, ask about couples and groups who engage in particularly sadistic sex. Liam, get the word out on the street that we're looking for people with sadistic tendencies, men and women. Particularly small women."

Liam looked shocked and Craig realised he hadn't told them about the woman's footprint at the scene. He brought them up to date.

"If there is a woman involved she didn't do it alone, so we're looking at couples or groups."

Annette leaned forward. "What would you like me to do, sir?"

"Come with me, Annette, and you too, Jake. We're going back to High Street to have another go at Dr Warner."

They turned to walk off the floor and Liam yelled after them. "I'll tell Jack to heat up his whip."

Chapter Ten

Ian Carragher left the science park and pulled out onto the Saintfield Road, indicating towards Belfast city centre. Dr Winter, the pathologist, had been kind, but despite his entreaties he wouldn't let him view the body, veiling his refusal in a mysterious. "Really, it wouldn't help." Instead, he'd sat him down in a small office and brought him tea, then he'd gone through the reports that proved the woman they'd found had definitely been Eileen, his wife of twenty years. The DNA said so, so it must be true.

They'd talked for a while longer and then Dr Winter had left him alone to think until he was ready to leave. Now he was driving into town to make funeral arrangements for the woman he'd loved. Ian Carragher corrected himself honestly; grown to love. They hadn't met in the first flush of youth and neither of them had been holding out for the romantic dream. Just as well.

They'd met in the Board room of a boarding school. Carragher smiled at the duplication then added a homophone. Bored. They'd met at a boring Governors' meeting that he'd dashed into, late and muttering apologies, only to see Eileen Burns sitting there. Primed and ready to do a presentation on the school theatre group.

There'd been something about her prim white blouse and tight chignon that had said 'beneath this front seethes passion just waiting to be unleashed.' He'd been married then, happily as well, so he'd restricted his thoughts about her to his quieter moments. Then his wife had died and things changed and after some complications had been sorted, he'd asked her out. They'd bonded over their common interests, and his joy at finally finding someone just like himself. It prompted him to propose, a decision he was never to regret. Eileen had been a willing pupil who'd become his tutor many years before, and now she was gone, taken while still in relative youth. He knew he would never meet anyone like her again.

Ian Carragher drove on automatic pilot, all his thoughts of twenty years before, barely focusing on the road in front, never mind on the road behind. He parked on the industrial estate on Boucher Crescent and scanned the road for signs of the funeral parlour, clutching the certificate declaring his wife dead. He didn't see the blow approaching but he felt his skull crack and himself fall. Then nothing, until he woke up again, in hell.

***

High Street Station

"You have a go at Warner, Annette. Liam and I tried yesterday. He's handcuffed so you're quite safe."

Annette peered through the two-way glass and felt her skin crawl. There was something about Gerry Warner that made her nauseous, but she didn't know what it was. She voiced her thoughts and Craig stared at her curiously then nodded her on to explain.

"Sometimes I get a feeling about people. An instinct, perhaps."

Craig nodded. He'd seen it in action many times and always put it down to a people sense, developed during Annette's years working as a nurse.

"Nursing?"

Annette shook her head, surprising him. "It's always been there. My Mum says I had it when I was little. If I got a bad feeling about someone, apparently I would scream and run straight back to her. It always turned out that they were a bad lot. Nursing probably made it stronger."

Animals sensed danger; perhaps what Annette felt was the same thing.

"And Warner makes you feel that way?"

"Yes. Very strongly. He makes my skin crawl."

Craig peered through the glass at the man in the interview room. He looked like a villain, yes, but not half as tough as many they'd had in there, and nowhere nearly as dangerous as men he'd seen Annette arrest before.

"Do you feel physically threatened because he pushed you? Would you like me to go in with you?"

Annette shook her head, confused. "No. It's not that. It's not physical. It's something deeper. I can't put my finger on it."

Jake interjected chivalrously. "If he says anything lecherous I'll come straight in."

She smiled at the young sergeant, controlling the urge to ruffle his hair. "That's not it either. But thanks." She shrugged. "It's probably my imagination and I'll laugh about it when I've finished."

She placed her bag on the floor by Craig's feet and left the viewing room, appearing on the other side of the glass a moment later. Annette took her seat and introduced herself professionally, running through Warner's rights and recapping Craig's interview from the day before. Finally she folded her hands on the table and stared Gerry Warner straight in the eye.

"Dr Warner. Could you tell me when you last saw Mrs Eileen Carragher?"

Warner said nothing, just folded his arms and stared back. Annette tried a different tack.

"We know that you had drinks with Mrs Carragher on Saturday, and we're trying to ascertain her whereabouts between then and Monday morning. We'd be grateful for your help."

Warner's posture shifted imperceptibly and Jake twitched. Craig motioned him forward to the mirror.

"Watch Warner's body language, Jake. Do you see how he's extended his leg towards Annette under the table?"

"Yes, sir."

"He's a sexual predator. Annette can't see him doing it but he's trying to touch her. If he does then he'll get a thrill from her being shocked."

Just then Annette surprised them both by pulling her chair back slightly from the table, removing herself from Warner's reach unless he dropped to the floor. Craig smiled. She was good. Years spent dodging male patients. He'd been right to put her in there. Warner had already revealed something about himself that he would never have shown with a man.

"You think I did it, don't you?" Warner's tone was oily and Craig could see his eyes roaming across Annette's body. "You think I killed Eileen after we met for drinks, don't you?"

Annette stared at him, unruffled. "Did you?"

Warner's nostrils flared. "Tell me. How was she killed? Was she bound and whipped? Strangled at the end?"

Craig could see his arousal at the thought. Annette's tone was cool.

"Is that what you like to do, Mr Warner? Hurt women?"

Warner sneered. "They enjoy it. The ultimate high." He licked his lips. "What do you like, Inspector? No, let me guess. You're the buttoned-up type, desperate for a real man to take control and make you scream."

Suddenly Warner lurched across the table, his progress inhibited by his hands being cuffed behind his back. Craig felt his hand on the door handle then he stopped, as Annette's clear tones rang through the air. She sounded perfectly in control. He peered through the glass. Annette was sitting with her arms folded, staring at Warner as if he was an insect on her shoe. She'd got his measure. This was a man who got off on women's fear so she was playing the other card.

"You wouldn't know how, Mr Warner. You'd need someone weaker than you to manage that, and that's not me." Her voice rose in volume. "Now what time did you last see Eileen Carragher on Saturday night?"

Warner didn't move an inch and neither did Annette. Craig and Jake watched from the viewing room waiting for one of them to crack. Finally Warner did. He smiled coldly.

"Touché, Inspector. Well played." He gazed at the clock. "When the big hand meets the little hand on nine, that's when Eileen walked back to her car in the city centre." He shrugged. "Where she went after that I have no idea."

If they were to believe him then Eileen Carragher had been abducted in Belfast sometime after eight-forty-five on Saturday night. It should be easy enough to check with CCTV and traffic cams, but Craig was more intrigued by Warner's choice of words. 'When the big hand meets the little hand...' It was like he was talking to a child, but then he was a teacher. Still...

Annette wrapped up the interview and Jack escorted Warner back to his cell. As she entered the viewing room Annette gave a sigh. "We can't hold him for much longer, sir. We've no proof that he's involved."

Craig nodded. "Not in Eileen Carragher's death, but then I never thought he was. But he's up to his eyes in whatever got her killed, and judging by yesterday's interview he's afraid the same thing will happen to him." He turned to Jake. "Charge him with Annette's assault, Jake, that should let us hold him a bit longer." Craig smiled kindly at her. "How are you? You handled him well."

She shuddered. "I feel like I need a good scrub. If that man hasn't raped someone I'd be very surprised."

"I agree. He's a sexual predator, no question. But you were right that he would need someone weaker than you. Does that explain your earlier feeling?"

Annette shook her head, surprising Craig again. "No. There's something else about him. Something even grubbier than rape."

The door knocked once and Jack Harris entered. "He's back in his box and the kettle's on."

Jack had no idea why they were all grinning at him but he was about to find out.

***

Ian Carragher had been easy to kidnap, much easier than his wife. Mai had guessed that he would be, and in a way she was saddened by the fact. It would've been far more satisfying if Carragher had struggled, but instead he just lay there, anticipating his demise with a half-witted smile.

Carragher gazed up at the woman standing beside him, marvelling at how pretty she was. Who would ever have guessed? He glanced down at the straps restraining him and squirmed in delight, his bald scalp gleaming under the spotlight rigged above his head. He was going to die, he knew that, but at least he would enjoy the pain, unlike Eileen. Pain had always been his thing, so what better way to go? He smirked at the girl.

"Take your time. I'm in no rush."

Mai swung her arm back and slapped him hard in the face, watching as her handprint rose on his skin. "Don't tell me what to do, you bastard! No-one does that."

Carragher's face took on a submissive look. "I'm sorry, mistress."

Mai stared down at him with contempt, and a frisson of pleasure ran down her thighs. The young man saw her reaction and quickly turned her towards him. "No."

She shrugged his hands off, dismissively. "Why not? He's going to die anyway. I might as well enjoy it."

He grabbed her again, more firmly, resisting her attempts to escape. "NO! We're better than that, Mai. Punishment and death, but no enjoyment. We agreed."

Mai stared at him for a moment, her dark eyes on fire, then reason returned and she started to cry. She fell into his arms, sobbing. "I'm sorry, baby. I'm sorry. Thank you for stopping me."

The young man dried her eyes and stroked back her tear-soaked hair, then he kissed her gently and led her from the room. He returned a moment later and walked across to Ian Carragher, hissing into his wrinkled face.

"You're going to die, old man, be very sure of that. But I guarantee there'll be no pleasure in it for you."

***

The C.C.U.

Davy leaned towards his computer screen, playing with the 3D animator until he'd created a clear outline, then he sat back and frowned. In front of him was the model of a woman, whose fingerprint size would match the one that John had found, and who wore size two-and-a-half shoes. After a moment he scratched his head, then rose and walked across the floor.

"Nicky."

Davy gazed at the top of her purple-streaked head, waiting for a reply. None came. Instead Nicky just gazed mournfully into space. He decided to try something.

"Nicky. The boss says he's getting married next week and w…would you like to come?"

There was no reply for a few seconds then Nicky turned towards him with a husky "what?"

"Aha. I thought that would get your attention. He's not really getting married. I just knew it w…would make you turn round."

She sighed heavily. "What do you want, Davy?"

Davy didn't know whether to be hurt or concerned. He'd been Nicky's pet since he'd joined the squad and her sudden lack of affection gave him an unexpected twinge. He turned away, hurt.

"S…Sorry to bother you."

Nicky stared after him then rose and walked over to his desk.

"I'm sorry, Davy. I've a lot on my mind, but I shouldn't be taking it out on you. What can I help you with?"

He smiled at her and turned his screen towards them both, gesturing at the image.

"I've created a 3D image of the w...woman we think was at the scene, and I just wanted to s...see what you thought."

"OK. Shoot."

"W...well, according to the sizing of her fingerprint and shoes, by my calculations she must be no more than five-feet tall."

"What size were her shoes?"

"Size two-and-a-half."

"I wear a size five and I'm five-feet-four, but so does my sister and she's five-feet-eight. There's a range of heights with any shoe size. Although her fingerprint does point towards the lower end."

Davy nodded and typed in some numbers then watched as the model changed to fit.

"OK, so the programme says the tallest she could be is five-feet-two. Otherwise she would fall over with feet that size."

"Unless you're Barbie."

"What?"

"Apparently if Barbie was real her dimensions would mean she'd have six-inch ankles. She'd fall over for sure."

"And bounce back up again."

Nicky smacked him playfully on the shoulder and smiled. "Davy Walsh. You're not too big for a telling off. That's all that BDSM stuff I heard you talking about earlier. It's corrupting you."

Davy grinned. "And we thought that you hadn't heard."

"I'm preoccupied, not deaf. " She gestured towards the screen. "Anyway. Your sums are wrong."

"How come?"

"Because unless I am deaf the chief said that her shoes had heels. That's why Dr Winter thinks she's more likely to be a woman and not a young girl. Mind you, some of the ten-year-olds who live down our way…"

Davy stared at Nicky and then at the screen, then he hugged her so hard that he lifted her off her feet.

"Nicky, you're a genius!"

She blushed and pushed him away embarrassed, then warmed to her theme. Fashion was her area of expertise. "What type of heels did the shoes have?"

"No idea."

She tutted exaggeratedly then lifted the phone and called the lab. Des Marsham answered cheerfully.

"Hello Des."

"Ah, Nicky. Lovely to hear your dulcet tones."

Nicky smiled. Her voice was anything but dulcet but she appreciated the thought. "Des. The woman's shoe print you found. What was the heel like?"

"What do you mean what was it like? It was just a woman's heel."

She raised her eyes to heaven. Men. "Have you any idea how many different heel shapes there are on women's shoes, Des? No, I bet you haven't. Right. Tell me the dimensions, just of the heel. Then tell me the shape of the sole."

One minute later Nicky was drawing shoes on a notepad with Davy gawping at her. The heel Des had described had been stiletto and the sole of the shoe had been pointed. That left two likely types of heel. A kitten heel, small stilettos about one-and-a-half inches high, and a full stiletto, anything up to six inches. Nicky lifted the phone again and put it on speakerphone. This time Des was well prepared.

"I like Jimmy Choo's new heel. It would go really well with my jeans."

Nicky laughed for the second time that day, this time at the image of the bearded scientist wearing stilettos. "Go back to the sole print for me, Des. How is the weight distributed? Uniformly throughout, slightly more towards the front, or all towards the front?"

There was silence for a moment while Des checked. When he spoke again his voice contained something bordering on awe. "It's all at the front. But how did you know?"

"There's only one heel narrow enough to fit your dimensions – a stiletto. And depending on the height of the heel, a small kitten heel, to one a full six-inches high, the foot would be arched differently. The higher the heel the more her foot would arch and throw the weight towards the front. From your print I'd say she was wearing stilettos of any height between three and five inches. If she was really small five inches would look ridiculous and potentially tip her over head-first, but she could have got away with three."

"Mrs Morris, you're a goddess!"

"Not the first time that's been said, but always good to hear. Bye Des."

Nicky clicked the phone off to see Davy frantically typing away. He turned the screen towards her again.

"Even if your theory's right that still makes the suspect five-feet-two or less. That's tiny, Nicky."

She frowned then pulled over a chair and sat down. "Yes, it is. It's hard to picture someone that size as a murderer."

Just then Liam entered the squad, followed closely by the others. His voice boomed across the room.

"What size?"

Davy explained and Liam turned to Nicky with an affronted look.

"Here, so you're saying that small people are less likely to kill? What about Napoleon then? And I suppose that means tall people are more likely. That's size-ist!"

Davy gave him a sceptical look. "It doesn't work in reverse. Usually…"

Craig sat down beside Nicky, pleased to see her smiling. He stared at the screen and nodded. "Davy and Nicky are right, Liam. Look at the model on the screen. Excellent work you two. OK. If the female is that small, with or without heels, then we were right. The likelihood is that her partner or partners included at least one man to do the heavy lifting. Eileen Carragher wasn't a light woman."

Jake sat forward to interrupt. "There aren't many adult women that height, sir. Is there likely to be some sort of register somewhere? Like on old passports."

Craig laughed, thinking of Natalie. "Big Brother doesn't require people to register their heights yet, Jake. Although you're right, the old passports used to carry it, but even then it was self-reported. My other thought is, in what groups are women likely to be small?"

Annette was the first to answer.

"Well…elderly women tend to be small and Asian women tend to be smaller than Caucasians, sir. And East Asian. There were quite a few Filipino nurses where I trained and they were all very petite."

"OK. I think we can probably rule out elderly women on the basis of strength. Even with two people, lifting Eileen Carragher would have been a challenge. They would have needed strength; so probably young. Asian, East Asian, women from the Indian subcontinent, all of those groups fit."

"Growth restricted people as well. People with chronic childhood illness, or a genetic predisposition."

"OK, again bear in mind strength, but Annette, you and Jake look into that." He turned towards Liam and was pleased to see that Nicky hadn't headed back to her desk. "Anything from Vice, Liam?"

Liam gave him a knowing look and then glanced at Nicky. She squinted at him in warning.

"If you think you're getting rid of me just when you reach the juicy part, you've another think coming, Liam Cullen."

Liam shrugged and continued. "It seems there's quite the BDSM scene in Belfast." He turned to Jake, pre-empting his interruption. "Whatever BDSM stands for nowadays. There are at least five clubs advertised in the city centre."

Annette frowned, trying to imagine where they were hiding, amongst the fashion shops and burger bars.

"And more underground parties held regularly at people's houses. They cover everything from the usual to a few more niche preferences."

Nicky couldn't stop herself asking. "What do they cater for?"

Liam voice took on a lofty tone. "There are limits to what I'll discuss in mixed company, Madam."

Nicky snorted at the same time as Annette. "Since when?"

"Since I heard what they do in these clubs. Let's just say some people have warped minds."

All their pleading couldn't persuade Liam and he turned towards Craig. "All right if I go with Davy to see D.C.I. Hughes? I think there's mileage here."

Craig nodded. Aidan Hughes was an old friend of John's and his from school. He was a real joker and he could see the Vice Squad giving him plenty to crack jokes about. Craig updated everyone on their interview with Gerry Warner and announced they were extending his holding time for another twelve hours.

"Take photographs of the Carraghers and Warner with you when you go to see Aidan, Liam. Let's see if he recognises them. There can't be that many people on the BDSM scene."

Nicky smiled coyly. "Oh, don't be too sure, sir."

She strolled back to her desk to the sound of laughter, leaving a distracted Liam in her wake, reminding them all of his little crush on her. Craig broke up the group and headed for his office then Liam yelled after him.

"And thanks for landing me in it with Jack Harris about the gimp suit. He's planning all sorts of hell for me now."

***

It hadn't taken as long to kill Ian Carragher as his wife. He'd basically wanted to die, welcoming it as some sort of release.

But that hadn't stopped Mai performing the same ritual and taking her time, adding an extra little treat just for him. After the third defibrillation failed even she knew it was time to stop.

She scowled down at the body and swore. How dare he die on her so quickly? She'd wanted to cut his throat at the scene, the same way as his wife. Now they'd have to find some other way to show their disgust. She slapped Carragher's moribund face in frustration.

The young man wiped the last smear of blood from the blade and placed it back in its case. He rubbed his brow with a bloodied hand and gently turned Mai to face him, watching as she dragged her eyes reluctantly away from the corpse.

"We need to decide how to leave him, Mai. Let's shower now, then have some sleep. We can think about it tonight."

Mai rested her tiny hand on his chest and gazed into his dark eyes. "You go on. I want to stay here for one more minute."

He nodded and turned, leaving her alone with their prey. Mai stared down at the pulseless man, his doughy face still intact. They wouldn't destroy the face this time; he was the worst scum of all and she wanted him recognised straight away. She stood for a moment longer then filled her mouth with saliva, spewing it onto Ian Carragher's face. Then she turned on her heel and joined her lover, to rest before they took the next step.

**

John wandered through Belfast's city centre, stopping occasionally at jeweller's shops then glancing quickly over his shoulder, in case he was seen by anyone he knew. He wasn't looking for an engagement ring, definitely not; he was just looking at watches. He needed a new one. Window-shopping, that's what he was doing, but people might get the wrong idea. People were like that.

He wandered for ten minutes in a state of denial and then

halted in front of a small jewellery shop that he hadn't noticed before. There was something old world about its bowed front window, shaped from panes of thick, leaded glass. Its contents glittered with antique silver, and diamonds so highly polished they made you want to peer closer to see if they were real. Before John realised it he was inside, smiling at the tinkling bell above the door. Much more romantic than CCTV, or door-opening buttons on the counter that you had to press.

A man in late old age emerged slowly from the back of the shop. He smiled in a way that made John feel like he was back at school, standing in front of his favourite teacher; Mr Pogue. He'd had a way of making you feel important without saying a word and the man possessed it too. He gave John his full attention and smiled.

"Can I help you, sir?"

The man had a soft, round countenance, deeply scored with the lines of age. When he smiled the ones round his eyes folded and spread, so that all that could be seen were two small, blue dots of light. John knew that this man had seen everything in life and probably already knew why he was there.

He was right. Without another word the man reached below the counter and pulled out a tray of sparkling rings. There were diamonds, gleaming alone and with other stones; green, blue, and even pearls. The designs were stunning, better than anything he'd seen all day. But how had he known when John had only come in looking for a watch?

"Is the lady petite, sir?"

John gawped at the guru in front of him and gave a mute nod.

"And dark-haired?

Another nod. He knew as a doctor that people telegraphed information before they opened their mouths, but this was sheer mind-reading.

"What colour are her eyes?"

"Light blue"

"And her favourite stone?"

John shook his head. He didn't know and he suddenly thought that he should. He knew how many degrees Natalie had and every research prize that she'd won, but not her favourite stone. Work had bonded them together, but now he needed to think of her as a woman and himself as the man wooing her.

He blushed and the man smiled kindly, reading his thoughts again. John noticed that he wore arm bands, elevating his shirt sleeves and revealing his weathered wrists and hands. He hadn't seen anyone wear those since his father had died. He'd worn them when he was gardening, the only time he'd ever unbuttoned his waistcoat when John was a child. A sudden sob caught in his throat and he choked it back. His parents had been dead for so long that he barely thought of them nowadays, yet suddenly he wanted them there, to tell them about Natalie. He glanced at the man and he was still smiling. He gave John a wise look.

"A big day soon."

"If she says yes."

The man nodded. "She will. Choose a ring and leave it here, then you can bring her in and see if it's the one she picks."

He lifted a tray from a small cabinet and set it in front of John, pointing at a canary yellow diamond with a Marquis cut. It was stunning. John took it out and held it to the light, watching as it glistened and shone. It was glorious and unusual, just like Natalie.

"It's perfect! Can I leave it over, for a deposit?"

The old man considered John for a moment, as if he could read his soul, then he shook his head and John's heart sank. It needn't have.

"Leave it for one week with just your name. Propose to the lady and bring her in. It will still be here for you, I promise. And it will be the one she picks, if I know my grooms."

The jeweller laid the ring on a velvet square and nodded John on. John gazed at him, confused. Did he want him to try it on? It wouldn't even fit his little finger! The man smiled encouragingly.

"Go ahead, sir. Take a picture with your modern phone."

John smiled, imagining a 1940s Bakelite handset in the back room. He quickly took a photograph and they parted friends, then John stepped back onto Royal Avenue in a daze, feeling as if he'd been in another time. Cars were still whizzing around the City Hall and people were still walking and talking and carrying the things they'd bought, but he felt different somehow. He was about to get engaged. He hoped. And he did hope it, really hope it, he knew that now. He smiled back at the small shop doorway one last time then headed cheerfully for his car, planning exactly how he was going to propose.

**

Fitzwilliam Primary School, Lisburn Road, Belfast.

Annette knocked on her tenth classroom door of the week and waited to be invited in. She'd seen all the teachers but one now, and none of them had offered anything of use. Mrs Carragher had been a good headmistress, if a bit hard to get on with at times. They really couldn't think of a reason why anyone might want to kill her. The last comment was delivered with a similar lack of enthusiasm across the piste, and Annette saw frosty encounters and turbulent staff meetings written on the faces of each one. She shrugged. Lots of people were unpopular at work; it didn't mean they were bad people. She smiled, imagining a sarcastic comedian's voice delivering the phrase like a punch line. But it was true. She'd heard enough stories from Pete to tell her that schools were just like small villages, and the village elder was rarely universally loved.

Annette peered through the door's frosted glass and just made out the shape of a man hunched over the teacher's desk.

She knocked again more firmly and the shape turned towards the door, beckoning her in. She entered, expecting to be greeted by rows of low-slung desks, but they were higher than before and Annette remembered that this was the senior class, readying themselves to transfer to secondary school.

The man scanned her coolly and his gaze gave Annette the same shudder that she'd felt with Gerry Warner. He was somewhere in his twenties and slim, with cold dark eyes and sallow skin. She supposed that he was good looking, but not in a way that would ever attract her.

"Mr Rooney?"

The teacher didn't respond. Not by blinking or by rising, and not with a word or a nod. He just stared at her as if she would disappear if he did it for long enough. Annette repeated the question, this time showing her badge. An unpleasant grin spread across the man's face and then he spoke. His voice surprised her. It was low and soft with a sibilant hiss that reminded her of a cartoon snake.

"Ah yes, the fuzz. I heard you'd been harassing everyone. What do you want?"

Annette matched his rudeness with fierce good manners. "I'm Inspector McElroy, Mr Rooney, and I'm here to ask you some questions. We can do that here, or, if you would prefer, at High Street station. It's entirely your choice."

Alan Rooney laughed, surprising her. "Ah, but it's not, it is? Bravo, Inspector. You've passed the test. Full marks for not being intimidated." He waved her to a seat. "Ask away. My life is an open text book."

Annette doubted it somehow, but she took out her notebook and turned to a clean page.

"How long had you known Mrs Carragher?"

He thought for a moment before answering. "When you say know, do you mean know as a teacher or know in any context?"

"Any context."

"Ah well… then I've 'known' her for ten years."

"In what context?"

"Biblically, Inspector. We were lovers."

Annette was so shocked that she almost bit her tongue, but she didn't show it. Years of nursing had taught her not to be surprised by anything people revealed. Instead she merely scribbled the words down and gathered herself for what came next. Rooney was still speaking.

"Well, when I say lovers, we weren't exclusive of course, but we were fairly consistent."

He smiled nastily to let the words sink in, watching Annette's face closely as he did. She stared back without blinking and she could see Rooney's annoyance grow at his words not having the desired impact.

"Aren't you shocked, Inspector? By a man screwing his boss thirty years older?"

Annette's tone was dry. "Very little shocks me, Mr Rooney. And there's nothing new about sex. It's been going on forever. Although as you're quite young I should imagine you were barely legal when you and Mrs Carragher became lovers?"

"Bravo again. I was just sixteen. She taught me a lot."

He smiled as if he was reliving the experience and Annette wanted to hose him down. Where was a water-cannon when you needed one? She swopped 'just sixteen' for underage in her head and Eileen Carragher became a paedophile. But she'd worry about the age of consent later. For now she had questions to ask.

"Could you tell me when you last saw Mrs Carragher?"

Rooney glared at her, irritated that his words were having no effect. Annette stared him out in silence until finally he shrugged, dismissing the conversational thread.

"Friday morning. I had a meeting with her at eleven o'clock to discuss the transfer test. It lasted for an hour."

"Not after that?"

He shook his head. "No. I had a half day. Off to Manchester for the weekend, to check out the scenery."

She had a pretty good idea which scenery he was referring to.

"I came back yesterday and found out she was dead. Pity. She was a great shag."

Bile filled Annette's mouth at his dismissal of their victim as only useful for sex, and she asked the question she intended to ask Gerry Warner when she got another chance.

"Do you frequent BDSM clubs in Northern Ireland, Mr Rooney?"

Rooney smiled again. It was even nastier than before and accompanied by a slow handclap this time. "Oh well done; you are a clever girl. You've guessed my dirty little secret. Yes, I'm part of the scene, although not at any clubs you'll ever find."

"What does that mean?"

He sprang to his feet surprising her, and headed swiftly for the door, throwing, "do some work yourself and you'll find out" back over his shoulder.

Then Alan Rooney was gone, leaving Annette gazing around the small classroom and wondering about the secret lives people led.

Chapter Eleven

Aidan Hughes was tall, so tall that he dwarfed the six-foot Davy, and came within an inch or two of Liam's giant height. But where Liam was broad and well upholstered, Hughes was whippet thin and pure muscle; even his forearms looked like they'd been carved. The look was accentuated by a deep tan and shock of bright blonde hair. Davy pictured him yelling 'play ball' on some American sports field; he definitely looked out of place in a wintry Belfast. That was, until he opened his mouth.

"Ach, it's the baul Liam. How's it hangin', man? And who's the male model? These young cops are getting better looking every day."

"How's yourself, Aidan? Been hitting the gym again I see. You need to lay off the protein drinks, lad; you're nothing but muscle and bone. And give that sunbed a rest for God's sake. You look like a stick of Wensleydale."

Hughes laughed loudly and Liam indicated Davy. "This is Davy Walsh, our resident Armani model. He's also our brainbox analyst. We're here to ask you about Vice in Northern Ireland."

"Why? Are you looking for some?"

Hughes laughed at his own joke then waved them to a seat and indicated the percolator, talking as he poured.

"Aye well, Vice is alive and well in Northern Ireland, in all its many-splendored forms. People trafficking, prostitution, drugs, you name it. Which particular type were you interested in?"

Liam waved Davy on and sipped his drink.

"BDSM generally, D.C.I. Hughes. Hard core in particular."

A grin spread across Hughes' face and he grabbed a seat,

sitting forward eagerly.

"BDSM. My favourite. Consenting adults getting up to all sorts, with bits and bobs from the hardware store."

Davy's eyes widened as images of pliers filled his mind.

"Is there a big BDSM s...scene here?"

"Big enough, lad. Depends if you're talking about the scene open to the public, or the bit that's underground."

"Both."

Hughes thought for a moment then he reached into his desk and pulled out a DVD. He slipped it into the computer and pressed start. Fifteen minutes later Davy had finally stopped blushing and even Liam was getting bored with sex. The DVD was wittily entitled 'Northern Ireland's Hottest Spots' and it was true to its name. It gave a blow-by-blow tour of Northern Ireland's street-level BDSM clubs, and showed footage from inside each one, including the menu of services they provided, often displayed on the walls. Some of them used euphemisms like 'school discipline' and 'water sports', but by no means all.

There were fifteen clubs dotted across the country in total, located in places that matched some of the region's best-known tourist spots. They ranged from so small that they would fit into someone's back room, to high-end glossy with hostesses and the works.

Liam shuddered. "I'll never look at the Giant's Causeway or Tyrella Beach the same way again."

Hughes removed the DVD and turned it over to the other side.

"Aye, I know. It makes it hard to find somewhere to take your kids on holiday without picturing someone half-naked carrying a whip." He paused for a moment and his tanned face took on a solemn look. "This next side isn't quite so vanilla."

Davy interrupted. "Vanilla?"

"It's a word used on the BDSM scene for people who aren't very sexually adventurous. They basically prefer straight sex with the odd silk scarf thrown in."

"Practically an insult then."

Liam guffawed loudly and slapped Davy on the back, spilling his coffee. "Good lad. Your humour's definitely improved since you met me."

Davy threw him a sceptical look and wiped himself down.

"Fire ahead then, Aidan. We're all men of the world."

Hughes grimaced and suddenly the atmosphere in the room changed.

"OK, you asked for it, Liam, but it isn't pretty. This is the underground BDSM scene and it's murky. Some of it is legal stuff, just parties held in people's houses, moving venue each time; still consenting adults. But on the edges we're looking at prostitution, forced engagement..."

"Rape?"

"Yes, and on a massive scale as well. Gang bangs, trafficking, hard-core videos, even snuff movies at times."

"Deliberate deaths or accidental?"

"Both."

Hughes paused and Liam knew exactly what was coming next.

"Kids? The seedy bastards are involving kids?"

Hughes nodded. "There's a big overlap in the hidden scene with all sorts of abuse. Physical, sexual, child abuse, violence against women..."

Liam interrupted. "Torture?"

Hughes gave him a puzzled look. "That's often part of it."

Liam leaned forward eagerly. "Torture where someone is sliced to death?"

Hughes grimaced. "God, no. That's a new one, even on me. What's this all about, Liam?"

Liam waved him on, thinking. As the DVD started he pulled out the photos of the Carraghers and Gerry Warner.

"Do you know any of these Muppets?"

Hughes peered closely at the pictures then pointed at Warner. "Him for sure. Gerry Warner. He's big into the underground scene. Gets up to all sorts. The woman too, maybe. She looks familiar."

"She was our victim. Found sliced and diced in the school where she was headmistress."

"God!"

Davy leapt into the few seconds pause that followed. "Do you get many professional people involved in the s…scene?"

Hughes nodded. "Nearly all the punters are. It can be expensive to buy the toys. We've had police, teachers, military, Judges, you name it. They often fall on the masochistic side. Submissives. They spend their days making decisions and telling people what to do, so they like to be bossed about at night. Mind you, some of them are the complete opposite; sadistic bastards. You'd be surprised at who's doing what to whom."

Davy glanced at Liam. They were both thinking of the trafficking ring they'd encountered the year before. It had included some very well-known men.

"W…We wouldn't, you know."

Hughes raised an eyebrow then turned back towards the screen and turned up the volume. They'd managed to ignore the moans and writhing in the background until now but after the first loud screams Davy glanced at Liam meaningfully. They both nodded and then stood up. Liam set down his cup and shook his head at Hughes.

"I don't think we need to the details, Aidan. I've had enough sex today to last me for a month. Well, a week anyway. How the hell do you do this all day?"

Hughes face saddened. "You need a sense of humour, that's for sure. But it doesn't stop it getting to you. You just have to keep thinking of the victims. That's what keeps you going." He ejected the disc and handed it to Liam. "Just in case you want to view it later in your case. I'll e-mail through a list of the underground haunts and the names of any big players on the scene."

He showed them to the door, more subdued than when

they'd arrived. As they walked back up to the tenth floor they both thanked God they worked in murder instead of Vice.

***

The C.C.U.

Annette knocked on Craig's office door but there was no reply. She could see his dark outline standing by the window so she knocked again, gently opening the door. He was staring out at Belfast Harbour; the place where the Lagan quit the city to marry its waters with the Irish Sea. Subsumed and surrounded, never to be quite the same again. As she stood waiting for Craig to turn she realised that he hadn't heard her. She was just wondering whether to exit and start again when Craig roused himself and glanced round, smiling when he saw who it was.

"Hello, Annette. Coffee?"

"Yes please. I just wanted to update you on something. I interviewed all the teachers at the school."

"Anything interesting?"

Annette grimaced. "Umm. Yes and no. Everyone says they had no reason to kill Eileen Carragher, but no-one seemed to like her very much."

"Isn't that par for the course for bosses?"

Annette laughed. "Is that what you think? That no-one likes you very much?"

Craig gave her a surprised look then he blushed. "Well, no. I mean, I don't know. I hope not, but giving orders is never popular."

"Depends how you give them, and whether they make sense." She smiled kindly at him. "You won't ask, so I'll tell you. No-one hates you, sir. In fact, we're all quite fond of you, really."

Craig's blush deepened and Annette laughed again. She sipped her coffee and continued.

"Anyway…Then I got to Mr Rooney, the one that Harlston had mentioned as being friendly with Eileen Carragher."

"And?"

"And he's a nasty little man. Horrible, in the same way Gerry Warner's horrible, but even more so."

She paused, reluctant to go into more detail. Craig urged her on in a gentle tone.

"Come on, Annette. There's a reason you're telling me about him now, instead of reporting at the debrief. What is it?"

"Well… Rooney admitted that he frequents BDSM venues, although he did say, none that we would find."

"And he knew Eileen Carragher intimately."

Her mouth dropped open. "Yes. How did you guess?"

"You were so embarrassed that it was a safe bet."

"It's worse than that, sir."

"How?"

Annette broke his gaze and suddenly found something in her handbag fascinating. "He…he said he and Eileen Carragher had been lovers for ten years."

Craig could see why she'd wanted to tell him privately, instead of announcing it in front of Liam. It conjured up all sorts of jokes.

"Really?"

"Yes. Well, not lovers in any relationship sense." She blushed. "He said she'd been a great… shag."

Annette's blush deepened furiously as she said the last word and Craig didn't know whether to laugh or cry at her embarrassment. Annette was quite prim, despite the job, and he knew that saying it had cost her a lot.

"Charming."

"That's what I thought. He was horrible, but he was quite open about it. She was thirty years older than him!"

"Men date people younger than them all the time, Annette, so why not women? Besides, it's not as uncommon as you might think. Did he give you any more details about the venues?"

She shook her head. "No. He basically told me to find them myself. But think about it, sir. She was virtually a paedophile. Rooney's only twenty-six. That means he was sixteen and she was forty-five when they first...well, you know."

Her voice tailed off and Craig thought for a moment. Eileen Carragher mightn't technically have been a paedophile but she hadn't been far off. Even if Rooney had consented, it was murky at best.

"They estimate that up to four percent of paedophiles are female, Annette, so she won't have been the first."

He nodded her on.

"Rooney said he last saw her at a meeting on Friday morning. After that he was in Manchester all weekend, doing God knows what."

"I think we all know what."

Craig sipped his coffee thoughtfully for a moment. Finally he straightened up and smiled. "Good work, Annette. OK, check out Rooney's alibi to rule him out for the murder, then go and see Ian Carragher to suss out if he knew about his wife's affair. They were married when she and Rooney started having sex."

"Won't her husband have been involved in BDSM as well?"

"Not necessarily. Couples don't do everything together. Lots of women take aerobic classes and their husbands don't go along."

Annette's smile told Craig that the analogy was unfortunate.

"It's obvious that Warner's into BDSM so I'd like to go back and ask him which clubs he attends, sir."

"OK. But check out Ian Carragher first and let's see what Davy and Liam have to tell us. We can re-interview Warner tomorrow morning."

"If some solicitor hasn't got him out on bail by then."

"And even if they have."

Chapter Twelve

Mai stared down at Ian Carragher's bloated body without any sense of joy. She'd expected to feel the same way that she had with his wife, but there was no pleasure here. He'd given in too easily; accepting death like it was a blessed release, instead of kicking and screaming his way into the dark night. Ian Carragher hadn't feared the unknown at all. Except where he was going wasn't unknown. If both the Carraghers didn't go to hell then there was no justice anywhere.

Mai kicked the body with her small foot and turned to walk back to the house. At the garage door she stopped, noticing a roll of barbed wire that had been there since they'd rented the place. It was perfect. She smiled happily to herself and strolled towards the kitchen, ruffling her hair and quietly humming a tune.

***

The C.C.U. 4 p.m.

"OK. Is everyone here?"

Craig scanned the open-plan office. Everyone was there except Annette. He gave her another few minutes then called the briefing to order. She'd be there soon, and anyway, her absence was no bad thing. It would give him time to repeat what she'd told him earlier. She'd asked him to relay it, and if he did it first then Liam's inevitable jokes would be out of the way before Annette arrived.

"OK. Annette's off seeing Ian Carragher, but earlier today she went to the school to finish interviewing the teachers. It turns out that no-one much liked Eileen Carragher, but they didn't hate her enough to kill her. She was having a sexual relationship with a male teacher at the school who was thirty years her junior. When I say relationship, it was consensual, casual sex, probably involving BDSM."

Craig rattled it out quickly and sat back, awaiting Liam's inevitable retort. Nothing came. He stared at Liam and then at Davy. They were sitting like bookends at either side of a desk and neither of them said a word. Craig called both their names and Davy stared blankly at him, then realised he'd been speaking.

"Oh hell. S...Sorry, chief."

Davy glanced at Liam and saw that he was staring at the floor. He lifted a book and slid it along the desk until it hit Liam's elbow and made him look up.

"Ow! What was that for?"

Davy tilted his head towards Craig and Liam realised that he was expecting a response.

"Oh, God aye. That's shocking, boss."

Craig smiled, knowing that Liam hadn't heard a word. "What was?"

"That thing you just said."

"That thing that neither you nor Davy heard, you mean?"

Craig repeated the earlier information and this time Liam raised his eyebrows as high as they would go. But that was it. Not a rude comment or a smutty remark, just vague surprise. Jake watched the scene, stunned. His old boss at Stranmillis had been easy going, but nothing like Craig.

"All right you two. Something obviously happened when you went to see Aidan Hughes, so what was it?"

Liam made a face. "That world he lives in is a shocker, boss."

Davy nodded. "Grubby is the w...word I'd use." He looked at Jake for someone his own age who would understand. "He showed us one side of a DVD, about all the known BDSM clubs in the North. There were fifteen of them!"

Jake responded in a shocked tone. "Fifteen? All for people who want to beat each other up, and presumably spend a fortune doing it. That wouldn't be my idea of fun."

Liam shook his head. "Nor mine. He looked at Craig. "That was just Side One. Aidan said the other side was really hard core. Hidden clubs across the province with incidences of gang rape, abuse, kids, snuff videos. Reminded me of the Ackerman case last year."

Craig nodded; his gut had told him there was something more lurking behind Eileen Carragher's death. "Any names or venues for the hidden clubs?"

Liam shook his head. "Aidan said they travelled round different places. Some are held in private homes."

"Torture?"

"Probably, but nothing like what was done to Eileen Carragher."

"Did…"

Craig was interrupted mid-question by a breathless Annette rushing through the double-doors.

"Sorry I'm late, but there's something you should know."

"Catch your breath, Annette. You can tell us in a minute." He turned back to Liam and Davy. "Did you show Aidan the photos of the Carraghers and Gerry Warner?"

"Aye. He recognised Warner straight off. He's heavily into the BDSM scene. Said Eileen Carragher looked familiar too, but not the husband."

"Annette went to ask Carragher tactfully if he knew about his wife's other life."

Craig turned to Annette, nodding her on.

"That's where I've just been. I went to his office to see if I could talk to him and they said he hasn't been in today. They thought he was taking some time off after his wife's death."

"Is that what he told them?"

She nodded. "Well, he said he was going to sort out the funeral arrangements this morning and when he didn't return, they assumed he was going home. Anyway, I went round to the house and knocked the door but there was no answer. Then I phoned his son Ryan at his restaurant, and he said his Dad had told him he was going to an undertaker on Boucher Crescent to sort the service out, but I phoned the funeral parlour and Carragher missed his appointment. He's disappeared."

Craig jumped to his feet. "He must have got the death certificate from John, they couldn't organise the funeral without it. Liam, call John and ask him what time Carragher left his lab. Davy, get me the address of the funeral home on Boucher Crescent." He crossed the floor quickly, beckoning Jake and Annette to follow.

"Nicky, we're going to Boucher Crescent. I'll call you from there if we need the C.S.I.s"

Jake looked puzzled. "C.S.I.s? Why would we need them, sir?"

"Because if I'm right, Ian Carragher's been kidnapped, by the same people who killed his wife."

***

Wednesday 5 p.m.

Boucher Road was a long, wide artery of a road running through South and West Belfast. Two miles long to be precise. It was lined with carpet stores and hardware shops, with a myriad of car dealerships thrown in. It was always busy, especially at weekends, when everyone in Belfast seemed to get the urge to view sofas and beds, or buy something that they didn't need. During the week it was used as a shortcut between Stockman's Lane and the M1 motorway into town; a very busy shortcut.

Stockman's Lane was where they'd been sitting for the past

half-an-hour, stuck at the traffic lights waiting to turn right, after taking Liam's bright advice that it was the quickest route. Craig was peering through the windscreen of his aging Audi willing the traffic to shift, when something caught his eye. The petrol garage up ahead reminded him of something. His eyes tracked across the road to a small white bungalow with a pillar-box red front door. It looked familiar and he was certain he'd been inside it, but then he'd been door-to-door in half of Belfast in his time.

The lights changed and Craig turned the car, glimpsing the house more closely, then he blushed. If Annette noticed his change in colour she wasn't rude enough to ask. Craig had remembered where he'd seen the house before; it belonged to Katy Stevens' mother. He'd called there the year before, during a case. He could still remember how nice her mother had been, and how pretty Katy had looked with her long blonde hair loose. John's double-date suggestion popped into his head and for a moment Craig wondered if he should, then he shook his head. It was too soon. Not for him, he wanted to move on quickly; needed to. He'd spent years on his own after Camille. But it was too soon for Julia, she'd been hurt by their break-up and hearing that he'd started dating so soon would hurt her even more.

Annette's warm voice broke through his thoughts. "The funeral parlour is on Boucher Crescent, the next left turn."

"Thanks. What number is it?"

"Six hundred and four."

Craig counted down past the car showrooms and discount stores, until finally they reached a small turning. It led to a low white building with a car park behind. There was only one car there that wasn't a hearse and the hairs on Craig's neck suddenly stood on end.

"Jake, find out what Ian Carragher drives."

"Already have, sir." Jake nodded towards the car. "That's it. The dark green Volvo. The registration matches."

Craig parked fifty metres away and climbed out, signalling the others to wait. If forensics needed to work the place it was better they only had his footsteps to rule out. He walked towards the Volvo slowly. If Ian Carragher had been taken from here, it would have been at the boot or the driver's side. That's where any clues would be.

Craig headed for the passenger door and scanned it expertly. Nothing. He worked his way around the bonnet to the driver's side; still no signs of a struggle. Something dark on the ground caught his eye, halting him abruptly. It was blood. Dried and dark, but still blood. He increased his distance from the car and walked slowly towards the boot; more blood, a lot of it. Carragher had been abducted from here and not without a struggle. Craig pulled out his phone and dialled quickly, calling forensics to the scene, then he strode back to his car and got in.

"What did you find, sir?"

"Carragher was taken from here and he didn't go without force. There's blood all over the ground at the driver's side and boot. I've called forensics." He turned towards the back seat. "Jake, stay here and wait for the C.S.I.s then start Uniform on the interviews. We're over-looked from the back of those shops, so let's see if anyone there saw anything. Find out what time Carragher left John this morning, and you'll have the approximate time he arrived here. He would have come straight here with the death certificate. He was lifted before he saw the undertaker but find out if anyone else was here at the same time. Someone might have seen him, or seen who took him."

"You're certain that he was kidnapped?"

Craig nodded once. "Whoever took his wife took him, Annette, and if I'm not mistaken he's going to end up the same way."

***

111

Boucher Crescent. 9.p.m.

By nine p.m. the car-park had been taped off and the C.S.I.s had done their thing. Jake had interviewed everyone inside the funeral parlour and Uniform had completed their interviews elsewhere. That only left the shop assistants opposite to talk to, but they'd gone home at five o'clock. They would have to wait until tomorrow. Jake propped himself against a low brick wall and flicked back through his notes. A consistent theme ran through the interviews. Several people had seen a small van or people carrier in midnight-blue. No-one remembered the registration completely, but two people had said it started with DFZ. It shouldn't be impossible to find and Carragher's abductors would have known that, so either it wouldn't trace back to them or they just didn't care.

One witness said she'd seen a small, dark figure and another a tall, dark man. Which was it? Neither or both? Jake rubbed the back of his neck tiredly and then realised the time. Time to go home. He walked to a liveried patrol car and clambered in, looking forward to a good night's sleep.

Chapter Thirteen

It was dark. Dark in the way that only a street can be dark, when the lamps are shattered and the drapes are drawn and everyone's long asleep. Dark in the way a starless night leaves a country road un-illuminated, reminding the world of how people used to live before someone lit their way. Pitch dark.

So dark that the two slim figures were barely visible, moving quickly between the van and road. A van whose colour blended with the night. They didn't mind their names being known; it was inevitable that they soon would be. But not before they'd completed their work and arranged their escape.

Mai lifted Ian Carragher's feet, leaving the bulk of his weight to be carried by her man. She smiled at the coil of wire around their victim's waist and took faltering backward steps towards the yard. The wire was perfect. Strong enough to bind him so that he didn't fall, and symbolic of captivity.

She slid Eileen Carragher's pass card into the gate, watching as it creaked open. They moved quietly in perfect step, arranging her husband vertically against the railings then twisting the wire deep into his flesh to hold him tight. Mai smiled up at the building. If the police missed their message this time then they weren't as good as she thought.

***

Fitzwilliam Primary School. Thursday, 9 a.m.

"Oh crap. Not another one."

Craig nodded tiredly and Liam scratched his head. They walked through the school gates and considered the sight in front of them, because that's what it was; a sight. A mess of blood and hair, with strips of skin embedded in both, tied to the railings with barbed wire. Every piece of the body's surface anatomy had been erased just as before. Only Ian Carragher's face told them that it was a man at all.

Craig dragged his eyes away and scanned the playground. It was full of Uniforms and C.S.I.s, not a child to be seen. It was Groundhog Day, except it was Thursday instead of Monday and the body was Ian Carragher's instead of his wife's.

"Why here?"

"What?"

Craig repeated the question. "Why here? Again? The link was obvious with Eileen Carragher, but the husband was a surveyor, not a teacher."

Liam furrowed his brow in thought then the penny dropped. "She worked here and Annette's pervy Mr Rooney works here. Who knows, maybe the husband built the place?"

Craig thought for a moment then shook his head. "Too easy, but I think you're almost right. It's to do with a school all right, but not necessarily this one."

Liam gave him a sceptical look. "Where'd you get that from? This is where all the action is."

"It isn't where Gerry Warner works and he's a big part of this equation. Call it gut instinct. You believe in that, don't you?"

"Aye, aye I do. OK then, which school? And what does all this have to do with the BDSM scene?"

"Both the Carraghers were into it and they were tortured, which happens in BDSM. That's as far as I've got." Craig nodded towards the car." Let's head back to the Squad, I want everyone to chip in."

Twenty minutes later they were seated out on the open-plan floor. Craig had commandeered a white board from the briefing room and he was standing beside it with a marker in his hand.

"OK, let me summarise first, then I'll open it up. Here's what we know so far. Eileen Carragher and her husband met in 1989 at a school in Bangor. They married and had two sons. He worked as a surveyor and she as a teacher, then as headmistress of a primary school. So far, so normal. Except behind the scenes Eileen Carragher had another life, one where she engaged in an affair and BDSM, as did at least two other teachers that we know; Gerry Warner and Alan Rooney."

He stopped for a sip of coffee and scanned the group. Annette was scribbling notes down furiously and Jake was doing the same, although with less energy; he'd had a late night. Davy was biting his nails and staring into space and Liam was seeing if his foot could reach the page he'd just dropped and pull it towards him, without him having to reach down and pick it up. Craig smiled. They were all listening, even if it didn't look like it from the outside. He was just about to restart when Davy suddenly frowned.

"Boss, did you s…say the Carraghers had two sons?"

"Yes."

Davy shook his head. "S…Sorry, but they didn't. I think that was my fault. I should have made it clear. The two boys were his. Eileen Carragher was their step-mother."

Craig thought for a moment then nodded him on.

"OK. The s…sons are Ryan, thirty-four; he's the one with the restaurant, and Jonathan, twenty-three. Their mother died when they were young, in 1994."

Annette interrupted. "That means they were three-years-old and fourteen. What did she die of, Davy?"

"Cancer. I don't know what sort."

Craig nodded slowly, as if he was working something out. "So when he met Eileen in '89, Ian Carragher was married to his first wife and the younger boy hadn't been born. By the time they married, he was a widower with two young sons."

"Yes."

"That's important. I'm not sure why yet, but I know it is.

115

OK, Davy, thanks for that. Let's keep going. Right, Eileen Carragher was the killers' primary target because she was killed first."

Liam interjected. "And they chose her school to dump the bodies."

"Yes, although there may have been another reason for that as well. But if she was the primary target, then that means she was the one that our killers wanted to hurt most."

"They managed it."

Annette raised her pen to interject and Craig nodded her on.

"Couldn't it just be that they wanted to hurt her first, but not necessarily most, sir? They killed her first but they killed her husband as well, and just as brutally."

"Yes...yes, they did. OK, she was the first, but that doesn't mean that there aren't others on the list. The fact Ian Carragher was left recognisable is significant in some way as well."

"Sir."

Craig nodded Jake on.

"Well it's just...we know that Eileen Carragher, Rooney and Warner were all into BDSM, because Rooney confirmed he was and D.C.I. Hughes recognised the others. But what's the link between Ian Carragher and the BDSM scene? If you think BDSM definitely has something to do with their deaths?"

"Good point. We don't have anything concrete to say the husband was into BDSM yet, but the absence of proof doesn't mean it isn't true."

Liam nodded sagely. "Right enough. We all know when a scrote's guilty, but proving it's another thing."

"And Ian Carragher was definitely involved in something, or our killers believed he was, otherwise he wouldn't be dead. OK. If Eileen Carragher was first and her husband was next, I think we can assume that our other BDSM participants, Warner and Rooney are at risk. I've nothing to base that on definitively, but it's worth warning them to be careful." Craig perched on top of a desk and turned towards Davy. "That brings us back to the primary case."

Davy had stopped biting his nails and was playing with his hair now, lifting strands of it to examine his split ends. Everyone stared at him to see if he was listening and he looked up and repeated Craig's last sentence in a dry tone. "I can multitask you know, people." He pulled himself upright and turned towards Craig. "Yes, boss. What do you need to know?"

"Anything on the M.O. yet?"

Davy shook his head. "Nothing in the W...Western world at all, or in the Arab or African states, so I'm looking at Asia now for methods of torture. The knife as well. Essentially it's a razor-sharp meat cleaver, but with a serrated edge. There are no records of a knife exactly like that being s...significant anywhere in Eastern or W...Western culture, and it's not in any of Des' books. The closest is called a Chinese Cleaver, used in cooking, but it has a bevelled edge not s...serrations. Maybe they s...serrated it themselves to cause more pain? There's nothing out on the W...Web yet, so they possibly didn't video the killing, or it's not for public consumption. S...Sorry I can't give you more."

Craig smiled. Davy had ruled out one hundred variables in two days. He couldn't complain.

"That's great Davy, it tells us a lot."

Davy gave him a puzzled look. "It does?"

"Yes. I'm presuming when you said the Web, you meant that it wasn't on the Dark Web either?"

Davy looked impressed. The Dark Web was barely known about outside the hacking world. It was a collection of underground websites, some selling drugs, porn and all sorts of other nasty things. The sites were only accessible through modified internet browsers so it required determination or desperation to access them.

"Yes. I mean no, it's not on Dark either."

Liam screwed up his face in confusion. "Oh, God, would one of you two speak English. Don't tell me there's another

117

internet out there? It's taken me years to get used to this one."

Craig watched as Davy buried Liam in tech-speak, until Liam finally waved him away. Davy slowed his voice down exaggeratedly and spoke in a soothing tone.

"Basically perverts buy programmes that let them access w… websites that normal people can't see. And they aren't s…selling cuddly toys."

"Why didn't you just say that then?"

A laugh went round the group then Craig pulled them back to the case.

"OK. So from what Davy has told us we know our killers aren't doing this for applause or money, or that video would have been on the Dark Web or auctioned to the highest bidder by now. We also know that they've researched this method of killing in detail. It's elaborate and not obvious e.g. not something they're likely to have seen in a movie."

He glanced at Davy for confirmation.

"I ran it through all the movie databases, chief, and it doesn't match anything. I'm running searches of libraries and books on the s…subject of torture now."

"OK, so they didn't just see it in a film and decide to imitate it. They went out looking for it."

"Or they already knew about it, sir."

Annette had a thoughtful look on her face and Craig signalled her on.

"Well… you know we decided the female in this partnership was petite?"

"Yes, and?"

"We played about with possible ethnicities and came up with Asian, East Asian and Indian mainly, as well as people who were growth restricted for whatever reason."

"Yes. Where did you get with all that?"

"Still working on it. But what if it's not the knife but the method of killing that's unique to a particular culture? What if the woman's ethnicity and the method of killing are from the same place?"

Craig's eyes widened. "Yes! But take it further, Annette. What if the method isn't showing up on Davy's searches because it's no longer used?"

Davy leaned in. "You mean an ancient method?"

"Maybe. What happens if you put the parameters into historical databases, Davy?"

Davy rushed to a computer and typed-in four words at lightning speed. 'Torture, multiple cuts, Asia'. Nothing came back. He thought for a moment, deleted one word and added another. Craig held his breath as he watched him then exhaled noisily as a smile spread across Davy's face. Davy pressed print and handed Craig a warm sheet. It held two words.

"Ling Chi? What is it? And what did you type in to find it?"

Davy grabbed a second sheet and re-joined the group, throwing Liam a triumphant look. That was another tick on his side of their long running contest; his technology versus Liam's street sense.

"First I typed in torture, multiple cuts and Asia into the historical database, but nothing came back. Then it dawned on me that it might not have been categorised as torture, but as legal, s...so I took out torture and entered 'execution' and voila, Ling Chi." He extended his arms in a flourish.

"It was legal! To do what they did to the Carraghers?"

Craig's voice showed the shock they all felt. Davy warmed to his theme and started reading from the sheet in his hand.

"Ling Chi translates as S...Slow Slicing, the lingering death, or death by a thousand cuts. It was a form of torture and execution used in China from approximately AD 900 until 1905, when it was banned."

"1905! They still allowed it a century ago?"

Craig gave Jake a dry look. "I imagine people in the future will say that about lethal injections and the Electric Chair. Carry on Davy."

"Ling Chi was reserved for crimes viewed as particularly

severe, s...such as treason and killing one's parents. The condemned person was killed..." He paused and glanced meaningfully at Annette. His message was clear; 'brace yourself; you're not going to like the next bit.' She nodded him on.

"The condemned person was killed by using a knife to methodically remove portions of the body over an extended period of time. The process involved tying the person to be executed to a w...wooden frame, usually in a public place. The flesh was then cut from the body in multiple s...slices. In later times, opium was sometimes given."

"At least they showed a bit of mercy."

"Either that or they didn't want them to pass out, boss."

Davy read on to the conclusion. "Ling Chi had three purposes: as a form of public humiliation, as a lingering death, and as a punishment after death, because by mutilating the body the belief was that the s...spirit would never find peace: Xiao Jing. Cutting the body goes against the Confucian principle of filial piety or Xiao."

Liam let out a whistle. "Good old Confucius. And to think we worry about whether the handcuffs are on too tight. Bloody hell, those guys knew how to punish a scrote."

The room fell silent for a moment while everyone pictured the Carraghers' last moments. Eileen Carragher's lab tests hadn't come over from John yet, but the smart money said she hadn't been given any pain relief. Craig wondered if her husband had suffered a similar fate.

"Davy, call John and find out what Eileen Carragher's tests said, please. They must be back by now."

Two minutes later Davy put down the phone. "No sedation or pain relief in her blood. Her last meal w...was Bombay Mix."

"That fits with her meeting Warner for drinks. She must have been lifted right after she left him."

Liam startled, remembering something. He gave Craig a sheepish look. "Oh aye, sorry, I meant to tell you, boss.

Uniform found Eileen Carragher's car parked in the centre of town last night, a stone's throw from the bar where she and Warner met for drinks. It had been clamped on Monday morning. The C.S.I.s are going over it now."

Craig wrote all the things they'd discussed up on the board. He circled Ling Chi repeatedly then turned to face them.

"If they chose Ling Chi as a method of killing they thought the crime was severe enough to warrant it."

"No-one kills for treason nowadays, boss, but what if the Carraghers killed the parents of one of our killers?"

Craig shook his head, not at the suggestion but at its limitations. "Yes, that's possible, but I think we need to look further, Liam. It might not have been a crime that the state views as severe, but it obviously felt severe to our killers."

Annette interjected. "But if this Ling Chi thing is meant to cause public humiliation, then why not put a video of Eileen Carragher's murder out on the Web?"

"Something stopped them doing that, Annette, and I think it's because they wanted the death to be private. Their reasons for killing are personal to them. The public display of the bodies after death might have been enough."

Craig paused and they watched as he worked out the scene in his head. After a moment he spoke.

"OK. Let's say that the Carraghers did something to our killers, something so severe that it made them feel that they deserved the Ling Chi punishment and death. And let's say that our female killer is Chinese and knew about Ling Chi. Chinese would fit with her shoe size and likely height. Would that help your search for the knife, Davy?"

"It might."

Liam leaned forward enthusiastically. "I could go back to Aidan Hughes on Chinese women involved in the BDSM scene, boss. Do you think the man is Chinese as well?"

"Might be, but we've no evidence to say he is. Stick to the woman at the moment."

"We've no age range, sir. And without that we're looking at a lot of people. There's been a big Chinese population in Northern Ireland since the 1960s."

Craig raked his hair. "Good point, Jake." He thought for a moment then sighed. "OK, at the risk of sounding unimaginative, let's go for the fit adult range; twenty to fifty."

"Wouldn't sixty be better, boss. Given that's around Ian Carragher and Warner's age? If this is someone who knows them well enough to hate them, then they could be the same age group."

"Fair point, Liam. Sixty it is then, Davy."

Craig thought for a moment longer then tightened his tie and grabbed his jacket. "Right. That's about as far as we can get for now. You all know what you're doing." He headed for the door. "I'm off to the lab to see whether Ian Carragher suffered the same fate as his wife."

***

The Lab.

Craig arrived in John's office just as he was writing on a small card. He pushed it hastily into his top drawer and Craig knew from John's flustered look that the words were for someone else's eyes. He smiled to himself and grabbed a chair.

"Is that percolator boiling? I could do with a cup."

"Why? Have you only had five this morning instead of your usual ten?"

Craig laughed. Everyone knew about his caffeine addiction but only John was brave enough to slag him about it. He scanned his friend's face. Something had changed since their meaningful conversation two nights before.

"I take it you've made up your mind?"

John swung round from the percolator so quickly that he knocked the milk carton off the bench. Craig caught it before it hit the floor.

"Good catch. And with your left hand too."

"You can give me a round of applause later. Have you?"

"What?"

Craig sighed, knowing John was being evasive. "Made up your mind."

John ignored the question and handed Craig a mug, then he sat down behind his desk and busied himself with a file, closing the subject.

"Eileen Carragher's blood and stomach contents tests have gone across to Davy."

"I know. How many days have you been sitting on them?"

John blushed. He'd collected them on Tuesday, the day that he'd bumped into Katy Stevens, but he'd forgotten about them and left them on his desk. He nodded, acknowledging his mistake. "Longer than I should have, but you already know that."

Craig smiled. "You're allowed to be pre-occupied sometimes, John. It's called having a life. Besides, Davy would have been shouting for them if they'd been urgent. Any joy on her time of death yet?"

John shook his head. "I can get it down to the time of darkness that night, but the overnight frost makes it hard to be precise. Do you need it exact?"

"Not really, the range will do. We know she left Gerry Warner just before nine o'clock on Saturday night and her car was found clamped on Chichester Street, near the bar. They probably abducted her as she walked back to it then kept her alive until Monday morning at the playground when they cut her throat."

"The last cut was the deepest."

"Isn't that a Rod Stewart song? And a romantic one too, if memory serves me"

John laughed. "You're not back on that topic again, are you? Actually the song said 'the first cut' and yes, it is a Stewart number. In Eileen Carragher's case it's factual. The last cut was the deepest. The cuts on her body were shallow and rough, designed to produce maximum pain. The last one on her throat was so deep that it almost severed her spinal cord."

Craig screwed up his face. "Have you ever heard of Ling Chi?"

John's face fell and he banged his forehead with his palm. "Of course... that's what it was! I'm stupid. I should have known." He looked at Craig enthusiastically. "I saw one, you know, on a study trip to China."

"When? They stopped doing it in 1905."

John shook his head irritably, the way he only ever did when he was talking about his work. "No, I don't mean I saw an actual execution, I mean I saw a body that had undergone Ling Chi. It was preserved in a private collection. It was fascinating."

"It was disgusting."

John gazed at Craig as if he'd just remembered he was talking about a human being. "God, yes, you're right. Of course you're right. It is disgusting. But..."

"From a medical perspective, seeing what the human body can tolerate, it's fascinating to you as a doctor. Is that what you meant to say?"

"That's exactly it. How did you know?"

"Twenty years of listening to you talk about your work."

John gave him a sheepish smile. "You really believe it was Ling Chi?"

"Don't you? And the husband, what about him?"

"I'm going to start the post-mortem now if you'd like to stay."

Craig drained his mug and set it down. "No thanks. I'll give that a miss. But check his bloods urgently, will you?"

"You think there'll be something to find?"

Craig nodded. "My money's on some form of pain relief. It would make sense if the killers didn't hate him quite as much as his wife."

"Why did they hate them at all?"

Craig stood up to go. "Ah now, that's my bit. By the way, if you've decided to propose to Natalie I'm really glad. She's funny and kind, and perfect for you."

A blush covered John's cheeks. "You think so?"

"I do."

They smiled together and then John said quietly. "I do too."

Chapter Fourteen

High Street Station.

Gerry Warner tapped his feet on the floor of his cell in a rhythm that he knew from somewhere. He racked his brain for the tune, amusing himself by segueing into memories from the past to match each wrong melody he named in his quest. He'd almost remembered the right song when the cell door opened, cutting short his daydream. He jerked round to see who'd disturbed him.

Craig's lean shape filled the doorway and he nodded Jack Harris to escort Warner from the cell. Warner's saturnine face twisted in an un-teacherly scowl and he stubbornly refused to rise.

"No. No more questioning without my brief present."

He folded his arms and leaned back against the cell's cool wall, in a gesture of defiance older than time. Craig imagined he must see it from ten teenagers a day. He shrugged.

"Fine. Whatever you want, Mr Warner. I was only going to ask you a couple more questions, then let you go." He turned to leave. "But if you'd rather stay here…"

Warner jumped to his feet and headed for the door so fast that Jack was caught on the hop. He fell back against the wall, surprised. Craig swung around, ready to intervene, just as Jack steadied himself and grabbed Warner's arm. They needn't have worried. Warner was just eager to follow Craig, the thought of going home for a shower and a change of clothes had made him forget he was a prisoner, instead of in charge.

He raised his hands in surrender. "Calm down, boys. I just want to get out of here. Ask me your questions then let me go the hell home."

One minute later they were sitting in the interview room with coffees at their elbows, and Craig turned on the tape. Instead of Jack watching from the viewing room as he always did, he stood by the door menacingly, despite Craig's assurance that he would be fine.

Craig stared at Warner for a moment, not quite sure what he could see. Yes, he was a teacher; a respectable pillar of society to the outside world. But Craig had seen his lascivious response to Annette and Aidan Hughes had confirmed that he was well known to Vice. What Gerry Warner did in his free time wasn't respectable at all.

Craig checked himself mentally. What Warner did outside work wasn't his business, unless it was illegal. He might think BDSM was grubby but what consenting adults did to each other in private wasn't a crime. Warner having drinks with Eileen Carragher wasn't a crime either, even though she was another man's wife. Although he knew if Liam had his way there'd be a whole section in PACE just for that.

So what had Warner done that they could charge him for? Well, he'd tried to run away from them at the school; not smart, but not illegal. And he was lying about something by omission; Warner knew something about why Eileen Carragher had been killed but he wasn't saying what. Again, not a crime. The only thing they had him on was assaulting Annette, and he'd already been charged with that.

Craig rubbed the back of his neck. They had to let Warner go, but before they did, he was going to pump whatever he could out of the man. He sipped his coffee and then started.

"Mr Warner, you know that Eileen Carragher is dead."

"Yes. You informed me of that several days ago."

Warner's tone was sarcastic and Craig could see Jack's eyebrow rising menacingly in response.

"I want to ask you a few questions which may not seem relevant to the enquiry but bear with me, please. Do you frequent BDSM clubs?"

Warner snorted and folded his arms defensively. "You obviously already know the answer, Craig, so don't play games."

"Fair enough. Do you also attend private BDSM parties?"

"Private clubs you mean?"

Warner smirked and Craig knew he was going to make him drag every scrap of information out of him. He shrugged mentally. He'd done this dance a thousand times with a thousand different criminals. He didn't care how long they paced around the floor; he would win in the end.

"Private clubs then, Mr Warner. In people's homes."

Warner sniffed and stared at Craig, then he smiled. "You should come to one, Craig. A handsome man like you would do well with the ladies, especially when they find out about your job. It's surprising how many women fantasise about being handcuffed."

Craig ignored him and continued, his voice insistent. "Have you been to private BDSM groups, clubs or parties in other people's homes, Mr Warner?"

"Again, you know the answer to that, Craig, so why bother asking?"

"Where?"

Warner unfolded his arms and leaned on the table, waving a finger in Craig's face. "Tut, tut. That would come under the heading of things I need to know and you don't."

Jack moved forward from the door and Warner sat back, smiling defiantly.

"I'll tell you this much. No-one knows where the parties are until the day, then we're all taken there in a van. No-one knows the exact address except the driver, and they move around so much that unless you've a damn good memory it would be hard to remember a single place."

"General location would do for now."

Warner thought for a moment then nodded. "OK. Generally, Malone Road and out near Cultra. Specifically, lots of big houses set in their own grounds, where people can get naked and scream without being heard."

A look of distaste flickered across Jack's face but Craig just smiled and shook his head. Warner wasn't going to tell them any more than he already had. He took a different tack, watching Warner's thin face carefully as he spoke.

"Do you know of a Chinese woman or girl, very tiny, who is on the BDSM scene?"

It's amazing how many emotions the human face can display; four thousand in all. In ten seconds Gerry Warner had managed to show half of them; the shocked, guilty, caught-out and 'Oh Fuck' half.

Craig watched as each word of his question registered on the man opposite, assessing their impact in turn. The first one that registered was 'Chinese', resulting in Warner's eyes widening then filling with the clear question. "How the hell does he know?" By the time Craig got to 'woman, very tiny' something else had entered the mix. Craig puzzled for a moment about what it was and then he recognised it. It was fear. Warner was afraid of this woman, whoever she was. The acrid stench of his sweat filled the room, underlining that Craig was right.

Then something different. As soon as he reached the words 'BDSM scene' Warner's tension dropped, his shoulders sloping downwards in relief. His eyes dropped to the table and he shook his head. Craig understood instantly. The Chinese woman wasn't part of the BDSM scene, or she wasn't part of it now. Or… that wasn't where Gerry Warner knew her from. They were on the wrong track. Warner knew exactly who he was talking about, he just knew her from elsewhere.

"Who is she, Mr Warner?"

Warner's eyes fixed on the Formica table and for a moment they sat in silence, only the sound of the tape-recorder's whirring breaking the quiet. Craig rephrased his question.

"You know this woman, but not from the BDSM scene nowadays. That much is obvious. And you're afraid of her; that's also clear. Why? Why would any man be so afraid of a tiny woman?"

Warner shook his head again and then raised his eyes. They were unreadable.

"I know her but I'll never tell you from where, Craig, no matter how long you hold me. Do your worse, because trust me, nothing you can do will ever get close to her."

***

12.45 p.m.

They'd had to let Warner go with a date for his court appearance and a clear warning to watch his back. Craig couldn't tell him about Ian Carragher's death until the next of kin had confirmed it, but he'd hinted as hard as he could that they had reason to believe Warner might be next. His offer of protection was waved away.

Craig was walking down High Street on his back to the ranch when his phone rang. It was Davy.

"Yes, Davy. What's up?"

"Two things, boss. One, Liam says he'll pick you up at Custom House S...Square in five minutes. You're going somewhere to meet D.C.I. Hughes."

"But D.C.I. Hughes is three floors down at the CCU."

"Not today apparently. Liam w...will tell you more when he sees you."

"What was number two?"

"OK, I've found the knife, serrations and all. I'll have the info ready for when you get back."

"Suppliers?"

"There's only one here."

"Good. If Annette's there, Davy, can you put her on? And

130

thanks, that's great work."

Five seconds later Annette's came on the phone. "Yes, sir?"

"Annette…"

The sound of a car rushing past as he crossed Victoria Street to Custom House Square drowned out the rest of Craig's words.

Annette squinted at the phone. "I didn't get that. Too much noise. Where are you?"

"Waiting for Liam at Custom House Square; he's taking me on some mystery tour to meet Aidan Hughes. I've just been at High Street with Warner. We've had to release him; I'll brief you later on it. I couldn't tell him about Ian Carragher, but I've warned him to be careful. Did you manage to get hold of Rooney to do the same?"

"Yes. He was offered protection but he refused. Jake saw him. I didn't fancy another encounter with that slime ball. I wanted to scrub myself for hours after last time."

Craig laughed. He knew what she meant. Warner had the same effect on him.

"I've got something else for you to do, Annette. Davy's found the sole supplier of the knife. Can you go and check them out?"

A sharp rumbling in Craig's stomach reminded him that he hadn't eaten since the night before. They would have to grab a sandwich on the way. He glanced at his watch.

"Look. It's almost one o'clock. Get some lunch before you go. Take Davy and Jake to 'The James' on me and I'll square up with you when I get back. We're briefing at three-thirty. And Annette…"

"Yes?"

"Drag Nicky to lunch with you and tell her I said it was an order. She needs cheering up."

***

Liam was picking lettuce from his teeth and moaning when they pulled up outside the uber–modern detached mansion on

131

the Upper Newtownards Road. It was set back from the main carriageway in several acres of ground and whoever it belonged to definitely wasn't poor. Craig undid his seat belt and swung round to face him.

"Why the hell did you get salad in your sandwich if you hate lettuce so much?"

"I didn't know they were going to ruin a perfectly good cheese bap with bits of grass, did I? They should have listed the ingredients on the cling film. It's false advertising, that's what it is."

"Take it up with your M.P."

They climbed out just as Aidan Hughes appeared at the house's front door. Craig indicated their surroundings.

"Slumming it, Aidan?"

"Aye well, I only go to the best parties."

"Party?"

"Yep! That's why I wanted to meet you here. There was a BDSM party held here last night that got a bit exuberant. Three assaults and a rape allegation."

"Just a regular Friday night in the student quarter."

Hughes laughed. "You've been hanging out with Liam too long, Marc. And here's the lovely D.C.I. Cullen himself."

Liam loped towards them wearing a grumpy expression.

"What's wrong with you?"

"Lettuce."

Craig raised a hand to halt the diatribe that was about to follow. "Don't ask. Right. Tell us about the party."

Hughes waved them inside the house. Its wide hall and spacious rooms were painted white, and furnished in a style that was much more than modern; it was decades ahead of the curve.

"Let me guess. The owner's an architect or a designer."

"Got it in one. Edgar Tate. He's designed half the new buildings in Belfast." Hughes led the way to a small room at the end of the hall. "We can sit in here. The C.S.I.'s have already done their stuff."

He grabbed a chair and nodded the others towards a low-slung black leather couch. They sank into it and Liam spoke about something other than lettuce for the first time in half-an-hour.

"This is really soft. You wouldn't think it to look at it, would you? I wonder how much it cost."

"More than any of us can afford, I imagine." Craig turned to Hughes. "Fire ahead."

"Right. Uniform were called to a fair old disturbance here at about five a.m. When they arrived the scene that greeted them wasn't their usual. Instead of drunken youngsters, or even a couple having a domestic, there were round fifty…" He stopped abruptly and consulted his notebook, reading aloud. "Fifty-eight, semi-naked adults of between twenty-five and seventy. Carrying whips and wearing various costumes, including a dominatrix and two full leather gimps."

Liam shrugged. "Sounds like one of my mother-in-law's dinner parties."

Craig burst out laughing and they descended into a moment of banter before Hughes picked up the reins.

"You can imagine Uniform's response, especially since it was two rookie constables who answered the shout. They started arresting everyone for being perverts and it took until ten o'clock this morning for their Inspector to sort it out. "

"So who's in the cells at the moment?"

"Five men who appeared to be involved in the assaults. The alleged rape victim is being examined up at Antrim. It's going to be a hard sell, given she'd already had sex with four men beforehand, but that's the problem of the sex-crimes team."

"And your problem is trying to find Tate?"

Hughes shook his head. "Not so much. Throwing a private sex party is neither here nor there; they can shag each other stupid for all I care. It's the drugs, prostitution and coercion bits that I'm here for."

133

"You fairly know how to live, Aidan."

Hughes smiled sarcastically at Liam and Craig leapt into the gap.

"Which drugs did you find?"

"A fair amount of cocaine and some heroin. They were chasing the dragon halfway down the Newtownards Road. I've handed that bit off to Sergeant Rimmins in the Drugs Squad."

Liam interrupted. "Is that Karl Rimmins?"

"Yes. Do you know him?"

"We met him on a case last year, boss. Remember? He looked like he was using drugs himself."

Craig nodded. Karl Rimmins had been a constable when they'd met him on a murder case at St Mary's Healthcare Trust. He'd had a dark, dangerous look that fitted in well when he went undercover, but his accent had been pure Malone. Hughes continued.

"Karl took the drugs bust and we held onto the prostitution and forced sex side. Most of the hookers were well known to us, girls well over the age of consent who were getting decently paid for the party. But there's one girl I think you should meet. She's new and by the looks of her she didn't come willingly. She's been badly beaten."

Craig's face darkened. "Is she in hospital?"

Hughes shook his head. "Wouldn't go. I think she was afraid to leave our sight in case she was snatched."

"Any idea by whom?"

"No. But judging by how scared she is, she's terrified of them." Hughes paused. "Listen. I've no idea how old she is, Marc. She looks well underage but she won't tell us anything, so maybe you could have a try? I've a W.P.C. sitting with her at the moment."

Hughes led the way back into the hall and up a short flight of stairs to a mezzanine. At the end of the corridor was a room with its door lying wide open. Craig could see the W.P.C. leaning forward, as if she was talking to someone young. He was unprepared for just how young.

Craig gasped inwardly at the sight that greeted them. Liam gasped as well, only not as quietly. On the settee was a young girl no taller than four feet. Her hair was white blond and straight, pushed back from a fine-featured face that bore the stains of cried-off make-up and a developing bruise on her chin. There were other darkening bruises on her legs and arms, but Craig knew that her thin T-shirt and skirt would be concealing the worse of her injuries. People who caused visible bruises like this knew how to leave others much worse, where they wouldn't be seen.

Craig stood six-feet away from the girl so as not to make her more afraid. Then he noticed Liam's face reddening, signalling that he was about to explode. Craig grabbed his arm and dragged him outside.

"She's a kid! What sort of bastard does that to a kid? I'd like to get them alone for five minutes."

"We all would, Liam. But she doesn't need this now. Get hold of yourself before you come back in."

Craig re-entered the room with Liam following a moment later. If the girl had heard anything she gave no sign of it, just sat staring into space. Craig walked over to the W.P.C. and spoke quietly.

"Has she told you anything?"

"Nothing, sir. Not even her name. She didn't seem to mind so I looked in her bag."

She indicated a pink backpack on the floor with a kitten logo on the outside. It was the sort carried by girls at primary school.

"There was nothing inside but a hanky and a strawberry lip-gloss."

"Was the hanky paper or material?"

"Actually it was material, sir. White cotton, very worn but quite good quality. It had a logo on it. A little castle."

Craig nodded. "Get a copy for D.C.I. Cullen, please. He'll see if our analyst can match it."

He turned to see Liam and Hughes both standing by the door, wary of approaching the girl. Craig walked slowly to the end of the sofa farthest from her and sat down on the arm, then he said "Hello" very softly.

The girl turned her small face towards him uncertainly and gazed into his eyes. Craig smiled and sat patiently, while her gaze travelled to his hands and suit and shoes and then back again to his face. Craig willed her to see some kindness there but he knew that she could probably only see a man, just like the ones who had hurt her. He was wrong. After a long moment while their eyes locked and everyone in the room held their breath, a faint smile tugged at the edge of the girl's mouth. It was a breakthrough, and it was followed by another one.

"Bonjour, monsieur."

The girl's voice had a high-pitched pre-pubescent tone and her accent was pure French. They had a battered young French girl sitting in a house off Belfast's Newtownards Road. What the hell was going on?

Craig smiled gently and replied. "Bonjour, ma petite. Quel est votre nom?" (Hello, little one. What is your name?)

"Aurelie."

"Quel âge avez-vous, Aurelie?"(How old are you, Aurelie?)

"J'ais onze ans." She was only eleven. Craig hid his shock and disgust and pressed on.

"Parlez-vous anglais, Aurelie?" (Do you speak English?)

She shook her head and made a 'tiny' gesture with her hand.

"Ce n'est pas un problème. Votre mère. Où est-elle?" (That's not a problem. Your mother, where is she?)

A tear that had been threatening to fall since they'd entered, spilled over from the corner of the girl's eye. It rolled alone down her cheek as Aurelie shook her head and said that she didn't know. "Je ne sais pas."

Liam watched the conversation in open admiration. He would have barged in like a bull in a china shop, blasting about getting the men who'd done this and scaring the life out of the child. Craig's approach had already yielded her name and age. Craig spoke soothingly and they watched as the girl slowly leaned towards him, sensing that he was kind.

"Ne pas avoir peur, ma petite. Tout va bien." (Don't be afraid, little one. Everything is good.)

Liam had reached the limits of the French Danni was making him learn for their camping holiday, but it didn't matter. They all got the gist. The girl's name was Aurelie and she was eleven years old. She was terrified and seemed to have no idea where her mother was. Liam bit his tongue to prevent himself saying what he thought. If he got his hands on the bastard who'd hurt her he was going to kill him.

Craig said something else to the girl and she took the hand of the W.P.C. They walked slowly towards the door then the girl stopped and turned back to Craig, her eyes imploring him to come as well. Craig turned to Liam.

"Liam, they're taking her to High Street station and I'm going along to translate, until they find a native French-speaker. She might give us something. Take the handkerchief back to Davy and see what he can learn from the logo. I'll be back around three for the briefing." He turned to Hughes. "Can I call down and see you after that, Aidan? About four o'clock?"

"Sure." Hughes smiled at the girl. "Well done, Marc, I'm surprised. I didn't notice you paying that much attention in French class at school."

"I didn't, but we spent a few summer holidays with our cousins on the French/Italian border. You either picked up the language or they'd rip off your pocket money."

They went their separate ways and Craig climbed into a squad car with Aurelie. He wasn't certain that the girl's presence at the party had anything to do with their double murder, but he didn't believe in coincidence either.

***

2 p.m.

It was taking Annette forever to find 'The Cutting Edge' knife shop and she expected it to be as naff as its name suggested when she did. The computer had given the shop's address as Joy's Entry but Annette had been through that alleyway a million times since childhood and she'd never noticed it there. She'd parked at High Street Station, promising to have a cup of tea with Jack another time and headed for the narrow alley. Annette scanned its four-centuries-old brick walls as she walked, wishing they could tell her all the things they'd seen.

Belfast's Entries were narrow conduits in the city centre that ran mostly between the shopping meccas of High Street and Ann Street. Some of them dated as far back as 1630. Joy's Entry was one of the most famous, named after Francis Joy McCracken, who in 1737 had founded the oldest English language general daily newspaper still in publication in the world. The paper, The News Letter, was still in business, like some of the entry's original pubs.

There'd been dance classes held in the entries for generations, the sound of youngsters tapping and leaping, reverberating through the allies' walls. Pete's Mum had gone to them and she'd told them stories of laughter, even during Belfast's fatal 1941 Blitz. Annette pictured young girls and their boyfriends cuddling in the darkness during World War Two. The perfect place for a kiss after they'd waltzed the night away at the luxurious Grand Central Hotel across the street; where Castle Court shopping centre now stood.

Annette shook herself from her romantic dream and scanned the narrow street. It had atmosphere and history but none of the shops that lined its walls were the one that she was looking for. She tutted in frustration and turned to look at the map Davy had given her again. As she did so Annette noticed a small, red door flush with the entry's wall, with a tiny brass plate that said 'The Cutting Edge' embedded beside its bell. She revised her opinion of the shop from naff to strange and pushed hard at the door. It was locked. She peered through the low glass fanlight and saw a shape inside waving and shouting 'bell'. As Annette pressed it the door opened remotely for her to step inside.

Annette didn't know what she'd expected a specialist knife shop to look like, but it certainly wasn't this. The red door swung inwards to reveal a high-ceilinged vault of a room, stretching back further than she could see. Shining swords and machetes hung from the walls, each one lovingly polished to within an inch of its life. Racks of others in varying sizes stood to attention against one wall, while a horseshoe of glass cabinets glistened in the centre of the room. It was like Aladdin's Cave! She wouldn't have been surprised if someone dressed as Ali Baba appeared any moment wielding a sabre. Instead, a young man with his arms covered in tattoos popped up from behind a counter on one side.

"Just give me a minute will you? I'm in the middle of sharpening a blade."

He disappeared again and Annette heard the high-pitched whine of a knife-grinder doing its thing. She gazed around her as she waited. The glass cabinets were filled to the brim with knives of every sort. She recognised a Swiss Army Knife inside one, red lacquered and intricate. It had about twenty attachments and Annette wondered which man in her life she could buy it for. High on one wall were exotic blades that she'd never seen before, secured with clamps that would take a key to unlock. The place was a psychopath's paradise; she could understand now why the front door had to be secure.

The young man popped up again just as the machine's whining slowed and stopped. He walked round the counter to greet her, cheerfully extending his hand. The tattoos on his arms were matched by more on his chest. Annette loathed tattoos but somehow they didn't make him unattractive; the look was more

David Beckham than circus strong man.

"I'm Hugo. What can I help you with?"

She flicked open her badge and he added "Officer."

"Do you own the shop, sir?"

He shook his head. "Sadly no. It belongs to my uncle, he's asleep upstairs. I help him out sometimes."

Before Annette could recover from the revelation that the shop had another floor the young man had disappeared up a spiral staircase. He reappeared one minute later with an elderly man with sparse grey hair. He climbed gingerly down the stairs and took a seat, while his nephew made tea for them all.

"This is an amazing place you have, Mr..." She consulted her computer printout. "Archer?"

The old man nodded. "Frederick Archer. Yes, it is, but sadly it's getting too much for me now." He indicated a travelling staircase like the ones libraries used. "I can't climb it like I used to, to reach the knives higher up." He smiled at the young man. "But most of our customers are by appointment now and Hugo helps me out when he can." Archer sipped at his tea. "What can I help you with, officer?"

Annette outlined the knife that they were trying to match, leaving out the exact reasons why. Archer senior peered at the computer image Davy had given her, then he nodded.

"Yes. We supply it. A lovely blade; used by meat restaurants. They're two hundred pounds each. I've sold five of them this year."

"Is the edge serrated like that when it's sold?"

He looked more closely and nodded again. "Yes. It's unusual I know, but excellent for chopping large cuts of meat."

Archer signalled his nephew to fetch his order book then ran his finger slowly down a page. "Yes, here it is. Three were bought by a steak restaurant in town; Millennia, I have their details if you require them. They've been a customer of mine for years. The other two were bought by a young man."

"How did he pay, Mr Archer?"

"I've written here; cash. In early January."

"Do you ask for names and addresses? After all, knives can be dangerous."

The old man nodded with more force than Annette thought his thin frame possessed, then he spoke in an offended tone.

"I certainly do, officer. I'm a responsible merchant. This shop has been in the Archer family for two hundred and fifty years."

Annette saw that she'd offended him and quickly apologised, pausing for a moment before pushing him a little more. "Could I have his name, please?"

As soon as Archer had showed her the name Annette knew that he'd been had. It belonged to a member of a boy-band that her daughter Amy loved. Annette knew the address would be fictitious too, but she didn't say so, just wrote them both down and carried on.

"Can you describe the man to me, Mr Archer?"

He smiled, mollified by being of use. "I can indeed. He was tall." He turned towards his nephew and gestured him to stand. He was six-feet-four. "He wasn't as tall as Hugo, but not much less. And he was young, well under thirty I'd say. He had dark hair with that stuff in it. The kind that makes it stand up."

Hugo leaned in kindly. "You mean gel or wax, Uncle."

Archer sniffed. "I may well. It's all girly muck to me. Men never used to wear such rubbish."

Annette smiled. Frederick Archer was around seventy and she would bet that he'd used plenty of Brylcreem in his younger days. She carried on, working out ways to ask about the man's ethnicity without seeming racist.

"Did you notice anything about his eyes, Mr Archer?"

Archer gave a wide smile. "I did indeed."

Annette wanted to punch the air in celebration, until Archer said what he'd seen.

"He wore dark glasses the whole time he was here, never took them off. In January too."

Annette slumped, disappointed, then she tried a different

tack. "Did you notice anything about his voice? Anything that might have hinted that he wasn't from here?"

He shook his head. "No, no, I don't think so. He didn't sound foreign, just normal, like a local. That was all I really noticed." He tapped his chin thoughtfully. "There was one other thing. He was carrying a hold-all, one of those plastic ones, with unusual markings down the side."

"Do you know what they were?"

"No, I'm sorry. But I might be able to describe them."

It was more than Annette could have hoped for. They drank tea and talked for a while longer then she rose and shook two sets of hands, requesting that they come in to see a sketch artist the next day. Annette left by the small red front door, smiling to herself and knowing that she was one of the few people in Belfast that had ever been inside a real-life Aladdin's Cave.

Chapter Fifteen

Mai watched as Gerry Warner left the police station, rubbing his eyes as he tried to adjust to the bright late-winter sun. He looked different, older, but then it had been ten years. There was something else about him as well. She racked her brains for a moment, searching for the right word. Then she found it; Warner looked scared.

She smiled her full-lipped smile, pleased that they were having that effect. Warner must know about the Carraghers by now, so he knew that she was coming for him next. Either him or Rooney, she hadn't decided yet. It depended on her mood. The master or the pupil; decisions, decisions. So many men, so little time.

Mai watched for a moment longer as a taxi drove up and Gerry Warner clambered into the back seat, glancing anxiously around. Run away, old man. For now. You won't be running anywhere very soon.

***

John knew that Natalie was wondering why he'd phoned her at work, but she seemed preoccupied so he crossed his fingers that she wouldn't catch onto what it was really about.

"I've been given a complimentary dinner tonight at The Merchant Hotel. Will you come with me, Nat?"

Natalie glanced down distractedly at her theatre Crocs while she waited for her next patient to be prepped for operation. The Crocs were pink, with small cartoon figures dancing across the toes. Mickey Mouse was starting to look grubby; time for a new pair.

"Is this some drug company trying to keep you sweet, John?"

"God, no. You know I'm not into that sort of thing. It's for a paper I wrote. There was a prize for the best."

"Good for you, pet. I'm sure you deserved it."

She paused for so long that John thought that perhaps she'd caught on. He was just kicking himself for not inventing a better cover when Natalie acquiesced.

"OK then. But let's not make it late one. I'm on call again tomorrow night. I'll have finished by five tonight, so how about seven o'clock?"

John punched the air and struggled to keep his voice calm. Seven was perfect. It would give him time to run home and change and then prime the restaurant's Maître D. When John's voice hit the air it sounded much less cool than he wanted, so he coughed to cover its excited pitch.

"Fine. I'll pick you up at six-thirty."

Natalie dragged her eyes away from her feet and squinted suspiciously at the phone. Pick her up? John knew she liked to get there under her own steam, so why was he going all '50s prom date on her?

"I'll meet you there." She paused before continuing. "Are you all right, John? You sound a bit strange."

"Who, me? What? No. I'm fine. Just mega busy at work."

He knew from the wariness in Natalie's voice that he'd almost pushed it too far, so John feigned nonchalance until she got off the phone. Then he pocketed his mobile and scanned the dissecting room. Only the Carraghers' dead bodies were there and they were covered in sheets; they couldn't laugh at him through dead eyes. He was so far gone he didn't even think of the lack of logic his thoughts implied.

John walked into the hallway, let out an excited whoop and did the victory dance for five full minutes, then he straightened his tie, composed himself and went back to being a grown-up for two more hours.

***

3.30 p.m.

"Right, everyone. This is going to be short and focused. We've a lot to get through and I'm starting to get grief from Headquarters."

Liam slurped his tea then shoved another biscuit into his mouth and started talking, much to Annette's disgust. "Aye, well. They probably want us to solve these two before they kill another one."

Craig nodded. "To paraphrase the Chief Constable's words... OK. I'm going to bring you up to speed on our excursion earlier today. Then Annette on the knife, and Liam, Jake and Davy on whatever else you've managed to find."

He sipped at his coffee and sat back, recounting how they'd gone to the mansion on the Newtownards Road and outlining the details of the arrests. Craig watched Jake's eyes widen as he described the outfits worn by some of the party goers, but let it pass. They didn't have time for a ten minute fashion discourse from Liam, no matter how funny it was likely to be.

"OK, that brings me to the girl. They found her hiding under the stairs during the raid and D.C.I. Hughes put her in an upstairs room with a female officer."

Annette cut in. "When you say girl, sir, do you mean eighteen or so?"

Craig shook his head sadly. "Unfortunately not, Annette. I mean little girl. She's eleven."

An uncomfortable murmur ran through the circle and Craig raised his hand to still them.

"You'll all get a chance to comment, but for now please just let me report."

He carried on. "OK. She'd been beaten and God knows what

else. Uniform's taken her to the children's hospital for examination. It's disgusting that a child should have been at the party and there'll be plenty more to say on that, but there's an added complication."

Liam nodded knowingly. "She's French."

Craig raised his eyes. "Remind me never to tell a joke in front of you, Liam. Yes, as Liam said, she's French. Native French-speaking with only pigeon English. All I've managed to glean from her is that her name is Aurelie, she's eleven-years-old, from France and she doesn't know where her mother is."

"Didn't they get a translator at the station, boss?"

"No. We never got there. She felt faint in the car so we headed straight for the hospital instead. But I'm pretty fluent and they had a French nurse who also tried to get through to her. They were talking for quite a while, but the girl only said what she'd already told me. She doesn't know where her mother is or how long she's been in Northern Ireland. Just that she comes from France. She doesn't seem to know which part, but she's pretty shocked at the moment so she may tell us more in a few days."

Annette shook her head. "Not necessarily, sir. It depends how traumatised she's been. And the doctors won't let you interview her again until they're certain that it won't harm her."

Annette was right. They would just have to do their best with what they had.

"OK. One thing we did find in her possession was a cotton handkerchief with a small logo embroidered on it." He turned towards Liam and Davy. "Any joy on that yet?"

Davy raked his hair. "Yes and no, boss. Yes, I can identify the logo. It's French. The symbol of a posh preparatory school in the Loire Valley. I sent the girl's photo over to them and to the French police, but the school's come back with a 'non'. I even tried with the name Aurelie, but they have about twenty girls called that in every year. W…We've nothing from the Gendarmes yet."

146

Craig had a thought. "What age range does the school teach, Davy?"

"Six to twelve-year's old. W...Why?"

"You know that computer software that Des has? The one that shows what people look like as they age?

Davy nodded hesitantly. He couldn't see the relevance.

"Can it be reversed? Can they take a picture of someone now and see what they were likely to have looked like years ago?"

Davy screwed up his face in thought for a moment then his expression brightened and he started to babble excitedly.

"If I put in the parameters ..."

Craig raised a hand and smiled. "Before you bury us in tech-speak. Yes or no?"

"Yes. Yes, I think so. I need to s...speak to Des."

"Great. After we finish here, please. He'll need a good full-face shot of the girl, so you'll need to get the hospital's cooperation on that."

Liam cut in. "Could someone tell me what's happening here? Are you saying that the girl might have gone to this posh school but they don't recognise her because she left a few years back?"

Craig nodded. "That's exactly what I'm saying, Liam. The hanky was old and worn."

Davy jumped in eagerly. "The s...school said the girls are given them in their first year."

"If she was given the hanky when she was six years old that would explain why it's worn. We're lucky she kept it. The school might not recognise her because she left there years ago. Either to move on to another school." Craig's face darkened. "Or for some other reason."

"You mean she was kidnapped, sir."

Craig nodded. "That's what I'm thinking, Jake. If she was taken some years back then they wouldn't recognise her picture now. Children change a lot in a few years. We need to find out who she is and this is our best lead."

Liam nodded slowly. "OK. Let's say we find out who she is,

and we find her parents and they're normal people who want her back. Happy ending all round, but it still doesn't explain what the hell she was doing in a house in Belfast, beaten black and blue."

Craig sighed heavily. "Liam's right. This is complex. The likeliest scenario is that she was taken some years back, which is why she can't remember her surname or where her mother is. Then she was brought to Ireland by someone and used for God only knows what. That party won't have been the first."

A pall fell over the group. Craig let them mourn the girl's innocence for a moment then pulled them back to the case.

"OK. Let's go back to the Carraghers. What else do we know?"

"Not much, boss. Their bank accounts are clean. The place down in Newcastle was bought with an inheritance from Mrs Carragher's mother."

"We must have enough for a search warrant now. Liam. Get one and take Jake down with you tomorrow morning, please. Pull the place apart. I want their townhouse searched as well."

From the side of his eye Craig could see Annette's eyes widen. She was surprised at him sending Jake with Liam. Craig caught her gaze and held it. He'd done it deliberately. She and Jake had been paired too often recently and it was starting to feel like Annette thought Jake was hers to command. Annette had great people sense, but Liam's nose for the street was second to none and Jake needed equal exposure to them both.

Craig broke her gaze and turned his eyes front again. Liam was asking a question.

He shook his head. "Sorry, Liam. I missed that."

"I said what do you want us to look for?"

"You'll know it when you see it, but bring any computers and papers you find back for Davy to search." He turned to see Davy scribbling on a pad and smiled, knowing he was already writing a de-aging programme.

"Davy. Annette will get a warrant for the Carragher's home

and work computers. Is there anything else you need?"

Davy thought for a moment. "I s...should be able to access their e-mail accounts and anything they've put on the Cloud from their computers, but is anyone looking at their phones? They must have several between them."

He was right. It was a rookie's omission.

Craig nodded. "Davy's right. That's my fault. We should have accessed those on day one."

"Don't go blaming yourself just yet, boss. Remember, on the face of it Eileen Carragher was an innocent victim. We'd no grounds to go poking through her stuff, and the husband would never have given us permission."

Liam was right as well. It was only now that they could legitimately get a warrant; two deaths and several sordid social lives in.

"Thanks, Liam. OK then, let's get both houses and their offices searched. Phones, computers and papers back here for Davy to do his thing." He remembered something. "Liam, did Aidan recognise the Chinese woman's description from the BDSM scene?"

Liam's face dropped. With all the confusion at the house party he'd forgotten. "I'll get on to that now."

Craig smiled. "Don't worry about it. We'll nip down after the briefing." He turned towards Annette. She'd recovered from her momentary possessiveness and had her notepad out, ready to report. "Any joy on the knife, Annette?"

Annette thought back to her visit to the small shop and smiled. It had been surreal.

"Yes and no, again. Yes, they stock it, and they're the only place in Northern Ireland that does. That's always supposing that it was definitely bought here. There are four shops in the Republic that sell them as well."

"We'll look at those if we hit a dead end."

"That's what I thought. Anyway, they've sold five of them in the past year. Three to a restaurant in town that specialises in steak dishes." Davy made a face and she nodded. "I know, that's what I thought. Too close to home. The other two were sold to a young man. He paid in cash and gave a false name; a member of a boy-band."

Craig smiled ruefully. "When was that?"

"Early January."

"Chinese?"

"The shopkeeper wasn't sure. The man wore dark glasses the whole time. He did say he didn't sound foreign, as he so delicately put it."

"He wouldn't if he'd grown up here. Did he have a local accent?"

"He did mention local, but he couldn't be any more specific than that."

Liam interjected. "That'll be a yes then."

Jake cut in. "If he's Chinese but Northern Irish by birth then there would be no way of telling his ethnicity except by seeing his whole face."

"Which might well be why he was wearing sunglasses in the middle of January? OK. It's a definite maybe. Annette, did you see one of the knives?"

"I did even better than that. I bought one!"

As she said it Annette reached into her handbag and drew out a brand-new serrated cleaver, waving it around. Liam sat as far back in his chair as he could.

"Watch that thing, girl."

She brandished it playfully at him. "I'm going to get my own back on you, Liam."

Liam stood up and backed away. "I remember when you let a gun slip out of your hand at the firing range, McElroy. Don't be doing the same with that thing."

Craig smiled at the floor-show, wondering what Joe Public would make of it if they walked in now. "OK, at the risk of sounding like everyone's Dad, put it down, Annette. Actually, hand it to me. I'll give it to John to match."

Annette grinned and passed the cleaver over, then turned back to her notes. As he listened Craig perused the blade from all angles. The main shank was sparkling stainless-steel, two or three millimetres thick, but the blade's cutting edge was as thin as a sheet of paper, rucked with regular serrations that made it sparkle like ice. It looked lethal and he didn't want to think about how being cut with it must feel. Annette was still talking.

"Anyway. The man who bought them paid in cash."

"Typical. Millions of credit cards in the world and he couldn't even use one of them."

"But the shopkeeper remembered something that might help, sir."

Craig roused himself from the blade's hypnotic effect. "What?"

"He said the man put the knives in a PVC hold-all with unusual markings."

"What kind of unusual?"

"A red and gold pattern. I'm putting him in front of a sketch artist tomorrow."

"Good. That's helpful." Craig leaned forward, preparing to sum up.

Annette looked put-out. "I hadn't finished, sir."

Craig raised a hand in apology. "Sorry. Carry on."

"The shopkeeper said that the man was young. Not a kid but definitely under thirty, he would swear to that. He said his clothes were modern and he had 'stuff' in his hair that made it stand up. His nephew said it was probably gel or wax."

Annette stopped again and Craig waited to see if she'd reached an end. She had.

"Good, thanks Annette. When the shopkeeper comes in, get him to do a sketch of the man as well, please. He might be able to remember his mouth, nose or other things."

Craig stretched and yawned, then locked his hands behind his head. "OK. This is looking more like a young couple; male and female, with the female Chinese. We'll ask Aidan what he knows about her when we go downstairs, but there's plenty to get on with meantime. Liam and Jake, organise warrants for the searches of the homes and offices, and go to Newcastle tomorrow and see what's what. Annette, while they're away would you mind supervising the search of the Carragher's house here with Uniform, and get your witness in front of a sketch artist?"

"Will do."

"Thanks. Davy, start with the phone dumps until you get the computers. Anything you can find will be useful, but particularly if and how often the Carraghers were in contact with Warner and Rooney. And see if you can find any calls from the Carraghers to their Newcastle house; they shouldn't be calling it at all unless someone else is living there as well. And check any calls to the organiser of the house party. Aidan can give you his details."

Jake interrupted. "Is this to build up a picture, sir?"

"Yes, mainly. But you never know when a little gem might appear. Unfortunately there's still a lot of leg work to do, but we're getting closer."

Liam's voice boomed across the room. "If we know we're getting closer you can bet that the killers do too, boss."

Craig paused. Liam was right. Their killers must know that time was running out for them. That could be good or bad. It might make them careless enough to make a mistake and get caught, or it could make them kill more quickly to get to the end of their list, if there was one. His money was on the second option.

"You're right, Liam. That's why Warner and Rooney need to be watched. Get patrols to drive by their houses and repeat the offer of protection."

"You can take a horse to water, but…"

Liam was right again. For men with Warner and Rooney's proclivities, being watched would definitely cramp their style. The team could offer them protection until they were blue in the face but they couldn't make them accept.

***

Gerry Warner towelled himself dry and then walked into the bedroom of his three-bedroomed terrace house. It was sparsely furnished, the dry beige colour scheme broken only occasionally by an exotic souvenir from one of his overseas holidays. He crossed the room to pick up a carved teak elephant and stared at it, trying to recall exactly when it had been bought.

It had been on one of his trips to Thailand but he couldn't remember which one; there had been so many. Once a year when he was married, then more and more after his divorce, until he'd travelled nearly every month. To Thailand and Cambodia, then across the world to Mexico and Brazil. Countries where he could do the things he wanted to, barely censured, and buy anything that his heart desired.

Each time he'd travelled he'd thought that the trip would be his last and he would finally settle into a 'normal' life. He shook his head. He'd never managed it, always searching for something to satisfy him but never complete. He'd envied his colleagues with their dogs and marriages and rounds of golf. BDSM had given him the closest thing to peace he'd ever known and now even that was going to take its revenge.

Warner shrugged and combed his thinning hair. He was going to die like Eileen Carragher had; it was only a question of when. He glanced at the door leading off his bedroom that everyone thought was an ensuite then he lifted the key from the dresser and turned it over slowly in his hand. After a moment's thought Warner slipped off his dressing gown and walked naked into the room. If he was going to die he might as well enjoy himself while he could.

***

"Chinese, you say?"

Craig nodded and Liam wandered absentmindedly around Aidan Hughes' office, pausing by the right-hand wall. It held shelf after shelf of videos and DVDs. He hadn't noticed them when he'd been there before. They were neatly arranged and colour-coded according to some unknown key. Hughes saw him staring and twisted his mouth in a smile.

"Wondering what they are, Liam?"

Liam tossed up between admitting that he was interested, or feigning 'I don't know what you mean'. Curiosity won and he plumped for the first.

"Is it your Sci-Fi collection then?"

Hughes shook his head grimly. "I wish to God it was."

He walked to a shelf and pulled down a laminated sheet, handing it to Liam without a word. Liam's eyebrows shot up and he turned even paler than he normally was. He glanced at Craig to see if he already knew.

"I've seen Aidan's list before, Liam. It's grim reading."

It certainly was. The sheet held a column of coloured blocks and against each was one word. Bestiality, Torture, Snuff... Liam's jaw dropped further as he moved down the page. Finally he placed the sheet on the desk, turning it over and pushing it away. Hughes watched, knowing what was going through Liam's mind.

"Don't worry. I'm not a pervert. Just thank God you work in the Murder Squad." He waved his hand at the wall of porn. "These are videos lifted from suspects. We had to view them all for evidence then catalogue them from the mildest to the hardest core. These are all SAP category five; the worst you can find. I sub-categorised them according to genre."

Liam found his voice. It was quieter than it usually was. "Why keep them here? Shouldn't they be in evidence?"

Hughes shook his head. "They're copies and mostly old cases; most of the perps are banged away or impossible to find. I keep these for the Squad's new recruits. They have to watch them during their first year. It makes them un-shockable."

Liam mimicked being sick. "Remind me never to transfer to Vice."

Craig interrupted. "I spent some time in Vice in London. It's hard going."

Hughes shrugged. "Someone has to catch the weirdoes. For all the crap we have to see and listen to, I can't tell you how good it feels to lock one of them up and throw away the key." He returned to Craig's original question. "What sort of Chinese, Marc? Man or woman? Kid? And what are you looking for them in connection with?"

"The case Liam asked you about the other day. The one he showed you pictures from."

"Warner and the woman I recognised from the BDSM scene?"

"Yes. We think a Chinese woman, young probably, but we don't know her age, might be connected to the murders somehow. Warner reacted pretty strongly when I mentioned her. We need to know if she's on the BDSM scene now, or ever has been."

Hughes rubbed his chin thoughtfully. After a minute he moved to the video collection and pulled down a tape marked with a green key. Craig checked the laminate sheet. Green meant torture. Hughes slipped the tape into the machine and waited for it to start. As it flickered into life he hit pause.

"Listen. This is grim, I warn you." He glanced at Liam, remembering his reaction from a few days before. "Do you want to leave, Liam?"

Liam struggled with his macho-ness for a moment until Craig took him off the hook. "Aidan, does this have children in it?"

Hughes nodded and Craig looked at Liam kindly. "Liam, this isn't the time to tough it out. You have small children; you don't need to watch this. Disappear and come back in five."

Liam grabbed at the 'out' like a drowning man and was

through the door before Craig could say another word. Craig turned back to the screen and nodded. They watched in silence for a moment, with the sound down initially and then Hughes jacked it up. What Craig saw and heard brought tears to his eyes, and after two minutes Hughes pressed 'stop'.

Neither man spoke, the only sound in the room the straining of the video tape attempting to restart. Finally, Craig broke the silence in a tight voice, indicating the screen. "How old was the girl, Aidan?"

"We're not sure. The tape was found doing the rounds in 2008, but it was pretty degraded so it had probably been taken years before. We estimate she was about six when it was shot."

"Do you have any idea who she is?"

Hughes shook his head. "Was, more likely. No child could survive that level of torture for long."

Craig stood up and paced the room, trying to erase the girl's screams. He was grateful that Liam hadn't heard them. Hughes was still talking.

"The tape was almost certainly made in Northern Ireland; those accents were local. And she's the only Chinese girl I've ever seen on a local tape, that's why she came to mind. There's been no adult Chinese woman on the BDSM scene that I know of, not in my time anyway, and I've been in Vice since 2009. "

"Who was the boy?"

The memories of the girl screaming were forced into second place by the image of the underage boy who'd wielded the whip that hit her. The boy had hit her again and again, encouraged by a man out of shot. A man whose voice jogged something at the back of Craig's mind. The boy had cried and said sorry to the Chinese girl each time the lash struck her. Both children pawns of some warped bastard whose face they couldn't see.

Hughes shook his head. "No idea. He's probably dead as well." He stared at Craig solemnly. "The children, and a lot of the adults in these videos, don't survive. The bastards view them as playthings to arouse themselves with. Once they've served

156

their purpose they get rid of them and get a new toy."

Craig could feel tears pricking his eyes again. "I admire you, Aidan. I couldn't do this without wanting to kill someone."

Hughes laughed. "Who says we don't."

Just then Liam's large shadow appeared at the door and Hughes beckoned him in. Craig summarised the tape for Liam, leaving the worst details out. Liam winced, then he snapped his fingers as if he'd had an idea.

"Could we get screen shots of the kids' faces, Aidan?"

Hughes squinted at him for a moment, puzzled. "The boy had his back to the camera, but the girl, yes."

Liam turned to Craig. "What if we got Davy to age her for us, to see what she would look like nowadays?"

Craig smiled admiringly. Liam's time-out had done him good.

"Brilliant idea. OK, you organise that. It's a long shot but who knows what we might find."

Craig stood up to go and Hughes started talking again. "I'll put the feelers out to see if anyone's heard anything about a Chinese woman."

"Could you dig into the Carraghers a bit more for me too, Aidan? Gerry Warner and a younger man called Alan Rooney as well. They're all linked to our case."

"Which is...?"

Craig smiled. "Which is a nasty double murder, but I can't give you any more detail yet. Sorry."

Hughes shrugged; secrets were part of the job and they all had their own. Craig and Liam walked back up to the tenth floor. Liam formulating photo-arrays in his head and Craig wishing that his head contained anything but the video he'd just seen.

Chapter Sixteen

5.30 p.m.

"We need to meet."

Alan Rooney glared at his mobile, resenting the other man's tone.

"I don't need to do anything, Warner."

"For God's sake put your ego to one side, and meet me. The Carraghers are dead."

"What! I know about Eileen, but there's been nothing about a man being killed on the news."

"They're keeping it quiet, but I could read between the lines. They offered me protection, said I was at risk."

Rooney sneered. "Me too, but that doesn't mean Ian's dead."

"It does. They didn't offer us protection after Eileen's death, so something else has hit the fan since then. I've tried Ian's mobile and work and there's no answer. Something must have happened to him. Ryan hasn't seen him either. I rang him and asked."

"I didn't know that you two were friends." Rooney's voice held the hint of a smile.

Warner's was much cooler. "We aren't, but Ian's his father. He should know where he is."

"So what if Ian's dead? That doesn't mean we're next on the list. There probably isn't a list."

"Do you want to take that chance?"

Rooney thought for a moment then gave a shrug. "OK, we'll meet. But I'm warning you now; if there is a list it's every man for himself."

***

6 p.m.

John straightened his tie and glanced in the mirror. Not bad, in a preppy, nerdy sort of way. But women liked nerdy men nowadays. You only had to look at the Top 100 list of men they thought were 'hot' to see that. John adjusted his black-wire glasses and stared at himself again. What did he care who women liked nowadays? He was only interested in one woman; the best one that he'd ever met.

He walked to the table and gazed down at the flowers he'd ordered, knowing that they were over the top. He didn't care. Tonight he was going to woo his girl in the way she deserved and he desperately hoped that she wanted to be wooed. John grabbed the bouquet and his car keys and headed out the door. He wanted to get to the hotel early to check that everything was prepared. After all, he didn't propose every night and he only planned on doing it once.

***

Craig knocked the top off a bottle of beer and drained it in three gulps, then he opened another one desperately, hoping that he could get drunk enough to shut out the girl's screams. Three bottles later he was nowhere near drunk but the screams had gone. What was in their place was the boy from the tape.

He'd been Caucasian, about ten-years-old. Pale and thin and naked, except for a grubby little vest. They'd caught a glimpse of his profile once, when he'd turned towards the man's voice, begging to be allowed to stop. The boy's words had been thick with tears and his eyes rubbed raw, as if he'd been crying for a week. But the voice had been relentless.

"Do as I tell you. Hit her again."

He'd said it over and over, threatening to kill the boy's family if he didn't comply. Craig doubted if the man would have been able to find them never mind kill them, but the fear was enough to frighten the child. That was how power worked. Create the illusion that you have it and the rest just flows.

Craig wondered where the two children were now and if they were even still alive. Had they survived their abuse? And if they had, what were they now? Still victims? Normal and well balanced? Or abusers themselves? And what was it about the voice on the tape that had made him feel like he'd heard it before?

Craig shook his head hard in frustration and grabbed a bottle of red wine from the rack. Beer hadn't worked so he'd have to try something new. He'd drink all night if he had to. Anything to wipe the images out.

***

8 p.m.

The two cars pulled up simultaneously and Gerry Warner climbed out first. Rooney hung back for a moment, scanning the shopping centre car-park as if it was some sort of trap. It was deserted. Warner had found the only supermarket in Belfast that wasn't open late on a Thursday night.

Rooney squinted through the windscreen suspiciously, searching for anything out of place. He knew Gerry Warner of old; he's always been a tricky bastard, so why should he play straight now?

Warner stood with his arms folded, waiting for his protégé to emerge. By the looks of it Rooney's paranoia was getting worse. Warner shrugged. He'd never liked Rooney much and he didn't care if he was losing it now, he just wanted his help finding the Carraghers' killer before they killed him.

Eventually the car door opened and Rooney emerged. He strolled arrogantly across the tarmac towards the older man.

"As trusting as ever I see, Alan?"

"As untrustworthy as ever, Gerry?"

Warner laughed at the repost. Rooney scanned the snow-covered car-park then blew on his hands.

"It's too bloody cold for this. And how come this place is empty on late-shopping night?"

"It's derelict. Follow me."

Warner turned towards the supermarket's entrance and forced the glass doors apart with his hands, walking into the echoing foyer. Rooney whistled admiringly.

"Great venue. We could get up to all sorts in here."

"I was planning a party here before the shit started hitting the fan." Warner stared seriously at the younger man. "The plods think a Chinese woman had something to do with the Carraghers' death."

Rooney didn't move an inch and for a moment Warner thought that he hadn't heard. He went to repeat the words and Rooney scowled and turned away. "I heard you."

"Then you'll know what this means. We need to clear out. Now. Unless you fancy being the next one to end up as Steak Tartare."

Rooney wheeled round to face him. "Where did they find Ian?"

"They didn't tell me, they haven't even confirmed he's dead. Why? What does it matter?"

Rooney looked thoughtful. "The Governors closed the school on Monday for the rest of the week. Mark of respect for Eileen. Only teachers were only allowed in the odd time, to work. They could have left Ian's body there and I wouldn't know."

Warner looked irritated. "So fucking what? If he's dead I don't care if they hung him from the Cavehill. It's me that I'm worried about."

Rooney snarled his next words. "You stupid prick. You mightn't care, but if they used the school again it means something."

"What? What does it mean that's so important?"

"If Ian was brought all the way there instead of just being left where he dropped, it means that whoever did it isn't working alone. And don't forget the symbolism."

Warner nodded slowly as realisation dawned. One school was pretty much like another when you were trying to get a message across.

***

The Merchant Hotel. Belfast. 7.30 p.m.

By seven-thirty Natalie still hadn't arrived and John's nerves were in shreds. He was also on his second bottle of wine. He'd given the flowers to the Maître D, with instructions to bring them and champagne once he asked about dessert. Natalie never had dessert, preferring a starter and a main course, so he was safe. Perfect planning, even though he did say so himself.

He had it all worked out. Light chit-chat during the first course, a natural hiatus after the second and plenty of wine throughout. Relaxing, elegant and the perfect setting for the big moment. He could see it now. Natalie would be wearing her favourite dress and smiling lovingly at him across the table, then he'd take her hand in his and kiss her knuckles, like he's seen them do in the movies. Why her knuckles he didn't know, but it always looked good when George Clooney did it. She'd stare at him like he was a God and hang on his every word and then he'd say 'Natalie. There's something I've wanted to ask you for months.' Not strictly true, it had been more like forty-eight hours, but that didn't sound as good.

She'd say 'Yes, darling.' Well, all right, probably not darling, maybe 'pet' or 'dear'. Something affectionate anyway. Then he'd drop on one knee in front of everyone, her eyes would light up and he'd ask her to be his wife. Cue Natalie crying and screaming 'yes' yes'. No, hang on, that was the restaurant scene in 'When Harry met Sally', wasn't it? Well she'd say a definite yes, however she said it, and then he'd call for dessert. It might seem a bit incongruous to want chocolate mousse at such a romantic moment, but he needed the flowers brought in.

John smiled drunkenly and topped up his glass, certain that the details would iron themselves out. After all, Natalie would be so overwhelmed with emotion that she'd notice nothing but him.

John's daydream was rudely interrupted by a thud, as Natalie dropped her rucksack on the floor by his chair. She grabbed his wineglass and tipped her head back, draining it in one gulp; then she sighed heavily.

"That bastard Owen really needs to be dealt with. That's the third evening I've been off that he's called me back into theatre at five o'clock."

John leaned forward to say something soothing but Natalie waved him back, warming to her theme.

"Of course, it's only because he's older than God that he gets away with it. There ought to be some rule to make surgeons retire when they get irritating."

John bit his tongue very hard, thinking how few surgeons would still have a job by that criterion.

"And then there was the anaesthetist! Well he's been sniffing his own drugs, that's for sure. Gas-men, huh! They only choose the job 'cos they're already half asleep."

John folded his arms and let Natalie rant about every injustice in her world, smiling his way into another glass of wine. After five minutes she stopped abruptly, suddenly remembering where they were. She cast a look around them and then stared at John's suit. Her face fell. She gazed down at her jeans and T-shirt and blushed deep red.

"You're all dressed up!" It was accompanied by an accusing

163

look and an affectionate tone.

John nodded drunkenly. "I am."

"And I'm not. I'm so sorry, John. I meant to go home first and change, but what with theatre…"

John raised his hand gently and made a soothing noise. "It doesn't matter, Nat. You're here and that's all I care about." He handed her the menu. "What would you like to eat? Some of the starters look good."

Tears rushed to fill Natalie's eyes and John stared at her, aghast. What on earth was she crying for? He hadn't even asked her yet!

"Don't be nice to me, John. I'm late and scruffy and I've been ranting for ten minutes. And the place is beautiful, and you look…"

A tear rolled down her cheek and she sniffed and dashed it away. It was followed by another, released by tiredness and shame. John wanted to kiss them away and take her in his arms, but he couldn't; they were in the middle of a restaurant surrounded by the great and good. Unless…

He caught the Maître D's eye and he was over at the table in a flash, holding the dessert menu in his hand.

"Yes, sir?"

John smiled and the man smiled back. "Two of your best desserts, please. And hopefully everything else soon after."

Natalie gazed at him, bewildered. "But we haven't eaten dinner yet, and I'm so scruffy and…"

Johns saw Natalie's lips move but he didn't hear another word. They were drowned-out by a rush of blood to his brain. To hell with his plan! John reached over and pulled Natalie towards him, kissing her hard. Natalie gawped at him, her eyes widening. They widened even further when John dropped on one knee and took her hand. He stared up into her wide blue eyes then he let his gaze roam over her pert face and long dark hair.

"I'd planned this very differently, Nat, I'd…. Oh hell. I don't care. I love you. Would you…"

Before John could say the words Natalie whispered "yes", so softly that he barely heard. His eyes widened questioningly and she said it again.

"Yes! Yes, yes, I'll marry you, John. I love you so much. Yes."

The tears ran down her cheeks unchecked now, but this time they were tears of joy. John lifted her in his arms and swung her round, much to the surprise of the other guests. Then the room full of diners rose to their feet in a round of applause and the next thing Natalie knew she was holding flowers, and John was shaking hands with people he'd never met. They drank champagne and ate and planned for hours until John suggested that they book a room upstairs. Then they talked on and on, until the hotel was quiet and the street was dark and they fell asleep in each other's arms.

Chapter Seventeen

Friday. 10 a.m.

"Any joy at the Belfast house, boss?"

Craig stared through his office window at the grey river below. The waves were pointing their edges like fingers, reaching out to touch the hovering gulls. Each wave wore a white glove of surf and they danced as politely as if they were performing a gavotte. Craig knew from the darkening sky that any politeness would soon be gone; the waves would be metres high and lashing at every boat moored in the port. He stared ahead at nothing while Liam waited for his answer.

Liam watched Jake drive expertly down the A24 and admired the Mourne Mountains looming ahead of them through the mist. After a moment he prompted Craig. "Are you still there?"

Craig shook himself from his daydream and focused. "Yes. Sorry, Liam. I was a million miles away. There's nothing at the house so far, but at least Davy's got the computers now."

"Don't forget their office ones at work."

"Already lifted."

Craig paused as something occurred to him. Where were Ian Carragher's two sons all this time? They'd been remarkably quiet for the past week. More than the relatives of two murdered parents would normally have been. He asked Liam the question.

"Oh, aye, the sons. The eldest one is Ryan and the younger one's Jonathan. Thirty-four and twenty-three, that's all I know."

"Quite an age gap."

"Aye, well. People will keep on having sex. I suppose Carragher was looking for a mother for them when he met the wife."

"Where are they?"

"Ryan's the one who runs Tagine, the Lebanese restaurant on the Ormeau Road. He's the one Carragher asked to have called on Monday, when the wife died. I talked to him for a minute; seemed normal enough."

"And the younger boy?"

Just then Liam's eye was caught by a van selling strawberries by the side of the road and he signalled frantically for Jake to stop. Danni had asked him to get some if they saw a stand. He pulled a note from his pocket and waved at Jake to get out. Craig listened to the background conversation and smiled. He heard the car door open and close and asked his question again.

"Aye, sorry, boss. The younger boy. I couldn't get hold of him. Went off to school at thirteen, then Uni in London straight after that."

"To study what?"

"Some sort of history. That's all Ryan said. He'll be back for the funerals, whenever they are. Ryan's organising them."

"They should be early next week. I'll check with John if he's finished with Ian Carragher's body."

Craig cast another look at the river, imagining the Irish Sea where Liam was heading. He remembered a phrase from an old melody 'Where the mountains of Mourne sweep down to the sea', and wondered if the Carragher's house would have such idyllic views. He pulled himself back to the case.

"Are you still there, Liam?"

"Aye. I'm waiting for Jake to get back with Danni's groceries. What is it?"

"I've been so fixated on the Carragher's murders that I forgot the most basic thing. Where was it that the Carraghers were working when they met?"

167

"Some school in Bangor. Davy has all the details. But it closed down years ago, boss, in 2004. It's a dead end."

Craig muttered something and then the line went dead. Liam was still staring at the phone when Jake climbed back into the car. Liam gave him a confused look. He couldn't be sure what he'd heard Craig say, but he thought it had been 'MGM'…

***

Mai had tossed a coin. Heads Warner, tails Rooney. Rooney lost. Pity. She would have liked to kill the Sorcerer next, but they'd have to make do with his apprentice. They'd use the school again to dump his body. The police were watching it during the day but they wouldn't waste manpower covering it at night.

She thought for a moment longer then rolled towards her lover and stroked his face, waking him up with a kiss. He opened his eyes one by one, as if reluctant to face another day, then he gazed at Mai, drinking in her beauty as if he'd never noticed it before. He kissed her nose and then her lips, before moving purposefully towards her breasts.

Mai shook her head and laughed. "You always were a morning boy." She retreated from him gently and sat at the end of the bed, wearing a serious expression. "We need to finish them quickly, before the police get in the way."

The young man's voice was pleading. "Can't we leave them, Mai? We've done enough. The police will get Rooney and Warner and then follow the trail. We could go away somewhere and get on with our lives."

His body tensed as he braced himself for what he knew would follow next but he hadn't anticipated its strength. Mai's delicate face contorted until her eyes were wild and red, burning against her twisted muscles and veins. She bared her teeth and stretched her neck until it bulged and then she screamed with every ounce of strength she had. The sound ripped through him, full of anger and hatred, but worst of all was the back-note of pain and loss. She had lost so much. They both had. But he was made of different stuff. Quieter for sure, but stronger as well in a way. The nightmares didn't torture him now, but they still stole her sleep every night.

He reached across and took her in his arms, young and strong, strong enough for them both. Mai struggled but she couldn't free herself and eventually he felt her relax and lean in, letting him rock her into a mercifully dreamless sleep. As he watched her eyes close he knew they had to keep going until the end, or she would never find peace.

***

Craig opened his office door so abruptly that Nicky dropped the yoghurt she was eating onto her lap. She watched as it ran across her knee and dripped onto the floor, forming a trail of congealing goo. She swung round, ready to give Craig a lecture about surprising people, but the fire she saw in his eyes made her stop. He'd had an idea, one of his inspired ones, and it didn't do to break his flow.

Craig strode across to Davy's desk. "Davy. I need you."

Davy glanced up at the words and was surprised to find Craig standing in front of him.

"Yes, chief. W…What for?"

"Where's Annette?"

"With the sketch artist I think. Her w…witness arrived thirty minutes ago."

"Right."

He wheeled round to see Nicky heading for the door, holding her dress out like an apron.

"Nicky, where are you off to?"

Nicky thought about swearing and then reconsidered, smiling sweetly instead. "I'm taking my dress for a walk, sir."

Craig screwed up his face, puzzled. "What? Oh, OK then. When you've finished doing that, can you get Annette?"

Nicky stopped mid-step, trying to decide whether to keep walking or call Annette now. She'd need at least ten minutes to wash her dress and dry it with the hand-dryer in the loo, and she knew she'd get no peace until Annette was back in the squad. She sighed, lifted the nearest phone to the sketch artist and asked him to send Annette back upstairs. Then she walked sedately to the ladies toilets, checked that they were empty and then swore at the top of her voice.

Annette pushed through the floor's double-doors and hurried straight over to Davy and Craig.

"Yes, sir. What did you need me for?

Craig smiled apologetically. She was out of breath. He hadn't meant to rush her that much, but he was on a roll.

"I need both of you." He turned to Davy. "The school where the Carragher's met. Tell me about it."

He grabbed a chair and motioned Annette to do the same while Davy tapped at his screen.

"Marcheson's International school. It was outside Bangor, County Down, on the coast halfway between there and Donaghadee. It w...was a boarding school for the children of wealthy couples w...who lived abroad."

Annette snorted. "You mean a dumping ground for people who should never have had kids. They have them because they want a trophy baby, then once they start to need attention they dump them on nannies or schools. Poor little tots."

Davy nodded. "Tots are right. By the looks of it, the s... school had a nursery."

Annette cut in. "Three years old! They dumped their children in a boarding school at three! They should all be sterilized."

Craig smiled, recognising his mother's viewpoint in Annette's words. Mirella Craig was a typical protective Italian Mama; if she had her way both her adult children would still be living at home.

"Go on Davy."

"The school had classes for three to s…seventeen-year-olds, boys and girls. It looks like they had great facilities; concert hall, gym, pool…"

"Are there any images?"

Davy nodded vigorously, setting his long hair flying around his face. He turned the computer screen towards them and Craig saw screen-shots of an Olympic size swimming pool and three tennis courts. Well-scrubbed children in uniform were pictured laughing and working at their desks.

"Looks idyllic but it's a bit too perfect for me. Any dirt on it?"

"No. I ran it through all the databases when it first came up. Not a thing."

"Why did it close down?"

Davy frowned. "Yes, that was a bit s…strange. It closed in 2004." He tapped his keyboard quickly then nodded. "The school closed for the s…summer in June 2004. In the August it was announced that it w…wasn't going to re-open and all the kids were going elsewhere."

"Where? Local schools? There can't have been too many that could offer the same facilities."

Davy shook his head. "No, you're right. Anyway, the school's still there but it's a hotel now, called The Down Hartley."

"Damn!" The vehemence of Craig's exclamation took the others aback. He explained about the video Aidan Hughes had played, sanitising the worst detail. It wasn't sanitised enough for Annette.

"Dirty buggers. They should all be shot."

Craig nodded. "I wish I'd never seen it, to be honest, but if I hadn't then I wouldn't have known what I was looking for. I have a hunch that it was filmed in that school, but we'll never know now. It was bound to have been remodelled when it became a hotel." His MGM comment to Liam had referred to a film shoot.

Davy shook his head. "Don't be so quick on that, chief. Give me a minute."

He waved them away and turned back to his empire, leaving Craig and Annette to make coffee and talk. Annette squirmed for a moment then said the word she hated most in the whole world. Even saying it made her feel like she needed a bath.

"Paedophilia, sir? So you don't think the Carraghers were just into BDSM?"

Craig shook his head and perched on the edge of Nicky's desk.

"There's something very nasty going on here, Annette, and my gut says that the Carraghers were up to their necks in it. It's more than BDSM with willing partners; you don't get killed for that. The video of the Chinese girl was locally made; child pornography, with elements of BDSM and torture thrown in, and we know the Carraghers were into BDSM."

Annette corrected him. "Eileen Carragher was. We have no proof about the husband."

Craig nodded, conceding. "But it's unlikely he didn't know what she was into, and even if he just turned a blind eye he was still culpable. The way they were killed says that this is someone getting revenge."

"And you think it's a child they harmed?"

"Possibly. Or someone who loved that child." He raked his hair. "And then there's Aurelie."

"But we've no proof she had any links with the Carraghers, or our murder cases, sir. She was found at a party thrown by Edgar Tate."

Craig nodded. "That's true, but at the moment I want to explore every option, then we can eliminate them one by one."

Annette shuddered. "If it's been going on since the Carraghers met, then that's twenty years. But Davy said nothing was ever reported at the school."

"That's true, but let's say it was happening there and was never discovered. When the school closed, their perversions didn't suddenly disappear. They had to find other places to pursue them." He shook his head and shrugged. "This is all speculation at the moment. Based on a small shoeprint at Eileen Carragher's scene that's hinting one of our killers is a Chinese woman, and an old locally made video."

"You really think the Chinese girl on the tape could be involved in the Carraghers' deaths?"

"Maybe, or maybe not. That child could be dead and gone and this woman might be someone else entirely, except that I don't believe in coincidences."

Davy beckoned them over and Craig kept talking as he walked. "I don't know, Annette. It's all speculation at the moment and pretty wild speculation at that. But…" He turned towards Davy. "What have you got for us, Davy?"

Davy was looking pleased with himself. "After you said the s…setting for the video might have been destroyed when the school became a hotel, I thought of something. They w…would have had to get planning permission for the building's change of use and it was likely the architects would have taken a lot of photos, so…"

"You hacked their database." Craig tried to look disapproving. "You're not allowed to do that."

Davy looked put-out and shook his head. "I didn't hack it! W…Well, not really. They posted everything on the Cloud. It was just a matter of wriggling through their s…security settings." Davy gave Craig a defiant look that made Annette laugh. "But I can wait for a warrant if you'd like, chief." He held his finger above the escape button. "If you really don't want to look, I can easily erase it now…"

Craig thought for a moment. He just wanted to confirm the video's setting for his own information. It wasn't something that they were likely to use in court, if they ever got that far, and by then they'd hopefully have found something else. He nodded, convincing himself. They could get a warrant on some basis if they needed it and visit the architects and hotel in person.

173

"OK, show me." He tried to sound disapproving but knew that he was failing. "But Davy, you can't…"

"I know, but this is urgent. Don't w…worry. I'll cover my cyber trail."

It wasn't the first time Craig had thought Davy would make a fortune as a crook. He smiled and gestured him on. Davy flicked through screen after screen of renovation images, showing the before and after of the luxury hotel. The architects had done a good job of taking classrooms and making them into bedrooms and ensuites. Craig shook his head, disappointed. There was nothing resembling the setting that he'd seen in the torture video. Finally Davy clicked on a file marked 'basement' and Craig held his breath. The room in the video had been dark, almost dingy. It was unfurnished and there'd been bare pipes on the walls. A basement or a garage would fit.

They scrolled slowly through the images until suddenly Craig shocked them with a loud yell.

"That's it, there!" He jabbed his finger hard against Davy's screen. "There. Print it out for me."

Annette squinted at the small screen image, then again at the larger print one. It was a boiler room on the lower ground floor. Craig punched the air. There was no mistake. It was definitely where the video had been shot. They hadn't renovated the school boiler-rooms when it had become a hotel.

Craig's triumph was short-lived and he slumped abruptly onto a chair, staring into space. Annette's face said that they were thinking the same thing. If the video had been shot in a school then how many more children had been abused?

***

Newcastle, County Down. 11.30 a.m.

By the time they arrived in Newcastle Liam had munched

his way through one punnet of strawberries and was eyeing the other one hungrily. Jake reproached him in a solemn voice.

"Didn't your wife specifically ask you to get those for the children? What's she going to say if you arrive home with none?"

Liam shot him a grumpy look then stared guiltily at his stained hands. He hit back with skewed logic.

"I can get some more on the way back, or there's a supermarket near our street, they'll sell them as well. She'll never know the difference."

"Those are wild strawberries." Jake pursed his lips trying hard not to laugh, and piled on more guilt. His next words were said in a tone that Liam hadn't heard since he'd been an altar boy. "God will know."

Liam stared at Jake to see if he was really being religious or just taking the piss. Then he hit his arm a playful thump.

"Ow! What was that for?"

"For pretending to be a holy roller and making me feel like I was back at school."

But the guilt had worked. Liam waved goodbye to the second punnet and glanced down at the map.

"Up here on the right. Next turn."

Half-a-minute later they were in a twig-covered lane lined with leafless trees. In front of them lay a steep road leading to a large wooden fascia-ed house. It had a flat front and a glossy front door. Jake pulled the car to a halt and stared at it admiringly.

"Very nice. That's based on a Georgian design. It looks like some of the houses you see in Dublin, or the wooden versions in some parts of the States."

"Thank you. Laurence Llewellyn-Bowen. Right. This is it. Let's see who's behind that door."

Two minutes of door-knocking and window-peering later they had their answer. No-one was behind it, not unless they were stone deaf. No-one else could possibly have ignored Liam's

175

yells. The house was empty and when Liam stopped yelling the silence that fell was oppressive. He'd called Ryan Carragher to say they were doing the search and he hadn't said a word, so Liam doubted that they'd find anything hinky, but he was impatient all the same.

He shuddered suddenly. "I don't like this place. Reminds me too much of the Adams' case."

The Adams and their daughters had lived in a house not dissimilar to the one in front of them, before the father had hanged himself and the wife had murdered three people before killing herself.

Jake glanced at him curiously and Liam shook his head.

"Too sad and before your time. Ask the boss."

Liam pulled the crumpled search warrant from his pocket and lifted the car radio, connecting with the local station. One minute later Uniform were on their way. He strode across to a ground-floor window and scrutinised it, expertly assessing its lock. Uniform would bring an Enforcer to break down the front door, but if he was right they could get inside with a lot less damage, and save the State a hefty bill.

He knew they should wait for back-up but his impatience won. Liam lifted a sharp chisel from the car's boot and slid it expertly between the window's wooden frames, popping the lock. He slid the bottom frame upwards and beckoned Jake across.

"In you go, lad."

Jake looked at the window then at his designer suit and shook his head. "No way. This is new."

Liam scanned Jake's suit ruefully and sighed "Then more fool you for wearing it to work. You'll learn. In you go anyway, because if I try to get through that gap I'll be picking splinters out of my ass for weeks."

Jake folded his arms stubbornly. "Let's wait for Uniform."

Liam propelled him towards the window. "And let them steal our search! What sort of a detective are you?"

Ten seconds later Jake was lying on the carpeted floor of what looked like the house's dining-room, thankful that he'd had a soft landing. He picked himself up and brushed down his suit, then scanned the room with an expert eye. It held a mahogany dining-table and a matching side-board with a silver serving dish set on one side. The Carraghers lived well. Jake's daydream was rudely interrupted by Liam's yell.

"Well, don't just stand there like a bump on a log. Go and open the front door for me."

Jake did as he was told, throwing a question at Liam as soon as he entered the house's parquet-floored hall.

"What was the fricking hurry?"

Liam gazed down at the younger man and shook his head dolefully. Young peelers nowadays. They knew nothing.

"Here's the thing, lad. There's them; Uniform, and us; The Suits. Now, most of the time we walk through life hand in hand picking roses, except at a crime-scene. At a scene you have to establish who's top-dog, stat, otherwise all sorts of terrible things might happen."

"Like what?" Jake tried to make his question sound less sceptical than he felt.

Liam's eyes widened as if he was picturing Armageddon. "They might find something first, then we'd never hear the end of it. Or they might mess up our forensics, or worse."

"Worse than messing up the forensics?"

Liam nodded solemnly. "They might eat all the biscuits." He guffawed loudly. "I'm only joking lad. It's just an old tradition. It's our scene and we invite them in, not the other way round. Not that they'd agree of course." He started walking down the hall. "Now stop standing there and come on. I want to be through this house before they arrive."

They moved quickly from room to room, scanning each one from the doorway, to avoid annoying the C.S.I.s. There was nothing obvious to see and any cupboards could be searched when Uniform arrived. It was just a well-appointed residence.

Nothing to hint at Eileen Carragher's kinks.

Five minutes later they'd been through the whole place and Liam had disappeared. Jake was about to search for him when he noticed a low oak door positioned discretely in an alcove in the hall. It looked so innocuous that at first he thought it was a storage cupboard. He pulled it open, expecting to find kitchen rolls and tablecloths, but instead he found a hollow darkness that indicated something beyond.

Jake flicked the switch outside the door and a light came on, illuminating a steep flight of steps leading down. He went to look for Liam and found him in the garden, staring at the house's rear. Liam's face was screwed up in puzzlement.

"What's wrong?"

Liam shook his head slowly. "I'm not sure yet, lad. Just... something feels wrong."

"I've found some stairs leading down from the hall. There's definitely a basement."

Liam waved him ahead, still looking perplexed. "Lead on MacDuff."

Jake nipped to the car and grabbed a flash-light then they walked back together to the small door.

"Boyso, that was well tucked away. You wouldn't see it unless you were looking very hard."

Jake nodded. "It was probably for servants when the house was first built. Shall I go first?"

"Up to you, lad. But watch your step and switch the torch on. Even with the light it looks to be a dingy place."

Jake flicked on the flash-light and stepped gingerly onto the top step. He could see that it was bare stone, but what he couldn't see was the film of grease that covered it. Jake's foot slipped away from under him and he dropped the torch, then he started to fall head-first down the stone steps. His descent was halted immediately just as he heard a loud ripping noise; Liam had caught his jacket. Liam yanked him firmly backwards and Jake fell hard against him, knocking them both to the floor.

After a moment's recovery Jake clambered to his feet. "God, thanks, Liam. I'd have been a goner if you hadn't been here."

Liam stared up at him, trying to find a breath. "You're heavier than you look, lad. You fair winded me." He stood up slowly and brushed himself down. "What made you lose your footing?"

Jake beckoned Liam over and shone the flash-light on the top step then he reached down with a finger and rubbed it. The step was covered in thick oil.

"It's a booby trap, Liam. Those steps are concrete. If you hadn't been here I'd have broken my neck." He glanced balefully at his torn jacket and then smiled. It was a small price to pay for his life.

Liam grinned, not at Jake's thanks but at what it all meant. "No-one sets a booby-trap unless they've something they want to hide. There's something nasty down there, lad, and it fits with what I was looking at outside."

Liam headed back to the garden with Jake in tow and he pointed at a faint stone outline on the ground. It marked out a long rectangle extending at least five hundred metres in one direction, and off into the trees width-wise for three.

Jake stared at it curiously. "What is it?"

"It's an underground building, that's what it is. I saw one once on my Granny's farm. It was huge inside, like a small village. They used it as an air-raid shelter during World War Two, then for storing fruit and curing meat. But I'll bet you a fiver there's no fruit in this one."

The hairs on Jake's neck stood on end and he shivered in the cool country air. As they waited in silence for Uniform to arrive, Liam stared grimly at the ground, trying hard not to imagine what they were going to find beneath the earth.

Chapter Eighteen

2 p.m.

Craig stared at his mobile, willing it to ring. There was no word yet from Liam and Jake and he was desperate to hear what they'd found, but he was loathe to call them and breathe down their necks. This was what delegation was about, much as it pained him to let go of the reins even for five minutes. He turned over the last page of a file Nicky had left for him to sign and tapped its cardboard cover restlessly. Nicky hadn't so much left it for him, as hurled it on his desk before lunch then marched defiantly out of the office without a backward glance. He didn't mind her mood; he minded what might be causing it. She'd stubbornly refused to discuss it, so now desperate measures were required.

He strode to the door of his office and called Annette in, ignoring the hostile vibes emanating from Nicky's desk. Annette bustled across the floor and took a seat on Craig's nod, then he closed his office door firmly on Nicky's ever-listening ear.

"Coffee or Tea, Annette?"

"Tea please, sir. If I have any more coffee my jaw will lock."

As Craig made it she started talking, about the case in general and the hotel in particular. "Did you want me to go there and take a look? My witness has nearly finished his sketches, so I could drop him home then pop down."

Craig shook his head. "It's not going anywhere and Davy's still trying to find out exactly why the school closed. We'll get to it later, then I'll send in the C.S.I.s. To be honest I'm more interested in your sketches and the Carragher's sons, plus whatever Davy's computer-aging comes up with."

He handed her the cup and placed a packet of biscuits on the desk. After a few sips of his coffee Craig sighed and set his mug down. "Actually, Annette, I didn't call you in about the case."

She glanced at him, concerned. "Are you OK? That video sounded bad."

Craig realised what she was thinking and smiled at her kindness. "Yes, I'm fine thanks. It's not about me."

Her eyes widened in alarm. "Not Liam?"

As he shook his head and said, "everyone's OK," Craig smiled at her immediate concern for her rival. She and Liam had jockeyed for position on the squad for years, always keeping score. But if it ever came to it he knew that they would die for each other. He fervently hoped that it never did.

He leaned forward and dropped his voice, as if the walls had ears. They both knew that they had, and they were Nicky's. Craig normally didn't mind her eavesdropping. All she heard was boring stuff about work and general intelligence, and it was part of a good P.A's job to keep abreast. If he had a really private call to make, he walked down to the river and made it there. But he didn't want Nicky to eavesdrop today, because the topic of conversation was her.

"Annette. There's something badly wrong with Nicky and she won't tell me what it is."

Annette nodded. She'd noticed it a few days before. A lack of smiles when Nicky was usually so cheerful. A lack of banter when Liam tried to wind her up. And a lot of attitude and frowning, making her look miserable and warning anyone with any sense to stay away. She thought she'd seen Nicky's eyes red today at lunchtime, as if she'd been crying, but when she'd asked her the question it had been answered with silence and Nicky walking away.

"You're right, sir. I've been seeing the signs for days." She folded her hands firmly on top of the desk and spoke in a decisive voice. "What would you like me to do?"

Craig smiled. It was like an episode of 'Mission Impossible'. 'Your mission, Annette, should you decide to accept it.' All that was missing was the tape self-destructing.

"Thanks. I knew you would help. She won't tell me what's bothering her."

Annette interrupted. "She won't tell me either. I've been asking her all week."

Craig nodded. He'd known that it wasn't going to be simple.

"You don't have to do this, Annette, and say no if you'd rather not. But would you mind going to see Gary and trying to find out what's wrong?" He sipped at his coffee and looked suddenly embarrassed. "I'm really fond of Nicky and I hate to see her unhappy. If there's something I can help with, then I'd like to."

Annette nodded firmly. "I'll do it. Mainly because I like her too, but also because if the quality of her coffee gets any worse this week, I'll have to start using the vending machine, and I draw the line at that."

They laughed for a moment and then Craig scribbled down a list of things that he thought it might be. He trusted Annette's diplomacy to take it from there.

***

Newcastle. 2.30 p.m.

Jake watched as the uniformed-officers sprayed something on the basement steps, waited for a moment and then washed the oil away. Two minutes later the steps were safe to walk on and Liam led the way into hell.

Liam already knew that's what they were going to find, from the booby-trapped stairs and the underground building's outline. But he felt it as well, on some visceral level. He didn't hold much with 'sensing' things, preferring to call his gut reactions 'hunches' or copper's nose, but he was sensing things now all right and all of them bad.

When they reached the bottom of the stairs Liam saw that the dingy ceiling light was never going to be enough. They needed to see their way clearly; if there'd been one booby trap there could be plenty more.

He yelled back over his shoulder. "Get that lighting cable down here and send out for more if you have to. We'll need enough for about ten rooms."

He knew the number because the walls and sub-walls of the subterranean structure had been clearly demarcated above. Inside the thick concrete outer walls there'd been a long corridor with small rooms off either side. The walls were thick, so he already knew they were probably sound-proof, and the lack of daylight wouldn't have made them pleasant places to be. At the end of the corridor there was a larger room that ran the structure's full width. Liam somehow doubted that it was a Jacuzzi.

He sent up a prayer that he was wrong in what he was thinking. That his imagination was working overtime, and the whole place would turn out to be a storage facility for furniture or wine. But the oil slick on the stairs said that it wasn't likely.

Once the corridor was well lit Liam signalled Jake to follow him, motioning Uniform to stay behind and search the house. He carried a high-beam lamp with him as he walked, swinging it from side to side to see where they were. They were in a narrow hallway with walls of bare stone, like a cellar. Each block was chiselled, as if it had been hewn from the ground. Jake touched one and recoiled. It was icy cold and water glistened on its surface like a clammy sweat.

The ceilings were so low that even the five-feet-eight Jake had to hunch and Liam was almost doubled in two. As Liam lit the way Jake saw something on the corridor's floor that made him freeze. Liam was several feet further on before he noticed that Jake had stopped. He motioned him to keep walking then saw that Jake's eyes were focused on a small doorway that he'd missed.

Liam walked back and stared at it. It was made of steel with two slots cut away, one at eye-height and the other near the ground. He recognised their purpose immediately. The top slot was for viewing and the other was for food. They were in a prison!

But it wasn't the door that had made Jake freeze. His eyes were focused further down. Liam shone the light at floor level and saw what had caught Jake's attention. He shuddered violently. Jake pulled an evidence bag from his pocket and for a moment Liam thought he was going to disturb the scene, but the sudden sound of retching said it had been for a different use. Liam knew how he felt; his worse fears had just been confirmed.

Wedged between the door and the wall was a child's doll. Its face was grubby and its dress was torn, but that wasn't the worst thing. The worst was that Liam recognised it as one he'd bought for his toddler daughter at Christmas. It was the latest thing for little girls and there had been a waiting list. The doll hadn't been abandoned there years ago, discarded by a generation gone by. It had been left there in the past few weeks.

Jake forced the words out. "That doll was new. My niece got one for her birthday." He paused and then said what they both already knew. "The Carraghers had no grandchildren."

Liam said nothing as he turned ahead again; not wanting to look behind the door until he knew the scale of what they faced. He stormed down the corridor with Jake trailing in his wake, scanning the floor for more signs of whoever had been here last. The place was a maze; the walls they'd seen above hadn't given a true indication of the number of rooms inside. Off anterooms and conduits there were smaller, inner doors. Each time they thought they'd reached the last, another one appeared in the gloom.

Liam stormed past them all, desperate to reach the last. On

and on, their nostrils filling with the stench of damp, and more, until finally a door appeared ahead of them, truncating the corridor and signalling that their journey was at an end. Liam swung the lamp high, scrutinising the door. It had no hatch or peep-hole; this room was different. He turned to Jake with a solemn look.

"This isn't going to be pretty, lad. There's no shame in you turning back."

Jake peered at him in the gloom and Liam could see his cheeks were stained with tears. He shook his head and Liam understood. They both had to see what was in there, although what they saw might live with them for the rest of their lives.

Liam placed his latex-gloved hand on the handle and pushed the door inwards as he did. The room was ink-black. Nothing moved; not Liam and not Jake, not even their chests to take a breath. Liam lifted his hand slowly, holding the lamp at arm's length until the centre of the room was lit, although the corners stayed dark. The ceiling was high and suddenly he could stand at full height. Liam's heart sank at what that meant. Adults spent time in here.

The room was large and cold and their breaths, when they took them, misted in the air. They could feel the damp washing over them, seeping into their bones and covering them in filth. This was how evil felt, and how it looked. Draped on the longest wall, hanging shining against the stone, were instruments that Liam had never seen before, but he would never forget again. Sharp knives and chisels, chains and spikes arranged in rows for size, the tiniest looking as if it would fit a doll. Whips with razor tips along their lashes, leaving nothing to imagine about the pain they could inflict.

Liam closed his eyes for a moment to shut out the images and he felt the urge to retch. He pushed it down hard, allowing the cold air to slow his pulse, until he felt his nausea ebb away and he opened his eyes again. Still standing in the doorway he swung the lamp first one way and then the other, casting the light into each corner. What they saw there made both men gasp. Discarded in one corner was a pile of toys, thrown there haphazardly as if left by children overnight, except Liam knew that their owners would never retrieve them.

In another corner lay a pile of rags, bloodied and torn. Liam squinted through the light and saw a tiny foot, filthy and bruised but human nonetheless. He strode over and knelt down beside it, already knowing that the child was dead. He knew that he shouldn't touch them, but he couldn't not. Liam reached forward gently and smoothed the child's hair back from his face, tears running openly down his cheeks.

It was a little boy no older than eight and he was smiling, as if he was at peace. He probably was, for the first time in God knew when. Liam felt for a pulse, already knowing that it was a thankless task. The boy was cold, too cold for them to ever warm him up. Liam sat back on his hunkers and wiped his eyes, as Jake spoke the first words since they'd descended the stairs.

"Liam... Sir. We need to look in all the rooms, in case there's someone still alive."

Liam gazed up at him blankly; as if he was a million miles away, then after a moment he nodded and rose to his feet. He stared at the boy and Jake knew that Liam wanted to lift him and carry him into the sun, but he couldn't. If they were going to catch whoever had done this, the C.S.I.s had to do their work.

They searched the rest of the room in silence, trying not to stare at the bloodied walls and the human bones scattered randomly on the floor. Then they walked back into the hallway moving from room to room. Halfway down the corridor Jake halted abruptly outside a door.

"Did you hear that?"

Liam listened then shook his head, motioning Jake on. Jake stayed where he was and listened again. To their right was a small door, slightly different from the rest. Instead of two slots being cut into it, it had a normal lock. A faint light was flickering from underneath. Jake pointed to it and Liam's eyes opened wide in surprise.

"How did I miss that?"

"We both did." Jake held his finger to his mouth, signalling silence, and listened again. Finally he nodded. "There's definitely something moving behind that door."

Liam's free hand went to his Glock and he nodded Jake to open the door wide. He slipped off the safety, ready to shoot, but he didn't need it. Inside the room, hunched in a corner, was a boy of around four-year's old. He was half-starved, filthy and barely dressed, but he was alive. Liam would have yelled in victory if he hadn't been afraid that he would scare the child to death. He rushed in then saw the boy cower and realised the sight of a six-feet-six man probably wasn't the most welcome thing.

He beckoned Jake in. "Here, you look a bit friendlier than me, lad. Talk to him."

Jake entered slowly and hunkered down three-feet from the child, watching as he scanned him for signs if he was friend or foe. Something about Jake's open-faced blondeness must have said friend, because the boy finally stared into his eyes, holding his gaze. After a moment Jake spoke.

"My name's Jake." He gestured towards Liam. "And this is Liam." The boys gaze shifted to Liam then quickly back to Jake. "What's your name?"

The boy looked blankly at him as if he didn't know and Liam shook his head. God only knew how long he'd been down there. He might have forgotten his name, if he'd ever known it. Jake held out his hand and then realised the boy's feet were ripped to shreds. Liam interjected.

"Tell him we're the police and he's safe. Warn him that I'm going to pick him up."

One minute later the boy was upstairs in the house's bright hallway, his eyes covered with Jake's hanky to shield them from the unaccustomed light.

"Get an ambulance, and I want a W.P.C to go with him to the hospital."

Liam pointed towards two sergeants, beckoning them over to one side. Jake knew from their changing expressions that he was telling them what they'd found downstairs, and tasking them to go down and check every single room for signs of life. They nodded hesitantly and then Liam called the local C.S.I.s. When he'd finished he strode out of the house into the afternoon sun. Jake joined him just as Liam was wiping his mouth, the smell of fresh vomit blowing away in the seaside air. Jake gave him a rueful smile.

"I wish I was drunk right now, sir."

Liam laughed, despite himself. "I know what you mean, lad." He dragged a hand down his pale face. "God, I need a beer."

Jake pulled the car-keys from his pocket and tossed them in the air. "Then let's go and get one. The C.S.I.s will be here for hours and we can't go home until everything's done." He gestured towards the house. "They know what they're doing and they can call us at any time."

Liam looked at his watch. It was four o'clock and they hadn't even had lunch yet. He gave a weak grin. "You're on, lad. And let me tell you, with that sort of attitude you'll go far."

As Jake drove them into the centre of Newcastle and found a bar that overlooked the sea, Liam phoned Craig to tell him the worst. Except that the worst wasn't over yet.

Chapter Nineteen

5 p.m.

Craig put down the phone and gazed out at the river, willing its waves to wash away the words Liam had just said. This case was getting filthier by the day and he had a strong feeling that it hadn't reached its blackest point yet. The late winter sky was darkening, ready for evening, echoing Liam's words and his own mood.

After a moment's sombre thought, Craig shook himself and walked out onto the open floor, beckoning Davy and Annette to take a seat.

"We need a quick debrief."

Annette looked surprised and glanced at the clock. "Aren't we waiting for Liam and Jake?"

Craig shook his head. "They're staying in Newcastle overnight." He paused, toying with repeating Liam's exact words. "It was the descent into hell, boss." He thought better of it and motioned Annette to report on her witness' sketch. He'd get to the worst when she and Davy had finished.

Annette lifted some stapled hand-outs and passed them round, tapping the page on top. It held the black and white likeness of a young man; once again the C.C.U.'s sketch artist Ernie had excelled himself. Davy stared at the drawing in awe.

"Cool. This looks almost real. Does Ernie take commissions, Annette?"

She shook her head. "No idea. Why don't you ask him? Are you thinking of getting Maggie done?"

189

Davy blushed and nodded. "It's her birthday soon and I thought it w…would make a nice gift."

Craig stared at the sketch as they talked. The man was in his twenties, slim and dark, with his hair worn in a modern, spiked style. He had regular features and pale skin, as if he never saw the sun, but it suited him, making his dark eyes more intense and throwing his bone structure into sharp relief. The eyes were Ernie's speculation of course; the man had worn sunglasses the whole time he'd been in 'The Cutting Edge'.

After a moment's more staring Craig shook his head; it didn't look like anyone that they'd met during the case. He didn't know what he'd been hoping for, but finding their man wasn't going to be as easy as all that. He set the hand-out to one side and turned to Annette.

"Great likeness, Annette, but no-one we know."

"That's just what I was thinking."

"Did Mr Archer say anything about the man's voice, except that he had a local accent?"

"Sorry, no. He just said it was 'normal'."

Annette peered closely at the picture, willing some information to leap out. There was none. She turned the page over and Craig suddenly realised there'd been another page underneath. He lifted his hand-out and stared hard at the drawing. It was a red kite, set inside a white and gold circle.

"This is the logo from the hold-all he was carrying?"

Annette nodded and Craig turned to Davy, about to ask him to run it for I.D.; Davy's smile said he'd already done it.

"It's a Chinese restaurant in S…South Belfast, chief. The Red Kite. It's just down the road from the one owned by Ryan Carragher."

A Chinese restaurant! It was way more than coincidence and Craig didn't even believe in that.

"Thanks, Davy. Let me have anything you can find on the owners and whoever works there. Run the sketch through the usual checks and let's see if we get a hit." He paused for a moment then with one eye on Annette he added another request. "While you're at it, run Ryan Carragher as well."

Annette gawped at him, surprised. "On what basis? If we start running people randomly it will come out in court."

Craig smiled. He'd known Annett would object and he didn't mind. She was a stickler for procedure and she balanced Liam out; and him when he was in one of his moods. But this time she was wrong.

"We should already have run him, Annette, and the other son. Both their parents are dead; they have to be suspects now. We've been following a phantom woman with small feet and that's fine, I'm sure that it's the right way to go. But we can't ignore the fact that thirty percent of murders are committed by family members." He turned back to Davy. "Run both Carragher boys, Davy, and the logo. Then we're getting them both in for interview."

Craig paused and sipped at his coffee for what seemed like a long time. Annette knew that there was something he was reluctant to say, so she gave him a way to start.

"Liam and Jake must have found something pretty special not to be coming back this evening."

It was a statement, but Craig heard the subtle question mark at the end. He nodded slowly. Special wasn't the word he would have used. Horrific, disgusting or evil described their find more effectively. Before he told them Craig grabbed at the last diversion he could find.

"Any word on why the school closed, Davy?"

Davy smiled, showing the whitest teeth that Craig had ever seen. Maggie had been beautifying him again. Craig smiled to himself. At least she'd stopped him painting his fingernails. She'd even got him wearing a tie some days and he didn't seem to mind. The power of love. He wondered what was next, eyeing Davy's long hair. No, not even Maggie would try to change that. A man's hair was his own business. Samson had brought down a temple because of it after all.

He realised that Davy was speaking.

"It was hard to get to the bottom of it, chief. The architects and planners said they knew nothing; they came in after the fact. So I w…went to the education board. That's when I got s…somewhere."

He crossed to his computer horseshoe, beckoning them to come and look. The right-hand screen held the pictures of the school's before and after renovations. On the central one was an e-mail from the head of the education board; Nigel Ross. Davy pointed to one line towards the end.

'Certain concerns at the school led us to ask parents to remove their children. More specifically there were allegations of inappropriate behaviour between some teachers and pupils."

Annette raised her eyebrows. "They wouldn't have just left it like that. There had to have been an investigation."

Davy shook his head. "That's w…what I thought, so I called Mr Ross. But no, there was nothing. It w…was a private school that took in the children of rich people who travelled or lived abroad. No-one made a complaint. They just took their kids and disappeared off round the w…world."

Craig interjected. "No social service or police involvement, Davy? Surely there must have been that?

"No. Nothing."

Craig dragged his hand down his face thoughtfully. It had been 2004 and thinking on child abuse wasn't as tight as nowadays. People were still wary of 'offending' professionals, holding them in awe, and parents often didn't want a scandal and hushed things up. It was how so many schools and religious institutions had got away with abuse for years. Something occurred to him.

"How did they find out in the first place, then?"

Davy stared blankly at him.

"Who made the original allegation?"

Realisation dawned on Davy and he shook his head. "It was anonymous, apparently. A phone-call to the education board."

Annette nodded. "No-one would have bothered to trace it unless the police had got involved."

Craig frowned. "Do we know who took the call, Davy?"

"Nigel Ross. They asked for him by name."

"Did he say if it was child's voice?"

"No, but give me a minute."

Davy turned quickly back to his desk and lifted the phone. After a brief conversation he turned back to them.

"Definitely an adult. A woman with a local accent. Well spoken."

Craig snapped his fingers and smiled. "Someone at that school knew that something was going on and blew the whistle."

Annette's face dropped. "But there could have been a hundred women working there, in one or other capacity, sir. Teachers, cleaners, canteen workers..."

Craig shook his head. "I doubt it, Annette. We're talking ten years ago, remember. Perhaps in a girls-only school, but Marcheson's had boys up to seventeen-years-old. The majority of teachers would still have been male. I'll lay odds on it. Right. Davy, get the names of every staff member and find out where they are now, any females that are still alive, give their names to Annette to follow up."

Annette's face fell and he shook his head.

"There won't be more than a handful that fit, Annette. If the Head of Education thinks they were well-spoken then they probably were. I think we're looking for a female teacher and I want to know what they knew."

Craig sat back and stared at the floor for a moment. When he spoke again his voice was dark. "I'm going to tell you why Liam and Jake are staying in Newcastle overnight. It's pretty bad, so prepared to be shocked."

Over the next five minutes he outlined their find at the Carraghers' house. The underground prison with its booby-trapped entrance and external outline, spotted by Liam's eagle-eye. The dank corridor with cells off each side, and the little boy found barely alive. Finally he told them about the torture room, with its chains and manacles, spattered blood and rags. He talked on as Annette screwed up her face in revulsion and Davy looked as if he was going to explode. Craig's voice broke as he delivered the final blow.

"They've found four bodies down there so far, all children. We don't know how many more they'll find buried in the grounds."

Craig hadn't looked at them as he'd recounted Liam's words, deliberately avoiding their eyes so that he could make it to the end. Now he did and what he saw there was the normal range of human responses to the work of the inhumane. There was silence for a moment, almost in respect. Finally Craig broke it.

"Give Liam and Jake some space tomorrow when they return, please. It's bad enough hearing about it, but remember they actually discovered it and saw the children."

"It w…was a dungeon, chief."

Craig nodded. That's exactly what it had been. He thought of the young boy they'd found and then of Aurelie, safe and warm now in temporary foster care, but still unable to help them find her Mum. But they could grieve for them later; there was too much to do right now.

"OK. Annette, tomorrow morning I want you to start searching for the teacher who called Nigel Ross and get the Carraghers boys into High Street. I'll interview them myself. When Liam and Jake return they can visit the Chinese restaurant."

He turned to Davy. "Davy, if there is a hyper-drive on your computers then get it working on this. I want those aging and regressing photos by tomorrow close-of-play and I want this sketch run through every database you can find. Follow up Aurelie's school and the Gendarmes, as soon as you have a photo of what she would have looked like a few years back. And let's pray she has parents who will be glad to see her. Get copies of every photo down to Aidan Hughes as well, just on the off-chance that he recognises someone."

Craig lifted the sketch of the young man and turned back to Annette. "Annette, do the same with this sketch, please. Get it to Aidan and ask him to rack his brain. I want to know if he's seen this man at a club, with or without a Chinese woman." He stopped for a moment, remembering something. "The man who organised the house party, Edgar Tate, do we have anything on him yet?"

Davy leaned in, his face flushed with excitement. "Yes, sir." Craig smiled. He must be excited, that was the first time Davy had called him 'sir' in months.

"Vice have him locked up."

"Good. Leave that with me. I'll see if I can meet him after I interview the Carragher brothers."

Craig glanced at his watch. It was nearly six o'clock. He thought of Liam and Jake and the evening they had ahead of them, and made a decision.

"OK. That's it for tonight. Go home you two, and great work. This is a dirty case and it'll get dirtier. So let's crack it ASAP and get back to good clean murders again."

He smiled, knowing there was no such thing. Then he was off his chair and out the door. Heading to Newcastle, to see if he could be any help.

Chapter Twenty

It had been surprisingly easy to lift Alan Rooney, on a quiet Friday afternoon with no children around. The school had been deserted, apart from teachers catching up on paperwork, and the caretaker in the yard, brushing away the fluttering remnants of crime-scene tape. He'd swept the detritus of the week into small piles, ready to be shovelled into large metal bins set against the wall, then he'd readied himself to close up for the weekend.

They watched him from a distance, in the relative comfort of the small van they'd hired. Mai scanned the car-park, searching for the familiar olive skin belonging to one young man. She stared at Rooney's sports car sitting alone against a wall, its sleek lines announcing its owner as important. Only in his own mind. To her Alan Rooney was what he really was. Cruel. And soon to be dead.

They took him easily, with far less of a fight than she'd pictured in her mind. The look in Rooney's eyes when he'd seen her had been a silent shrug, as if he'd known that it was coming and that there was no way out. Mai felt thwarted. As if his struggle had been part of some unspoken contract that he'd reneged on . Her anger bubbled and then subsided quickly as they forced him into the van, Alan Rooney's last sight of normal life his car's number plate, then darkness as they blindfolded him for the trip. There was no point in her getting angry and there was no need. Getting even was much more fun.

***

Newcastle. 9 p.m.

Craig raked his hair sadly and stared at the row of body-bags on the lawn. Seven so far and they hadn't finished yet. He stared into the distance, as the dog-handlers and men with scanners set up camp at the garden's farthest end. They'd go over every inch of ground and every bush, searching for bodies and bones or whatever they could find. They could be here for weeks.

He felt Liam walk up behind him before he heard his voice. It was surprisingly soft and Craig could hear a mixture of pain and exhaustion in every word.

"I'm sorry the Carraghers are dead, boss. They should be here to answer for this."

Craig nodded and turned, catching sight of Jake leaning against a tree. He was smoking and Craig knew that he didn't. Stress. Craig half-smiled at Liam.

"Do you feel as rough as you look?"

"Aye. And then some." Liam rubbed his face, transferring some of the grime on his hand to his cheek. Craig said nothing. It was unimportant.

"I hope we find every one of the bastards and get to throw away the key, boss." He shuddered. "Although I don't know how many years would be enough for this."

"There aren't enough. Perhaps that's why our killers are meting out justice themselves."

"Aye, well. You wouldn't trust the system much if teachers can do this."

Liam kicked a loose twig at his feet, watching it fly across the ground. Craig could see a question coming. It wasn't the one he'd expected.

"How come they escaped?"

"Who?"

"The Chinese girl and whoever she's working with." He gestured at the row of bodies. "If she was a victim and the Carragher's normally killed them, how come they let her go?"

Craig stared at him, uncomprehending at first and then in open admiration. "Liam, you're brilliant!"

Liam looked shocked at the compliment, then claimed it as if he got one every day. "Aye well, Danni says that, but I don't like to be big-headed." He laughed, casting a look around to avoid offense, then gave Craig a puzzled look. "Why am I brilliant? Apart from the obvious, I mean."

"Because you've just pointed out something that I'd missed. You're right. How did she get away?" He indicated the house. "There's no way anyone got out of there." Craig thought for a moment and then realised. "She didn't escape from here. If she was the girl in the video she would have been at the school until 2004. They bought this place in '95."

"What?"

Craig was so excited he almost shouted the answer. "The hotel!"

Liam screwed up his face, puzzled. "What hotel?"

Craig realised he and Jake had been on the road when Davy had made his find. He brought him quickly up to date.

"So you're telling me that the Down Hartley Hotel used to be the boarding school where the Carraghers met? I took Danni there for our last anniversary."

"Yes. We've seen the architect's photos before it was renovated. One of the shots of the boiler-room matched the backdrop of Aidan's porn video with the Chinese girl."

Liam shook his head vehemently. "Oh hell, no. I'm definitely not telling Danni about this." He paused, thinking. "So they were at it when the hotel was still a school and the girl escaped from there?"

Craig went to agree but stopped mid-nod. Something still didn't fit. If the Carraghers had been this security conscious here, he couldn't imagine they'd been any less so at the school. So how had the girl got away? Or, was it because she'd escaped that they'd become determined it wouldn't happen again and built tis prison? The options raced through his mind as he tried to settle on one. He couldn't, and he wouldn't be able to until they got more bits of the puzzle.

Craig turned quickly towards the car, beckoning them to join him. "We're heading back to Belfast."

Jake coughed and threw his cigarette on the ground, stamping it out with his heel.

"Those things will kill you, Jake."

"But, sir, we can't leave."

Craig halted mid-stride. "Listen. This was great work, but look around you. This is a forensics job now and they'll be here for weeks. You have to trust the locals. They'll keep you in the loop."

He turned to Liam. "Liam, is the local Superintendent up to speed?"

"All the way."

"Fine." He pointed to the most senior uniformed officer. "Go and tell him we're going back to Belfast and he's to call you the minute anything changes. I'll call the Super on the way and do the same."

Craig stopped and squinted at both of them. "What time did you two have a drink?"

"Three hours ago, and only one."

He threw his car keys to Jake. "Jake, breathalyse yourself before you drive. If you're sober take my car and go home and get some rest. You know where I live?"

Jake stared at the keys, taken aback. "Yes, sir. It's on the duty roster."

"Good. Collect me tomorrow morning at eight o'clock. We'll be working all weekend by the look of it. Liam, let's go. I need to bring you up to date on some other things."

They were halfway to Liam's car when Liam realised Jake was staring at Craig open-mouthed. Liam nodded. "You've never him on a roll, have you, son?"

Jake stammered out a 'no'.

"Aye well, after long periods in seclusion the snow leopard

springs, and all that crap. Watch and learn." He waved cheerfully. "See you tomorrow. And watch his clutch. It slips."

***

The sixty minute drive gave Liam plenty of time to recount the full horror of what they'd seen, then crack every inappropriate joke he knew. Craig wanted him to get it out of his system before they debriefed in the morning. In his book there was no need for anyone who didn't have to, to know the full details of what they'd found. If it could be summarised and sanitised then that's what they'd do, but meanwhile Liam needed to vent. He'd reached the stage of macabre jokes when Craig's mobile rang. Craig nodded Liam to answer it as he turned off the A49.

"Superintendent Craig's phone."

The sharp intake of breath at the other end was followed by a female voice, machine-gunning out a stream of words, none of which Liam understood.

"Here now. Start again, please. I didn't catch one word of that."

A deep sigh was followed by an exaggeratedly patient voice. "I say, where is my son? Why he not here for dinner?"

Liam recognised the broken English of Mirella, Craig's Italian mother, and hastily pressed speaker. Mirella muttered long enough for Craig to realise who it was and smile. He yelled at the phone in Liam's hand.

"Hi Mum. I can't talk, I'm driving."

"Why you driving? Where are you? And why you not call and say you will be late? I cook your favourite."

Without waiting for an answer she reverted to her native tongue, having what Liam gathered was a rant. Craig answered her in Italian, making Liam smile. It was always a surprise when he heard the boss speak Italian or French. He was fluent in both but he never used them at work, so when he did it felt like a window into his private life.

After a minute of conversation during which Liam only recognised one word, 'cheeky', Craig said 'Ciao, Mama' and signalled for him to cut the call.

Liam guffawed loudly. "I recognise that tone. You're in the shit for forgetting to call."

"Got it in one. But it's worse. I completely forgot it was Friday night."

Mirella Craig had designated Friday evening the time for family dinner and expected her children to attend each one. Short of a letter from the Prime minister or a Papal dispensation there was no acceptable excuse. Murder investigations just didn't cut it.

Liam nodded in sympathy. "Here, do you think women learn that voice at school? Like, is there a special class called 'voices you can use on men'? 'Cos your Mum sounded just like Danni in a snit."

Craig laughed. "No, I think they're born with it. Julia had it down to a fine art. In fact, she didn't even need to speak to get her irritation across."

Liam laughed again and then hesitated. Craig had opened the door by mentioning Julia McNulty, but he wondered if he should walk through. Craig read his mind and smiled.

"Spit it out, Liam. I know there's something you'd like to say."

"Aye well." Liam adopted a tone of concern. "Are you OK, like? With the whole McNulty thing?"

Craig laughed. "The McNulty thing! I've heard it said lots of ways but that's a new one. You mean, am I all right about my relationship with Julia ending?"

Liam nodded furiously and Craig knew he was blushing in the darkened car. "Aye. That's it. I'm not prying, boss, but…"

"It's fine, Liam, don't panic. Yes, I'm OK with splitting with Julia. It wasn't working."

"Aye. The distance. It's a fair hike to Limavady and back all the time."

Craig shook his head in the dark. "It wasn't just that. There were other things too. If there hadn't been then we would have found a way to deal with the mileage."

"Hard work, boss?"

"Very hard work. And a wise man once told me if a relationship was right it shouldn't be that hard."

"That's a good one. Who told you that?"

Craig glanced at him and smiled. "You."

Chapter Twenty-One

Alan Rooney peered into the darkness defiantly, trying to focus the two shapes by his side through his blur of pain. He sucked in some air and yelled his next words.

"Just fucking well finish it, will you? We all know how I'm going to end up, so don't drag it out."

His words fell flat against the walls of the garage then sank into the absent response. Mai smiled. Not a secret smile or a half-smile, but a full-on grin that made her partner cringe to see it. She was enjoying this all too much.

He touched her arm gently and motioned her towards the door, leading the way into the house. Once there he faced her in the lamp-lit hall, taking her hand tenderly and holding it to his face. He was a quiet man, using few words where others would have used far more, and he asked little of her, the guilt of their past subverting all of his rights. But when he did speak Mai listened, and he spoke now.

"Mai, please let's do this quickly."

She gazed up at him, seeing the pain in his soft dark eyes. She watched him plead for mercy, always kind, even to the people that had brought them to this state. She thought about what he was requesting; mercy for Alan Rooney, the kindness of a quick death. Then she remembered how many times they'd both pleaded for the same and she shook her head. She searched for the words to explain why it had to be done this way and found only one.

"Peace."

The young man touched her soft black hair and understood,

as he always did, then he nodded and turned towards the stairs, refusing to take part. Rooney's pain would give Mai a moment's peace and he couldn't deny her that. But he refused to hurt anyone ever again.

***

The C.C.U. Saturday. 9 a.m.

"Anyone seen the boss?"

Annette popped her head above her cubicle wall. "He called and said he and Jake would be twenty minutes late."

Liam headed for the percolator, knocking it on just as Davy wandered onto the floor, looking like he'd been caught in a shower. Liam glanced out the window. It wasn't raining.

"You been in a flash-flood, son?"

Davy shook his head hard, setting droplets of water flying across the room. He looked like a highly-strung stallion after a long run and his expression was less than happy.

"S…Some dickhead of a driver's just driven right through a puddle and drenched me."

Annette wrinkled her nose, knowing that the water would have been full of rubbish and dirt. She walked over to him wearing a sympathetic expression.

"Go to the men's changing rooms on the fourth floor, Davy. You can have a shower and wash your hair. There's even a hot rail to dry your clothes."

He shot her a look that said, 'would that really be all right?'

She nodded. "The Super won't be in for twenty minutes, so you'll just have time."

Annette grabbed Davy's bag and set it by his desk, handing him her security pass and shooing him off the floor. When she turned Liam was struggling with a coffee filter.

"Liam, give me that, for goodness sake. I don't know how you manage to get dressed in the morning."

204

Liam gave a coy smile. "Neither do I the way Danni behaves."

He laughed and Annette shook her head to remove the image. "That's way too much information."

Just then Craig and Jake wandered onto the floor. "What's too much information?"

"You honestly don't want to know, sir." Annette glanced at the clock. "I thought you said you were going to be late?"

Craig scanned the open-plan floor. "I'll explain in a minute... Where are Davy and Nicky?"

Annette beckoned him to one side. "Davy's gone to have a shower – he got drenched by a car. I told Nicky to stay at home today. I've found out what's been going on and I think she needs the rest."

"Fine. Tell me after the briefing." He turned back to the others. "Let's have a quick coffee while we wait for Davy, then we'll start."

"Boss, did you ever find out if Ian Carragher had pain relief while they did the deed?"

Craig's eyes widened then he headed quickly for his office. He'd forgotten to call about Carragher's results in all the uproar the day before. He rang John's mobile; no answer then he tried the lab and it was answered in one ring.

"John Winter; pathology's my specialty."

Craig stared at the handset, wondering what John was on. The answer came to him immediately.

"You proposed! And by the sound of it Natalie said yes! Congratulations."

"Marc?"

"Congratulations. When did you ask her?"

John's voice filled with pride. "Thursday night. We went out to dinner at The Merchant. I planned everything perfectly. She even liked the ring I'd held over. We're going to collect it later today."

He'd ignored practically every suggestion Craig had made.

Good man.

"You can tell me everything when we meet, but have you set a date?"

John coughed so hard that Craig had to wait a minute for his next words. "No, we did not! God, give us a chance to be engaged."

"Don't leave it too long, that's my advice, or the moment might be lost."

Craig had made that mistake with Camille.

"Thank you, Henry the Eighth… Right, as you didn't know that I'd proposed when you called, you didn't phone me about that. So what can I do for you?"

"Ian Carragher's blood tests. Any sign of sedation or pain relief?"

John rubbed his forehead. He thought they'd already had that conversation, but he'd been so confused all week, maybe not.

"No on both counts. Nothing in his stomach contents either. He wasn't given any pain relief, quite the opposite in fact; his wounds had traces of acid in them."

"Acid? What sort?"

"A weak sulphuric. Strong enough to hurt like hell but not enough to kill him. I'd say they poured it on his cuts to make them hurt even more than his wife's."

It was interesting. No, it was more than interesting, it was important. Ian Carragher's picture hadn't registered with Aidan Hughes at all, so they'd wondered if he was an innocent pawn. Obviously not, as far as his killers were concerned. If anything it looked as if they'd hated Carragher even more than his wife. John was still talking and Craig caught the word 'oil'.

"Oil? What type?"

"Engine oil. The sort you'd find in the average saloon."

Something occurred to Craig. "Is sulphuric acid used in car batteries?"

"Yes. Especially in older cars." John paused, working it out.

"Ah, I see, you're thinking of a garage."

"Yes. But it could be anywhere. We don't know if it's a commercial garage or just one in someone's house."

"It's something anyway. Right now, I need to go. There's a big find in Newcastle and they've asked me down to supervise. Don't suppose you know anything about it, do you?"

"Too much for comfort. Will you be back tonight?"

"Yes. Around eight. Bar Red?"

"I'll see you there."

Craig dropped the phone and walked onto the floor, to see a squeaky-clean Davy towel-drying his hair. He poured him a coffee and then beckoned them all to sit, updating them on John's findings first.

"God, boss. Battery acid? I've never heard that one before."

"Live and learn, Liam. But it means that rather than Ian Carragher being innocent, they may have hated him even more than his wife." He turned to Annette. "Any joy on the sons, Annette?"

"The eldest, Ryan, is coming in here this morning. I'm putting him in the relatives' room. I thought it was better than High Street."

"Good, that's best. We have nothing to say the sons are guilty of anything yet. They're more likely to have been victims. What about the younger boy?"

"Jonathan. He's hard to pin down. He did history at Uni but mainly drifted after that. Ryan won't say much about him."

"OK. Find out if he's hiding something or just being protective. Any joy on aging the photos?"

"Davy's got them in a pack. He's going to hand them out in a minute."

"Excellent."

Craig turned towards Liam with a gentle warning look. They'd debriefed the gory details about Newcastle the evening before and he'd done the same with Jake that morning. They would both see the force's psychologist as soon as the case wound up, but meantime they'd agreed a PG version for the rest of the team. "Liam?"

Liam turned to the group, looking subdued. He'd talked to Craig and slept as much as he could the night before, but he was haunted by the things he'd seen and it showed on his pale, freckled face. His deep voice was uncharacteristically quiet.

"It was grim." He stared pointedly at Annette and Davy. "You don't need to know the details, believe me, and I wouldn't inflict them on you. All I'll say is that they built a dungeon where they kept kids and did unspeakable things to them. We found one boy alive but there were nine others dead as of eight o'clock this morning. The C.S.I.s and dogs are down there working the grounds, with ultrasound, so God knows how many more bodies they'll find. That's it."

He nodded at Jake to take over and he repeated the story, staring into space and adding. "Imagine the worst video game based in hell that you can think of and then multiply it by ten. I hope I never see anything like it again."

The room was silent for a moment. Annette's face was blank and Davy picked frantically at his nails, while Liam and Jake stared at their feet. Finally Craig broke the mood.

"OK, we'll hear more on that over the next few days. John's been asked to consult by the pathologist down there." He smiled and his tone became upbeat. "By the way, there's some good news. John and Natalie are engaged."

Annette grinned. "Our first team wedding! Brilliant. I can't wait to tell Nicky."

Liam shook his head in mock despair. "Another man bites the dust. Ah well." Then he guffawed. "There's bound to be a party. Great excuse to get drunk."

"Like you need an excuse!"

Annette smirked. "You'll have to buy Danni a new outfit, don't forget that."

Craig let them banter for a moment then added. "There's no date set, so I wouldn't hold your breath for the wedding. I think we're looking at a long engagement there. Anyway, let's move on. Davy, what have you got for us?"

Davy lifted a folder from his desk and distributed the handouts inside, talking as he did. "There are three s...sheets, each containing images. The top sheet is what we think the girl from the porn video looks like now. The boy's back was to the camera, so unfortunately w...we couldn't get a clear shot of him."

They were looking at the photograph of a young woman. Her eyes were Chinese but there was something else. Craig said it first.

"This girl is mixed race. Chinese/Caucasian, I'd guess."

"Yes. It w...wasn't as obvious when she was a child, but her features altered as she grew."

"There's no chance this is wrong, Davy?"

"None."

Annette interjected. "Most people seeing her would still describe her as Chinese. That's probably why Warner reacted when you mentioned it."

"You're right. OK, good, Davy. What's the next shot?"

They turned to the second sheet. It held a series of photographs, starting with Aurelie as an eleven-year-old and working backwards through her school-age years. At every age she was a slight little girl with white-blonde hair.

Craig stared at the photos for a moment, remembering the terrified little girl he'd spoken to two days before.

"I've s...sent these across to the school in the Loire and the Gendarmes."

"Excellent. Liam will get you a headshot of the boy they found in Newcastle. Do the same for him please."

"Where shall I send them?"

Craig shook his head. The boy hadn't said a word yet. He was hoping they'd find records at the house that would give some clue to his past life.

"We'll sort that out later. What's the final page?"

Annette answered him. "The sketches of the man who bought the knife and the logo on the bag he was carrying. You saw them yesterday."

The others stared at the images. The man's eyes were pure speculation so any I.D. was useless unless they had a face to match. He could be western or he could be Chinese. The logo was more interesting.

"It's a Chinese restaurant on the Ormeau Road. Liam, Jake, I'd like you to pay it a visit. Take the images with you, please."

They stared at the pictures for a moment longer then Craig brought them back to the report. He nodded Jake on and sat back, thinking. Their killers were a young Caucasian or Chinese man and a Chinese/Caucasian woman of a similar age. There was something niggling at him and he knew it was important, but every time he reached for it, it slipped away.

Jake's clear voice cut through his thoughts. "I was collecting the boss this morning when we picked up a call. It was at Fitzwilliam School again."

Liam sighed heavily. "Ah, God, not another one. That school's turning into a graveyard."

"Yes, another one. Alan Rooney, judging by the papers found beside him."

Annette leaned in urgently. "His face had been destroyed, like Eileen Carragher's?"

Jake nodded. "And they'd strapped him to the merry-go-round. It was a miracle he was found before some kid saw him on Monday. I've no idea how they keep getting through the locked gates."

"Houdini."

Davy shook his head. "It's a key pad system; it w…would be easy enough to hack."

"Did the caretaker find him?" Annette's voice was as sympathetic as they all felt. All except Liam.

"That poor bugger's having a bad week. I've heard of leaving litter, but…"

"Liam!"

"Ach, away on with you. You've got to laugh about it or...." He searched for something to indicate gravity, settling on. "Or you'd have to get drunk."

Annette pursed her lips. "And there's me thinking you were about to say 'you'd have to cry.' But that would require a heart."

Craig shot Liam a quick look that said he'd seen his tears the night before, then he gave Annette another look that said 'you're wrong.' She read it immediately and clammed up. Craig interrupted Jake's report with an apologetic nod.

"Sorry, Jake, I'll take over if that's OK." He stared pointedly at Liam and Annette. "It's the only way to keep these two from killing each other. OK. Yes, it was Alan Rooney. Killed in the same way as Eileen Carragher and her husband, with his face removed like Mrs Carragher's had been. I'm sure John will find the same forensic traces. Apart from any detail we get from the scene, I'd say that any vague doubt we had that Rooney might not have been involved, has now gone. That only leaves us with one suspect still alive. Gerry Warner."

He turned to Liam. "Pick him up and bring him into High Street. I'll interview him with you later. Annette, when you see Ryan Carragher, show him the sketches of the woman, the man and the logo on the holdall. In fact, show him Aurelie's sketch as well and watch his face. We don't know whether Aurelie was anything to do with his parents, but with the discovery of the boy in Newcastle I'm not ruling it out."

Davy signalled to speak. "If both the Carraghers were involved with kids, then w...what are the odds the sons weren't aware?"

Craig shook his head. "Slim to none I'd say, but we have to treat them like grieving family or potential victims, until we know for sure. OK. I'm meeting Aidan to interview the owner of the house. But first Jake, you and I are taking a trip to see Aurelie in half-an-hour. You can visit the restaurant with Liam when we get back. Bring the sketches and a live photo of the

Carraghers, please. If the social worker allows me I'm going to see if she recognises them." He stood up. "Annette, what time is Ryan Carragher coming in?"

"Twelve o'clock."

"OK, good. Can you come into my office for a moment, please? Everyone else, sorry, but we're going to be working most of the weekend, there's a lot to do."

Ten minutes later Annette had told Craig everything she knew about Nicky's tax problem. Craig dragged a hand down his face and stared out at the Lagan. The day was unexpectedly mild, with that mix of sunshine and light frost that usually said Halloween. The sun was lighting the river with silver and a gentle breeze was urging it along so quickly that it looked like a sheet of molten glass. He stared at it for so long that Annette finally coughed; reminding him she was in the room.

Craig turned to her with a smile. "What's the bottom line?"

Annette frowned and pulled out her notebook, flicking to a page. "Six thousand, eight hundred and forty-two pounds. But it might as well be a million pounds for them."

Craig nodded and reached for his wallet, ignoring her open mouth. He pulled out a card and handed it to her. "Take a note of the numbers, then on Monday morning phone the VAT people and pay the bill. They're not to tell Nicky that someone paid it, please, they're to say it was an error on their part, but emphasise to Gary that he needs to keep up-to-date with his returns in future."

"Just in case he gets them in the same mess again."

He nodded then smiled at her. "I don't want any talk of this in the office, please, Annette."

"But Nicky will want to thank you."

"Nicky will never know there's anything to thank me for, if the VAT people do as they're asked. It'll be worth it to see her happy again. Her grumping about was bad enough but it was affecting her coffee-making as well." He waved her out. "Now, go and have a break until Carragher arrives. Jake and I will be with Aurelie, then I'm going to see Aidan Hughes."

"What time are we briefing tomorrow morning? Just, Pete wanted to take us all out for breakfast."

Craig's eyes were already back on the river. "Eleven o'clock. Even we deserve a lie-in on Sunday."

***

Social Care Foster Home, Antrim Road, Belfast. 10.30 a.m.

Aurelie was as ethereal looking as Craig remembered her, but much tidier. Her white-blonde hair was combed neatly back from her face and anchored in a low ponytail. Her purple leggings and pink fleece dress made her look exactly like what she was, an eleven-year-old girl who should be dreaming of ponies and new friends, not sitting in a room full of strangers with only a social worker to hold her hand.

The little girl's face had lit up as soon as Craig entered the room. She went to rush towards him, but her stocky companion held her back and rose instead, drawing them quickly to one side. Her voice was a stage whisper as she gave them instructions, and one eye watched Aurelie as she stared at Craig.

"You won't ask her anything difficult, will you, Superintendent? It's just that she's cried since she was brought here until a couple of hours ago, and we don't want her upset again."

Craig glanced at Aurelie, seeing the tell-tale redness around her eyes. He nodded and the social worker motioned them to sit. Craig perched beside Aurelie on a small settee. He leaned forward towards the girl, introducing Jake in French, then explaining that they were in touch with the Gendarmes and trying to locate her family. On the word 'famille' her face lit up and she clapped her hands happily.

213

"Maman, Maman. Vous avez trouvé Maman? Où est-elle? (Mummy, Mummy, you've found Mummy. Where is she?)

Craig shook his head gently and watched as her face fell and tears started to roll down her cheeks. He smiled at her, ignoring the social worker's gimlet stare, then softened the blow by explaining they were doing everything they could to find her mother and wouldn't stop until they had. Aurelie nodded and gave a wet half-smile then Craig said something to her in French that made her laugh. Jake made up his mind to learn a language. It looked like it might come in handy someday.

When Aurelie seemed slightly happier Craig motioned Jake to hand him the folder that he'd been holding on his lap. It held photographs of the Carraghers and the others, and the exterior of the Newcastle house. He wanted to see if she recognised it. The house's interior could wait indefinitely for her I.D. Craig chatted softly for another moment then composed his face in a serious look that signalled his next words would be important.

"Aurelie. Ne soyez pas effrayé, s'il vous plaît." (Aurelie, don't be frightened, please.)

She nodded hesitantly.

"J'ai des photos de certaines personnes. Dites-moi si vous les connaissez. " (I have pictures of some people. Tell me if you know them.)

Her eyes widened instantly and she jerked back in her seat. Craig held her gaze. The gentleness in his eyes was clear to everyone, but there was a second message that only she could see. 'Help us. You're safe now but we must catch these people.'

Her companion leaned forward and shook her head. "No. Mr Craig. She's not ready for this." A small hand touched her knee, surprising her, and she turned to see the girl nodding.

"Are you certain?"

Aurelie understood what the social worker had asked, if not the exact words. She nodded again and the woman motioned Craig on, watching Aurelie's face carefully as he withdrew the photograph of the Chinese girl. Aurelie gazed at it bewildered

214

and then touched the woman's hair and eyes. For one moment Craig wondered if they'd met before then she shook her head and he realised it had just been a child's curiosity about another race.

He smiled and took the photo back then slid the Carraghers' picture from the file and placed it face-down on his knee. It was the most important one to show Aurelie after the girl's. It wasn't an I.D. parade; that would have been redundant now that the Carraghers were dead, but if Aurelie recognised them it would join the dots between them and her abduction; the house could wait for another day. Craig held the photograph on his knee for a moment before asking again.

"Certain?"

Aurelie nodded. "Certain, monsieur."

Craig turned over the photograph slowly, watching Aurelie's face carefully as he did. She reacted instantly; the horror of what she'd lived through etched immediately on her face. Tears ran thick and fast down her cheeks and Craig thrust the image at Jake to conceal it, then he leaned forward and gently took her hands as Aurelie stared at him, wild-eyed.

"Je suis désolé, Aurélie. Ils sont partis maintenant. Vous saviez tous les deux?" (I'm sorry, Aurelie. They've gone now. You knew both of them?)

She nodded again then sobbed so hard that Craig thought his heart would break. But her knowing the Carraghers was a connection between them and her being at the sex party. It could be a vital link in the case. Craig soothed her softly with words Jake didn't understand until eventually Aurelie's sobs subsided and she sniffed and dried her eyes. Then she whispered something, so softly that even Craig, six inches away from her, couldn't hear. He asked her to repeat it.

"Encore, s'il vous plaît, Aurelie."

Her young voice rose and the word she said was clear in any language. "Diable."

The Carraghers were devils. It was enough for today and it

gave Craig the noose to hang Tate and Gerry Warner with.

***

Rooney had died too quickly. His cowardly screams had echoed through the garage, until eventually she'd got bored with them and ramped up the Heavy Metal to drown them out. Mai had done exactly what she'd done before, but those times her lover had watched her, arms folded, even if he'd declined her offers to join in. She knew why he didn't watch this time. The first time had been exciting, so exciting that it had led to her laughing hysterically afterwards for hours. The frisson had been less with the second, although he was even guiltier in ways. By the time she'd got to Alan Rooney she'd almost yawned.

Mai remembered his young, sallow skin. It should have given her more pleasure to kill him; after all, he'd had more years left to do evil, filthy things. But instead it had given her less. Rooney had been boring in life and boring as he died. She was bored.

She gazed across the table and reached for her lover's hand. "Only one more left."

He shook his head. "Let's leave it, Mai, please. We've done enough to stop them."

He wasn't even slightly surprised when she screamed in his face.

"Leave it! Leave it? Are you mad? Leave Warner alive after what he did? What he'll do again, given half a chance."

Mai grabbed a knife from the dish rack and drew the blade swiftly across her arm, watching fascinated as the red droplets slid down it and then fell into the sink. He moved quickly to her side, seizing the knife and casting it away then he pulled her to his chest and stroked her hair. He buried his face in the silky strands and whispered, soothing Mai as she cried.

"There now. It's OK. We'll kill him, I promise. Then we'll go

216

so far away that they'll never find us again."

***

11.30 a.m.

"Boss, we can't find Warner."

Liam's voice boomed through the Audi's speakerphone as Craig drove down the Antrim Road towards town. He nodded Jake to lift the handset.

"What do you mean you can't find him, Liam?"

Liam stared at his mobile, puzzled, then he remembered.

"Hello, lad. I forgot you were going with the boss. Any joy with the girl?"

Craig could hear every word Liam's loud voice said and he yelled at the handset. "We'll tell you later. What about Warner?"

"Aye, well. I've been to his house, the school, the pub he hangs out in, even the gym where he plays squash. No joy. I've an all-points out on his car and Uniform's keeping an eye out around town."

Craig shook his head and sighed. It wouldn't matter how hard they looked. Gerry Warner had gone. The only question was where.

"Tell Liam to have the airports checked, if Warner's lucky he's managed to skip the country."

"Or?"

"He's been taken. My money's on the latter."

Jake started to relay the words when Liam cut him off. "I heard. I agree with the boss. Warner's dead. It's only a matter of when and where he turns up."

"They won't leave him at the school this time; it's been completely sealed off."

"Where, then?"

Craig interjected. "I don't think it'll be far. They won't want to drive around for long with a corpse in the boot." He shrugged. "It doesn't matter. We'll find out eventually."

He glanced at the clock. "Look, it's almost twelve o'clock now. Jake, I have to go back to the office to see Ryan Carragher and Aidan, but you and Liam should just check out the restaurant then call it a day until we hear something about Warner. We'll meet for a briefing tomorrow morning at eleven."

Jake relayed the message and clicked the phone off.

"Where's your car, Jake?"

"Basement of the C.C.U., sir. I'll meet Liam there."

Ten minutes later they drove pass the elderly gate officer and Craig parked his Audi in the nearest spot. He took the lift seven floors and went straight to Aidan Hughes' office; after he seen him he'd see what Ryan Carragher had to say.

***

Annette had managed to persuade someone to speak to her at the VAT office on a Saturday; perhaps miracles did happen after all. They'd taken the payment eagerly; however, they were less eager to say that it had been their mistake. Annette tried politeness, begging and finally veiled threats of legal repercussions if they ever jay-walked, but the stolid sounding woman at the other end of the line was having none of it. As she repeated herself for the tenth time Annette found herself mouthing the woman's words, hard Belfast accent and all.

"We can't go around making 'ceptions to the truth, nye can we? Else people'd never learn, nye would they?"

It was a rhetorical question. The woman was already so convinced of her own infallibility that even a grunted assent was a waste of breath. Annette bit her tongue hard and tried another tack.

"OK, then. How about if you just said it was paid by an anonymous donor? That's not a lie, is it?"

She paused, expecting an immediate 'no', but instead there was silence. Annette thought she could actually hear the woman's neurons firing while she considered her reply. The longer the silence continued the more hopeful Annette could feel herself becoming. She stamped on her optimism, squashing it; time enough for celebration if the woman said yes.

The silence was finally broken by a long drawn out, "welll…" that brought Annette's optimism surging forth again. "I suppose that wud be aw-right. I'll have ta check with my supervisor."

A moment later a man came on the line. His voice signalled an uncertain age somewhere between forty and death. Annette thought they probably felt like the same thing, working in the VAT office.

"Mrs McElroy?"

Annette was taken aback by her civilian title and paused for a moment while she remembered who Mrs McElroy was.

"Oh. Yes, that's me."

"May I ask you why Mr Craig doesn't wish his kindness to be known?"

Annette smiled. How to explain a boss who hid his generosity behind a complaint about the quality of Nicky's coffee? She did her best and to her surprise the supervisor laughed. In the VAT office! There was probably a financial penalty for such things.

The VAT man spoke again, with an amused tone in his voice. "Very well, Mrs McElroy. You may tell Mr Craig that his secret is safe with us. We will imply, imply mind you, not say, that we made an error with the bill. I'll phone Mrs Morris now with the news. But I will meet with her husband personally to go through the books and point out how to avoid such a mess again."

He paused, and for a moment Annette thought Mrs Stolid was coming back on the line, but it was still her boss. The man chuckled again. "I must say, this is the most unusual request I've ever had. It's quite made my week. Goodbye."

Annette bade him goodbye and hung up the phone, congratulating herself on not saying "you need to get out more".

Then she gathered her notes for quite a different conversation and went to the relatives' room to wait for Ryan Carragher to appear.

***

The Red Kite Restaurant, Belfast.

Liam pushed open the heavy glass door and led the way into the Red Kite's interior, expecting to hear the sound of flowing water, reminiscent of Chinese restaurants from his youth. His nostalgia dissipated abruptly as he looked around. The spacious restaurant was painted white and gold, with red kite stencils covering one wall and a T-shirt bearing the restaurant's logo displayed on another. Black-wood tables and a similarly coloured floor completed a décor that was bang up-to-date. The nose stud of the young waitress who approached them underlined it.

Jake smiled at the modern interior and made a note to come back with his partner, Aaron. Then he took out his badge. The girl looked startled and he rushed to reassure her.

"Sorry. We were just hoping you could answer a few questions for us. About some of your customers."

She smiled, relieved and then pointed them towards a table in the corner. Liam half expected her to bow but instead she said in a clear Belfast voice. "Hang on here and I'll get my Dad."

Before Liam had time to be politically incorrect a man younger than himself appeared, extending his hand.

"Good day officers. I'm James Wong. What can I do for you?"

He sat opposite Liam and smiled pleasantly, as Jake removed the images from a folder and set them face-down on the tablecloth.

"Aye, well. We've a few questions to ask about your

customers, Mr Wong. But first, could you take a look at these pictures and see if there's anyone you might know."

Jake turned over the sketch of the girl and Liam watched the restaurateur carefully as he ran his eyes down the page. He screwed-up his face in puzzlement then after a few seconds he shook his head.

"I thought I knew her, but it's not the same girl."

"Who did you think it was?"

"A girl who used to come in here a long time ago, when I was a young man." He smiled. "I noticed her because she was pretty."

Liam leaned forward, knowing that there was something more. "Did she come in on her own?"

Wong shook his head. "No, always with two boys. One very little and one so high." He indicated a boy somewhere in his teens. "Sometimes an old man came with them." He laughed. "I thought he was old, but now I think he was probably the age that I am now."

Jake asked the next question quickly, before Liam ended them up with a complaint. "Were they all Chinese, Mr Wong?"

Wong shook his head again. "No, only the girl. The others were white, like you."

Ian Carragher and his sons? But the woman with them was too old to be their mystery girl.

Liam waved Jake on, knowing he was doing them both a favour by not letting him speak. Jake turned over the second page; the sketch of the young man.

"Do you recognise him, Mr Wong?"

Just then his daughter reappeared with a pot of tea. She set it down and then stared closely at the two sheets.

"I know them."

Liam turned to her quickly. "Which one?"

"Both. I don't know their names, but they've been in here together several times. Mostly at the weekends."

Jake interjected eagerly. "You're sure it's this girl? Please look closely."

The girl leaned in and then nodded. "Definitely. She's mixed race; Chinese and white. He's white. They're a couple. Very lovey-dovey."

The man who'd bought the knives was white and the girl was his lover. So who was the woman that James Wong had seen years before?

Jake's voice was eager. "Did they ever pay by credit card? Or did you overhear anything they said? A name, maybe?"

The girl shook her head. "No. Always cash." She smiled. "With a big tip." She hesitated. "I didn't hear their names but... He did call her something once, but I thought it was a joke."

"What was it?"

"Miss Whiplash."

***

Craig wandered onto the seventh floor and knocked Aidan Hughes' door, relieved to find that the murder team weren't the only sad gits working on a Saturday. Hughes yanked the door open, looking unfeasibly cheerful for a man who had to deal with perverts all day. The personality was probably a job requirement; either that or he was on the happy pills.

"Hey, Marc. How's it going?"

He waved Craig in, not waiting for a reply, and continued talking. "I heard about Liam's find in Newcastle. Quite the coup. I can't wait to see it. I'm off down there Monday."

"It was grim."

"Grim, maybe, but fascinating never the less. I'm going to ask if I can write my thesis on it."

Craig screwed up his face. Hughes was starting his doctorate in criminology; he could think of nicer topics to research for the next three years. He changed the subject.

"What's happening with the house party? I went down to see the girl this morning."

"And? Anything new?"

Craig nodded. "She recognised the Carraghers' faces. And not in a good way."

Hughes long face lit up. "You're sure?"

"Positive. I had to leave it at the I.D. She was too distressed to go on. Davy's working with the Gendarmes to see if we can find her folks." He paused, shaking his head quietly. "You know Liam and Jake found a boy still alive in that hell-hole?"

Hughes' jaw dropped. "No! I hadn't heard. Has anyone talked to him, yet?"

Craig knew Aidan was thinking of what he could learn from being there when they did. It was ghoulish but he couldn't blame him. He spent his days talking to murderers and found their motivations fascinating, what Aidan dealt was just another type of scum. Craig shuddered. He still couldn't do Aidan's job. One video had been enough.

"The boy hasn't said a word yet. Liam's leading on it with the locals so I'll get him to keep you in the loop." Craig repeated his original question. "So what about the house party?"

Hughes grinned. "You know we got the organiser. It was definitely the architect who owns the house; Edgar Tate. Turns out he was the one dressed as a gimp. We didn't recognise him until he took off his mask at the station."

"And?"

"God, you want blood, don't you? OK. He has a big design practice in the centre of town. Very successful."

"And wealthy, judging by the house. Is there a Mrs Gimp?"

Hughes guffawed. "There is indeed. But she and the kids were on holiday at her mother's when the party kicked off. Swears she knew nothing about her hubby's other life."

"True or false?"

"True, I think, judging by the speed she filed for divorce this week when she found out about the party." Hughes perched on the desk facing Craig and his face darkened. "I know what you're going to ask, Marc. Does anyone own up to knowing anything about the Aurelie?"

"Well, do they? She didn't get there by herself and someone caused those bruises."

"And the rest."

The words hung in the air between them, neither man wanting to discuss what else the girl had been through. Craig asked the question again and Aidan shook his head.

"They're all giving us the same story. It was a BDSM house party arranged for consenting adults. Nothing illegal occurred."

Craig's face contorted in anger. "Tell that to the eleven-year-old crying her eyes out." He clenched his fists and headed for the door. Hughes blocked his way with his hands raised in peace.

"Wow! I remember that temper from the rugby field. You control it better nowadays, I'll give you that much."

Craig stared at him, then realised how ridiculous he must look, standing there with whitened fists. He gave a sheepish grin.

"Sorry, Aidan. It's not your fault, I know. It's just...if you'd seen Aurelie today..."

"I know. I see them every day, remember. But hey, there's a bit of good news as well. Turns out Tate didn't have the wit to use cloakroom tickets."

Craig shot him a puzzled look. "For what?"

"Oh, that's right. I forgot you elegant boys in Murder don't lower yourselves that way."

He waved Craig back to his seat and reached into a desk drawer, pulling out a book of raffle tickets.

"Most parties where they have hookers, they give the punters tickets to hand over in exchange for services rendered, so that no money changes hands. Tate wasn't that smart, he let the hookers get paid in cash. That's an offence."

"Yes!" Craig punched the air. "I want in on his interview."

"Sure. It's on Monday. Couldn't do it before then, he got himself a good brief."

"I don't care if he's got himself Clarence Darrow. It still won't be enough."

***

Craig whistled his way the one flight up to the relatives' room. He stopped whistling at the end of the corridor and rang Annette.

"Yes, sir?"

"I'm at the end of the corridor. Can you come and meet me?"

Five seconds later the room's door opened and Annette stepped outside and joined him.

"Is Ryan Carragher here yet?"

"Yes. He arrived ten minutes ago."

"Good. He can cope on his own for a moment. Follow me."

He led the way into the main floor coffee area and poured them both a cup.

"You're looking enigmatic, Annette. Something interesting?"

Annette smiled proudly and pulled out his credit card. "I managed to get it done today. I paid the VAT and the supervisor said he'll cover it up, but he'll go and meet with Gary anyway and help him get the returns right in future."

Craig slipped his card into his pocket and smiled. "Excellent. But actually, that wasn't what I meant. I was referring to Carragher."

"Ah…Well, he seems genuinely upset about his parents. If he knows anything about the life they led, he's giving nothing away."

"OK. I'll have a go and see if anything shows. Before we go in I want to update you." He brought Annette up to speed on Aurelie and the house party, adding. "Liam's going to be busy with the Newcastle side, so would you like in interview Edgar Tate with Aidan and me on Monday? He's stonewalling so far."

She sat forward, excited. "I'd love to. If Aurelie I.D.ed the

Carraghers, the next thing is to see if she recognises Tate from the party, isn't it?"

He nodded. "And the house in Newcastle. But she's very fragile, so I want to take it one step at a time. After we see Tate we'll know if we need to arrange a line-up."

"We might not get him on the prostitution angle, but maybe on child endangerment, sir? She was a minor in his house during an orgy. That might open a few doors?"

Craig's face lit up. It might indeed. "Excellent. Speak to the child protection team and see what grounds you can find. I want everything watertight before Tate's interview."

"By the way, sir, I chased up the anonymous call to the education board, tipping them off about Marcheson's, but I've hit a dead end. There were only three female teachers there in 2004; one's dead and the other two are denying knowing anything."

Craig shrugged. It was just a loose end and once everything unravelled it wouldn't even be that. "OK, thanks for trying. Let Davy know, please" He stood up and drained his cup. "Right. Now let's see how innocent Ryan Carragher really is."

***

Liam held up the coloured rattle and waved it at his fourteen-month-old son. He watched as he stretched for it and then giggled as Liam moved it playfully beyond his reach. Rory's laughter soon turned to annoyance when Liam moved it again. Liam smiled as he recognised the same temper he'd had as a kid.

He felt a sudden pain in his ear as Danni cuffed it. "Stop tormenting your son, and give him his rattle. I'll buy you one of your own if you're that fond of it."

"That hurt."

She smiled and wagged her finger at him playfully. "Then don't be a naughty boy."

Liam gave a lascivious smile. "Come here and I'll show you a naughty boy."

Danni made a face and indicated Erin playing quietly in the corner with her doll. "Behave yourself; your children are in the room." She followed up with a smile that held promise for later on. "Now, help me get the kids ready. I said I'd take them down to see Mum this afternoon."

Liam stood obediently and stared down at the little group. They were his world and his job was to protect them. There wasn't much that made him lose his temper nowadays; the benefit of age he supposed. But if anyone hurt Danni or his kids then he would break them in two.

As Liam slipped Erin's tiny arm into her anorak, she smiled up at him with a look so trusting that he thought his heart would break. He smoothed her red hair down over the hood and thought of the prison that they'd found the day before. Some of the bones had been from children no older than her.

The first Liam knew that he was crying was when a tear splashed onto his daughter's coat. It was joined a second later by another rolling down his cheek, then a third and a fourth until Erin's tiny fingers reached up and touched his face and her baby voice repeated words that she'd heard somewhere.

"There, there. Not cry. Daddy not cry."

Her small face crumpled in sympathy and her tears started to flow, matching his. She was crying for a reason she didn't understand, protected by her innocence. Liam really wished that he was.

***

The door to the relatives' room was lying open as they approached, and Craig saw a well-built young man standing with his back towards them. He was gazing out of the window onto Clarendon Dock, eight floors below. The Dock had been built on reclaimed land beside the Lagan thirty years earlier, and the window overlooked office buildings and café's, stretching to the river several hundred metres away. Craig preferred the view from his office. No buildings loomed between him and the water and the lack of space there was left to build on meant they never would.

They stood in the doorway and watched the man. It was interesting how much information could be gleaned without someone uttering a word. Ryan Carragher was tall, taller than his father; perhaps it had come from his mother's side. His hair was thick and dark and fell to the nape of his neck, and his shoulders and arms were muscled, saying that he was fit. Craig's sharp eyes took in his clothes at the same time as Annette's; jeans and trainers, the uniform of the young all over the world. Craig wondered what Carragher was thinking. If he was looking for distraction from the events of the past few days he would find plenty out on the Dock.

When Ryan Carragher turned around they learned even more. He was wearing a dark T-shirt and on its front was the same logo as in Frederick Archer's sketch; The Red Kite. Craig was becoming more curious about the restaurant by the hour. What was its connection to their case?

That was where Craig's luck ran out; Ryan Carragher didn't look anything like the young man in Archer's sketch. Where the young man had been pale and slim, Carragher was tanned and well built, and on his cheek was a large scar so livid that it couldn't possibly have been missed.

Annette's eyes widened when she saw the logo and Craig shot her a look that said 'not yet.' He wanted to see what Ryan Carragher told them before they gave anything away. Craig walked forward with his hand outstretched and Carragher shook it, his face wearing a puzzled look. His confusion wasn't about the handshake, Craig was sure of that. It was generic, as if he was confused about recent events in his life.

Craig motioned him to the sofa. "Thank you for coming in, Mr Carragher. Did you get a cup of tea?"

The younger man gave a weak smile. "I'm tea-ed out, thanks."

"Right then. My name is Superintendent Craig and you've already met Detective Inspector McElroy. We're two of the detectives handling your parents' case."

Carragher nodded, watching as Annette handed Craig a coffee then sat down.

"Are you both working on their cases, or one each?"

It was an unexpected question, but valid.

"We're part of a team that is working on both your parents' cases."

Carragher stared at him. "Why? Do you think their deaths are related?"

Craig glanced at Annette, momentarily confused. What had Carragher been told about his parents' deaths? He asked the question and Carragher filled-in the gaps.

"My step-mother was found dead in the playground of her school on Monday. Then my father was found dead three days later, I don't know where. The officers didn't say but I assume they suffered some sort of accidents."

Craig scrutinised the man's face, searching for lies. "Who notified you of the deaths, Mr Carragher?"

"Uniformed officers. They were very vague. I went to the mortuary and identified my father's body but only his face was uncovered and the doctor didn't go into details about how either of them had died." Carragher gave Craig the dazed look that he'd seen often in the next-of-kin, but something about it made Craig feel uneasy. "I suppose I should have asked for more information, but I assumed an accident or maybe heart attack, for my father."

Irritation flooded through Craig for a moment, then he realised. Uniform couldn't have given a cause of death until there'd been a post-mortem, and John might have withheld the mention of murder in case it prejudiced their case, fudging it with 'cause unknown'. Either that or John's head had been elsewhere all week, which was more likely.

Craig's ire subsided as he remembered Liam saying Ian Carragher had found it hard to accept his wife had been murdered. He may not have told his son; if people were in denial there was little that you could do. His mood changed to optimism. The fact that Ryan Carragher seemed to know nothing could be useful.

Craig changed tack to a more conversational tone. "Could you tell me a bit about your father and mother, Mr Carragher, and your early upbringing?"

Carragher paused for a moment, as if searching for an ulterior motive for the question, then he shrugged, like a man with nothing to hide. "It was pretty ordinary, really. My father was a surveyor and we moved around a bit with his job. My Mum stayed at home with me and my younger brother."

"Jonathan isn't it?"

"Yes. He's twenty-three; eleven years younger than me. Bit of an accident I think but they doted on him." His face darkened. "Unfortunately my mother Marianne died in 1994, when Jonathan was three-years-old. Breast Cancer."

"I'm sorry."

Carragher nodded. "It was hard, probably even harder on Jonathan. He grew up without a mother." He brightened slightly. "Although Tian Liu was a great help."

Craig saw Annette shift imperceptibly at the mention of the Chinese name. He nodded her to ask the question.

"Who was Tian Liu, Mr Carragher?"

"She was our au pair and a live-in nanny for Jonathan. Dad hired her when Mum got sick."

Craig interjected. "How old was she?"

"In '94? About twenty I think. Yes, that's it. She was twenty." He smiled, remembering. "I remember because I had a huge crush on her and she told me that I was six years too young; I was fourteen."

"How long did she live with you?"

"Until Jonathan was four or five I think. I left home at sixteen to go to catering college. In 1996." He sneered. "Dad married the bitch not long before that."

Craig raised an eyebrow and motioned Annette to ask.

"You mean your step-mother, Eileen?"

"Yes."

"Why do you call her the bitch, Mr Carragher?"

"Ryan, please. And I call her that because that's what she is, was. I hated her from the day I met her. My Dad was a nice man and she dominated him completely. Undermined and harangued him until he would have done anything for a quiet life."

Craig frowned, watching Carragher's face carefully as he ran through the list of petty humiliations Eileen Carragher had subjected his father to. The more he talked the more uncertain Craig became that Ryan Carragher knew nothing of his father's other life. He lifted the folder Annett had brought and then tuned back into what Carragher was saying.

"Jonathan bore the brunt of it. Especially when she sacked Tian Liu after they got married. Jonny really missed her; she was the only mother he'd known for years."

Annette was asking all the right questions so Craig just sat back and watched.

"When did she sack her?"

"As soon as she got her feet under the table."

'95 or '96. Interesting.

Craig interjected. "Do you see much of your brother nowadays?"

Ryan shook his head. "Not much. He went away to Uni in England to study History and Chinese."

Chinese again.

"He said he wanted to specialise in oriental history and he needed to speak Chinese for that, but I think part of it was about Tian Liu. It was mainly Cantonese he learned and that was what she spoke."

"When was the last time you saw him?"

Annette asked the question in such a conversational tone that Carragher answered without a thought. "Last week, actually. He's back in Belfast for a while staying with friends."

"Do you know their names?"

"Sorry, no. They're much younger than me so I don't pay much attention."

The atmosphere in the room was pleasant and grew more so as Carragher talked about his mother and the father, and the brother that he obviously loved. What had happened to make such a normal family so dysfunctional? Eileen Carragher? One person; was that really all it took?

After five more minutes chatting, Craig slipped in a question. "That's an unusual T-shirt. What's the logo?"

Carragher looked down at his T-shirt, stretching it out so he could read what was on the front.

"Oh, this? I just grabbed it this morning because it was clean. I got it years ago from a restaurant Tian Liu used to take us to. It was huge on me then. I used to sleep in it." He smiled wistfully. "It was her favourite place to eat. She said it did the best Cantonese food in Belfast."

"Did?"

"Well, it still might do for all I know. I never get out of my own place long enough to try any others."

Craig sat forward purposefully and Annette shot him a questioning look that he ignored. Instead, he removed two sheets of paper from the folder she'd brought.

"Thank you, Mr Carragher. I think that's almost it for today. We'll need to speak to you again when we have more information."

"Fine." Carragher made to stand up and Craig motioned him back to his seat.

"Before you go, there are just a couple more things. Did you know a Dr Gerry Warner or a Mr Alan Rooney by any chance?"

Carragher heard the past tense immediately. Warner and

Rooney must have bitten the dust as well!

Craig had used it deliberately, to see how Carragher would react, but nothing about his behaviour suggested guilt. He hadn't committed the murders; Craig would stake his reputation on that. Ryan Carragher used the present tense in his answer just in case it had been a trick.

"Yes. I know both of them. They were friends of my step-mother mainly, although my father knew them as well."

Ian Carragher had known Alan Rooney, the man his wife had been cuckolding him with for years! Craig nodded and then slid the sketches across the table. "Final thing, I promise. Could you look at a couple of images for us?"

"Sure...I think. Are they anything to do with my Dad's death?"

The omission of his step-mother from the question said, 'I hated her', loud and clear.

"No, not directly, but we think the people in them might be able to help with our enquiries."

"OK, then. Fire ahead."

The first sketch Craig turned over was the aged-up photograph of the young girl from the video. He scanned Carragher's face as he stared at it then leaned in to peer more closely. Recognition filled his eyes; it was followed quickly by a puzzled look. Annette interjected excitedly.

"You know her?"

"No...well, maybe. I'm not sure. She looks too young."

Craig spoke in a calm voice. "Too young?"

Carragher looked at him, a look of genuine confusion on his face. "For a moment I thought that she was Tian Liu. But she isn't. Tian Liu would be forty now and this girl's only about twenty."

"Is age the only reason you don't think it's her?"

Carragher shook his head. "No. She looks very like her, but there's something about her features as well."

He stared for another moment then put the photograph

down triumphantly. "I know what it is! This girl's related to her somehow. And she's mixed race; Tian Liu was pure Chinese." He chuckled. "This girl looks like Tian Liu's love child with a white man."

It was what they already thought, but Ryan Carragher had just told them who the girl's mother was. Craig pushed him further for confirmation.

"You're saying she looks enough like your old nanny to be her daughter with a white man?"

"Yes, yes. I suppose I am." Carragher shook his head. "But that's impossible. After Eileen sacked her, I heard Tian Liu went back home to Hong Kong. She probably married a Chinese man and has kids of her own by now."

Maybe.

Craig thanked him, then set the other sheet of paper face-down on the table and glanced at Annette. His message was clear. 'Watch Carragher's face as I turn it over.'

Annette did and what she saw was exactly the same as Craig. The moment Ryan Carragher saw the sketch of the young man his eyes widened in recognition. He hid the look quickly, but not before they'd both seen it. He glanced away, avoiding Craig's gaze.

"Do you know this man, Mr Carragher?"

Carragher leapt to his feet, readying to go. "No, I'm sorry. I've never seen him before in my life."

He glanced at his watch in the universal mime of 'I have somewhere else to be.'

Craig smiled inwardly and rose, motioning him towards the door. "The Inspector will show you out, Mr Carragher. Thank you. We'll be in touch."

He extended his hand and shook Carraghers for long enough that the young man had to meet his eyes. Craig's stare said he knew that he'd recognised the man in the sketch, and Carragher's blush said that he knew he'd been caught-out.

"Do we have your contact details, Mr Carragher?"

"Yes. I gave them to the Inspector."

"Right. Goodbye then."

Craig waited until he heard the lift doors closing then he telephoned Davy at home.

"Sorry, Davy. I need you back in for an hour. We've just got a new lead."

Chapter Twenty-Two

The C.C.U. 4 p.m.

"I want you to find me a recent photo of Jonathan Carragher, Davy. Driving licence, student card, whatever you can get. And I need to locate a Chinese woman of around forty years old, called Tian Liu. She was over here from Hong Kong working as a nanny, somewhere between 1990 and 1996. There must be something on her at immigration, or the Chinese Embassy in London?"

Davy smiled weakly at Craig and waved him away from his desk. He'd been stretched out on the couch in Maggie's apartment just settling down to watch a DVD, when his mobile had rung, ruining their lazy Saturday afternoon. He'd been trying to watch 'Elysium' for months now and each time he pressed 'play' he was interrupted. He gave up. He was doomed never to see Matt Damon reach his goal.

He'd told Maggie to go on and watch it without him, in the hope that she'd be so grateful that she wouldn't make him watch some girly rubbish tonight. Maggie Clarke was a news journalist with the Belfast Chronicle and they'd been dating for fourteen months, ever since they'd met on a murder case at Stormont. Not the most romantic of introductions, but things were going really well. Except, for a hard-nosed reporter Maggie showed a disturbing desire to watch slushy Rom-Coms in her time off, no matter how often Davy said no.

Craig took the hint and wandered off towards Nicky's desk. He was just filling the percolator and setting out three mugs when a loud clicking sound drew his gaze towards the doors. Nicky was storming across the grey-carpeted office faster than he'd ever seen her move. Annette saw her coming and ducked down behind her cubicle wall, leaving Craig to greet her alone.

"Oh! Hi Nicky. I didn't expect to see you in today."

Nicky lifted the percolator from his hand without a word and steered Craig towards his office, closing the door hard behind them. Craig didn't know whether to laugh or object, so instead he stared mutely down at her blue-tipped hair and waited for her to speak. The VAT issue was at the front of his mind but he was saying nothing, in case her mood wasn't about that at all.

"Sir."

Nicky's husky voice was firm but unreadable, although her one word address said she wasn't taking any crap. Craig glanced at her face in reflex and glimpsed Annette's silhouette at his half-glass door. He willed her to come in. No such luck. She was taking the discretion part of valour seriously today.

Craig tried to break Nicky's gimlet gaze, searching for somewhere else to look and trying hard not to stare at her silver lame leggings and frilly top. Which strange fashion magazine had she been reading this week?

"Sir."

Oh God. She'd said it again; that meant he was in real trouble. Craig willed himself to bluff it out, rushing to his own defence before she said it a third time.

"Now, listen, Nicky…"

"No, sir. You listen."

Craig wasn't going to argue. Years with girlfriends, a sister and an Italian mother had taught him that arguing with women was a zero-sum game. Never do it unless you're prepared to fight to the death and ignore their tears, and he never could do that. So Craig did as he was told; he listened. But instead of the stream of invective he expected to hear, Nicky merely stared into his eyes for a moment longer then reached up, turned his cheek firmly towards her and kissed it lightly. Then she said the words that told him she'd worked everything out.

"I know what you did, sir."

She stared at him again, as if waiting for him to cave in and admit his evil deed. Craig said nothing so Nicky kissed his cheek again and said. "Thank you. You've saved our lives."

Then she spun round and yanked open Craig's office door, smiling as Annette almost fell in. Nicky hugged her as well then clicked her way quickly off the floor, leaving them both blushing in her wake.

Davy peered up from behind his computer screen, puzzled. "W…was that Nicky? Why didn't she say hello?"

Craig wandered over to him. "Don't take it personally, Davy. She didn't say hello to me either." Craig sat down and linked his hands behind his head, still smiling at the brief interlude. It was so typically Nicky Morris that he wanted to laugh. Annette did. She was still laughing when she joined them at Davy's desk.

"Right. What have you found?"

Davy squinted at Craig sceptically. He'd only had five minutes! If he hadn't been so good at his job he might have thought the boss was taking the piss.

"OK." He turned a screen towards them. "Here's Jonathan Carragher in 2011 w…when he was at Uni. And here's the s… sketch Annette's witness produced."

Craig's eyes flicked between the two images and he nodded. There was no doubt that it was the same man. The young man who had bought the knife that had killed the Carraghers was their youngest son, Jonathan! Craig corrected himself. He was Ian Carragher's son, not Eileen's.

Annette spoke first. "It's definitely Jonathan Carragher, sir. So the sunglasses weren't hiding the fact he was Chinese. He's as Caucasian as us. He must just have been wearing them to hide his identity. Pity he forgot about the logo on his hold-all."

Davy leaned forward curiously. "The Chinese Restaurant logo? W…What about it?"

Craig answered. "Sorry, I forgot to tell you. Ryan Carragher was wearing a T-shirt with it on the front. Apparently they do a range of merchandise you can buy."

"Only in the s...shop, or on-line as well?"

Craig shook his head slowly. "I hadn't even thought of that. Can you check it out?"

"OK. But if Jonathan Carragher bought the knife that killed his parents..."

Annette interrupted. "The type of knife that killed them. We won't know for sure until we have an exact match."

Davy shrugged. "W...Whatever. The type of knife then. That means he must have killed them."

"Whoa. Not so fast." Craig raised a hand to still their speculation. "It's interesting certainly, but it's not a slam dunk yet. What have you found out about the woman?"

Davy tapped on his keyboard and another face appeared on the screen. It was the passport photograph of a young Chinese woman.

"That w...was Tian Liu's photograph back in 1992, when she first came to Belfast. S...She was eighteen in it."

"She started to nanny for the Carraghers two years later, sir."

"Good. Davy, anything on her nowadays?"

Davy shook his dark head. "No. It's pretty s...strange actually, and I can't be certain until the embassy gets back to me, but I can't find anything on her after '95. It's like s...she dropped off a cliff."

Craig's heart sank. He knew instantly what had happened to Tian Liu, but he needed to check something first.

"Davy, can you put the aged-up photo of the little girl from the video beside Tian Liu on the screen?"

Davy tapped again and the two women appeared side by side. Tian Liu at eighteen and their mystery girl. Annette gasped. They were almost identical.

"She's her daughter all right. But her father was white."

"Who? Ian Carragher, sir?"

Craig nodded. "That would be my guess, Annette. Lonely widower with a pretty nanny; he wouldn't be the first. But we won't know for sure until we find the girl and compare DNAs."

Davy shook his head firmly. "Not true, chief. I can give you a pretty good likeness of their possible offspring from Tian Liu's and Ian Carragher's photographs. Give me ten minutes."

"Thanks, Davy. That's brilliant. Also…"

Craig hesitated slightly. He asked a lot of Davy and he was about to ask more, but he knew Davy was capable of it.

"Ryan Carragher is in contact with his brother, I have no doubt about that. He told Liam that Jonathan was coming to the funerals and the only way he could have known that was if they'd been in touch. So…"

"You w…want me to see if I can find Jonathan Carragher's phone number by tracking back from his brother's?"

"Can you?"

"Yes. But it will take me until Monday. I'll need to speak to the mobile phone provider and that's hopeless at the w… weekend."

"OK. It will have to do. My bet is that Ryan phoned Jonathan as soon as he left us today. About half-an-hour ago."

Davy made a note of the timing and then waved them both away. "Give me ten minutes to play with these images."

Craig did as he was told and beckoned Annette to one side. "Nicky knows, Annette. But how?"

Annette shook her head. "God knows. Nicky is the most streetwise person I've ever met. Either the VAT man said when he called her, but I honestly don't think he would have. Or she worked it out by herself."

"Even a hint would have been enough for her to latch onto. She's like a bloodhound when she gets a trail."

Annette smiled. "Sherlock Morris. But even so, sir, all she would have guessed was that someone had paid her bill, she couldn't have known it was you…"

As Annette said it her voice tailed off. Of course Nicky

would have known. Who else but Craig would have cared enough to do it and been that generous? Nicky knew Craig well enough to know it's exactly what he would have done, and one look in his eyes would have been confirmation.

Annette pointed an accusing finger at Craig.

"She knew because you told her."

Craig spluttered out his coffee. "I did not!"

"Not by what you said, but in your response when she stared you down. She did stare you down, didn't she?"

Craig blushed to the roots of his hair. Nicky had got him with the oldest interrogation trick in the book. She'd stared at him and he'd caved in, in some miniscule, fraction of a second way, telling her everything she'd needed to know without uttering a word.

"Clever girl. Pity she's not a detective, there wouldn't be a murderer who wouldn't confess."

They laughed for a moment and then Annette sipped at her coffee thoughtfully, giving Craig a pointed look.

"What's on your mind, Annette?"

"It's Liam and Jake. Newcastle sounded pretty rough. It's bound to have affected them both."

Craig nodded. "I told them to see the counsellor once it's all wrapped up."

"Which they won't, of course. Well, Jake might; the younger men seem more evolved, but Liam will think it's all mumbo jumbo and soldier on."

Craig nodded. "OK. I'll have a word and try to get him to talk to someone."

"You too."

"I didn't find the prison."

"But you saw everything that they did."

Craig frowned and Annette raised her hands in peace. "OK. I've said my bit. I know better than to push any of you stubborn bunch." She grinned. "I'll ask Nicky to push you instead."

241

Craig was just about to object when Davy beckoned them over, smiling triumphantly at his work. Each of his three screens displayed different images. The first held images of Tian Liu and Ian Carragher, the second their possible male offspring and the third the female. Craig glanced from screen to screen several times before speaking.

"That's remarkable, Davy. Really remarkable."

Davy blushed slightly and shrugged. "It's just a programme, boss. It applies algorithms based on s…sex differences and age and…" He extended his long arms in his latest favourite gesture. "Voila, as they say."

Annette was staring in silence at the third screen. It held six images of female children. One of them matched their mixed-race girl exactly. She pointed to it.

"There she is."

Craig nodded. There was no question that the young man and woman they were looking for were both Ian Carragher's children. His son Jonathan with his first wife Marianne, and his daughter with his children's nanny, Tian Liu.

It raised all sorts of questions. Where was Tian Liu now? Craig suspected that she'd never returned to Hong Kong after she'd given birth. She was most likely dead, and her daughter with Carragher had ended up in a porn video being beaten by a boy not much older than herself.

If the girl was mixed up with Jonathan Carragher then how had they met, and did they even know that they were half-brother and sister? Had they killed the Carraghers and Alan Rooney together? The girl couldn't have been raised by the Carraghers; from what they knew of Eileen Carragher she would never have allowed it. Mothering her new husband's bastard daughter would have been step too far.

And Ryan hadn't recognised her, impossible if she'd been raised in their father's home. Even if he was away at college he would have seen her on visits home. So; what? The girl was adopted by someone else after she was born? Or farmed out to relatives?

Craig shook his head. It was getting confusing and they were all tired. Time to call it a day and come back fresh tomorrow. Maybe by then they'd have found Gerry Warner. He hoped for Warner's sake that they found him alive.

Chapter Twenty-Three

Sunday morning.

Warner was the last of them. The final one in the small group that had made their childhoods hell. He'd seemed so big then, so tall and powerful, and he had been when they were only six and ten. His giant hands and stale adult breath had stopped all their escape attempts with ease.

Mai touched her lower back gingerly, gently running a finger over her raised scars. They were Keloid now, from years of cutting and healing. The wheals had been red then white then red again, as the edges of the scars were split repeatedly by the whip, wielded to fulfil Warner's perverted needs. Mai closed her eyes; forcing herself to remember and feel the hatred for him again, as fresh as she'd felt it every day for years. Tears seeped between her dark lashes and tip-toed gently down her cheeks, their years of gushing and being ridiculed for it, teaching her to cry silently or attract more pain.

She pictured Warner's face, younger and lean, with dark hair slicked back from his forehead where the grey now appeared. Hair that she'd grown to hate for what the sight of it heralded, long before she could reason why. She could hear his voice instructing the boys to hit her, his brown eyes gleaming as he watched them cause her pain. Forcing each boy to strike harder than the last, although most of them could barely see her through their own tears. Little boys with high-pitched voices saying "I'm sorry, I'm sorry" to the little girl that they were forced to hurt, again and again.

They'd begged her forgiveness for an act that they were mere puppets in, but she hadn't hated them. They were children like her, trapped in a macabre Punch and Judy show. All except Alan Rooney. He'd been an eager pupil, offering to strike harder and longer without a single tear, his eyes bright with a pleasure that had mimicked Warner's own. Warner's ever-willing apprentice as a child, and worse as an adult. That's why they both had to die.

Mai shook her head, shaking out the images that filled her mind. The dank, damp basement room of the school that her 'loving' parents had sent her to. Or so the story went. She'd never known them and she'd never been sure what was true. The other children had suitcases and money, with letters and presents coming from home. They called their parents by name and held their photographs close at night. She'd had no names to utter and no images to gaze at in the dark.

It hadn't mattered. All the money and power and photos and names hadn't saved any of them from their fate. One by one they'd come for them, leading them down the dark corridors into the night and then further, beneath the building into hell. Hell. Mai sneered at the word. If she was destined to go there when she died could it really be any worse than that room?

Night after night. Warner in the corner, shouting instructions while he stroked his thighs, her trying to avert her gaze from what he did next. Eileen Carragher laughing and drinking in the corner, while Warner inflicted pain on them, and then forced them to watch their bestial adult acts and join in.

Mai's face brightened as she remembered the night that she'd met her love. Him a slight, pale boy not much older than herself. Shivering in his thin vest and squinting half-blind into the dark, then gasping when he'd seen her chained to the boiler-room pipes. She'd loved him at once for his full mouth and thick dark hair and then even more for his stubborn refusal to lift the whip. He'd fought and cried when they'd forced it into his hand, and stood arms down, obstinately denying them their thrills. Warner had beat him until he'd buckled and lay bloodied on the ground, then she'd met his eyes with hers and nodded, silently giving him permission to carry out their will.

Mai smiled as she remembered how light his touch had been. How high he'd flicked the lash so that it barely skimmed her, all momentum gone. They hadn't realised what he was doing, as she timed her screams to match its rise and fall. She'd loved him then and she loved him now, for all his gentleness and care.

Mai turned towards her lover Jonathan Carragher and smiled, remembering their first meeting and grasping his hand as they gazed at the man on the garage floor. Gerry Warner struggled harder, tightening his bonds, expertly tied by Mai after years of watching him do it to her. She bent down close to him, breaking her silence with a whisper.

"Well, Mr Warner. Time for science class."

Gerry Warner tried to scramble away, his eyes wild and red, but there was nowhere for him to hide. Mai peered closely at the man that she'd been so afraid of as a child, knowing that he couldn't hurt her now. His body was thin and weak, all his youthful muscles wasted and gone. His face was lined and his hair fell in a clumsy curtain now around his face. Warner looked old and indigent and for a moment Mai saw a flicker of pity on her lover's face. She turned to Jonathan Carragher fiercely and gripped his arms.

"No! He doesn't deserve your sympathy after what he did to us."

Warner's incongruously strong teacher's voice forced its way through his gag. "Who are you? Why are you doing this to me?"

Mai kneeled to face him and then laughed into his face. Her voice was sharp. "Don't you remember, Mr Warner? Your favourite little girl? Down in the basement night after night, pretending to be a respectable teacher during the day?" She stood and bowed mockingly to him and then turned her back.

"Perhaps you'll remember me better if I turn around?"

Realisation widened Gerry Warner's eyes and he struggled harder, writhing futilely on the floor. Oh God, he was really going to die. Like this? He always thought it would be in his sleep when he was old. Not this. Not now. He had to escape. There must be some way. Mai watched the frantic reasoning fly across his face and laughed again.

"I know exactly what you're thinking. How did I get here? And how do I escape? The same things I thought for years until they finally closed the school and I slipped away in all the mess."

She knelt down beside him again, pushing her face close to his. "You, a teacher! You taught me nothing but how to be cruel. For years I earned a living the only way I knew. The only way you taught me. On the scene, but this time making sure I held the whip."

She turned towards her lover and smiled. "Until he found me and cared for me. He'd looked for me for years, and now we're together every day and no-one can tear us apart."

Warner's eyes flicked towards a corner of the dark garage. He could just make out the shape of a tall young man. He couldn't see his face, but if he was the man he thought he was he wondered if the bitch knew what that meant. A frisson of pleasure ran through Warner at the thought of hurting her again. Mai saw his look and frowned, puzzled by what it meant. She ripped off his gag and slapped him full on the face, the noise of the slap making her partner wince. Warner smiled. It was a snide smile and his eyes held something that bothered her, as if he knew something that she didn't, couldn't, know.

Mai screamed at him in frustration. "What are you smiling at? WHAT?"

She slapped him again, her arm swinging down in an arc and her open palm connecting with a loud smack, knocking Warner's head back and splitting his lower lip. She watched as blood gushed and ran across his chin, but still Warner didn't break his gaze. Instead he slowly extended his tongue and swept it round, licking his own blood with a look that said it was nectar from the Gods.

Mai beat his head with her fists and screamed full in his face. "Tell me you bastard, tell me what you know, or I swear I'll kill you now."

Warner smiled between her blows. "You're going to kill me anyway, so why should I tell you? I have information and you want it. That's the basis for a trade, I'd say."

She spat into his face then jumped to her feet and started kicking his stomach hard. The young man stepped forward to restrain her, just long enough for Warner to see his face. Warner's smile spread and they both saw it. He'd been right.

Mai kicked him again, in the side of the head, making Warner black out. But not before she'd seen his triumphant smile. She turned to her lover with a tormented look.

"He recognised you, Jonathan."

"Of course he did. He knew my parents and saw me grow up through the years. Besides, it was him that brought me down to the boiler room each night."

Her eyes were frantic. "No! That doesn't explain why he looked so pleased. Why would he be pleased that we're together now?" Her voice rose into a panicked screech. "I don't understand. Why was he pleased?"

Jonathan Carragher stroked her hair gently and soothed her like a child, shaking his head. "It's nothing, Mai. He's just playing games. Trying to wind you up and make you believe that he knows something we don't, so we'll let him go." He smiled down at her then kissed her gently on the lips. "That's all it is. Remember, he's a sadist. He's gaming you, that's what they do. Don't let him."

Her sobs subsided as Jonathan's anger grew. Warner had been a family acquaintance almost since Eileen Burns had entered their lives. He'd watched as she'd dominated his kind father, diminishing him day by day, until she had him where she wanted him and destroyed all their lives. First the bitch had sent Tian Liu away, ignoring his pleas to keep her on. Then she'd brought him to the school she taught at and started her sadistic games. She'd recruited Warner into the school, ostensibly to teach science, but really to ruin their lives even more. Gerry Warner had had free reign to use all the children there in his perverted little games.

Jonathan shook his head, remembering how once he'd been old enough the bitch had used him too, trying to make him cruel and break him down. She hadn't succeeded and now she'd paid the price. His father too, for not protecting him. In some ways his father Ian had been the worst of all. He was supposed to protect his child, not let him be used in such cruel games. Then Alan Rooney, the next generation of scum, who used the younger children to satisfy his perverted needs, first at the school and then in his father's house near the Mournes.

It was the house that had been the final straw. When the school had closed Jonathan had hoped that they would stop, or at least confine their games to adults. But the first time they'd forced him to visit their underground dungeon he knew that they hadn't and he'd insisted on being sent away to school, with the intention of never coming back.

Jonathan sobbed. He should have acted then; gone to the police or made an anonymous call. But he hadn't and he didn't know why, not until he met Mai again by accident one day. He'd looked for her futilely for years then one day he'd gone to the restaurant Tian Liu used to take them to, and she was walking out as he walked in. Jonathan thought back to the moment. He'd stopped in his tracks and called her name. "Mai."

He expected her to scream and hit him, call him a bastard and telephone the police, even though they'd both been children when they'd been forced into their malicious games. But instead she'd turned and then smiled as she recognised him and they'd walked back inside to talk for hours. The pain they'd suffered as children had grown into a sort of love and they clung together gratefully, the only people who wouldn't be repelled by their scars. But they couldn't have peace, not while their tormentors were still roaming free to do it again.

Jonathan took Mai's hand and led her from the garage, before Warner woke up and mind-fucked her again. Warner was just pretending he knew something to play for time, trying to delay the inevitable moment when he died. But Mai was too fragile to deal with his sadism now so Jonathan made up his mind.

He'd never killed anyone or anything, only watched her do so, reluctantly, to make sure that she didn't come to harm. Nothing had ever seemed important enough to him to kill for. But now Mai was. She would sleep and he would kill Gerry Warner before she woke again. She could do whatever she wanted to do with his corpse.

***

The C.C.U. Sunday. 11 a.m.

"OK. A quick debrief before we get out there again."

Craig sipped at his morning coffee, regretting yet another late night out with John, after they'd met for 'just one drink' at Bar Red. He looked rough and he knew it. He'd cut himself shaving and his eyes were an interesting combination of red and blue. Ah well, it wasn't every day that his best friend got engaged.

Craig straightened up, preparing to start, and then he heard a familiar clicking sound. He greeted its creator without turning.

"Good morning, Nicky."

Nicky laughed cheerfully. "Good morning, sir. I'm just in to catch up on some stuff. Everyone OK for coffee?"

Liam saw the quick glance exchanged between Craig and

Annette and knew that something was up. He approached the matter with his usual tact and diplomacy.

"Here. What did I miss? And how come Nicky's smiling when she's had a face like a Lurgan Spade all week?"

The kick Annette gave Liam's shins made a crack so loud that everyone turned to look.

"Ow! What the hell did you do that for? I was only asking…"

The look in Annette's eyes said that he'd get another kick if he didn't shut up, so Liam reluctantly concurred. He squinted at her in a way that made it clear retribution would be forthcoming and Craig interjected in a voice like a tired parent.

"Right. If you two have quite finished, let's get on with the case."

Craig summarised his meeting with Aidan Hughes and handed over to Annette for an update on Ryan Carragher. She ended by telling them about his T-shirt, then Liam updated them on their trip to the restaurant and Craig nodded Davy to pitch in. Five minutes later everyone knew that the Carragher boys' Chinese nanny, Tian Liu, had been dismissed soon after Ian Carragher remarried, but not before she'd had his illegitimate daughter. They also knew that the daughter was the six-year-old girl in the porn video, and that the young man who'd bought the knife used in the murders was Ian Carragher's younger son, Jonathan.

Liam held up his hand to slow Davy down. "Hang on. Am I hearing this right? You're saying that Jonathan, the younger son, is working with this half-Chinese girl, who's his half-sister?"

Davy nodded. "Yes, that's exactly w…what we're saying."

Liam scratched his chin. "The waitress at The Red Kite was sure they were a romantic couple."

"Are you s…sure?"

Liam nodded. "Positive. I'll come back to that in a minute. So hang-on, we're really saying that the younger son, Jonathan, and his half-sister, whatever her name is, are on a killing spree?

251

And so far they've taken out the father, the step-mother, Rooney and now Gerry Warner's probably next, but the older brother Ryan knew nothing about it?"

Craig nodded. "Says he knew nothing… Yes, that's about it, Liam. But it's worse than that. The video of the young boy and girl…"

"The video that I thankfully didn't see."

"Yes. It was shot in the boiler room at the Marcheson's school in Bangor, so the likelihood is that any abuse that was going on there…"

Liam finished Craig's sentence. "Kept going at the house in Newcastle. With the same kids?"

Craig shook his head. "Kept going yes, but it's unlikely that the same children were involved. Once the school closed their parents would have taken them home."

Annette leaned in. "Except for the girl and Jonathan Carragher, sir. If Ian Carragher was their father then they had nowhere else to go."

"Perhaps, Annette, but I'm not so sure. We need to find out when the Chinese girl appeared on the BDSM scene. If it was after the school closed in 2004 then she can't have been locked up in the Newcastle basement."

Liam jumped in. "Here, boss, the waitress said she heard Jonathan Carragher call the girl Miss Whiplash once. She thought he was joking, but maybe not, if she was into the BDSM scene."

Craig nodded. It fitted.

Jake leaned forward, cutting in. "If the girl escaped, sir, it would have to have been before the Carraghers moved to Newcastle." He shook his head, picturing the dungeons they'd found. "There was no way anyone could have escaped from there."

"OK then, let's speculate a bit. Let's say that the girl escaped during the Bangor school's closure, and ended up on the BDSM scene around Northern Ireland when she was still a child."

Annette shuddered. "She was a baby. She would only have been nine-years-old when the school closed."

"She grew up fast, Annette. From Liam's Miss Whiplash comment and Warner's reaction, I'd say she became a successful dominatrix too. Warner was terrified when we mentioned a Chinese woman and he wouldn't have responded that way if he'd only known her as an abused child. Then somehow the girl met Jonathan Carragher again and they teamed up; maybe as partners or maybe even as lovers, if the waitress at The Red Kite is correct."

"But that's incest!"

Craig smiled at Annette's surprise. "Well, first, they mightn't know that they have the same father. I don't think Ian Carragher advertised that the fact he'd fathered an illegitimate daughter, judging by Ryan's lack of recognition of her photograph. And second, even if they do know, compared to the things they've been made to do in their young lives, incest is pretty small beer."

Davy shook his head. "I don't think they do know they're s… siblings, chief."

Craig turned towards him, curious. Davy's tone of voice said he knew something that they didn't.

"What have you found out?"

"It's probably nothing, but before I left last night I ran an experiment. I asked D.C.I. Hughes for the video and I managed to get one clear image of the boy."

"How? He never turned towards the camera."

Davy gave a thin smile. "He was reflected in an old panel of glass leaning against the boiler room w…wall. I captured the image and inverted it, then aged it up and got this." He passed round sheets of paper printed with two photographs. "The first is Jonathan Carragher's s…student card; the other is the aged-up image of the boy in the video."

Craig stared at the images for a moment then shook his head

in despair. They were the same boy. Ian Carragher had used his own son to beat his daughter with Tian Liu half to death, just to give his friends a thrill. His only concession to Jonathan's anonymity was that he'd been filmed from the back.

Annette said what they were all thinking. "Animals! They all deserved to die. To do that to any child is bad enough, but to do it to your own children…It's inhuman."

No-one else said a word, their expressions ranging from fury to complete incomprehension. The silence was broken by a click from Nicky's percolator. She'd been too far away to hear what was being said and she shouted cheerfully across the floor.

"Fresh coffee anyone?"

It was the prompt that Craig needed to break the mood. "Yes, please."

When Nicky handed Craig a plate of biscuits it opened the barn door again for Liam to stomp through.

"Here! Where's my biscuit, then?"

Nicky sniffed and turned on her heel. "Still in the packet."

"Here, boss, that's favouritism. I'm reporting that to the Equality Commission."

Craig smiled and held out the plate. "Have a Rich Tea and shut up, Liam. We have a lot of work to do."

**

2 p.m.

Liam was back on the road to Newcastle, grinding his teeth at having to view the scene again, when his car-phone rang; it was Craig.

"What's up, boss? Give me some good news, for God's sake."

"Man United have won the F.A. cup."

"What? When?"

Craig laughed at his eager reaction. "It's February, Liam. Unless they've moved the fixtures I was joking."

Liam covered his mistake quickly. "Oh, aye. I knew that. I was just testing you. I mean, what sort of Muppet would think the F.A. Cup was played this time of year?"

"Very funny. Anyway, I was just calling to say that Aidan's been on the phone."

"About the Chinese girl?"

"Yes. She didn't ring a bell with him so he asked around. Seems there was a young Chinese girl, and I mean very young, on the BDSM scene for about seven years between 2004 and 2011. She worked as a dominatrix in the later years and then disappeared."

"Disappeared, disappeared? Or just took herself off?"

"No one knows. She could be dead or she could be sunning herself in the south of France, but my instinct says that she's back, spending a rainy February in Belfast with Jonathan Carragher."

"Aye well, she'll turn up eventually, I'm sure."

Liam sighed heavily and Craig knew it had more to do with his destination than the girl. Craig could hear a question forming in the silence.

"Boss...do I really...?"

Craig interrupted him. "The other reason I called was to tell you to come back. Des has been called down to help John with the forensics. Until they've finished completely he says he doesn't want you there. His exact words were; 'If Liam comes down we'll end up in the nearest pub and get no work done'."

Liam's first instinct was to shout "Result!" but his sense of duty kicked in, so instead he swallowed hard, barely able to believe what he was about to say.

"God knows I don't ever want to see that place again, boss. But I think one of us should try to speak to the boy we found alive. I'd better keep going."

"Don't worry about the boy. I've been in touch with the social care team and he's being brought to Belfast; to the same foster home as Aurelie."

Liam said something else but it was drowned out by the sound of a lorry racing past, followed by a selection of four letter words. Craig heard Liam's car indicator clicking and then the sound of his engine grinding to a halt as he parked.

"That's better, Liam. I couldn't hear a word you said."

It wasn't true but it allowed Liam to erase anything that he'd prefer Craig hadn't heard.

"Aye, well. What I said was, are you going to let them see each other? Aurelie and the boy?"

"No. Not yet. They need to be interviewed separately otherwise it will weaken our case. Although, at the rate our killers are going, I don't think there'll be anyone left alive to charge with their abuse. But we still have to build the case."

"Has the boy said anything yet?"

"Not a word, apparently. We don't even know where he's from. Davy's working away on a possible I.D. There's a chance he might be from here, but Davy says he thinks middle or eastern European. He's dark, so somewhere like Romania or Bulgaria perhaps."

"Aye, he was very dark. Well, if you're sure there's no reason for me to go down, I'll head back to the ranch. There's plenty for everyone to do."

"Actually, no there isn't, Liam. Davy's gone home; he's set his programmes running and they'll alert his mobile if he needs to come back in. He's limited in what else he can do because it's Sunday. There's no sign of Warner yet, and unless he turns up with some fresh clues there not a lot more we can do today. Annette and Jake have already gone home, so my suggestion is that you do as well."

"And do what?"

Craig laughed. "Whatever you normally do on a Sunday afternoon. Take the kids to the park; watch a Disney DVD, whatever. Just come in raring to go tomorrow morning. We're briefing at eight o'clock."

He stifled a yawn and Liam laughed. "And you're going

home to sleep off that hangover. Pity for the Doc that he can't do the same."

Chapter Twenty-Four

Monday. 2 a.m.

Jonathan had almost finished Warner off, when Mai walked back into the garage and saw what he'd done. Instead of screaming and crying as he'd expected she just gazed down at Warner's bloodied body.

"Is he dead?"

Jonathan shook his head and pushed his hair back from his face with a gloved hand. "Almost, but you can have the final cut."

It was safe to allow her close now; Gerry Warner was long past words. He couldn't hurt anyone anymore.

Mai stared down at the immobile body, her eyes unreadable. But Jonathan knew what was going through her head. She was remembering every time Warner had touched her against her will and every time she'd suffered pain at his hands, either directly or through one of the helpless pawns he'd forced to beat her. He knew what she was thinking because he felt the same way. Warner hadn't just used him to inflict pain; he'd used him in other ways too.

Mai smiled slowly and turned to her lover, stroking his face gently with her small white hand. Warner had laughed at their tears, now they were the ones laughing. And yet…where was the peace she'd expected to feel, now that their last abuser had gone? The thought of it had kept her going through years of disgust and self-harm, struggling to survive by using the only skill that she'd learned.

Even when Jonathan had re-entered her life she'd felt angry and restless, never able to settle, moving from house to apartment and then back again. In their first year together she'd made him paint the rooms four times, each time certain that it would make everything right, until she saw them finished and knew that they had to be changed again. She'd flitted from room to room and chair to chair, with Jonathan always still, in the centre, like the eye of her storm. She'd start to read and then set the book aside, as she wore herself out searching for something that she couldn't define and didn't understand. Peace. She'd never had peace, so how could she possibly know how it felt. The closest she'd ever come was when she was in her lover's arms.

Mai stared down at Gerry Warner's unmoving body and lifted the knife. Perhaps when he was dead peace would finally come. She swung her arm down, landing the blade on his neck with certainty, then she drew it across in one smooth sweep as she'd done three times before. Warner gurgled once as the blood spurted upwards, soaking her face and hands, then there was nothing except silence.

Mai watched as the spurting slowed and then stopped, gazing blindly at it until Warner's pulses ebbed away and only they were left alive. She watched for longer, willing his soul to wander the afterlife in torment and give her some peace as it fled. Jonathan watched her with tears in his eyes, reading her thoughts. No ghost could give Mai the peace that she craved. Her heart ripped open afresh each day, every year of abuse written on it, like a freshly inflicted scar that couldn't heal. Jonathan held his breath as he watched her, knowing the agony she would suffer, once she realised that killing them still hadn't bought the tranquillity she'd pursued for years.

He kept on watching, as Mai deferred the inevitable realisation, saying. "Once we've displayed him, that's when it will be over and we can have a normal life."

They dealt with Warner's body and loaded it into the van, to be displayed somewhere symbolic, now that they couldn't access the school. Tomorrow it would be found, and tomorrow Mai would feel her pain again. And again and again forever, with no hope of peace for her broken mind.

Jonathan drove in silence towards Gerry Warner's final resting place and while Mai gazed eagerly at the road ahead his heart sank. For now she was hopeful, but soon that hope would die and her pain would begin again, then he would have to decide their path. There were only two choices; get Mai the help she needed, or both their deaths.

***

The C.C.U. Monday. 8 a.m.

Nicky lifted the phone before it rang a second time, her smile saying this was going to be a very good day.

"Murder Squad. Can I help you?"

The voice on the other end was familiar, although it normally sounded less flat.

"Hello, Nicky. Is the Super there?"

It was Jack Harris. They used his interview rooms at High Street so often that he usually had a laugh and a joke with Nicky when he called, but not today. Nicky stared at the phone, puzzled, and rang through to Craig. Craig dumped his sports bag in the corner and grabbed the receiver.

"Yes?"

"It's Sergeant Harris, sir. He doesn't sound very happy."

"Put him through. And Nicky…"

"I know. Coffee."

Craig smiled and answered the call, still expecting to hear Jack Harris' usually cheerful voice.

"Morning, Jack. What can I do you for?"

The sigh that followed said this wasn't a social call.

"Sorry to start off your day like this, sir, but a body's been

260

found on my patch."

Craig tightened his grip on the phone. Gerry Warner. It had to be.

"Where?"

"Aye well, that's the problem. It couldn't be any more public. It's been found in the grounds of the City Hall. There's chaos up there."

Belfast City Hall! Craig shook his head for a moment. It didn't fit. OK, they'd made Fitzwilliam Primary School inaccessible by sealing it off, but another school would have fitted their killers' message better, and there were hundreds of those around. Craig closed his eyes for a moment in thought. The City Hall symbolised authority and the killers probably felt they'd been let down by every system in the book. Plus it was bound to cause headlines; he could just imagine the Chronicle's front page later that day.

Craig was silent for so long that Jack thought he'd lost the call.

"Sir? Did you hear me?"

"Yes, sorry, Jack. I was just trying to make sense of it. Is the body recognisable?"

Jack's voice showed his distaste. "Well, it has a face, but…"

"Where in the City Hall?"

"The courtyard near the back. It's near where people get married and they've ceremonies planned for today."

Where Ian and Eileen Carragher had got married as well, most likely. Craig understood now. The killers were commenting on the travesty of that marriage, in the only way they knew how.

"OK, Jack. Who's there now?"

"The body was found by a cleaner at six o'clock. Uniform's been there since then. It's cordoned off, but there isn't a hope in hell of keeping this quiet; there are reporters all over the place already."

Craig smiled, knowing that Davy's girlfriend Maggie was

probably one of them. Jack was still talking.

"We're waiting for forensics and the medical examiner, some Dr Augustus. Doc Winter's off on his travels somewhere."

"Newcastle. It's linked with our case, and so is this."

"Aye, well. That's what I thought."

"You were right to call me, Jack. Can you meet me there in ten?"

"Will do."

Craig clicked the phone off and pulled open his office door, just as Nicky approached with his coffee in her hand.

"Everyone's ready for the briefing."

Craig took the coffee gratefully and gulped it down, then headed for the double-doors.

"Sorry, everyone. Briefing's postponed until twelve. Liam, Annette, come with me. Jake, can you call D.C.I. Hughes and ask him if we can move Edgar Tate's interview to this afternoon. I want you and Annette to come with me to that."

Craig and Liam were in the lift so quickly that Annette struggled to keep up.

"Wait for me."

Liam held the lift doors, shaking his head exaggeratedly from side to side. "That's those high heels, girl. Get yourself a pair of trainers and you'll be able to keep up."

"You shrink a foot and see how much slower it makes you."

Craig pressed the button for the garage. "Stop the bickering you two, or I'll stop your pocket money."

Liam changed tack. "What's the hurry, boss?"

"A dead body outside the City Hall, and it's one of ours."

Annette gawped at him. "Someone killed in the grounds?"

Craig shook his head. "Killed elsewhere and dumped in the grounds more likely. I think it's our killers but I don't have any details yet. Jack said the body was recognisable, but…"

Annette gave Craig a puzzled look. "But it's not a school, sir."

Liam laughed. "No shit, Sherlock."

Craig shot Liam a warning look and turned to Annette.

"They couldn't get near the Fitzwilliam School this time, because we have it sealed-off tight. My thoughts are that they left it at the City Hall as two fingers up to authority. It was also left near the Registry Office, where they perform the marriage ceremonies, so it may have been a comment on the Carragher's marriage. That's just my speculation at the moment, but either way the press are all over it so we need to get there quickly."

"I can just see the headlines."

They all winced, knowing that the press was going to have a field day. They'd managed to keep reporting to a minimum at the school but this was different.

It took five minutes for Craig to drive from Pilot Street and park on the pavement near the Scottish Provident Building at Donegall Square West. As they approached the Hall from the side entrance Liam couldn't resist a quip.

"Here. The last time there were this many peelers at the City Hall was when they voted the flag down in 2012."

Annette thumped his arm. "You've the tact of a brick. Some people were annoyed about that."

"Ow! I was only saying."

Craig flashed his badge at the guard by the entrance and he waved them in. "It's in the courtyard, sir."

As they approached the focus of attention Craig could see that something didn't look right. Even less right than dead bodies normally looked. Instead of the sheet being spread lengthways, to hide a corpse, it was covering a mound with a prominence on top. Craig strode over to the sergeant in charge. The man was sweating and pale beneath his natural tan and Craig had already worked out the cause. Craig extended his hand, introducing himself. The sergeant shook hands firmly, belying his pallor.

"I'm Sergeant Rutter from Stranmillis, sir. They sent me down to assist High Street." He gestured towards the covered pile. "I have to say, this is a first for me."

Craig nodded. If it was what he thought it was, it would be a first for all of them, although Liam had seen some sights during The Troubles that were much worse. Rutter waved Craig on to take a look, so he gloved up and tentatively lifted the edge of the sheet, peering underneath.

Staring back at him was the disembodied head of Gerry Warner. The neck was bloodied but the face looked just like the man they'd interviewed a few days before. His eyes were closed as if he was sleeping; he looked far more placid than he deserved. At least he wouldn't be harming any more children now.

As Craig stared at the head the penny dropped. Of course... He knew that the voice on the porno tape had rung a bell, now he recognised who it belonged to; Gerry Warner. He'd been using children for years, now, if they were right, two of them had taken their revenge.

Craig was jerked back to the present by Liam's booming voice. "What have you got, boss?"

Craig beckoned him over and lifted the sheet. Liam let out a long whistle.

"Boyso, he must have really pissed them off."

As Annette joined them Craig dropped the sheet quickly and straightened up.

"I'd like to see, sir."

"Are you sure, Annette? It's basically Gerry Warner chopped into bits. The lump at the top is his decapitated head."

Annette's eyes widened and she turned on her heel and stood beside the sergeant. "Here is close enough for me."

"Very wise. Sergeant Rutter, do you know when we can get the remains moved? The press are having a party out there."

Liam interjected. "Aye, and our old friend Ray Mercer is there, front and centre."

Mercer was The Belfast Chronicle's star reporter, not because of the elegance of his writing but for the sensationalist trash he spewed out. It wasn't art but it did guarantee them readers.

Craig frowned. "Where is he?"

"Over by the front gate, boss. Never you worry; if he puts one foot on the grass I'll have him."

"Stay away from him, Liam. Remember what happened the last time you two met at close quarters."

Liam thought back to the encounter and smiled, then checked himself as he caught Craig's warning glance.

"Aye, all right. God, there's no fun in life anymore."

Just then the small, slim shape of Mike Augustus walked towards them, accompanied by a flock of white-suited C.S.I.s. Des Marsham dandered in behind them at a leisurely pace. Craig grinned when he saw Des coming. His beard was halfway down his chest these days and there were flecks of white amongst the black that he hadn't noticed before. In a few more years he'd make a brilliant Santa Claus.

Des smiled pleasantly at Annette and nodded at Craig. Liam cracked the first joke.

"Here, Des, Movember's over. Can you not afford a razor?"

Des grinned and stroked his beard. "Now, Liam, there's no need to be jealous, just because I'm a real man." He patted Liam's smooth cheek. "Worse than a teenage boy."

Craig laughed and interrupted. "Nice to see you again, Des. I thought you were down in the Mournes with John."

"I came back last night. Annie gave me my orders. What have we got?"

"I've made the I.D. already, but do the usual stuff."

"How did you I.D. him? I heard he was in bits."

"His head's intact and we interviewed him last week. His name's Dr Gerry Warner. He's a suspect in our case."

"Was a suspect."

"True. Listen; when you've done your thing can you just confirm the type of knife for me. If there are any prints so much the better, but I'm pretty sure we know who it was."

Des arched an eyebrow curiously.

"I'll tell you when I'm sure, Des." Craig stopped suddenly and thought again. "Actually, I have a better idea. When's John expected back from Newcastle?"

"After lunch. He's done what he can down there. They're shipping any remains they've found up to the lab for a closer look."

"Good, then how do you both fancy coming to a briefing this afternoon around four?"

Des smiled and his lips disappeared in a carpet of hair. He made Annette think of an aging teddy bear. It was a nicer image than what was under the sheet. Craig smiled, reading Annette's thoughts.

"I'll take that as a yes then and see you both there. There's a lot to catch you up on."

Craig headed for the car, deep in thought. Liam hung a few feet behind him with Annette, watching Ray Mercer carefully out of the corner of his eye. The hatchet-faced reporter spotted them and forced his way through the crowd of onlookers, catching up with Liam as he emerged from the Hall's side gate.

"Any comment for the Chronicle, D.I. Cullen? Our readers have a right to know."

Liam spun round towards him, his pale face blank. "It's D.C.I. Cullen, Mercer. And your readers will have to wait for an official statement."

Mercer's face twisted into a sly smile. "D.C.I., well, well. Police brutality obviously pays."

Annette saw Liam's expression change and moved quickly to intervene. "Move along, Mr Mercer. There's nothing for you here."

Mercer grinned at her but the smile didn't reach his eyes. "If it isn't the faithful sidekick. Frumpy Cop herself."

Liam saw Annette's face fall and he was just about to move in, when Craig stepped between Mercer and his prey. He turned to face him then moved so close that only Mercer heard his words. Whatever Craig said it had the desired effect. Mercer spat out a few expletives for bravado, then disappeared into the crowd. Craig headed back to the car and no-one spoke until they were parked in the basement of the C.C.U.

Annette turned towards Craig, deliberately catching his eye. "What did you say to Mercer, sir?"

Liam leaned forward over the back seat. "Aye, what was it? Whatever it was he looked scundered."

Craig stared straight ahead for a moment then he sighed exaggeratedly, as if he'd made up his mind to confess.

"I told him there were a lot of murderers who hadn't liked his reporting on their cases, and some of them would soon be out on parole. His home address might accidentally find its way into their possession."

Liam's jaw dropped and Annette gawped at him. "Sir, you didn't. That's threatening behaviour."

Craig smiled inscrutably and climbed out of the car, leaving them wondering whether he had or not.

***

Davy was sitting head-down focussing on something when the group entered the squad-room, and Nicky smiled at them as if they were her children, back for the school holidays after not having seen them for weeks. She jumped to her feet and pulled out a box, opening it to reveal a selection of cream cakes.

"The coffee's on and you've been working so hard all weekend that I thought a treat was in order."

Before she could finish her sentence Liam had dipped his hand into the box. He lifted a chocolate éclair and slipped it vertically into his mouth, with all the delicacy of a python swallowing its prey. Annette averted her eyes and stared into the box for what seemed like forever, finally settling on a cream slice. She was just about to lift it when she thought better of it and turned abruptly towards her desk. Nicky stared after her curiously.

"What's the matter, Annette?"

Annette smiled thinly. "Oh nothing. I just need to lose a few pounds."

Nicky scrutinised her with an honesty that no man would dare employ. Annette was a size twelve and muscular. She circuit trained and took a dance class. She wasn't fat, just strong, and that was exactly what Nicky said. Annette stared down at her legs. They were muscular but lean, but Ray Mercer's caustic remark had hit home.

"Do you really think so, Nicky? It's just that Ray Mercer called me Frumpy Cop."

Davy's ears perked up and he loped across the floor at speed. He put his arm around Annette's shoulder comfortingly.

"Mercer's a rude bastard and he hates w…women. Maggie tells me all the time about cruel things he says to girls in the office."

Annette stared up at him eagerly. "He does?"

Davy nodded firmly. "Yes he does. His w…wife left him and he's got even w…worse since then." He swooped on a cream donut. "Ignore him. Honestly."

Davy smiled and wandered back to his desk and Annette decided the cream slice was a good idea after all. Silence reigned for a moment while they ate their cakes, then Liam slurped his coffee and considered Annette with what he thought was an expert eye.

"Mercer didn't say you were fat anyhow. He said you were frumpy. That's different."

Nicky hissed at him. "Liam. For God's sake!"

His eyes widened innocently. "What? I was only saying…"

"You were only saying far too much. Annette's style is her own business."

Craig thought it was time to intervene. "OK. That's it. Liam, leave Annette alone. Annette, ignore Mercer, he's a sad little man and he's hardly a fashion plate, is he? You have two minutes to finish the cakes Nicky very kindly provided, and then everyone get back to work."

He wandered into his office to the sound of Nicky

whispering. "Come shopping with me next Saturday, Annette and we'll see what we can do."

Craig smiled and shook his head, picturing Nicky's eclectic results.

***

"What time are you interviewing Tate, Aidan?"

"One o'clock. Can you make it?"

Craig glanced quickly at the clock. It was twelve-forty. They were waiting for Warner's body to be processed, Davy had all the checks running for his various I.D.s and they had an alert out on Jonathan Carragher and the girl, by description if not by name. John and Des would update him on everything else at the briefing. There seemed little to stop him nipping off for an hour.

"Yep. We'll see you there in ten."

He dropped the phone quickly and pulled open his office door.

"Nicky, I'm heading to High Street to interview a suspect with D.C.I. Hughes. Find me there if you need me."

He glanced around the floor. Davy was staring intently at his screen. Annette was nowhere to be seen, but she wouldn't be far, and Jake was sitting at his desk, head bowed. Craig walked over and stared at his screen. He was typing-up his account of the Newcastle discovery. It could wait.

"Right Jake, find Annette. We're taking a trip to High Street. D.C.I. Hughes has Edgar Tate waiting for interview."

Jake's face lit up. Craig thought it was probably because the interview was the lesser of two evils, although it was a toss-up which was worse. Write a report on finding children's remains in an underground prison, with all the memories that evoked, or spend an hour listening to a pervert deny that he'd done anything wrong.

Ten minutes later they were pushing through the steel door

of High Street Station. Jack was nowhere to be seen so Craig tapped on the reception window. A pair of dark eyes appeared from underneath the desk. They were followed by a familiar grin.

"Hello, Sandi. Could you buzz us in, please?"

Sandi Masters smiled at Craig and Annette then gave Jake a curious look. Craig took the hint.

"Have you two not met before?"

Jake shook his head.

"Sandi, this is Sergeant Jake Mclean. He's with on secondment to us from Stranmillis. Jake, this is Constable Sandi Masters. She keeps Jack in line."

Sandi smiled and buzzed them in. "Sergeant Harris is in the back. He wasn't feeling very well so I told him to take a break."

Craig shot her a concerned look and pushed through the staff-room door. On a worn couch set against one wall, Jack Harris was sipping tea and looking pale. An image of his father having his heart attack the year before filled Craig's mind and he walked over to Harris anxiously.

"Jack. Are you OK? Sandi said…"

Jack waved away his concern and, as if to underline how well he was feeling, he bit firmly into a biscuit. He smiled at Jake. "Hello again, lad. Is the Super here keeping you busy?"

"He is indeed."

Craig watched Jack's face closely. Something was amiss but it wasn't physical. He grabbed the nearest seat.

"What's wrong? You're not dying or you wouldn't be eating biscuits and chatting." His father could barely speak when he was ill. "So what is it?"

Jack waved his hand vaguely in the direction of the cells. "Ach. I'm just being a stupid old man, I suppose, but there are some crimes that I really can't take."

Craig nodded. They all felt revulsion at this case.

Jack continued. "Sandi hasn't seen the file, so she doesn't know what's bothering me."

Craig would lay money on Sandi not knowing because Jack was protecting her. Jack talked on.

"I don't mind what these weirdoes get up to in their free time, but involving that little French girl..." He shook his head in disgust. "I have a granddaughter that age and if anyone touched her..." His face flushed. "Well, he wouldn't be walking for long, that's a fact." He shook his head in disgust. "Innocent, that's what children are, and that bastard in the cells throws a party to ruin one of them."

He lapsed into silence and the others said nothing. What was there to be said? None of them disagreed. The only person who did was sitting in a cell. If Edgar Tate was guilty their job was to make sure he stayed there for a long time.

Just then Aidan Hughes bounced energetically through the door. He read the mood immediately and tempered his own, pouring a cup of tea and gulping it down. Then he rubbed his hands together.

"Right lads and lady, what do you say we give Mr Tate and his brief a run for their money? Marc, you happy that I lead and you chip in?"

Craig nodded. He might have the rank but animals like Tate were Aidan's stock in trade.

Craig turned to Jake and Annette. "Observe from the viewing room, please. Jack, I take it you want to be as far away from this one as possible?"

"You're dead right, I do." He glanced at his watch. "In fact, I think I'll lock the doors for an hour and take Sandi out to lunch if you're OK with that?"

Craig nodded. "I'll get Nicky to take your calls and we'll hear the front door if it rings."

"Right then. I'll see you at one o'clock." Harris grimaced. "I don't envy you your task."

They headed into the interview room. Hughes first, then Craig. Jake and Annette peeled off into the viewing room. Now that Gerry Warner was dead, everyone likely to be murdered had gone. That left them with two killers to catch, a house full of bones and two children who couldn't help them. Edgar Tate was their best chance of getting answers, even if they had to cut him a deal.

The door to the interview room swung open and the two men seated at the table turned. One with startled eyes, the other looking bored. The bored one stood immediately and extended his hand, only to find it barely touched by Aidan and ignored by Craig.

It was curious the way solicitors always stood when the police entered interview rooms. Craig had long ago stopped believing that it was good manners; he'd seen too many of them drunk in town to credit them with that. No, he had another theory. They stood to ensure that the police knew who the good guy was and who the bad, in case they were mistaken for the accused. They obviously weren't sure people could tell the difference without a hint.

There often wasn't much difference; plenty of lawyers sailed close to the wind. Their experience last summer with Judge Dawson was proof that the judiciary weren't above reproach. Dawson was doing twenty years in Maghaberry to prove it.

Hughes took his seat across from Tate and Craig sat beside him, facing Tate's brief. They turned on the tape and ran through the legalities and formalities, then they sat in silence, no-one saying a word. Craig gazed at Edgar Tate across the table. It was a freezing day and he was cold in his heavy suit, yet Tate was sweating profusely in a thin shirt. The sweat of a guilty man. Correction. The sweat of a guilty man who'd been caught. He doubted if Tate had produced a drop of sweat when he was partying and abusing kids.

Tate ran his hand nervously under his dark shirt collar and Craig noticed its designer motif. He had plenty of money, there was no doubt of that, but the law didn't care how much he had in the bank. He stared at the man's greying hair, cut in a style that gave his age away. Tate was in his fifties somewhere and

Aurelie was a child.

Craig wanted to beat him to a pulp, but instead he smiled, so coldly that Tate glanced away. Aidan had interviewed men like this a thousand times before and Craig didn't know how he could stand it. Tate hadn't said a word yet and he already wanted to kick away his chair.

Suddenly the silence was broken by Aidan Hughes' strong voice. "Mr Tate, your solicitor will have told you how much trouble you're in. What I don't want is for you to use this interview to deepen that hole. This is your opportunity to give us something, anything that might be used as mitigation in your case."

He tapped the pile of papers sitting in front of him.

"We have you organising a party where prostitution occurred."

Tate leaned forward to object but Hughes raised a hand to still him. "The party occurred in your home and you were present and conscious and wearing a costume that clearly indicated that you were joining in. Whoever organised the party, you allowed it to happen on your premises; you are responsible. There were also Class A substances being used; charge number two. Now, I couldn't care less what consenting adults get up to in private, as long as there's no prostitution or drugs involved. Even allowing for that, a court might be inclined to be lenient if we could put forward mitigation."

Craig watched the solicitor as Aidan said 'mitigation' and his ears pricked up. Aidan was throwing them a bone on the first two charges. But there was always the caveat…

"However, there was a female minor present at the party. A little girl of eleven year's old. She was in a position to witness sexual behaviour, which at very least is child endangerment." Aidan leaned forward so suddenly that Tate jerked back and his voice grew hard and loud. "And what's more the child was bruised, and there were signs that she had been sexually assaulted. Courts take a very dim view of that, Mr Tate, and I take an even dimmer one."

Tate started to bluster, his eyes wild with panic. "I didn't know she was there! She was nothing to do with me!"

Hughes sat back slowly and Craig smiled to himself. He didn't know how Aidan interviewed scum like this, give him ordinary decent criminals any day, but he was a master at it, there was no doubt of that.

"Ah, you see, now that's our problem, right there, Mr Tate. The girl was at your party, in your house and she was physically and sexually abused. Unless you can tell us how she got there, we'll have to charge you with all of that."

Aidan Hughes shook his head exaggeratedly, his face grim. All that was missing was the black square on his head before he condemned Tate to death. Edgar Tate's eyes widened and he turned frantically to his brief, whispering something in his ear. They watched the exchange knowing exactly what was coming next. They were right. The solicitor turned to Hughes.

"I'd like five minutes alone with my client."

Hughes nodded curtly and they stood and left the room. As they stood in the corridor outside Aidan Hughes rubbed his face. His next question surprised Craig.

"Do you smoke, Marc?"

"No, sorry. Do you need a cigarette?"

"Yes. I don't smoke, but there are times when I almost wish I did."

Craig smiled. He knew what Aidan meant. He had the odd cigar at times of strong emotion, like Italian family weddings and when Man United was in the cup. Now seemed like one of those times. An image of Julia's twenty-a-day habit popped into his mind, crushing the inclination.

The interview room door opened and the solicitor emerged, beckoning them back in. He spoke first.

"My client is willing to give you some information, in exchange for the charges about the girl being dropped, and a recommendation for leniency on the other charges."

Hughes glanced at Tate and then back at his brief. "It depends what he tells us."

He folded his arms and sat back in his chair, waiting to be convinced. The solicitor motioned Edgar Tate on. Patches of perspiration had soaked through Tate's expensive shirt now, making his underarms and chest wall black. His voice squeaked its way through his first few words and then Tate gradually found his pace. What followed was a tale of 'poor me' and 'not me' and 'a big boy did it and ran away'.

Eventually Craig had had enough. He glanced at Hughes, seeking permission to interject, and then he spoke. Craig didn't just speak; he banged his palm down hard on the Formica table's top.

"Enough! I've heard nothing that would make me change my mind about the charges." He pointed his finger at Tate. "You really expect us to believe that the girl magically appeared in your house, and you didn't even know she was there until the police arrested you? That's rubbish! You brought her there and you're going to prison for a very long time."

Tate leaned forward desperately. The sinews in his neck stood out like cords and his eyes were wild.

"I didn't know anything about her. I don't even know what she looks like. I wouldn't involve kids for God's sake. I have two of my own."

Poor kids. Craig could see that even the solicitor agreed. Craig kept up the pressure, his voice more intense with each word.

"Who then? Who brought her there? You know, so don't lie to us. Give us their names."

Tate looked frantically at his brief then pleaded with Craig. "I can't. He'd kill me. Honestly he would, he's killed before."

He? Was there only one man behind Aurelie's abduction?

"Then help us get him off the street. Give us his name!"

Craig's last words were shouted so loudly that Jake would have heard them even without the intercom. He peered through the two-way mirror, marvelling at Craig's change in tone. This wasn't the smooth, quiet boss he knew. It was a man who would stop at nothing to get the truth. He was just wondering how far Craig would go when Tate blurted out the name.

"Ryan. His name's Ryan Carragher. He supplies children to some of the real perverts." Tate raised his hands in denial. "I have nothing to do with it and I had no idea that he'd brought one to my party. He knows my rules. One party every six months, when my wife takes the kids to America to visit her Mum. Consenting adults only."

Craig slumped back in his seat, stunned. Ryan Carragher! The Carraghers had been running a family business, with only Jonathan innocent of any abuse! Jonathan had been a victim. Did he know what his big brother had been doing? He shook his head, no, he couldn't have. Ryan had taken them all in with his act. The grieving son who they hadn't wanted to shock by telling him about his parent's sordid private life. What a joke! This was the uneasy feeling he'd had when they'd met Ryan in the relative's room.

Hughes stared at Craig and then at Tate, then he spoke into the tape. "Five minute break while I confer with my colleague. D.C.I. Hughes and Superintendent Craig are leaving the room."

Aidan rose and Craig followed quickly. They walked silently down the corridor then pushed through the fire-door to the car-park outside. Craig sucked hard at the fresh air.

"Shit, Marc! Had you any idea?"

"None. I spoke to Ryan Carragher two days ago, as a relative. There was something about him that made me uneasy but I'd no idea that it was this! He gave nothing away."

Hughes was pacing. "This was a family factory. I've only heard about something like this once before, in the States. The whole family was in on the abuse. Shit! I can't believe this."

Craig shook his head. "Not all of them. Jonathan Carragher and Ian Carragher's illegitimate daughter were both victims.

Now they're getting their revenge."

Hughes spun round to face him. "That means they'll kill Ryan Carragher next."

Craig shook his head slowly. "I'm not so sure. He and Jonathan are still on speaking terms. They wouldn't be if Jonathan knew Ryan had been involved."

"So he managed to hide his involvement somehow. How?"

"Ryan's over a decade older than Jonathan. He went away to college soon after Ian Carragher remarried. Perhaps Ryan was already a paedophile, or perhaps when he found out what his father was up to he saw a niche that he could carve out for himself."

"Children for parties?"

"Perhaps. But the Carraghers and Warner were already using children at the school. When that closed they moved to Newcastle and they would have needed another supply as well."

"But where does Ryan get them from?"

Craig stared at him blankly.

"The children. The Carraghers lost their supply once the school closed, so where did Aurelie and the kids they held in Newcastle come from? She's not local and the chances are the boy isn't either. Is it random abduction or something more organised?"

Suddenly Craig knew. The words had been screaming at them and they hadn't wanted to hear it. Child trafficking. Aurelie and the other children had been trafficked and brought to Northern Ireland by Ryan Carragher. It had to be how they'd ended up at the Newcastle house. That meant that Ryan Carragher might only be the local boss of a larger kidnapping ring.

"They were trafficked. They must have been. This could be huge. If Ryan Carragher is getting those kids from abroad he isn't doing it by himself, and there must be a big enough market here to make it worth his while."

Hughes' expression alternated between horror and glee. He

settled on the latter. "We can crack this, Marc. Between us and Interpol we can get these bastards, I feel it in my bones."

Craig thought for a minute then nodded. "OK. At the moment Ryan Carragher thinks he's safe. He's playing the grieving son and Jonathan has no idea what he did. We need to find a way to use that."

"And we need to keep Tate quiet, or he'll tip Ryan off and blow everything."

"We'll persuade him of that while Davy sees if he can find a trail from the house back to Ryan Carragher. And we need to see what the Uniforms in Newcastle have found."

"Surely the kids will be able to I.D. Ryan Carragher?"

"Perhaps, but we need to be careful how we involve them, otherwise some slick bastard of a lawyer will get him off. And you can be sure of one thing; Ryan will be able to afford the best. Whoever he's involved with abroad won't want him going down and starting to talk."

Craig paused for a moment and Hughes knew he'd had an idea.

"What've you thought of?"

Craig glanced at his watch. "OK, quickly. I've got an idea for a sting. Tell me what you think and then I'll run it past the CC…"

Five minutes later they'd agreed the details and Craig turned to re-enter the building.

"OK. Let's go back in and charge Tate with the drugs and prostitution. We'll say we're going to investigate Ryan Carragher and expect his full co-operation, and that any hope he has of a deal will go down the tubes if he tries to tip Carragher off. I'll see what else we can dig up before the briefing." He glanced at Hughes. "It's at four o'clock. Can you make it?"

Hughes grinned, showing a set of large white teeth. "I wouldn't miss it for the world."

***

Jonathan gazed down at Mai's sleeping form, watching as she cried and fought invisible foes in her dreams. He wondered what came next. All of the people who had hurt them were dead, Mai had had her revenge and none of them would ever hurt children again. But it still wasn't enough to give her peace. He leaned over and kissed her pale cheek, surprised again by how soft her skin was.

Mai looked so defenceless that Jonathan shuddered, remembering the first time that Warner had told him to hit her. He'd refused for as long as he could, as her thin arms shook, rattling the clumsy chains they'd used to suspend her. Mai had been so young and frail, but even then her courage had shone through her eyes. She'd told him to go ahead, without making any judgement. She'd known he hadn't wanted to do it, he was as much a victim as she was; and years later her acceptance had turned to love.

He would have done anything to give her peace, so when she'd suggested they take revenge he'd gone along with it, in the hope that it would mend her tortured heart. But it hadn't. Their abusers were dead now and any children still at the house would be freed, yet still Mai was crying in her sleep. He didn't know what more he could do.

If he took her to a doctor it would all come out, and besides, the one time he'd suggested it she hadn't spoken to him for a week. That only left one thing. Jonathan shook his head at its finality and resolved to find another way, then he wrapped Mai in his arms and drifted back to sleep.

***

The C.C.U. 3 p.m.

Craig had called them all into his small office, and there were people sitting or standing against every wall. He apologised for the crush.

"I wanted to speak to you in here in case anyone walked onto the floor. The investigation's at a very important stage and we have Drs Winter and Marsham joining us at four for the briefing. D.C.I. Hughes as well."

Liam interjected. "If he can drag himself away from the sunbed long enough." He laughed at his own joke and Craig joined in.

"Very funny. OK. Let's go round and see what's new. Davy, start us off please."

Davy was standing beside Liam against the back wall. They looked like very tall bookends.

"OK, boss." He opened a cardboard folder and distributed the sheets inside. On the top was a picture of Aurelie. "You have a picture of Aurelie as s...she is now. Turn the page and you'll see a younger girl, that's Aurelie w...when she was eight. The next page was when s...she was five and so on." He smiled at Craig. "We've had a bit of luck."

Annette leaned forward. "You've found her?"

Davy nodded and pushed back his smooth black hair. "W... We think so. I sent these through to the Gendarmes and the school in the Loire. The school phoned an hour ago with an I.D."

Craig leaned forward eagerly. "Who is she, Davy?"

"Her name's Aurelie Masson. Her date of birth is May 2002. S...She's eleven years old, as she said. The s...school didn't recognise her because she left there w...when she was seven, to move to another school. When they saw the five-year-old version they I.D.ed her straight away."

"And the Gendarmes?"

Davy nodded again. "They've located her mother and they're flying her over tomorrow. Apparently Aurelie was abducted from the garden of her own house." He swallowed hard. "S... she was taken just before her eighth birthday."

Craig slumped back in his chair. "Three years.... And they've been looking for her all this time?"

Davy nodded. "Apparently they've had police, private investigators, the w…works. The marriage broke down because of the s…strain, but the parents kept on looking."

Craig thought of the years that Aurelie had been a prisoner, trotted out for parties to be abused by scum. They were lucky she was still alive. Davy was still talking.

"The boy has turned out to be easier to find. It w…was a bit of a fluke actually. I put out his photos everywhere I could think of and got a call from the Lebanese police. They say he's called Nassib Bastany, and he w…went missing from Beirut a year ago."

Lebanon! How far did the kidnapper's reach stretch?

Liam jumped in. "That fits with the news from Newcastle. They said the boy didn't say a word and he isn't any better now he's with the girl. But if he doesn't speak English or French then maybe that explains it?"

Craig shook his head. "It wouldn't have stopped him saying some words in Arabic, if that's his native tongue. He could be mute from shock, or he's chosen to be."

Annette nodded. Elective mutism; she'd seen it with abuse victims when she'd been a nurse. Jake signalled to speak and Craig smiled at his politeness. Another few months with Liam and that would change.

"I spoke to the foster carers, sir, and they said the boy's eating OK and playing with toys."

Craig nodded and turned back to Davy. "Lebanon, Davy? Isn't that where they cook using Tagines?"

Liam looked puzzled. "What's a Tagine when it's at home?"

Annette smiled knowledgeably. "It's a special cooking pot used mostly in North Africa and the middle-East."

"And Cyprus."

Craig nodded. "It's also the name of Ryan Carragher's restaurant."

Liam and Davy looked confused. Craig put them out of their misery. He updated them on their interview with Tate, and his revelation that Ryan Carragher was trafficking children into the country to be abused.

"You're sure, boss?"

"Positive."

"Ryan Carragher, well there you go…"

Liam whistled and Annette shook her head.

"To think I was nice to him about his parents."

"You were right to be, Annette. Innocent until proved guilty. It probably reassured him that he wasn't a suspect."

Liam cut in. "He wasn't. Then. Do you want him picked up?"

Craig shook his head firmly. "No. I want him to believe he's still not a suspect. Ryan Carragher's to be treated exactly like a grieving relative." He scanned their faces sternly. "If anyone thinks they can't maintain that pretence with him, then tell me now. There's no shame in it."

Annette nodded. "If you don't mind, I'd…"

"Not a problem, Annette. I'll find it hard to pretend myself." He looked at the others. "Liam? Jake?"

"We'll be fine, boss. Just tell us what you want done."

Craig's voice became excited. "I know it's ambitious, but Aidan and I want the whole trafficking ring, or as many of them as we can get."

Davy broke in with a "Yay" and Annette smiled. It was like a meeting of the Famous Five.

Craig continued. "I've a call booked with Interpol at three-thirty and I'm meeting Chief Constable Flanagan at five o'clock, to see what we can do at this end." He glanced at the clock. It was twenty-five past three. "Let's keep going till Nicky puts the call through." He turned to Liam. "Liam, anything?"

Liam puffed out his cheeks then exhaled. "Aye. Plenty of news from Newcastle but none of it good. They've scanned the grounds with ultrasound and found more graves." He paused, as if reluctant to say what came next. "They're…they're nearly all child-sized, boss."

282

"Oh God."

"Aye…but it gets worse. They did the same in the basement of the Down Hartley Hotel and they've found bodies in the walls and floor. I've spoken to the management and they've agreed to shut it down until further notice." He shook his head. "There's three acres of ground there, as well two annexes. Forensics will be there all bloody year." His voice took on a more cheerful tone. "Still, anyone who fancies can have a free night's stay in a five star."

They all grimaced and chorus of 'no thanks' followed. It was interrupted by Nicky opening the door, squeezing Jake into the corner behind it.

"That's Interpol on the line, sir."

Craig nodded and everyone readied to leave. "OK. We'll pick this up at four o'clock. But good work everyone. We're getting there."

"Aye. And when we've sorted this lot out we might finally catch our murder perps."

***

Ryan Carragher chopped the meat into thick cubes and placed it in the Tagine. He covered it with herbs and apricots then left it ready for that night's evening meal. He smiled as he worked, thinking about the plods he'd spoken to two days before. They hadn't suspected a thing, treating him like a grieving son who was bravely suffering his loss.

His loving parents. That was a joke. Maybe his Dad hadn't been a bad man, but God was he weak. He could run rings around him by the time he was twelve. He'd even managed to convince him that throwing girls down in the playground and climbing on top of them had just been a game, no matter what the headmaster thought. Although he'd loved his Mum and missed her when she died, she'd always been more suspicious of his games.

If she'd lived he could never have realised his potential. As it was, he'd been well on the way to being a child-lover by the time Eileen Burns had married his Dad. With her dominatrix tendencies and her access to the BDSM scene, it hadn't taken him long to find his niche. He'd hated the bitch but she'd had her uses.

His Dad had taken some persuading, but Eileen kept him in his place. Soon he was chatting online with lots of like-minded individuals across the world and a new Northern Irish franchise had been born.

Ryan wiped his hands on a tea towel and pushed through the fire exit into the yard. He lit a cigarette and took a drag, then leaned back against the wall, deep in thought. The plods had found the French girl at the party and they'd managed to locate the Newcastle house. He shrugged. So what? Once it stopped being a crime scene he would inherit the land. Jonathan was so fucked-up he wouldn't even know he was entitled to half.

He'd sell up and start again somewhere else, abroad. That was one thing about child molesting, it was an international game. He racked his brains for anything at the house that could connect him to it or the French girl. There was nothing. His parents were the perverts, officer, he'd been totally unaware.

He was free and clear. Free to weep his way insincerely through their funerals and, after a decent period of time, get on with his life. Ryan smiled lasciviously, thinking of the young girl who was being imported the following day. By life he meant the boring day-to-day stuff everyone did, but as for pleasure... well, there was no need to slow down on that. He slipped his smartphone from his pocket and connected to the web. Then deeper; to the Dark Web and his favourite chat-room, where everyone spoke different languages, but the meaning was always the same.

***

The C.C.U. 4 p.m.

Everyone had arrived for the briefing, been tea-ed and coffee-ed, and all the banter had died down by the time Craig got off the phone. He emerged from his office like a mole into the light and Nicky thrust a cup into his hand. She lifted her pad to take notes.

"Are you sure you want to hear this, Nick? It's ugly stuff."

She nodded. "It's fine, sir. If it helps catch these creeps then I'd like to help."

Craig turned to the semi-circle of people, all men except for Nicky and Annette. He needed to do something about that. "Right. We've only got an hour."

Nicky leaned in. "Actually, sir. I made your appointment with the C.C. at five-thirty, just in case."

He smiled. "Correction, we've got about eighty minutes. Right, I'd like to hear from John and Des first, if that's OK?"

Des took a drink and signalled John to start. John took off his glasses and rubbed them against his sleeve, something he always did when things were getting dark.

"Right. I'll start with our adult murder victims then move on to the Newcastle house, if that works for everyone?"

He was answered by a series of nods.

"We have four adult murder victims now. Eileen Carragher, her husband Ian, Alan Rooney and finally, this morning, Gerry Warner. Eileen Carragher and Rooney were killed in the same way, sliced slowly until they almost bled to death, then finally finished off with a last cut to the throat. Both had their faces mutilated, they were then publicly displayed in the playground of the school where they worked. Ian Carragher died before they slit his throat and he was left at the school as well. His face was unmarked."

He took a sip of coffee and restarted.

"The symbolism of a school has since become obvious and you'll hear later about links with another school. The method of killing is one that was used in China between 900 AD and 1905. It's called the Ling Chi, the slow death, the slow slicing, or the death of a thousand cuts. It was reserved for particularly heinous crimes and designed to publicly humiliate, inflict maximum pain and destroy the body so that the soul had a rough time in the hereafter."

Liam boomed across the room. "Hell wouldn't be bad enough for this bunch."

John pushed his glasses up his nose and nodded. "Quite. There was an additional factor in Ian Carragher's case that Des will tell you about. But first I'll move onto Gerry Warner. He also underwent the Ling Chi, but in his case, and I'm assuming this is because the school was inaccessible, he was left in the grounds of Belfast City Hall this morning."

Aidan Hughes burst out laughing. "Seriously?" He turned to look at Craig and saw it was true. "God, you kept that quiet, Marc. I bet that put the Councillors off their Ulster Fries."

Aidan found soul-mates in Des and Liam and they all guffawed. Craig smiled and shook his head, motioning John to go on.

John gave a wry smile.

"There's a funny side to everything, I suppose. The two fingers up to authority by using The City Hall is fairly obvious, but there was something else different about Gerry Warner's body. He was decapitated and dismembered after death and his body parts were left in a heap."

Nicky spluttered and Davy said "Yuk!"

"That's a good word for it, Davy. It was vicious, but there was something more. The cuts used to kill and dismember him were much less frenzied than in the other bodies."

Craig leaned in. "We're pretty sure there are two killers, John. Jonathan Carragher and a girl. Carragher must have dismembered Warner; the girl wouldn't have had the strength. Couldn't the difference be explained by that?"

John shook his head firmly. "No it's something else. The Ling

286

Chi on Warner was also much less vicious and frenzied. I think one of your killers is calm and one is near breaking point. If the boy performed the Ling Chi on Warner and dismembered him, and the girl did the Ling Chi on the others that would make more sense. Either way, there's something about the Ling Chi in this case that was less vicious than before."

Craig interrupted. "Perhaps the boy did Warner precisely because the girl hated him too much. After all, Warner was the one who led her torture."

John shrugged. "Perhaps. Or perhaps she's just too near the edge." He turned to Des. "Des, can you tell us about the forensics for these deaths?"

Des nodded and brushed a crumb off his beard. Nicky was certain that something was building its nest in it.

"You already know about the woman's footsteps at the first scene, well, Warner's scene gave us even more. There are clear marks of a man's trainer, so we've made a cast of those for you to match, when you have your man. And there are fingerprints all over the place. The first scenes barely had a print to find, only that small one at Eileen Carragher's scene. This time we have prints on Warner's body, hairs on the sheet, everything. So either they think they won't be caught or they're starting not to care."

Craig interrupted. "I don't think they care anymore. They've done what they set out to do. Take revenge." He stopped, thinking about Ryan Carragher. The killers definitely didn't know about his proclivities or he would be dead as well.

"Well, either way, we have lots of stuff to go on with Warner, which is great. On the other bodies, none of them had any pain relief in their systems, so the pain you imagine was exactly what they felt. In fact…Ian Carragher had sulphuric acid in his wounds, guaranteeing him extra pain. So with all due respect Marc, I don't think they decapitated Warner because they hated him most, I think they just did it because they couldn't hang him and display him in the school playground. I think they

287

hated Ian Carragher more than any of the rest. He's the only one with acid in his wounds. The pain must have been indescribable."

Liam laughed incongruously.

Des took the bait. "OK, what's the joke?"

"Well, if Eileen Carragher was the dominant one, then Ian Carragher might have enjoyed pain. The killers probably thought the acid was a punishment, but he might actually have enjoyed it."

Des started laughing and Annette and Nicky exchanged a look of despair.

Craig shook his head and returned to Des' report. "I agree with Des. I think they used the acid on Ian Carragher because they hated him most. He was Jonathan's father. He was supposed to look after him. Eileen Burns, Warner and Rooney had no blood tie to Jonathan, but Ian Carragher did and he didn't protect him."

Aidan interrupted. "And the girl?"

Craig nodded. "I'll come back to her in a moment. Des?"

"Right. There were traces of engine oil on all of them, the grade used in the average car, so the place you're looking for either has a garage, or is a garage. I'll come onto the other forensics when John's finished."

John straightened his papers and brought a sheet forward from the bottom of the pile. He sighed heavily. "OK. The house in Newcastle, or should I say the hell-hole. I've been to Quantico and read the files of their serial killers, and I've consulted on genocides in Eastern Europe and Africa. Let me tell you, this ranks right up there with those." He yawned unexpectedly. The last week had taken its toll.

"Sorry, I'm wrecked. OK. The house is a large detached, set in its own grounds and it was owned outright by the Carraghers. It was bought in 1995 when they married and they moved their sordid little operation there when Marcheson's School closed in 2004. Thanks to Liam and Jake's eagle eyes they found a basement, which if you never have to see it, count yourselves lucky." John focused on his page, his eyes unreadable.

"The basement fed off a door in the main hallway of the house, and extended five hundred metres beyond the house." He turned to Liam with a look of open admiration. "I have no idea how you spotted that outline, Liam. If I hadn't known where it was I would never have noticed it."

"Bomb shelter. My Granny had one on her farm from World War Two. I recognised the raised edge. But Jake had already found the door."

John smiled at Jake and continued. "Well, however you found it, thank God you did, otherwise that little boy would be dead."

He paused and took a gulp of tea then made a face. Nicky took the hint and went to re-boil the kettle.

"Anyway. We got inside the basement and it had a long corridor with rooms off either side." John handed out copies of the floor-plan as he talked. "When I say rooms, I mean cells. Anyone who's been to Kilmainham Jail in Dublin and seen the original cells will know exactly what I mean. Stone walls, no light, and hot and cold running cockroaches."

Annette shuddered.

"There were twenty small cells, all with locked doors, but the real tragedy was the room at the end. It ran the full width of the building and it was full of the most obscene torture paraphernalia I've ever seen outside a medieval text book. Unbelievable stuff. The C.S.I.s are still working on it and they'll be there for a long time yet."

Nicky returned and pressed a fresh cup of tea into John's hand. He took it gratefully and drank as he talked. "In each of the cells was a pile..." He stopped abruptly, unable to speak, and signalled Des to carry on.

"In each of the cells was a pile of rags, which on closer inspection turned out to be remnants of children's clothes covering human bones. I'll hand you back to John on the bones in a moment, but for now I'll cover the forensic side. We have prints from every cell, some adult and some from children. We're working our way through them slowly and Davy's helping with that. We've also removed all the torture implements and we're dealing very carefully with any skin and hair we find on those. It's a treasure trove of information and we don't want to miss anything. Forensics will be the only way to I.D. the victims."

Jake leaned in to ask a question. "Did you find any other signs of life, Dr Marsham?"

Des shook his head sadly. "Sorry, no. The only things living were the boy and the cockroaches. He's a lucky little lad."

Craig wondered if the boy would think so when he grew up. The saddest thing about abuse was that the trauma lingered for years. Des continued.

"We moved to the grounds and we've been ultra-sounding there now for two days. Sad to say we've found a number of shallow graves."

Craig broke in. "All children?" He already knew the answer would be no.

Des shook his head. "There's one adult. A female. I can't be certain until we get John's full opinion, but I think she was young. Her skull was fractured. That may have been the cause of death."

Craig was pretty sure it would turn out to be Tian Liu, the girl's mother. He turned to John. He'd recovered enough to eat a biscuit. "John?"

"Des, have you finished on the house?"

Des nodded, glad of the chance to grab a Rich Tea before Liam had eaten them all. There'd been a whole packet at the beginning of the meeting and there were only four left.

John restarted. "The bones in the house are from children aged between four years old and sixteen. Both sexes. We can't be sure of numbers yet. I've had a quick look at the woman's body and I can't say anything other than her skull was shattered by a

290

heavy blow and I'm sure that was the cause of death. She was young, I can tell you that. In her twenties somewhere." He paused, trying not to think about the implications of his next words. "She'd also given birth in the previous few months."

It fitted. Tian Liu had had a daughter with Ian Carragher and been killed soon after, probably by his new wife. Craig bet that it wasn't before she'd been tortured. He took back the briefing for a moment.

"If the body is Tian Liu and she'd given birth soon before, it reinforces our theory that Ian Carragher had a daughter who was half-Chinese. The aged-up boy in Aidan's video was Jonathan Carragher. The girl he was being forced to whip was his half-sister, but I'm betting neither that of them know that even now. I'm pretty sure the voice off-screen belonged to Gerry Warner."

Des turned to Aidan. "I can match the voice patterns if you get me a sample of Warner's voice."

Hughes nodded then spoke. "Your killers are in an incestuous relationship, Marc."

"If they're having a romance, yes. But, as I said, I doubt they know."

John thought out loud. "Imagine if they did. After all they'd been through it could be the final straw. You find some sort of love with the boy who was forced to beat you, only to find out that he's your brother."

"It gets worse, John, but I'll come back to that in a moment. Anything on the hotel, Des?"

Des reached for the last biscuit just a Liam was eyeing it up. He grinned triumphantly at Liam then turned to Craig.

"Yes. Plenty on the hotel. We started in the boiler room and worked our way up from there. It's not good news. There are bodies buried in the floors and walls of the basement, children again. We're scanning the annexes and grounds now, but it's slow going. There are three acres of grass, trees and lake at the hotel. The divers are starting tomorrow."

291

Liam exhaled slowly. The case had started with one death and it was turning into dozens. Craig ran quickly around the room getting everyone to fill in their gaps, then finally he turned to Aidan.

"House party, Aidan."

Aidan paused for a moment, taken aback by what he'd heard, then he launched into the story of the party and the arrests they'd made. Eventually he got to that afternoon's interview with Edgar Tate. When he revealed that Ryan Carragher was involved in an international paedophile ring, their guests nearly fell off their chairs.

Des interrupted. "Let me get this right. Father and Step-mother are into BDSM?"

Craig nodded. "Yep. She was a dominatrix so he was probably the passive one."

Des continued. "Carragher had two sons with his first wife; Ryan and Jonathan, and an illegitimate daughter with the au pair. And he allowed Jonathan to be tortured, and be used to torture his daughter?"

Craig nodded again. "Ian Carragher married Eileen Burns and they started their abuse of children at the school, including Carragher's son and daughter. Then they carried it on at their house in Newcastle."

John interjected. "They may have started the abuse before they married. It would have made sense to be sure of each other before they tied the knot."

Des shook his head. "Hell of a courtship. Meanwhile the elder boy Ryan had left home, then he joins Mummy and Daddy and starts a paedophilic side business of his own. Now Jonathan and his half-sister are taking revenge by killing them all. Yes?"

"Yes."

Des shook his head ruefully. "And I thought my family was bad. The best of this bunch are the girl and her brother."

Craig smiled. "I don't think you'll get much argument on

that." He glanced at the clock. "OK, I've got to go in ten minutes so I want to update you on what else we've found." He gestured at Davy. "Thanks to Davy's skill and efforts we've found the I.D.s of the two children. The girl's mother is flying in from France tomorrow. The boy is from the Lebanon and Davy's liaising on that. I spoke to Interpol an hour ago and they say they've been aware of a child smuggling ring running out of Beirut for some time. The children are stolen all over Europe and the middle-east and shipped to wherever the paedophiles want them sent. They have a man undercover in Lebanon and I'm speaking directly to him tomorrow. Ryan Carragher is already known to them and they've said the perps communicate in a chat-room on the Dark Web. Davy can explain what that is when I've gone."

Davy nodded eagerly.

Craig summed up. "I've a meeting with the Chief Constable now, but before I go I want to suggest a few things. First, considering that Eileen Carragher's body was only discovered last Monday, we've come an enormous distance. This is a joint Vice and Murder case now and I want us to see it through together. There are two strands to it. The first is pursuing Ryan Carragher's paedophile ring, which is undoubtedly involved with the bodies in the Newcastle house. I think the ones at the hotel were probably down to Eileen and Ian Carragher and Warner alone."

Annette signalled to interrupt. "Sir, where does Alan Rooney come in? He wasn't much older than Jonathan Carragher so he can't have been involved until recently."

"It's a good point, Annette. My instinct says that he was an abuse victim; we know he was Eileen Carragher's lover from the age of sixteen, but I doubt if that was his first dance. If he was abused when he was underage, then he may well have taken part in one of Warner's basement sessions with the girl, or Jonathan Carragher. That might have been motive enough for them to kill him, or he may have been involved more recently with the Newcastle scenario. Although we don't know if Jonathan and the girl know about the Newcastle set-up yet. Des might find us something to help on that."

Des nodded and Craig continued.

"The fact is, if there wasn't a market in Northern Ireland for abusing children then Ryan Carragher wouldn't be shipping them in. D.C.I. Hughes will lead on the paedophile ring, with our support. When we have Ryan Carragher we can make the murder cases against him for any children's bodies we find. The second strand of the operation is the recent murders. We have four victims and two killers out there running free. Whether people have sympathy with their motives or not, vigilante justice is illegal and they've killed four people, so we continue to work the Carraghers' killers like we would any other case. Obviously the Murder Squad leads on that. "

Craig turned back to Des. "Des, we need the forensics at the Warner scene, stat. Also, can you narrow down the battery acid and engine oil any way you can. Davy will help with that. John, keep going with anything you can find on the P.M.s. By the sounds of it you have your hands full." He scanned the faces of his team. "I'm not going to breathe down your necks about how many hours you spending on each side of this, as long as we get results. So, is anyone interested in following through the trafficking ring with Aidan?"

Liam nodded.

"OK, Liam's working with D.C.I. Hughes on that. The rest, on the murders please and support Liam as and when."

Craig stood up, signalling that the meeting was at an end. "Right. Jake, can I have a quick word? Everyone else go home. That's enough for tonight. And remember, no-one mentions anywhere that we suspect Ryan Carragher. We need him to believe that we're looking elsewhere. I want to see what he does next. Davy, first thing tomorrow look at the Dark Web and see what you can find on paedophile rings. I'll link you up with Interpol. John, I'll give you a call later."

"Please do. Natalie's on call so I'm free to misbehave."

Craig shook his head. "No more whiskey for at least a week."

"That'll be two shandies tonight then, Doc."

Liam guffawed loudly and Des and Aidan joined in. Nicky rolled her eyes and just thanked God they didn't all work in the same office.

**

The Chief Constable's Office. 6 p.m.

Chief Constable Sean Flanagan rose from his chair and wandered across his office to the window. He lifted a steel ball in the Newton's cradle sitting on the sill and let it swing downwards in an arc; then he watched the rhythmic motion it initiated, without saying a word. Finally it slowed and stopped and he turned towards Craig with darkened eyes, his normally cheerful voice subdued.

"I thought I'd heard pretty much everything in my time, Marc, but the situation you've uncovered is…Well, I don't know what it is. There isn't a word bad enough for it."

Flanagan sat down heavily on the edge of his desk, clasping his hands so tightly that his aging knuckles turned white. "I suppose the question is, what help can I give you?"

Craig had been hoping that he'd ask and he was ready with his reply. "I want to set up a sting to catch Ryan Carragher, sir."

Flanagan raised his eyebrows in surprise. Stings and murder didn't usually go hand in hand, but he waved Craig on.

"As you know, we've been working closely with D.C.I. Hughes in Vice on this case. The murders of the Carraghers, Rooney and Warner are inextricably linked with child abuse they committed throughout the years. Abuse that will continue if we don't catch Ryan Carragher." Craig paused hopefully.

"Go on."

"There are two things. The historic abuse committed at

Marcheson's School, now the Down Hartley Hotel. And then, there's what's been happening recently at the Newcastle house. We believe that our killers were victims of past abuse at Marcheson's, while the Carraghers worked there, and that they've been killing to get revenge for that. But the two children that we found at the BDSM party and the Newcastle house are very much current victims. There are countless cases of murder still to answer at both locations, and with the help of forensics we'll solve those, but what I'm most concerned about at the moment is preventing any more abuse."

Craig paused and sipped at his now cold coffee. Flanagan glanced at the wall clock; it was after six o'clock, time for a real drink. He crossed to a cupboard in one corner and pulled out a bottle of Bushmills Whiskey, pouring them both a shot. Craig forgot his earlier vow of abstinence and took the glass, warming to his theme.

"Ryan Carragher will play the grieving son long enough to inherit the money from the Newcastle estate, then he'll start his activities again somewhere else. Unless we stop him in his tracks."

"All right. How?"

"I've spoken to Interpol and they already have a man undercover in the child trafficking ring. He's based in Beirut, where the main focus seems to be. Interpol are closing in at their end, but they know that the ring extends to the UK, including here. They'd like us to put Ryan Carragher under surveillance and build a case against him. They feel that if he's facing life in prison he'll make whatever deal he can and lead us to other paedophiles, here and overseas. The Met is doing the same with paedophiles in London, and they've forces in the Midlands, Scotland and Wales lined up as well."

Flanagan raised a hand to halt him. "D.C.I. Hughes is onside with this?"

"Raring to go, sir." Craig took another sip of his drink and let it slide down before restarting. "You know we have an excellent analyst in the Murder Squad?"

"Ah, yes. Isn't it that young Goth lad, Davy?"

Davy was an Emo not a Goth, but Craig thought correcting the C.C. when he was trying to show his street cred probably wasn't the best idea.

"Yes. He's excellent and he's linking up with Interpol on the internet communications the ring are using. Apparently it's on the Dark Web, where a lot of illegal activity is hiding."

Flanagan gave him a puzzled look. "Dark Web? It sounds like something out of a horror movie."

"That describes it pretty well, sir. It's basically a shadow internet with sites accessible by those in the know. Some deal in illegal substances. One of the sites, The Silk Road, hit the news recently; you probably heard it on the News. Anyway, Davy's digging into all that with Interpol and The Met, so he'll be tracking Ryan Carragher's movements online."

Flanagan halted him again. "OK. So Interpol are undercover in Beirut and the other UK forces are on side. Carragher is under surveillance electronically, and presumably you've got him under observation?"

"Yes, I've just tasked Jake McLean, our new sergeant, to supervise that, but..."

"But that's not the sting, is it?"

Craig shook his head. "No. Aidan and I would like to run an operation where we put a man undercover, to infiltrate Carragher's paedophile circle here."

Flanagan shook his head sceptically. "It won't work, Marc. He'd spot one of us a mile off, and besides, it would take forever to gain his trust."

Craig interjected eagerly. "Unless he already knows the man."

Flanagan sprang to his feet indignantly. "No! There's no way we're using a known paedophile to catch another one. It would be thrown out of court."

Craig stared unflinchingly at him and shook his head. "I'm not talking about a paedophile. Let me explain."

Flanagan reluctantly nodded Craig on and over the next ten minutes he set out his plan. When Craig had finished Sean Flanagan smiled and poured them both another drink.

***

As soon as his father had been killed Ryan had known who'd done it, or helped to do it at least. If it had just been his bitch step-mother who'd bought the farm, he would have put it down to the life she'd led. The fact that it was both of them narrowed it to revenge. It couldn't have been a kid so it had to have been someone older, someone they'd fucked-up at Marcheson's. Anyone who'd reached the Newcastle house would never have lived long enough. But most of the kids at Marcheson's school had been overseas students who'd gone back home. That only left two possibilities; his baby brother and the little bitch who'd disappeared from the school in the move.

Women were all bitches to him. Powerful and powerless in equal measure, but with the ability to fuck with a man's head like no-one else. That was why he preferred kids. Eileen had been the supreme bitch. She'd taken the cipher that was his father and imprinted her will on him like a hallmark from the first day they'd met. Ian Carragher been a man without personality, shaped by whatever woman he happened to wed. His mother Marianne had been as good a woman as Eileen Burns had been bad, and his Dad had just followed behind them like their slave, doing good or evil, as he was told.

Ryan laughed as the phrase 'lack of moral fibre' popped into his head. It had such a World War Two ring to it, but it described his father perfectly. Whereas he had far too much fibre, and all of it immoral. He laughed again, entertained by his own wit. But what about Jonathan? Poor motherless baby, but every inch his mother's son. Never angry, never cruel, Marianne through and through. Ryan thought for a moment then realised something. Jonathan could never have killed their father, or certainly not alone; he had to have had an accomplice.

When authors write phrases like 'everything became clear' or 'realisation dawned', it really doesn't do justice to the facts. Sometimes realisation slipped slowly through the barrier between the subconscious and conscious while you were asleep, and sometimes it crept up behind you and tapped you gently on the back. But at other times it clouted you on the head with a bloody great thump, and this was one of those times. The thump that hit Ryan Carragher was so hard that he wanted to give himself another one, just for being so thick! Of course... The girl the police had shown him! Tian Liu's double. How could he have missed it?

When he'd joked with the cops that she'd looked like Tian Liu's love-child he'd been right on the mark! He'd heard Eileen shouting at his father just before Tian Liu left for Hong Kong, but he'd been a teenage boy so he'd ignored it as boring adult stuff. When the Chinese girl had appeared at Marcheson's on one of his annual trips home, he hadn't given her a second glance, assuming that her parents were overseas. But now it made sense... She'd been Tian Liu's bastard. His father's bastard too. Now she was all grown up and working with his baby bro to get revenge. She was the bitch who'd escaped. Well, well... They'd done him a favour, killing four birds with one stone and making themselves into fugitives. Now he'd inherit the whole estate.

It wasn't long after his clout on the head that Ryan Carragher phoned his baby brother and told him that he knew he and an accomplice had killed their Dad, but not that he knew the accomplice was the girl. As long as they left the country he didn't care who his brother screwed. Two hours of talk and persuasion later and Ryan had worked out what to do. Jonathan and his accomplice would leave the country and he would organise their trip. He would inherit everything and the murder trail would go cold. Then he could get back to doing what he was good at, with the children that he loved.

The C.C.U. Tuesday. 10 a.m.

"OK. Here's what we're doing."

Craig scanned the faces in front of him, knowing that what he was about to say would shock them all. All except Aidan Hughes who was drinking his coffee and looking as if he didn't have a care in the world.

"I met with the C.C. last night. He's on board with our two pronged approach; pursue the murderers and help crack the paedophile ring. Davy's already been onto Interpol on the electronic side of the investigation. Davy, can you update us on that?"

Davy was staring at something on the ground and everyone's eyes followed his gaze. He was gazing at his feet with something approaching awe and they could see why. Instead of his usual heavy boots he was wearing new shoes. They were black lace-ups with narrow toes and smooth leather, not unlike Craig's own. They were very stylish and Jake was the first to say so.

"Cool shoes. Where'd you get them?"

Before Davy could launch into a fashion report, Liam kicked him with his size thirteen.

"Get on with it lad or we'll be here all day."

Davy did as he was told. "I've been onto Interpol, The Met, Manchester and a couple of the other English forces, also, some in S...Scotland and Wales. As you know, they believe that there's a paedophile ring operating out of Beirut. Interpol have a man undercover there and he says that a lot of the deals and arrangements are being done on the internet. In a chat room on the Dark W...Web. There are branches of the ring all over Europe, including the UK." He pulled a face. "Apparently Northern Ireland has one of the biggest. I'm digging into that s...side of things."

Craig picked up the reporting.

"Ryan Carragher is their man in Northern Ireland. According to what Davy's gleaned from the internet chatter, he's definitely the ring's organiser here. So he's the main focus of our joint operation. Davy's going to be into Carragher's phones, computers, even in his house, without him knowing." He turned to Jake. "That's partly where you come in, Jake. Jake's leading on the physical surveillance of Carragher, but he'll also be coordinating external listening devices with the surveillance team."

Liam cut in. "Here, can't we get a warrant to bug his place?"

"I'm working on that, Liam, but even if we do bug it there's a risk of him finding the bugs and that would blow everything." Craig scanned their faces gravely. "I can't emphasise how important it is that Ryan Carragher knows nothing about this. He can't know he's under suspicion or surveillance, or it will blow the operation and the paedophile ring here will go underground and be lost for years. Is that understood?"

There was a series of nods and Craig turned back to Liam. "The judge wasn't keen to give us a warrant to access Carragher's phone records, or remotely log-in to his computer. We managed it, but I think asking to bug the house as well would be pushing our luck."

Annette looked thoughtful.

"What's on your mind, Annette?"

"Well...It's just...isn't this going to distract us from the murders? I mean, that's our main remit really."

Craig smiled at her straightforward approach to life. "It is indeed and I'll come to that in a moment. OK. Davy's on the internet side, Liam's working with Aidan, as well as Jake supporting them on surveillance. I wouldn't be surprised if that turned something up on our murder cases. Jonathan Carragher's only living relative is Ryan. If Jonathan comes up for air he's going to contact him."

Annette nodded, starting to see the links.

"We're also awaiting a truck load of forensics from Des on

both cases, don't forget. Going back to Ryan Carragher for a minute. Obviously Aidan's team are plugged into networks all across the region, and they're putting out feelers on possible paedophiles, but they'll also be running a sting operation with us. Liam, I want you to help with that."

Liam sat forward eagerly, rubbing his hands. "A sting? Great stuff. We used to run those in the old days. They were good craic."

Craig laughed. "That's one word for it. OK. You all know that Aidan and I interviewed Edgar Tate. He hosted the BDSM party at which we found Aurelie."

Annette gave Craig a confused look. "Is Tate a paedophile?"

"No. That's exactly it, Annette, he isn't. We've got him on drugs and prostitution charges, but there's no hint that he's into kids."

"So what use is he, boss?"

Craig continued patiently. "Bear with me, both of you, and let me explain. We can't use a convicted paedophile in the sting, or they'd make sushi out of us in court. But neither can we use a police officer. They would be spotted mile off, as would anyone completely new to the world of Vice. Ryan Carragher would be suspicious immediately. He's not stupid or he wouldn't have stayed out of jail this long."

Realisation dawned on Davy first. "You're going to use Tate, chief. Excellent move."

Craig smiled. "I'm glad you approve, Davy. I was even more pleased when the C.C. OK-ed the plan last night. He took a bit of persuading and we were a few whiskies in when he said yes, but he hasn't retracted permission this morning so I think we're good to go."

Liam puffed out his cheeks in thought before he spoke. "So, let me get this straight. Ryan Carragher knows Tate from the parties, OK. But Tate's only ever been interested in sex with adults."

"Until now."

"OK. So you think he can persuade Carragher that he's suddenly interested in kiddies? Are you sure, boss?"

Craig sighed, not at the question, but at the idea that he wouldn't already have covered every base. He was about to say something sharp but he bit his tongue. Liam was only asking the questions the C.C. had asked the night before and he deserved an answer.

"It's a fair question, Liam. OK. Edgar Tate may not have expressed a liking for kids, and he denies he knew anything about the girl being brought to the party, but neither has he ever voiced open disapproval of Ryan Carragher's pastime in any way. On the negative side, Tate's a scum-ball who likes the younger prostitutes, late teens preferably. But, on the plus side, the fact Tate's been quite open about his preference for teenagers, doesn't make it such a stretch for Carragher to believe that he might be tempted into sex with even younger girls. Reasonable doubt, that's all we need. If we can make Carragher believe Tate is tempted, we might have our way in."

Hughes unfolded his arms and joined in. "You see Liam, perverts like to believe that we're all secretly perverts."

Liam guffawed. "I bet that's not the politically correct terminology, Aidan."

"Whatever it is, it's true. Tate is filth, but so far he's kept it legal age-wise. Carragher will always be looking for business, and he's like all of them, they need to believe that they're the normal ones, not us. So the more people they suck into their sick little world, the merrier. If I didn't think this would work, I'd say so, but I think it will."

Liam nodded, conceding that Craig was right. "What's Tate getting for his cooperation, boss?"

"Suspended sentence with no jail time, for allowing prostitution and drug use to take place in his house. Oh, and a sense of doing his civic duty."

Craig said the last words so sarcastically that everyone laughed.

303

"OK, so Liam will be helping Aidan out with that side. Tate will be wearing a wire when he meets Ryan Carragher and Davy will pick up on the recording side with Jake…"

Davy cut in eagerly. "Does that mean I can actually go out in the surveillance van?"

Craig thought for a minute then glanced at Aidan and Jake. They nodded and Craig turned back to Davy with a warning in his eyes. "Only when Tate is meeting Carragher. And you're a civilian so you'll wear whatever protection D.C.I. Hughes tells you to wear and stay in the van. Is that understood, Davy? The last thing I need is Nicky throttling me if you get hurt."

Davy smiled across at Nicky, his self-appointed 'office mum' then he gave Craig a small salute.

Craig threw him a wry look and continued. "Meanwhile Annette and I will be concentrating on the murders." He glanced at her. "Are you OK with that, Annette?"

She nodded vigorously. "More than OK. The farther away I stay from Vice, the happier I'll be."

Aidan grinned and Liam said what they'd both just thought. "Now, that's not what we heard …"

Annette's blushes and the ensuing banter declared the meeting well and truly closed.

***

Edgar Tate swallowed hard and then made the call; the prospect of ten years in Maghaberry on drugs and prostitution charges had focussed his mind like nothing else could. The phone at the other end cut to answerphone and Ryan Carragher's voice came on the line, suggesting that he leave a message. Tate's eyes widened in panic and he mouthed at Aidan Hughes, pleading to be told what to do. Hughes answer was clear; hang up. When Tate had cut the call Hughes gave him new instructions.

"OK. This time if the answerphone kicks in, say your name

and that you want Ryan to call you back on your mobile. If he answers you already have your script."

Tate glanced at the sheet of paper in his hand. It was a flow chart giving him the options of where to steer the conversation, for each question that Ryan Carragher might raise. Someone had done their homework. Tate didn't know that Vice had run this conversation before with a thousand different targets.

Hughes nodded at him to dial again and just at that moment Tate's mobile rang. His panicked look said that it was Carragher. He must have seen Tate's number and was phoning him back.

Tate stared at his vibrating handset and Hughes hissed loudly. "Answer it." Then he adjusted his earphones to make sure he caught every word.

Tate swallowed hard and answered the call, adopting his usual tone of voice. "Hello, Ryan. Thanks for calling back."

There was no sign of Tate's earlier panic. Not bad. They had a natural liar on their hands. No doubt he'd got plenty of practice negotiating building contracts. Ryan Carragher's voice came through loud and clear and Hughes gave the recording technician a thumbs-up.

"What do you want, Tate? Haven't you got a house to design or something?" Carragher laughed at his own weak joke and Tate relaxed, certain that he didn't suspect a thing. His arrest had been so low-key it had slipped under Ryan's radar.

"I want to talk business. Can we meet?"

Carragher's voice took on a suspicious edge. "What for? What do we have to discuss?"

Tate held his nerve. "Party business. I know you specialise and I'd like to broaden my interests."

There was silence on the line for a moment and Tate bit his lip. Had his tone been too cocky? After all, someone about to try out paedophilia for the first time might not be so cavalier. He held his breath and Hughes and his team held theirs, then, after a pause that felt deliberate, Ryan Carragher spoke again.

"You like your party games modern, I remember that. How modern are you looking to go? 2000? 2010?"

Tate looked wildly at Hughes. It was a question that they hadn't prepared for! Carragher was using euphemisms to describe the children he could offer, that much he understood. Their ages were being described by the year when they were born. But what should his answer be?

Hughes thought frantically for a moment and then scribbled a number down and held it close to Tate's face. '2002'. Eleven or twelve; Aurelie's age. Any younger would be too big a change from Tate's normal choice.

Tate nodded and spoke again. "No earlier than 2002."

"Pink or blue?" Boys or girls. Hughes wanted to throw up. This was bad, even for him.

"Pink. It's my favourite colour."

The line went silent for so long that Hughes would have thought the call had been cut if he hadn't been watching the technician's screen. After a full minute's silence Ryan Carragher spoke again.

"I remember now, you always did like pink, but more of the '95, '96 variety. Why the sudden change?"

Tate was prepared for the question and trotted out the answer written on the sheet.

"It's not sudden. I've been playing those games at home for years."

Carragher laughed, remembering that Tate had children. "Coming out of the closet are we? I wondered about that a few months back."

Tate scowled at the handset. Carragher was implying that he'd thought he was a paedophile for months. Tate opened his mouth to say 'fuck off' and Aidan Hughes shook a fist at him threateningly. His message was clear. 'Don't blow this'. The subtext said 'if you do, you're going to prison for years.'

Tate bit his tongue and laughed in return. "The closet's too small now."

Ryan Carragher paused and the men listening could almost hear his thoughts. He knew Edgar Tate; he'd seen him around the party circuit for years. Tate had never shown an overt interest in children, but he had always gone for the youngest hooker in the room, and some of them had looked barely legal. Young girls might well be Tate's thing. He wasn't ready to believe Tate just yet but a meeting couldn't hurt.

"OK. Let's meet. We can discuss party plans. I'll text you with the where and when."

The line went dead suddenly and Tate stared at the phone. No one spoke until the technician gave the thumbs up and disconnected the line, then Aidan Hughes let out a whoop and punched the air. They had their meeting! He turned to Tate and nodded grudgingly. Thanking a criminal for lying to another to save his ass seemed wrong; so a nod was as far as it went.

Edgar Tate smiled thoughtfully and Hughes squinted at him. He'd been a bit too smooth on the phone. He'd better just have been acting. The last thing he needed was another paedophile on his patch.

***

OX Restaurant. Oxford Street, Belfast. 1 p.m.

Craig beckoned the waitress over, ordered Annette another coffee and asked for the bill. The two of them were the murder team now and the office was buzzing with talk of the sting, so Craig had thought a change of scenery might clear their heads. He glanced out the window at the metal statue across the street; it was a statuesque woman holding a globe aloft. Officially it was known as 'The Statue of Harmony', a symbol of peace, but some wit had christened it 'The Doll with the Ball' years before, and it had stuck.

They were in OX, the new restaurant close to the law courts that John had introduced him to. The food was excellent and the setting great, but if he'd thrown a stone it would have hit a lawyer on the head. Annette smiled, reading Craig's mind and thanking heavens no bricks were available.

"It's a lovely restaurant, sir. Thanks for suggesting lunch." She grimaced. "The office discussions were becoming a bit too Vice-like for me."

Craig nodded and sipped his espresso. "That's why I wanted us to come here. Sorry about being overrun by Vice, but I wanted to keep a grip on the sting. I could have let them set up downstairs but then there would have been a delay in getting reports. And three out of four of you are working on it, so the squad seemed like the place to be."

Annette finished her coffee and Craig paid the bill then they stepped out into the winter sunshine and turned towards the Obel building, strolling slowly back along the river towards the squad.

"OK, now what do we have on the murders? Four bodies, Eileen and Ian Carragher, Alan Rooney and Gerry Warner. All tortured using the Ling Chi method then killed by having their throats cut. What else?"

"Well, they added acid to Ian Carragher's killing, to make it more painful."

"Yes, because?"

"They hated him more because he failed in his duty to protect his child."

Craig raked his hair thoughtfully. "OK. Initially Ian Carragher had been a good father and Jonathan had a nanny he loved, Tian Liu. Carragher had met Eileen Burns at Marcheson's School before he was widowed, but her negative influence only started after his first wife, Marianne, died of cancer. Then they started the abuse that continued until 2004 when Marcheson's closed."

Annette cut in. "Hence the symbolism of leaving the bodies at a school."

"Yes, that's clear enough. They met at a school and started

their abuse there. In the basement boiler-room, which is where Des says they're finding bodies now."

Craig stopped walking suddenly and stared at the river, letting it wash over his thoughts. Annette watched him in silence. Water seemed to give him some sort of peace; she noticed it anytime they were nearby. After a moment Craig smiled and they strolled on.

"OK. Let's say that Eileen was the dominant, but they were worse together than they would ever have been apart. A kind of Folie à deux or shared psychoses."

"Like Myra Hindley and Ian Brady."

"Or Rosemary and Fred West… OK…When Gerry Warner came to teach at the school the environment grew even more ripe for abuse. The Carraghers had bought the house in Newcastle when they got married in '95 and they continued the abuse down there when Marcheson's closed in 2004.

"Where did Rooney come into it?"

Craig searched for an answer for a moment. "His age suggests that he was a pupil at Marcheson's. Ask Davy to check. That would have made him a victim, but even if he started as a victim he must have become an abuser or he wouldn't have been murdered."

It was Annette's turn to stop walking. She stared up at Craig and shook her head. "No, sir. Rooney was only twenty-six years old. Even if he did abuse Jonathan Carragher or the girl when he was young, it would have been as Warner's victim, and they'd have known that. They wouldn't have blamed another child, so why did they target him when he grew up? And how would they even have recognised him?"

Craig's eyes widened. "Annette, you're a genius! You're absolutely right. There's only one reason they'd have killed Alan Rooney; if they knew he was still an abuser now. That can only mean one thing; they know about Newcastle!"

A look of confusion covered Annette's face. "What? But, of course Jonathan Carragher knew about Newcastle, it was where he lived with his parents after the school closed."

Craig shook his head. "Remember he went away to school at thirteen, but it's not only that. Jonathan Carragher must have known Newcastle was being used to abuse children and he must have seen Rooney there abusing, as an adult."

Annette nodded slowly. "So you're saying that they killed Rooney, not for what he did to either of them, but for what they knew he was still doing in Newcastle. They wanted to stop it to help the other kids?"

"Probably, and to exorcise their own ghosts."

"But, doesn't that mean they must know Ryan Carragher is involved? He was bringing the children to Newcastle to be abused and killed."

Craig furrowed his brow for a moment then his expression changed to a smile.

"What? You've just thought of something, sir. What is it?"

"OK, if Jonathan knew Ryan was involved, then we can assume that Ryan would be next in line to be murdered. Right?"

"Right."

"But then he wouldn't be talking to him on the phone about his parents' funerals. What if Jonathan just sees Ryan as his big brother who was away at college and didn't know that he was being abused at Marcheson's?"

"So he thinks Ryan's completely innocent?"

"It's very possible, if Ryan stayed well behind the scenes until Jonathan went away to University. And what's more, if Jonathan sees Ryan as his only living family he may even turn to him for help escaping."

It was exactly what Annette would do in their situation. "Will he? Help him, I mean?"

Craig shook his head. "I honestly don't know. On one hand Jonathan killed their parents and the fall-out has ruined Ryan's set-up in Newcastle. On the other, he's got rid of Ryan's competition; his parents, Warner and Rooney. Now Ryan has

310

everything to himself. If Jonathan leaves the country and keeps his head down, Ryan will inherit everything and he can keep running his paedophile ring in luxury. It's a hard one to call, but my money's on Ryan either helping them escape or killing them both. He won't want Jonathan caught, that's for sure. If he is then there's every chance Jonathan will unwittingly incriminate him. But the real question isn't will Ryan help them escape, but will Jonathan and the girl find out that Ryan was involved in Newcastle and kill him?"

Annette summarised the options in one line. "That depends on whether we expose Ryan as a paedophile and his brother finds out."

***

Jonathan wrapped Mai in his arms and they lay down to watch TV, trying to distract themselves from reality with mindless pap. Or rather, he was trying to distract Mai. To give her restless brain a break and stop her thinking about the past. He didn't hold out much hope of it working and even if it did, what then? Fill her every waking hour with trivia? Even if that was possible, not thinking didn't mean that she couldn't feel.

Jonathan reached for the remote and muted the sound, watching the flickering images race across the screen. Mai turned towards him quizzically, knowing that he had something to say. She was totally unprepared for what it was.

"We have to leave, Mai."

"The house?"

"The continent."

"For where? There's nowhere they won't find us nowadays."

Jonathan shook his head. "Venezuela. Even if they find us there, they can't bring us back."

Mai smiled into his eyes then traced his full lips with her own, whispering softly as she did. "And then what? Peace? There is none, pet. Not for us."

Jonathan held her at arm's length and shook his head. "There is. There will be. It's all arranged, we leave in two days' time and when we arrive I'm going to get you help. Doctors, therapists, whatever it takes."

He stopped abruptly, willing her to say yes, while Mai willed herself not to say no. She gazed into his eyes and felt his love for her. She had to go with him. Not because she believed in peace; she didn't. And not because she thought that she should. But because she loved that Jonathan loved her enough to try, and because she loved him so much.

Chapter Twenty-Five

Castle Court Shopping Centre, Belfast.
Wednesday p.m.

Ryan Carragher was always suspicious. It's what had kept him safe for so long. So it was natural that he'd insisted on meeting Edgar Tate in a public place. Two men having a coffee in Belfast's Castle Court shopping-centre; well-known, bright and full of high-street shops and fast food joints. What could be more normal? It was an event so innocuous that none of the mid-week shoppers would ever have guessed what the two men's discussion was really about; bartering children's lives for adult pleasure.

This wasn't some sleazy nightclub, wallpapered with bodies and lit with pulsing strobes, and they weren't lurking in a rain-soaked alley on a Friday night. That's where people believed such exchanges took place. Not here, near normal people, surrounded by fluorescent lighting and well-stocked stores. A shopping centre was bright and in the open, a place full of lively chatter, teenagers looking cool and worn-out mums exchanging their woes.

Meeting for coffee there was also a scenario that any half-decent barrister would find easy to defend, and anyone out to incriminate Ryan Carragher would find almost impossible to use. Liam smiled down from the security room above the mall and then scanned the bank of camera screens. Almost impossible, but not quite. Not when one half of the coffee-drinking duo would be wearing a wire.

Edgar Tate walked slowly through the centre's ground floor, released from a white van outside in Berry Street. He rubbed at his shirt collar, desperate to pull out the wire inside that was making him itch. But his future promised prison if he gave himself away, so Tate did exactly as he'd been told. He glanced around him like a normal shopper, but not too much; he was still the male of the species after all. Shopping should be treated like a hunting trip; know what you want and head straight for your prey. He would leave the window shopping to the fairer sex.

Liam watched Tate's progress, nodding approvingly. He was sticking to the plan. Not too fast and not too slow. If Ryan Carragher was watching him from somewhere he'd see nothing amiss. Liam tapped his microphone once and Jake picked up.

"Tate's reached the stairs and he's climbing them now. How's the reception?"

Jake had forgotten that surveillance vans were so small. He shifted around in the limited space, trying to get comfortable and banging his elbow on Davy's knee. Once all the equipment and people were inside, there was hardly room to swing the proverbial. He couldn't bring himself to think 'cat', remembering his tabby Caspian at home. He would be sunning himself in the conservatory about now, while Aaron worked away at the drawings his job as an engineer required. Jake shifted again and wished that he was there. A loud booming in his ear reminded him that he wasn't.

"Well, lad? The reception?"

Jake made a face and answered, reassuring Liam that it was fine. He could hear the changing echoes as Tate climbed up the stairs and knew exactly when he'd reached the top.

"He's outside the food court now."

Liam squinted at the handset, wondering how the hell Jake knew. He shrugged. He didn't understand machines and he didn't care how they worked, as long as they did as they were told. Jake signed off and Liam tapped the microphone twice.

Aidan Hughes' Belfast tones came on the line.

"Get off the bloody line, Cullen. We need to keep it clear."

Liam huffed. "I was only checking."

"Well now you know. Take a hike."

The line cut out abruptly and Liam mouthed an obscenity. He'd get Aidan later for that. He was plotting his revenge when Ryan Carragher suddenly appeared on a screen, walking along the lower floor of the mall. He was meandering slowly, as if he hadn't a care in the world. If things went to play he'd soon have more of them than he could handle.

The men headed towards their agreed rendezvous, in a noisy café on the first floor. Carragher had chosen well, almost as if he'd anticipated a trap. If Tate was being watched, the background noise of a café would put paid to their words being overheard. Carragher would have been right, if they'd only been using directional mikes. That was the problem with criminals; most of them were thick, but their arrogance invariably made them believe that they were smarter than everyone else. Carragher's arrogance hadn't allowed for the fact the police had joined the twenty-first century as well.

Carragher spotted Tate and indicated a seat, waiting until they'd placed their order before covering his second base.

"Raise your arms."

Tate didn't argue. He'd been expecting it. He endured Carragher's pat-down, masked as a lengthy man-hug, while Liam stared at the screen and smiled. It was going exactly to plan. Carragher hadn't thought of checking Tate's collar. When Ryan Carragher had satisfied himself that his companion wasn't wired he gave a cool smile. Liam tapped the mike three times, connecting with both Jake and Aidan Hughes.

"He's patted him down and found nothing. This should be interesting."

He signed off before Aidan gave him another lecture, and grabbed a seat, ready to watch the show.

Carragher led the conversation and Tate followed as he'd

been told to do. His nerves subsided slowly as they discussed Ulster Rugby and the latest local football match. Liam smiled. Craig should be listening to this; he was sports mad. They drank and chatted their way through a coffee and then the conversation reached a hiatus, punctuated by Carragher ordering another set of drinks. Liam was just wondering why his bladder didn't cave in, his would have ten minutes ago, when Carragher leaned forward like a man with something to confide. Instead he asked Tate a question.

"Why now?"

Tate stared at him, his expression deliberately confused. He'd known that the question was coming. It was one of the scenarios they'd prepared. "Sorry?"

"You heard me."

Carragher scrutinised Tate's face and waited for his reply.

"I've been thinking about it for a while. I told you."

"You told me more than that. Tell me again."

Tate hesitated for a moment, as a man about to admit he'd molested his daughters would. He felt a small squirt of bile fill his throat at the lie he was about to tell. He loved his daughters, but definitely not that way. But he loved them enough to stay out of prison, so he swallowed hard.

"I have two daughters. Fifteen and thirteen."

Carragher smiled lasciviously. "Great ages. Are they blonde or brunette?"

Tate wanted to lie about their appearance; telling the truth made it all too real. But he knew Ryan Carragher would have done his homework so he described the girls.

"Suzie, the fifteen-year-old, is brunette. Clare, my baby, is blonde."

Carragher leaned in and Jake could hear every sordid word. "Your baby. Is that what you say when you make love to her? Do you stroke her lovely blonde hair?"

Tate knew Carragher was trying to make him incriminate himself for insurance, so that if he went down he would drag him down too. Tate bit back the words he was longing to say and answered.

"She's my baby but she's a woman too. She loves what I do to her."

They locked eyes and whatever Carragher thought he read there satisfied him. He sat back in his chair and smiled, recognising a kindred soul. It made him indiscreet.

"I love them blonde."

Tate came back with questions from the list in his head.

"What's your preference? Boys or girls?"

"Girls. Under twelve. Before they get too knowing." He gave Tate a sly look. "Although sometimes I like them slightly older too. Perhaps you would share Clare with me sometime? I'm gentle."

Tate nodded, unable to say the word. Then he remembered the tape and croaked out a 'yes'. It sounded forced to him but it seemed to satisfy Carragher. He'd probably put his reluctance down to jealousy.

Suddenly Carragher leaned in again, as if he'd made up his mind. "OK. I'm going to let you in on a little secret."

Liam tensed, knowing that this was it. They already had enough to get a warrant on Carragher for his comments about the kids, but they wanted his smuggling route and connections as well.

"I ship them in."

"What?"

Carragher continued impatiently. "The kids. I ship them in from abroad." He gave a smug smile. "It's stupid to source them locally, that's where people always go wrong. The police here have informants all over the show. Plus, kids who speak English will always find someone to talk to. I get them from elsewhere and they don't speak a word."

Liam punched the air. It was the money shot! Ryan Carragher had just boasted his way to years inside.

Tate looked puzzled. "But how do you get them in? Don't

they need passports and stuff like that?"

Carragher laughed so loudly that a woman at the next table turned and smiled. "You're thinking like a law-abiding citizen, Tate. You don't think we bring them through City Airport, do you?"

Tate feigned an embarrassed smile, surprising himself with his acting talent. He wanted to punch Carragher in the face, except that he wouldn't soil his hands. He smiled again, more broadly this time, focusing on one thing. Carragher was scum and he was going to help put him away. He might use prostitutes the odd time, but they were always over the age of consent; the thought of someone touching a child made him feel sick. Edgar Tate sat forward eagerly. He wasn't doing this just to save his own skin now; he really wanted Ryan Carragher locked up. "So how do they come in?"

Carragher sniffed knowingly. "The docks down south. Dublin mostly. They load and unload containers every day. It isn't difficult to slip some extra cargo through the net."

"But how do they breathe?"

Carragher shrugged. "Some of them don't, but the majority make it through. Young and healthy, you see. They're all under fourteen."

"Where do you ship from?"

Liam winced. Tate was pushing too fast. Carragher would smell a rat. He needn't have worried; Carragher was on a roll, glad to have an audience.

"Greece and France mostly. But the kids come from all over. It changes every year. This year it's mainly Greek kids, easier to lift them there now because of the recession. A couple of years ago it was Eastern Europe. Wherever my supplier can source them from." Carragher smiled and Tate saw pure evil in his eyes. "Wherever there are men who love children, there are men who will supply them. My main man's in Beirut. Good guy."

Tate sat back and Liam exhaled. He was about to play it cooler, just like they'd agreed. He had Carragher on the hook, now he just had to reel him in.

Tate shot Carragher a sceptical look. "Sorry, but you're telling me there's a big enough market in Northern Ireland to make it worthwhile shipping kids in? No way!"

Carragher looked offended. "I'm not a liar!"

Liam spluttered his coffee all over the screen. This was a man who stole, smuggled, abused and killed children, and he was indignant about his honesty being questioned? If it hadn't been so serious he would have laughed.

Tate mollified him. "I didn't mean that, but it all just seems so incredible. Not that the kids can't be taken, but that there are enough men here that want them."

"Not only men. There are plenty of women who like a bit of young fun too. My step-mother was a case in point."

Tate's eyes shot open. It hadn't even occurred to him that women might be involved. He'd thought maternal instinct was a universal constant.

"Did she…?"

Carragher shook his head. "To me? No, I was too old. Not her taste. Now my kid brother, that's a different story. She'd been messing with him since he was five-year's old."

Jake's eyes widened. Ryan Carragher had known of his brother Jonathan's fate all along, and he'd done nothing to stop it!

"As for there being enough people here interested in what we ship…" Carragher tapped his pocket as if he had a notepad inside. "I have them all. Bank managers, Clergy, even the odd Judge or two. Very handy people to know in times of crisis." He stared coldly at Tate. "And now I have you. Next time I need a house designed for free I'll give you a call."

Tate heard Liam before he saw him. The sound of Liam's size thirteens thundering down the concourse made everyone turn and stare. Five seconds later the table was surrounded by police and the shopping centre crowd was agog. Ryan Carragher glared at Tate as both men were hauled roughly to their feet.

Tate feigned shock.

"What is this? We've done nothing wrong! What are you arresting us for?"

Liam read the charges and rights to both men and watched as Carragher scowled at Tate. Tate resisted arrest, as they'd agreed he would. He was so convincing that he fell to the ground and split his lip, making Carragher's expression change to doubt. Good. If Carragher believed Tate hadn't betrayed him it could be useful.

Liam hauled Edgar Tate to his feet and inspected his face. "This one needs the M.E. I'll get him to meet us at High Street."

They filed through the shopping centre followed by astonished eyes then Liam shoved both men in the back of an armoured car. As it drove away he wandered to the surveillance van and banged hard on the back doors.

"Wake up in there!"

The door was flung outwards and Jake jumped out and took several deep breaths.

"Well lad. Not bad for an afternoon's work. Did you get everything?"

Jake grinned and smoothed down his suit. "Every word. And it's enough to put Ryan Carragher away for life."

***

High Street Station

"I want to make a phone-call."

"You can want all you like but that doesn't mean you'll get it."

Jack Harris set his mouth in a determined line and folded his arms. He'd seen some scum in his time but Ryan Carragher was the worst, and as far as he was concerned he could rot. Jack left the cell and banged the door hard, locking Carragher inside, then he walked into the small staff- room wearing a grim look.

The room was crowded. Liam and Aidan Hughes were lounging on the worn armchairs and Jake and Davy gave Jack an exhausted wave from the couch. Craig was the only one standing. He was spooning coffee into mugs and waiting for the kettle to boil.

Liam was the first to speak. "Cheer up, Jack. It was a good shout."

Jack swung on him angrily. "Could you not have taken the scum somewhere else? Now I have to serve them tea."

Craig nodded. Jack found child-molesters hard to deal with. They all did, but they could interview them and walk away. Jack had to tend to their needs 24/7.

"Hopefully we'll get Carragher interviewed and arraigned by tomorrow, Jack, then ship him off on remand."

Jack wasn't mollified. "That's twenty-four hours too long for me." He took the coffee Craig offered and shoved Liam's feet off a stool, sitting down. After a sip of coffee he spoke again.

"He wants a phone-call."

Craig's face lit up. This might be their chance. "Did he say who to?"

Jack sniffed and scratched his balding head. "No, and I didn't ask. He can whistle for it."

Craig perched on the arm of Liam's chair and smiled. "Look, I know how you feel, Jack. This case is making all our skins crawl. But there's just a chance Carragher will phone his brother and we'll get our murders solved."

Jack sniffed again. "Aye well. That's grand for you to say, but I'll have to hand him the phone. I'll want to crown him with it."

Liam guffawed. "Good man. Glad to see you're not always placid 'Uncle Jack'."

"Don't you Uncle Jack me, Cullen. I remember you when you could barely shave." He turned to Craig. "Remind me to tell you about your boy here when he was at training college.

There was this young W.P.C…"

Liam leaned in quickly. "Here, now. No need for that. All that's in the past."

Craig laughed and returned to the case. "Let Carragher make his call, Jack. I think he's going to call his brother Jonathan and I want a trace."

Jack considered for a moment then nodded grudgingly, rising to his feet. "I'll do it now." He stared pointedly at Liam. "And when I come back to my staff-room I want a proper seat." He made for the door and then turned back to Craig. "Set up your trace properly, sir, because I'm not repeating this."

Five minutes later Craig was proved right when a young man's voice came on the line. There was only one person it could be.

"I'm in trouble. I need your help."

"What's happened, Ryan?"

"It's a long story but I'm in High Street Police Station. You've got to get me out."

Craig listened to the brothers' voices. They were almost identical, but something about Jonathan Carragher's was gentler and his voice held a note of anguish. He sounded like a victim and, unlikely as that sounded for a multiple murderer, Craig knew that it was true.

"But how can I come to a police station? They'll never let me go again. We have to get out of here. It's Mai's only chance."

Mai. So that was the girl's name. Mai Carragher? No. Mai Liu. Craig was certain that she didn't know the Carragher part.

Ryan's tone became aggressive. "You selfish bastard. You wouldn't be going anywhere if it wasn't for me. Get down here now."

The force in Jonathan's voice surprised Craig. "NO! Mai will die if we stay here. South America's her only chance. She needs help and when we get there I'm going to find it for her. I'm sorry, Ryan, but you'll be OK. Whatever the charges are they'll be bogus. You'll be out tomorrow, you'll see."

Ryan Carragher's voice cooled and his fury made him careless. "You snivelling little bastard. To think I asked Eileen to go easy on you all those years. You and your little whore."

There was silence for a moment while Craig held his breath, praying that Jonathan didn't hang up. After a long pause Jonathan Carragher spoke again, in a voice so cold that Craig's pulse slowed. "What did you say?"

"You heard me. I knew exactly what Step-Mommy Dearest was doing to you. All those years when you thought I knew nothing, coming home from college to the loving home. I knew everything! It would still be going on in Newcastle and making me rich now, it you hadn't decided to kill everyone and lead the filth straight to our door." Ryan's voice dropped to a hiss so low that Craig strained to hear. He caught one word, "sister", before he heard Jonathan Carragher scream.

"NO! It's not true, it can't be. She isn't, she isn't."

Ryan's voice came through loud and clear. "Oh yes she is, little brother. You've been banging your own sister all this time. You can't judge any of us."

A voice in Craig's ear said. "We've got a trace" then gave him a location. Craig dropped his headphones, signalled to continue the call as long as possible then he raced for the door. Ryan Carragher had just hung himself on tape; his venom stronger than his common sense. Craig didn't give a shit about him, but for some strange reason he did about the boy on the other end of the line.

Ryan had deliberately destroyed his young brother and it was anyone's guess how Jonathan would react to what he'd just heard. The call had been traced to a house high up in the Craigantlet Hills, near the Ballymiscaw Road. It would take the locals thirty minutes to get there on the narrow rural roads. Craig gunned his Audi out of High Street's car-park and sped towards the M3 motorway. He'd no idea what he'd do when he got there but he knew that he had to try.

***

Mai heard Jonathan's screams all the way from the bedroom, where she was packing for their trip. She raced to the landing just as he was running upstairs. He stopped at the top and gazed at her like he'd never seen her before.

"Jonathan, what's happened? What was that noise?"

Jonathan scanned her face mutely and his eyes filled with tears. Mai reached for his hand and he jerked it away. "Baby, what's the matter? Is it the trip? Are you worried about the trip?"

Jonathan shook his head, not trusting himself to speak, as his eyes caressed each feature on her pretty face. He loved her so much, but it had all been wrong. He shuddered, remembering every time they'd made love, each heartfelt movement seeming sordid now. Incest. It was such an ugly word. Neither of them had known, but now he did and everything had changed.

Memories that had faded with age flooded back to him and started to make sense. The whispered conversations between his father and Tian, when he was only four. Her leaving suddenly and a few months later a baby coming to stay. Then Eileen Burns and the pain that had lasted for years.

Jonathan gazed at his lover then stretched out his hand to encircle her slim neck. His fingers began to close then Mai smiled up at him and his anguish suddenly disappeared. They were both innocent and their love had been innocent as well. Jonathan lifted his hand to her face and stroked it gently; tracing her delicate features one by one and remembering the day when he'd first been told to hurt her. He'd fought it with every sinew until she'd given him permission to acquiesce. He'd wanted to protect her forever, and he'd missed her desperately when she'd fled the school. When they'd met again as adults it seemed natural that they'd fall in love.

And they had. A playful, passionate love, full of all the happiness that they'd both been denied. A love that had bound

324

them together, even as they'd taken their revenge. He stroked Mai's face slowly, knowing that if she found out she was his sister everything they'd built together would be destroyed, and her already fragile mind would crack. He'd tried to protect her for years and he was going to protect her now. Jonathan stepped onto the landing and held her close. Then he took his lover by the hand and led her to bed.

***

Craig reached the house before the local Uniform's, the back roads with their single tracks no match for the motorway route. He stared at the small brick cottage set back from the road, the only house for miles around, then he slipped his Glock from its holster and walked slowly up the path, glancing quickly at the garage alongside. This was where they'd killed them all, in this quiet country place. It felt so wrong that the rural peace had been disturbed in that way.

Craig clicked off his gun's safety lock, praying that he didn't have to fire. Yes, they were killers, but only ever from revenge; he doubted that they would try to fight their way out. His heart sank. He already knew that the situation wouldn't arise.

The house was silent and nothing but instinct told Craig that someone was still inside. He had to look. He should wait for the patrols to arrive but then it would be too late, if it wasn't already. He pushed gently at the low front door and it swung inwards, revealing a small, neat hall, touching in its normality. Craig stepped inside, listening intently for any sound, but there was nothing. Only the hum of the fridge said the house was lived in. Had been lived in.

He moved swiftly from room to room clearing them, until finally he reached the stairs. He climbed them slowly, eyes fixed above his head, but still nothing moved. He checked the bedrooms and bathrooms, until only one door was left. Craig moved to it quickly and said the official words.

"Armed police. Come out with your hands up."

No sound or movement answered him but Craig repeated the warning twice, already knowing that there was no-one left to comply. He entered the bedroom slowly and the sight that greeted him was the one that he'd known he would find the moment Jonathan Carragher had screamed down the phone. On the double bed lay a young couple, naked in each other's arms and half-covered by a white sheet stained with blood. The blood would be Jonathan Carragher's and the girl would have marks around her neck. Craig knew it as surely as his own name. Carragher had killed the girl he loved to save her from any more hurt and then he'd shot himself. It was what he would have done in his place.

Craig stared at the sad tableau for minutes; while the cars pulled up outside and armed officers cleared the rooms. Finally he smiled down at the star-crossed lovers and wished them peace, then he holstered his gun, raised his arms and walked downstairs.

***

Natalie and John's Engagement Party. Saturday 15th February. 10 p.m.

"Not exactly a happy ending, boss."

Craig shook his head and sipped at his beer. "I disagree, Liam. Ryan Carragher's giving us the names of paedophiles in Northern Ireland, scrambling for a deal like the spineless scum he is. Now he's someone I'd like to spend five minutes alone in a cell with."

Liam arched an eyebrow, wondering how many beers Craig had had. Craig was still disagreeing.

"We've got Tate for drugs and prostitution and I think he's been stopped in his tracks before he became a paedophile. And between Davy and Interpol, the kids we found are back with their parents and we're well on the way to cracking the whole trafficking ring. I think that's a good week's work. So does the C.C."

Liam caught the barman's eye and ordered another drink. "Aye, but what about the murders? Four dead and no-one to prosecute."

"We know who did it and they're dead. That's a stronger penalty than any of the courts here would have handed out."

Liam nodded and raised his glass. "Here's to them, then. Jonathan and Mai, the only two members of their scummy family with any honour at all."

Craig took another drink then glanced at Annette and crossed his eyes. She laughed and wandered over. Craig opened his arms in greeting.

"Annette, Annette, have a drink."

Annette smiled at her boss, avoiding Liam's eye in case she laughed. "Thanks, sir. I'll have a glass of white wine, any sort as long as it's sweet. I'll save the champagne for the main event."

She stared up at the ceiling. It was covered with glitter balls. There were silver streamers everywhere and the walls were decked with banners saying 'Congratulations Natalie and John'.

"Any idea why Natalie chose a seventies theme? She wouldn't even have been born then."

Craig nodded sagely. "Born in '78. Apparently she likes the style."

Liam guffawed. "God. Flares and flowery shirts. They were bad enough first time round. Mind you, the music wasn't bad. I used to boogie with the best of them."

"Boogie! That really dates you. Well here's your chance, Liam. The lights are going down."

The lights dimmed gradually, throwing the glitter balls into bright relief. When the DJ called out 'Saturday Night Fever' they were almost deafened by the squeals of delight, as every woman in the room dashed onto the floor. Annette was no exception and she dragged Liam with her.

327

Craig laughed solidly for five minutes watching them throw shapes, then he turned to the bar to order another drink. John appeared by his side.

"Well? How does it feel to be almost married?"

John smiled shyly and Craig ordered him a drink. John needed to be much drunker before he made his speech.

"Surprisingly good, actually. Now, we just have to sort you out."

Craig shook his head and laughed. "Oh no, you don't! I've heard about married people. They want everyone else to get married too, for company. I'm fine as I am, thanks."

John lifted his drink. "Oh well, then. I won't bother introducing you…"

Craig was staring at the dance-floor, watching Liam compete with Davy for the best moves. Davy was winning hands down. John repeated himself, standing in front of Craig to get his attention.

"Introducing me? Who to? Or should that be, to whom?" Craig puzzled drunkenly over the grammar for a moment then continued. "If this is one of Natalie's friends you're trying…"

"Katy."

"Katy who?"

Craig stepped to one side to reinstate his view of the floor show, just in time to catch Liam doing it Gangnam style. Wrong decade, but who cared. He just hoped someone was getting it all on tape.

John wasn't giving up. "Stevens. Katy Stevens. You remember. Blonde, cute, likes you for some strange reason. Well?"

Craig drained his beer and ordered another, intent on getting canned. He squinted at John. "Nope."

"What do you mean, nope? I thought you liked her."

"I do. I've had her number in my phone for months but the answer's still no. It's too soon and Julia would be devastated if she found out."

328

John's face dropped and he pointed an accusing finger. "You're still in love with Julia!"

Craig shook his head calmly then winced as the beer caught up. "God, John, you sound like you're sixteen. No, actually, I'm not still in love with Julia. I'm fond of her for sure, but we weren't right together. But she would still be upset if I started seeing someone this quickly. She'd think that I'd had them waiting in the wings. I want to give it another few months."

John glanced meaningfully across the hall. "You'll lose her."

Craig shrugged pragmatically. "Perhaps, perhaps not." He caught a glimpse of Natalie and waved. "Now go back to your fiancée. If I see Katy I'll chat to her, but I'm not asking her out until I'm ready."

The dance came to an end and Liam and Annette strolled back to join them. Craig smiled as he heard what the DJ was playing next, and pushed John onto the dance-floor.

"They're playing your song, John."

He stood with Liam and they laughed like drains as Natalie dragged her future husband around the floor to the tune of 'The Loco-Motion'. Setting the tone for their marriage as she meant it to carry on.

THE END

Fantastic Books
Great Authors

Meet our authors and discover our exciting range:

- Gripping Thrillers
- Cosy Mysteries
- Romantic Chick-Lit
- Fascinating Historicals
- Exciting Fantasy
- Young Adult and Children's Adventures

Visit us at:
www.crookedcatbooks.com

Join us on facebook:
www.facebook.com/crookedcatpublishing

Lightning Source UK Ltd.
Milton Keynes UK
UKOW02f2357280814

237719UK00001B/3/P